**"Why'd You Do It?" He Asked. He'd Forgotten About Being Angry That She'd Lied, And Now Just Wanted A Few Answers. "Why'd You Trick Me Into Staying Here?"**

She studied him for a quiet minute. Her fingers smoothed the arm of the chair with long, sensuous strokes that caught his attention and held it. He shifted a little in the chair, trying not to think about those fingers caressing his skin. He hadn't felt anything like this in years. It was as if his body were waking up from a deep sleep, and the first stirrings felt damn near painful. A half smile lingered on her mouth, and the slight curve of her lips was tempting.

"I don't know," she said. Her gaze met his. Something caught him, held him, and Sam knew he was sliding into dangerous territory— but for the life of him, he just couldn't look away.

Dear Reader,

Welcome to another passionate month at Silhouette Desire where the menu is set with another fabulous title in our DYNASTIES: THE DANFORTHS series. Linda Conrad provides *The Laws of Passion* when Danforth heir Marc must clear his name or face the consequences. And here's a little something to whet your appetite—the second installment of Annette Broadrick's THE CRENSHAWS OF TEXAS. What's a man to do when he's *Caught in the Crossfire*— actually, when he's caught in bed with a senator's daughter? You'll have to wait and see....

Our mouthwatering MANTALK promotion continues with Maureen Child's *Lost in Sensation*. This story, entirely from the hero's point of view, will give you insight into a delectable male—what fun! Kristi Gold dishes up a tasty tidbit with *Daring the Dynamic Sheikh*, the concluding title in her series THE ROYAL WAGER. Rochelle Alers's series THE BLACKSTONES OF VIRGINIA is back with *Very Private Duty* and a hunk you can dig right into. And be sure to save room for the delightful treat that is Julie Hogan's *Business or Pleasure?*

Here's hoping that this month's Silhouette Desire selections will fulfill your craving for the best in sensual romance... and leave you hungry for more!

Happy devouring!

*Melissa Jeglinski*

Melissa Jeglinski
Senior Editor
Silhouette Desire

Please address questions and book requests to:
Silhouette Reader Service
U.S.: 3010 Walden Ave., P.O. Box 1325, Buffalo, NY 14269
Canadian: P.O. Box 609, Fort Erie, Ont. L2A 5X3

# LOST IN SENSATION

## MAUREEN CHILD

Published by Silhouette Books
**America's Publisher of Contemporary Romance**

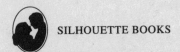 SILHOUETTE BOOKS

ISBN 0-373-76611-4

LOST IN SENSATION

This edition published by arrangement with Harlequin Books S.A.

® and TM are trademarks of Harlequin Books S.A., used under license.
Trademarks indicated with ® are registered in the United States Patent
and Trademark Office, the Canadian Trade Marks Office and in other
countries.

Visit Silhouette Books at www.eHarlequin.com

Printed in U.S.A.

**Books by Maureen Child**

Silhouette Desire

*Have Bride, Need Groom* #1059
*The Surprise Christmas
   Bride* #1112
*Maternity Bride* #1138
*\*The Littlest Marine* #1167
*\*The Non-Commissioned
   Baby* #1174
*\*The Oldest Living Married
   Virgin* #1180
*\*Colonel Daddy* #1211
*\*Mom in Waiting* #1234
*\*Marine under the Mistletoe* #1258
*\*The Daddy Salute* #1275
*\*The Last Santini Virgin* #1312
*\*The Next Santini Bride* #1317
*\*Marooned with a Marine* #1325
*\*Prince Charming in Dress Blues* #1366
*\*His Baby!* #1377
*\*Last Virgin in California* #1398
*Did You Say Twins?!* #1408
*The SEAL's Surrender* #1431
*\*The Marine & the Debutante* #1443
*The Royal Treatment* #1468
*Kiss Me, Cowboy!* #1490
*Beauty & the Blue Angel* #1514
*Sleeping with the Boss* #1534
*Man Beneath the Uniform* #1561
*Lost in Sensation* #1611

\*Bachelor Battalion

Harlequin Historicals

*Shotgun Grooms* #575
"Jackson's Mail-Order Bride"

Silhouette Books

*Love Is Murder*
"In Too Deep"

Silhouette Special Edition

*Forever...Again* #1604

---

## MAUREEN CHILD

is a California native who loves to travel. Every chance they get, she and her husband are taking off on another research trip. The author of more than sixty books, Maureen loves a happy ending and still swears that she has the best job in the world. She lives in Southern California with her husband, two children and a golden retriever with delusions of grandeur.

Visit her Web site at www.maureenchild.com.

For Susan Mallery—
a great friend and a wonderful writer.
Thanks for the good ideas and the fun plot groups.
Thanks for listening when I need to whine and thanks
for telling me what I need to hear—especially when
I don't want to hear it. May the wind always be howling.

# One

*No good deed goes unpunished.*

Truer words were never spoken, Sam Holden thought. And he should have kept them in mind. Because he was even now living them.

He just couldn't figure out how he could have done anything differently.

"I owe you, man," Eric Wright said from the passenger seat. Then he reached down and rapped his knuckles against the plaster cast encasing his right leg from the knee down. "Actually, I owe you two. Saving my skin *and* driving me home for my wedding."

"No, you don't owe me." Sam glanced at his friend. A purple and yellowing bruise smudged his forehead in stark contrast to his pale face. His dark red hair stood out in a weird sort of halo around his head. Lines of pain were drawn deep around his mouth, and his eyes were tired.

"You look like hell."

"Hey," Eric said with a small grin, "if not for you, I'd be looking cold and stiff right about now."

"Yeah, yeah." He brushed the latest round of thanks aside and narrowed his gaze. "You feeling okay?"

Eric grimaced. "You asking as my friend or as my doctor?"

"Which one will get me an honest answer?"

Laughing shortly, Eric shoved one hand through his hair, then scraped that hand across his eyes as if trying to wake himself up. "I'm okay. Just tired—" he looked at Sam again "—and grateful to be alive. Like I said, I owe you."

At thirty-two, Sam was tall, leanly muscled and too impatient for his own good. A black-haired, blue-eyed doctor, he had more female patients than male but much to their dismay, Sam never noticed more about the women than the symptoms they were presenting. He had only a handful of close friends and Eric Wright was one of them.

But in the last couple of weeks, Eric had been acting more like a *fan* than a friend. Sam had never been good with gratitude. He didn't like the slippery feel of someone's admiration. *Probably shouldn't have become a doctor then, huh?* But then, he'd had no choice. He'd been interested in nothing but medicine since he was a kid. At five, he'd borrowed his grandfather's stethoscope, listened to his dog's heart and found an irregular beat. Even the vet had been impressed. And that rush of discovery had pretty much sealed his future.

But having someone look at him with shining eyes and absolute trust made him want to run for the hills. Trust was a burden he didn't want to carry…it was just too damn fragile. An odd thought for a doctor, he mused. But there it was.

"You don't owe me, Eric." He'd said the same thing he didn't know how many times since the accident. Eric never seemed to hear him, though Sam continued to try. "Hell, I was in the car. What was I supposed to do, leave you in the wreck while I ran for it?"

Eric shrugged. "Most would. There aren't many people who'll climb *into* a burning car to drag somebody out." He waved a hand at the bandage on Sam's left forearm. "With a bum arm, no less."

"Just a sprain." The bandage was an irritation and, in his mind, not really necessary. But the ER doctors had insisted on it—at least for a few days. And the night of the wreck, he'd been too glassy-eyed from shock to argue.

It had all happened in seconds—and had felt, at the time, like they were moving in slow motion. A truck swerving into their lane. Eric ripping the wheel to one side. The scrape of metal against the guardrail. The long, eternity-filled seconds the car was airborne and the jarring slam when they hit the earth and rolled over. Sam had inched out of the broken side window, then crawled around to the driver's side. Unconscious, Eric was oblivious to the flames already licking at the undercarriage. But Sam had felt the heat against his face and the cold rush of fear in his bones. Somehow, though, he'd managed to free Eric from the seat belt and drag him to safety before the fire erupted into a blaze.

Luck was with them both that night. If it hadn't been, Eric's family would have been planning his funeral instead of celebrating his wedding.

"Still…"

Sam sighed and gave up trying to convince his friend. "Fine. I'm a hero. Super Doc, that's me."

Besides, if they were going to talk about payments due, Eric had it backward. Eric Wright had been a good friend—especially the last couple of years. By choice, Sam had always been something of a loner. More so in the last two years. But whenever Sam began pulling away from the few friends he did have, Eric had refused to allow it.

And for that, Sam owed *him*.

So here he sat, outside Eric's parents' house, with two long weeks to fill before he could head back home to L.A. Ordinarily, he would have driven up for Eric's wedding, then gone home the next day. But because of the accident and Eric's inability to drive,

Sam had somehow been suckered into a two-week vacation in northern California, specifically Sunrise Beach with Eric's family.

The prospect of which was enough to make Sam want to throw the car into gear again and peel away from the curb at warp speed. Unfortunately, he was a man of his word and there was no backing out now.

He shot a look at the Wright house. Sitting far back from the street, it boasted a deep, dark green lawn, despite the simmering heat of summer. Neatly tended flower beds, awash in splashes of brilliant color, lined the front of the old bungalow and dangled from brightly painted window boxes. The wide front porch had pots of ferns hanging from the rafters and planters with yet more flowers spilling from them perched on the railing.

The house itself was painted sunshine yellow with a dark green trim on the shutters and eaves. It looked comfortable, cared-for and sturdy, like a self-satisfied old woman. The street was quiet, tree-lined and only blocks from the beach.

To anyone else, this might have seemed like a great place for a little vacation. To Sam…he felt as if he were going into battle unarmed and naked.

"Come on," Eric said, opening the car door and taking Sam's last chance at escape out of his hands. "My folks can't wait to meet you."

"You know," Sam said, shifting his gaze past Eric to where people were already streaming out the front door like grade schoolers hearing the last bell before summer vacation, "maybe I should let you visit with your family first. I'll go to the hotel, check in, then come back tomorrow."

*Or the next day,* he thought wildly, watching the crowd of people pushing through the door grow and grow and grow. Just how many people were *in* the Wright family, anyway?

"Not a chance," Eric said, easing his crutches from the back seat. "If you have too long to think about it, you'll head back to L.A."

The fact that his friend knew him that well was mildly irritating, but Sam swallowed it back and forced a smile for the first member of the Wright family to reach the car.

"God, Eric, your leg!" An older woman with graying blond hair and wide blue eyes crooned the words. Eric's mother, probably, Sam thought as she reached into the car for her son.

"Look like hell, boy,"

"Thanks, Dad." Eric laughed and handed out the crutches. "Give me a hand."

The older man, burly with a square jaw, cautious eyes and a day or two's worth of gray stubble on his jaw, said, "Step back, honey." He waited until his wife was out of range, then took the crutches in one beefy fist and Eric's arm with the other, effortlessly propelling his son out of the car.

Sam stayed right where he was. Out of the swirl

of hugs and kisses and squeals. He had no doubt they'd get around to him eventually, but if he stayed quiet, he could put it off. The small mob tightened in some kind of group hug, with each of them trying to out-shout the other. Smiles, laughter, a few tears, and the family welcome celebration was in high gear. An old black Lab sat to one side and barked while a couple of kids, a boy about six and a girl even younger, danced around outside the circle of the jabbering adults, vying for attention.

It was like watching a greeting card commercial.

*Outsider.*

That's what he was, and at no time had it ever been clearer than right at that moment. Of course, that's how he wanted it, right? He didn't want connections. Ties. He'd done it once—made the commitment, made plans—and it had fallen apart, nearly undoing him in the process.

He'd learned the hard way that connections only left you vulnerable to pain. So whether he got lonely sometimes or not, he wasn't about to forget that lesson. He'd just sit here until the Wrights scrambled back into their storybook cottage and left him alone.

But that happy little thought lasted only moments. Until one of the women pulled away from the solid mass of humanity and leaned down to peer into the car at him.

"You must be Sam."

"Must be," he said and took one brief moment

to appreciate her—objectively, of course, as an art lover would admire a beautiful painting. Her skin was smooth and the color of rich cream. Her eyes were big and blue like her mother's. Her blond hair, pulled loosely back from her face into a ponytail, hung down on one side of her neck. The dark blue T-shirt and jeans she wore looked faded and comfortable.

"You're…"

"Tricia," she said, her lips curving as she studied him more closely. "Eric's sister. Well," she corrected a moment later, "one of them." She glanced back at the still-gleeful crowd. "There's the other one—Debbie."

He looked at the shorter, rounder blonde, currently wrapping her arms around Eric's neck tight enough to strangle.

"We're easy to tell apart. She's six months pregnant, I'm not."

"I'll remember," Sam said, though he doubted that Tricia Wright would ever be easy to confuse with anyone else.

She cocked her head, smiled and asked, "So, are you getting out of the car anytime soon?"

"Actually, I don't think so," Sam told her, suddenly looking forward more than ever to a nice, quiet night at the hotel. Give the Wrights time to enjoy their reunion. "I was just dropping Eric and his stuff off. I'll be going to the hotel until—"

"Oh, that's not gonna fly," she said, and slid into

the passenger seat. "Aah, that's better, was getting a crick in my neck."

Sam just stared at her, then shifted his gaze to where her family had calmed down enough to let the kids into the inner circle. Eric had the little girl balanced on one hip as he ruffled the boy's hair.

Family.

A part of him admired the strength in them. The bond that held them so closely. Yet, another part of him thought of those ties as binding chains that, once shattered, left a man suddenly, shockingly adrift. Better to avoid the ties altogether then, wasn't it?

"Nice car," Tricia said.

"Thanks." How to get her out of the car so he could turn on the engine and get gone?

She hit the eject button on the CD player so she could inspect the disc inside. Nodding in approval, she glanced at him. "Rock and roll, but not heavy metal. I like a man who can appreciate the classics."

Apparently, she'd settled in for the long haul. He scowled at her deliberately. That scowl had been used successfully to keep people at bay for most of his life. Apparently though, Tricia Wright hadn't gotten the memo on that one. She laughed. Not one of those dainty, musical, little wind chime laughs, either. It was full and loud and rattled around inside him until he was forced to shift uncomfortably.

"Sorry," she said, shaking her head. "Was that your 'scary' look?"

What was he supposed to say to that?

"Hey, Sam," Eric called out, "hit the trunk latch, will ya?"

Hallelujah. Anything to get this done so he could head to the hotel. He reached down by the side of the driver's seat, pulled the latch and heard the trunk spring open. Glancing into the rearview mirror, Sam saw what looked like the entire herd of Wrights assemble behind his car.

"So," Tricia said from beside him, "you're a doctor."

"Yeah." He kept his gaze fixed on the crowd behind his car. There seemed to be a hell of a lot of activity back there just to pick up Eric's two bags.

"What kind? Eric's never said, really."

He shot her an exasperated look. Those wide blue eyes were fixed on him. "Medical."

"Funny."

Sam sighed as she continued to stare at him. There was a steady patience about her that told him she wasn't going anywhere. Until he could make his escape, it looked as though he was going to be in a conversation whether he wanted one or not. "I'm a G.P."

"Good." She slid the CD back into its slot in the dash. "I hate specialists."

One eyebrow lifted. "Why?"

"I don't know," she admitted, smiling. "Maybe I watch too much TV, but specialists seem more concerned with the disease than the patient and that's not good."

"They're not all—"

She leaned back in the seat, flipped the visor down and checked her hair in the mirror. "I really do watch too much TV, you know. Comes from not having a life."

Way too much information, Sam thought and threw another look at the back of the car. Why weren't they finished yet?

"You're ignoring me, hoping I'll go away, aren't you?"

A pinprick of guilt stabbed at Sam, but he ignored it more successfully than he had Tricia. "Not really. I'm just…"

"Crabby?"

He scowled at her one more time. "No."

"There's that scary face again," she pointed out. "You should have noticed already that it doesn't work on me."

"What will?" Sam asked, desperate enough to try anything.

She chuckled and shook her head until her blond ponytail swung off her left shoulder to settle on her right. "Ah, that you'll have to figure out for yourself."

Trying to decipher Tricia Wright would take years, Sam thought. And he wouldn't be here that long. Two weeks, he reminded himself. Two weeks until Eric's wedding and then he could get back to L.A. Back to his practice. Back to the blessed stillness of his condo.

The trunk lid slammed closed and he smiled to himself. Couldn't go home yet, but he could escape to the tranquility of a hotel room all to himself. And right now, that looked like a close enough second-best.

"Sounds like they've got it all," Tricia said and swung her legs out the passenger side door. Then she looked back over her shoulder at him and grinned. "You might as well give it up and come along quietly."

"What?" He was hardly listening. Instead, he stared past her as the group of Wrights hauled luggage—Eric's *and* Sam's—toward the house.

"Hey!" He shouted it, but no one paid any attention. With no one left to ask, he glared at Tricia. "Where're they going with—"

"You didn't really think the folks would let the man who saved their son's life stay in a hotel, did you?"

He shifted his gaze to hers and saw the glint of humor sparkling at him. She knew damn well that he felt trapped. And it didn't seem to bother her in the slightest.

"So, Doc Crabapple," she asked, "you coming quietly or will I have to get rough?"

# Two

Food, Sam thought, seemed to be the universal signal for welcome.

And the Wright family had it down to a science.

The big, square kitchen was roomy and tidy, with the faux wood counters practically gleaming. Cupboards painted a blindingly snowy white lined the walls while a huge, farmhouse-style table crouched in front of a wide window. Afternoon sunlight slanted through the panes and poked between the red curtains, which were ruffling in a breeze slipping beneath the partially opened window. And on the table, in that splash of sunlight, lay enough food for a battalion.

Being without the fatted calf hadn't slowed Mrs. Wright down any. Instead, she supplied a turkey, a ham and every side dish known to man. The Wright family swarm surrounded the table, balancing plates and napkins and cups filled with everything from fruit punch to beer.

Sam had been scooped up and planted in the line taking a slow walk around the buffet and, hungry or not, was clearly expected to eat his way to unconsciousness.

"Have some of this macaroni salad," Eric's sister Debbie was saying as she plopped a heaping serving-spoonful onto his plate. "Mom makes the best."

"Don't forget my fresh corn." Mr. Wright, Dan, plunked a steaming ear, slathered with butter, on the corner of his plate and smiled with pride.

"You know," Sam said, "I appreciate all of this, but I should be—"

"Want another beer?" Eric called from behind the refrigerator door.

"No, thanks."

Debbie's husband Bill helped his daughter fill her plate while Mrs. Wright, Emma, focused on her grandson's demands for more stuffing. Eric's brother Jake leaned against a wall in the corner of the room, watching the melee over the rim of his cup of beer. Tricia had already been around the table, made her selections, and now was perched on the kitchen counter, watching Sam negotiate through the minefield of family. He felt her stare and sensed her amusement.

*Happy to help,* he thought wryly, glad that someone was enjoying all of this.

An only child, he'd been raised in quiet civility. His parents were older than his friends' folks and they'd treated him like a short adult. They'd included him in family decisions, fostered his love of books and school and taken him on vacations to the great museums of the world.

His experience with family life was completely different from the Wrights. In his parents' home, mealtime was a quiet, genteel hour with thought-provoking discussions on current events.

*This* was like a day at the circus. The noise level was tremendous and the eager conversations flying around the room defied all his attempts to understand them.

But none of them seemed to have any problem keeping up at all.

"Kevin," Debbie warned her son, "no cake if you don't—"

"—he's got beans," her mother said.

"—but no meat, and boys need meat."

"Boys can live without meat." The patriarch spoke up in a tone that defied a challenge. "They need milk."

"Milk is not for everyone, you know," Eric piped up. "Ask Sam. He's a doctor, he can tell you."

"Did you call and check on the caterers for the reception?" Debbie asked the question, but Sam had no idea to whom it had been directed.

"But if you don't have milk, your bones fall apart." Eric's father defended his stance.

"Yes, they've got everything under control." Eric's fiancée Jen answered, but Sam wasn't sure if she was talking about the milk or the reception. Wasn't sure if *they* knew. Or cared.

"Just look at Eric," Debbie's husband said with a grin. "He doesn't drink milk and his leg bone snapped like a twig."

"That was a car, not a lack of calcium." Eric swung his crutch at the man, but his brother-in-law was too quick and sidestepped the half-hearted blow.

"Same thing," Dan continued, apparently not caring if anyone was listening or not. "If Eric had still been drinking milk, he might not be wearing crutches for his wedding."

Sam's head swung back and forth, trying to follow the conversational tennis match, but he couldn't keep up. Nineteen forties–style music poured from the stereo in the living room, the family dog howled from beneath the table, and Eric and his brother launched into a new argument on the merits of SUVs versus sports cars.

A movement at the corner of his eye caught Sam's attention and when he followed it he spotted Tricia. Giving her family an indulgent shake of her head, she crooked her index finger in a 'follow me' signal.

The fact that he did only served to prove the level of his desperation.

She led him through the living room and onto the front porch. Once he stepped onto the whitewashed cement floor, she closed the door, cutting off most of the noise behind them.

He took a deep breath and let it slide from him in a rush. The relative silence was a blessing...an almost spiritual event.

Tricia spoiled it by laughing.

He shot her a look. "Amused?"

"Please. *Way* more than amused." She waved a hand, then walked to the end of the porch and took a seat on the bright red swing. Patting the padded cushion beside her, she coaxed, "Take a load off."

There's a choice, he thought. Alone with Tricia or back into the fray. He glanced behind him at the closed door and thought about the herd of people within. It took only a moment to make up his mind. Still holding a plate full of food he didn't want and a cup of cold beer he did, he walked toward her. Setting his plate on a small, square wooden table, he eased back into the swing beside Tricia and nearly groaned at the relief of the quiet.

"Are they always like that?" he asked, letting his head fall to the seat back.

"Loud?" she asked with a laugh. "You bet."

"How do they understand each other?"

"Shorthand," she mused and tucked one leg beneath her. Her other foot dangled and she used the toe of her sneaker to give them a push. The swing moved into a lazy back-and-forth pattern that induced relaxation. "With four kids in the family, you learn early to say whatever you want said or you'll never get the chance."

"What makes you think anyone's listening?"

"Hah!" She leaned her head back, too, and turned slightly to look at him. "They're *always* listening. Trust me on that. I used to try to sneak a sentence in without being noticed—"

"Like?"

Her grin broadened. "Oh, like, 'Is it okay if I go to Terri's party if her parents aren't going to be there?'"

"And they heard?"

"Oh yeah. Putting one past them was never easy, but they're great."

He glanced away from her long enough to look at the living room window just a foot or so away. Behind those dark green curtains lay unfamiliar and downright confusing territory. "I'm sure they are, but—"

"—but, being in there made you look really…"

"Uncomfortable?"

"I was going to go with trapped."

He turned his head to look at her again, meeting those blue eyes with a steady stare. Damn it, he hadn't meant to offend anyone and he hoped to hell the rest of her family wasn't quite as intuitive as Tricia. "Seems a little harsh."

"I thought so, too," she said with a smile that told him she, at least, hadn't been offended. "But still, I've never seen a man who looked more in need of a rescue."

"Maybe not a rescue, but the reprieve was good. Thanks." He took a sip of his beer, warming now in the afternoon heat. "I didn't mean anything by it—"

"Hey, I'm the first one to admit we take a little getting used to," Tricia said. "Especially for someone new."

"Thanks for that, too."

"No problem."

He looked at her. "Are you always so accommodating?"

"Oh," she said with another small chuckle, "almost never. You're catching me on a good day."

"Lucky me."

"Sarcasm. Or did you mean it?"

"Right now," he said, enjoying the fact that he was outside in the sunshine with relative quiet all around him, thanks to this one pretty woman, "I mean it."

"Then, thank you."

"You're welcome."

"See, how hard was that?"

"What?"

"We just had an actual conversation."

One corner of his mouth tipped up. "It was over so fast, I must have missed it."

"See? You're already learning about chats in this family. Want to go back in?"

His features must have mirrored what he was feeling because she leaned in closer and said, "No hurry.

You're the guest of honor, so you can pretty much do whatever you want to do."

"*I'm* the guest of honor?" Honestly surprised, he just looked at her. "I figured all of that food was on Eric's behalf."

"Not completely." Reaching out, she tapped her fingernails against the wrappings on his arm. "Heroes need big welcomes."

Sam shifted on the seat, putting a couple more inches between himself and the woman still leaning toward him. And something told him it wasn't nearly enough. "I'm not a hero."

As if sensing his need for distance, she sat back, but kept her gaze locked on him. "Couldn't prove that to Mom and Dad. Or to Eric's fiancée."

"I was there at the right time," he said simply, shifting his gaze to the yard and the street beyond.

"I'm glad."

He looked at her again, saw the warmth in her eyes and felt a like response flicker to life inside him. This he could accept. "So'm I."

She smiled and something inside him relaxed a little even as his other senses heightened.

Silence dropped between them and Sam reveled in it. He'd been too long alone to be able to adjust easily to being surrounded by people. In his world, there was his condo, the freeway and his office, with no points in between. Weekends only meant being in the office clearing up paperwork and getting a head start on the following week. His nights were spent either in his home gym or in front of his big-screen TV. When insomnia struck, as it often did, he stood alone on the balcony off his living room and watched the stars fade.

He shifted in his seat, a little uncomfortable with all of this sudden self-examination. Sam had never really stopped to consider the way he spent—or wasted—his time. Now that he did, he asked himself if he'd planned to become so insular or if it had just happened ...after Mary.

But then life itself had changed after Mary, hadn't it? The way he saw things, what he thought, felt, experienced. Nothing was as it had been...*before*. There'd been a pall over everything for the last two years and in response, he'd wrapped himself up in the muffling cocoon of solitude. Coming out of it now, even briefly, was as jarring as if he'd been dropped into the Amazon and told to survive with nothing more than a piece of string and a flashlight.

"You're really hating this, aren't you?"

The sound of her voice brought him back, gratefully, from his thoughts. "What?"

She chuckled, shook her head and drew her other leg up until she was sitting cross-legged on the swing. She looked completely comfortable and at ease with both herself and her surroundings, and Sam envied her.

"You heard me," she said, still smiling at him patiently as if he were a particularly dim-witted child.

"You're just trying to think of a way to answer that won't be insulting."

Irritating to be so transparent. As a doctor, he prided himself on his poker face. He never wanted patients to be able to read his diagnosis on his features before he'd had a chance to talk to them. In his personal life, he carried that trait over, keeping an unreadable—or so he'd thought—expression, unwilling to let anyone into his mind, his thoughts, his heart.

Well, except Mary.

But she'd been different.

Tricia Wright was simply…well, the word *different* about covered her, too.

"Your family seems very nice," he hedged.

"Don't forget noisy."

"That, too." Didn't seem wrong to agree if she was the one who'd said it first.

"And this isn't even as noisy as it gets."

"Don't know how it could get louder," he muttered, earning another of her low-throated chuckles. She sounded sexy, intimate, and at the thought, tension built inside him. Something he hadn't expected and didn't want.

"Oh, just wait," she teased, apparently enjoying his discomfort. "Tomorrow, Aunt Beth and Uncle Jim arrive with their three kids and then there's Grandma Joan and her new boyfriend Oliver—"

"Your grandmother has a boyfriend?"

"Well, not really a *boy*, though he is twenty years

younger than her," Tricia explained, "and let me tell you, that was a tough one for my father to take. Having a potential stepfather your own age is a big one to swallow."

Sam shook his head. He should have thanked his parents when they were alive, for being so…tame.

"And the day after, my cousin Nora gets here and she's bringing her son Tommy—lock up the matches."

"An arsonist?" he asked, appalled.

"Well, he's only seven, but he does seem to have his career picked out."

"Great."

"And there'll be *more* of us arriving during the next couple of weeks."

*More* Wrights? How could there be more? It made him want to run inside, grab his bag and hit the freeway, headed for home. But he couldn't, since he'd agreed six months ago to be an usher at Eric's wedding. So he'd settle for what he could get. "Good thing I already got my hotel room," he said, more to himself than to her.

But apparently, you didn't have to actually be speaking *to* Tricia to get a response.

"Oh, they'll be staying with family. No hotels allowed with *this* family. Mom and Dad will house most of them, they've got the most bedrooms. But Debbie and her husband get a few and Jake's putting up the bachelors at his place, God help them."

Sam shook his head, trying to keep the players straight, then gave it up. He'd only be here two weeks, he didn't have to know her family. But despite himself, he was caught up in the flow of her conversation. She hardly seemed to pause for breath.

"What's wrong with Jake's place?"

"Small, for one thing, and the man lives like a pig. He's never really there though, to give him his due," Tricia said thoughtfully. "He works for the government, something supposedly hush-hush. Hard to believe since he was never able to keep a secret when he was a kid." She sighed and trailed one hand along the arm of the swing. "Still, none of my business."

None of his either, Sam thought, grateful that he had an excuse to stay happily alone at his hotel room—a destination which was looking better and better all the time. In fact, no time like the present to make his escape. "With all those people coming in soon, I'll just grab my suitcase and head for the hotel after all."

"Nice try, big boy."

"What?"

She laid one hand on his arm, staying him when he would have stood up. "No hotel for the man of the hour, I already told you. You've already been assigned your quarters."

"I thought you were joking." A small sinking sensation opened up inside him.

"Nope." Tricia grinned and leaned toward him

again, and this time Sam caught a whiff of her perfume. Something soft and floral and summery, clinging to her and yet, drifting in the same light breeze that lifted the loose tendrils of her hair to curl about her face. This was not a good sign. Tricia Wright and her smiles and her scent were somehow more intriguing than they should have been.

But he wasn't going there, he decided, pushing those wayward thoughts out of his brain just as fast as they presented themselves. Holding his breath to avoid being seduced by the scent of summer flowers, he ignored the effect she had on him and concentrated instead on what she was saying.

"Yep, you'll be staying at my house."

Oh no. He just wasn't *that* good at ignoring temptation. And taking another long look at her, he decided that *any* red-blooded male wouldn't be able to ignore her for long.

"I don't think so."

"Scared?" she countered.

He laughed and didn't even manage to convince himself. "Of what?"

"Little ol' me?"

"Not so you'd notice," he said, although a part of him was very wary of both her big blue eyes and that scent that seemed to be reaching out for him, tangling him up in it as though he were being strangled by flowering vines.

"It wasn't my idea, so chill out. Mom and Dad

worked out the housing schedule." Her voice dropped. "They're really grateful for what you did for Eric. They consider you family."

He nearly shivered.

"And family does *not* stay in hotels," she said with another shake of her head. Her ponytail flipped from one shoulder to the other. "Don't worry, I didn't take one look at your masculine beauty and immediately work it so you'd be my houseguest."

He was never sure if she was serious or teasing. And right now, it didn't matter. "I didn't say that—"

"No, but you were thinking it."

"I'm not that easy to read and *no,* I wasn't."

"Ah," she said, holding up one finger like a hammy detective in an old movie, about to make his point, "but I only have your word on that, don't I?"

Sam grumbled and pushed up from the swing. Standing there looking down at her, he felt a little more in control. "Look, I appreciate the offer," he said, though God knows he didn't, "but the hotel will be more convenient all the way around."

"Can't get more convenient than my house. I live right next door," she said.

"What?" That sinking sensation widened…growing into something like a black hole.

"There." She pointed at the house just behind her. "That one's mine. Bought it a couple of years ago, thinking to get out on my own. But how on your own are you when you live next door to your parents?"

"I wouldn't know."

"Oh boy, I do," she said. Then shrugging, she added, "But it was a great deal and way better than throwing my money down a rent hole. And Mom and Dad don't just drop in, they're really good about that."

"Congratulations."

"You're very good at *that*."

"What?"

"Turning conversations around to avoid talking about what you don't want to."

Sam actually laughed. "From what I've seen, the conversations in your family are turning all the time."

"True," she said, pushing herself up and out of the swing. She stood just in front of him and when the swing rushed forward, bumping into the backs of her knees, she fell toward him.

Instinctively, Sam caught her. But he hadn't counted on the rush of warmth snaking up his arms to rattle around in the center of his chest. She was tall. The top of her head hit just below his nose. And she was close—too close. He stepped back, but not before he saw something flash in her eyes. "I just don't think—"

"You'll be a hero again."

The conversational Ferris wheel was turning again. "I'm not a—"

"Fine," she said, cutting him off neatly. "You weren't a hero with Eric. You were in the right place at the right time. But now, you have the chance to be a hero…for *me*."

Sam sighed and knew he was getting deeper and deeper into a mire he wasn't entirely sure he'd be able to get out of. She looked harmless enough, he thought—in fact, she looked the part of the quintessential, all-American girl. Which was actually trouble, not harmless. Add to that the fact that she seemed to have the unerring ability to see into corners of his soul he would prefer stayed shrouded in shadows…

She was more than he'd bargained for, that was all. Sam hadn't thought he'd be getting twisted up with Eric's family. He'd planned to be here, take part in the festivities and then leave again. But that clearly wasn't going to happen. As for now, just looking into her eyes, Sam knew he shouldn't ask what the hell she was talking about. But damned if she hadn't stirred his curiosity. "I surrender," he said. "Just how does my staying at your house qualify me for hero status?"

"If you're my guest, then I won't have to house the little fire starter."

"Your cousin—"

"Tommy."

"Right."

He thought about it for a long minute. Her eyes were wide and clear as she watched him and he knew that he'd be in trouble if he stayed around this woman for any length of time. She was a woman who saw too much, laughed too often. And made him feel…hell, made him *feel*. But he could manage for two weeks, he assured himself. Two weeks was nothing. He'd be able to have some peace and quiet. Her house was bound to be quieter than her parents' place. And he wouldn't have to spend a lot of time with Tricia. She'd be busy helping with the coming wedding. He'd have time to himself without insulting the Wright family.

It could work.

"Be a hero," she prodded. "Save the girl from a fate worse than death."

He'd probably regret it, Sam thought, as he looked down into her big blue eyes. He didn't want to be anybody's hero.

And yet, despite all that, he still heard himself say, "All right. I'll do it."

# Three

The scent of cinnamon and coffee greeted Sam on his first morning in Tricia's house. Sitting up in bed, he had one blank moment when he tried to figure out where the hell he was.

Then it all rushed back to him and he remembered agreeing to move into a perky blonde's house for two weeks. At the moment, he couldn't quite recall *why* but that didn't seem to matter anymore. He glanced around the room and told himself that he could have been staying in a generic hotel room. Instead, he was sleeping in a lavender room that smelled of cinnamon, atop a bed with a scrolled iron head- and footboard. He tossed the flowered quilt to one side and swung his legs off the bed. Lacy white curtains hung at the wide windows and danced lazily in the soft breeze sliding beneath the sash. On one wall of the big room, an antique chest of drawers stood like an old soldier, while on the opposite wall, a small television crouched atop a narrow bookcase stuffed with lurid murder mysteries.

Sam smiled to himself as he rolled out of bed. He'd taken a good look at the reading selections before going to sleep last night. And even with everything he'd seen in his residency and ER rotation, some of those book covers had been enough to turn his stomach. Intriguing woman, Tricia Wright, he thought. Romantic enough to enjoy lace and antiques and apparently grisly enough to enjoy a nice, gory murder or two. What did that say about her personality?

And why did he care enough to wonder?

After a hot shower in the old-fashioned, dollhouse-sized bathroom, he headed down a short flight of stairs. His elbow throbbed from slamming it into the shower wall, and he had a crick in his neck from trying to twist low enough to have the stingy fall of water actually hit the top of his head. But he was awake and now following the delicious scent of fresh coffee and what smelled like some kind of bakery heaven.

He moved quietly through the house, enjoying the near silence and appreciating a woman who didn't seem to have the need to hear the TV newscasters shouting bad news at her first thing in the morning.

Her living room was big and square and dotted with overstuffed furniture that practically invited you to sit deep and relax. There was a brick fireplace on one wall, its mantel crowded with family pictures in a dizzying array of frames.

But he kept moving, on the trail of coffee and when he reached the kitchen, he paused in the doorway, leaning one shoulder against the doorjamb. He crossed his feet at the ankles, folded his arms across his chest and, since she hadn't noticed him yet, took a moment to watch Tricia unobserved.

Her back was to him as she worked at her kitchen counter. In the bright, overhead light, her long blond hair shone like gold in a single, thick braid that ended just at her shoulder blades. She wore a tight gray T-shirt that clung to every curve and denim shorts that exposed long, sleekly tanned legs. She was barefoot and dancing in time to the music sliding softly from the radio on the counter.

As he watched, she deftly handled a rolling pin on the marble countertop putting her whole body into the task. Behind her, on the large kitchen table, an assortment of cookies in various stages of readiness were placed assembly-line fashion—some waiting to be baked, some cooling on wire racks and some waiting to be frosted and decorated. Since she obviously had a system, this must be a familiar routine.

Sam tried to think back and recall some of the things Eric had told him about his family. But it was all a blur of information and names Sam had never paid much attention to. That should teach him to listen more.

The first light of dawn spilled into the room in a thin trickle that warred with the glare of electricity and glanced off shining window panes to lie across the field of cookies. When Tricia started singing along with the radio, he smiled at her imitation of The King.

"I'd stick to baking if I were you," he said softly, then louder, added, "Does your audience get coffee?"

"Whoops!" She practically shrieked the word and whirled around all at the same time. Slapping one hand to her chest, she left a floury handprint on her T-shirt as she gasped for breath and then laughed. "You move like a creeper."

"And you sing like a baker." He stepped into the kitchen, still watching her. She looked good first thing in the morning, he thought. Which he really shouldn't be noticing. But as a male, it was sort of a given that he would.

"Didn't mean to spook you."

"Well, now that my heart's beating again," she said, "you're forgiven."

"Forgiven enough for a cup of that coffee?"

"I would never withhold coffee as a punishment," she said, already reaching for an oversized purple mug from the cupboard to her right. "It's just inhumane."

"You're obviously a superior human being."

"I like to think so," she quipped as she filled the mug with a rich, dark brew that smelled like heaven to Sam.

Turning, she handed it to him and said, "If you want to spoil this excellent Colombian roast, there's milk in the fridge and sugar in the pantry."

He shook his head and took that first glorious sip. As the hot coffee slid down his throat, Sam felt himself waking up. "I take it black."

She grinned and lifted her own mug in a toast. "My kind of man."

Now, most men, he figured, would have taken that statement as an invitation to get to know her better. To enjoy a little flirtation. A little word play designed to entice. But Sam withstood the temptation. He wasn't here to banter, wasn't here looking for a two-week fling. And if he were, it sure wouldn't be with a woman like Tricia. She just wasn't a "fling" kind of woman. Anyone could tell that just by looking at her. She had "permanence" practically tattooed on her forehead. She was picket fences and small children and holiday dinners and huge family gatherings.

In other words, she was everything Sam was *not*.

"Don't bet on it," he said.

She laughed, took another sip of coffee, then set the big blue mug down within reach on the countertop. "I said you were my *kind* of man, not *my* man. So you can take that *Oh-my-God-how-do-I-get-out-of-here* look off your face."

Instantly, he blanked out his features, but stiffened at the fact that she'd seen right through him. Again.

"Seriously," she said, picking up her marble rolling pin and waving it at him like a professor using a pointer, "you need to relax. Your virtue is entirely safe with me."

Sam scowled a little at her dismissal. Fine, he wasn't interested, but there was a *very* small part of him that still felt the sting of a beautiful woman's indifference. His grip on the purple mug tightened slightly. "And why's that?"

She gave him a brief look and an even briefer smile. But as brief as it was, it carried power. Like the first light of dawn breaking in a dark sky, that smile indicated that more spectacular things were ahead.

"I've sworn off men." She looked at him again. "Didn't Eric tell you?"

"Why would he?"

She shrugged and set the rolling pin aside to pick up a stainless steel cookie cutter. Deftly, she pressed it into the waiting dough, then turned it and pressed again, getting as many cookies as possible on the first roll. "Because the family's worried about me. They think I'm depressed or something."

*"You?"* He hadn't meant to sound so astonished, but how anyone could consider a woman who even *talked* with a smile in her voice depressed was beyond him.

"Thank you." She picked up a spatula and carefully began to scoop up the cut out cookies and lay them on a waiting baking sheet. "I love my family, but try to convince them of anything."

"What're you supposed to be depressed about?" He walked closer and leaned one hip against the cold edge of the counter.

She sighed dramatically and rested the back of her hand against her forehead in a pose worthy of Broadway. "I was *dumped*."

Surprise flickered to life inside Sam as he watched her. He couldn't imagine a man stupid enough to dump a woman like her—well, unless he'd been treated to an overdose of her family. "Eric didn't mention it."

At least, he didn't *think* so. But so often, when his friends were talking to him, Sam's mind was a million miles away. Eric might have mentioned being worried about his younger sister and the words would have sailed past Sam unnoticed. He'd been too wrapped up in his own misery the last two years to pay much attention at all to the rest of the world.

And for the first time, he began to feel a little guilt over that fact.

"Well yay, him," Tricia said, finishing up the latest batch of cookies. She picked up the tray and glanced at him as she turned for the huge, commercial-size oven on the opposite wall. She bent down, yanked the door open and shoved that tray, plus another, inside. When she straightened, she set a timer on the range top and turned again. "It's no big deal," she said, "it's just that I've finally decided to accept my fate."

"And what's that?"

She plopped both flour-dusted hands onto her hips, heedless of the white powder she was dribbling on her clothes and the floor. "I just don't have any luck at all with guys. So, I've decided to give up men and have a special relationship with sugar, instead."

He smiled in spite of himself. Waving one hand at the array of goodies on the table, he said, "Apparently you and sugar are quite serious about this new relationship."

"Oh, yeah. Sugar will never let you down." She held up three fingers in a half-assed Girl Scout salute. "It may give you cavities and make you fat, but it will *always* be there for you. No matter what."

"And that's the important thing?"

"What else is there?"

What else, indeed?

Moving away from the counter, he took a closer look at the cookies on the table. In the shapes of champagne flutes and beer mugs, the cookies smelled like glory and looked like a mountain of work.

Intrigued, he glanced at her. "Your sugar comes in the shapes of champagne and beer?"

She walked over to stand at his side. "Another good point about sugar. It can come in *any* shape or size and they'll all be the right ones." Then she grinned at him. "These were commissioned by Mom. Some for the bachelor party, some for the bridal shower. You guess which are for which."

"Not too hard to do," he said. "But I don't think I've ever had cookies at a bachelor party."

She sniffed. "You will at this one."

"Apparently. Do they taste as good as they look?"

"You tell me." She picked up one of the frosted, decorated beer mug cookies and handed it to him.

Sam looked at her as he bit into it. Then he closed his eyes to better enjoy the taste rolling through him. He'd never had anything like it. Sweet, but not overly so, the cookie had an underlying flavor that swept through him and yet defied description. When he swallowed, he opened his eyes again to find her watching him with a knowing smile on her face.

"You like it."

"It's great."

She gave him a half bow. "Thank you."

He took another bite, savoring as he chewed. "What's that flavor I'm tasting?"

"Family secret."

"Seriously."

"I am being serious."

"Your mom thinks of me as family."

She looked at him for a long minute and Sam felt a new and decidedly different kind of tension build up between them. Then she spoke again and the moment was gone.

"But you're not family, are you?"

"You're not going to tell me, are you?"

"Hey," she said, "if I go around telling people my secrets, I'll be out of business instead of growing."

"This is your business?" He looked again at the table, nearly groaning under the weight of the trays and platters and racks of cookies.

She practically beamed. "I'm Cookie Lady."

He shook his head. "What?"

She sighed and a wisp of blond hair on her forehead lifted into a brief dance. "Fine. So you haven't heard of me. I'm not well-known yet. But I will be," she told him, swinging back to the counter where more dough and her rolling pin awaited her. "I'm building a reputation with parties and promotional stuff. And in a month, I'll be setting up shop in my own bakery."

"Yeah?" Intrigued by the pleasure in her voice and the excitement fairly vibrating around her, Sam pulled out a chair and sat down. Snatching up another cookie, he ate, sipped his coffee and listened as Tricia described her blossoming business.

She looked at him over her shoulder and sent him a smile that would have staggered a lesser man. But he was immune. He hadn't noticed a pretty woman in two years. So he wasn't noticing Tricia, either.

Very much.

"I got such a great deal on this retail space on the Coast Highway. It's perfect," she said as she gathered up the dough, rolled it into a ball and wielded the rolling pin again. "Big storefront window for display, nice counters and a kitchen that will really give me some room to expand."

"Looks to me like you're doing a good business already," he said, finishing off his second cookie.

"Oh, it's been great," she agreed, "and go ahead, have another one if you want—"

He did.

"—but my business is growing faster than I'd even hoped, so I just can't continue to do it out of my kitchen, you know?"

"Is that what you want?"

"Huh?"

Sam shrugged, got up and walked to the coffee pot on the counter. Refilling his purple mug, he set the pot back on the warming tray and took a long sip before saying, "Most people would appreciate being able to work out of their home."

"Yeah," she agreed, "it's been great. And handy. The store will be more expensive to run, what with rent and having to hire somebody full-time to help me out, but the trade-off is that I'll be able to do more jobs."

He didn't even remember a time when he'd been as enthused about anything as Tricia was over her burgeoning business. He saw it in her eyes, heard it in her voice and he realized that he *missed* that feeling of challenge. Of betting on yourself. Of taking a risk and putting everything on the line.

"I'll move into the shop two weeks after the wedding, so the family will be able to help do the big jobs."

"You spend a lot of time together—your family, I mean."

"Well, we all live close by," she said, "except for Eric—but you already know that. So yeah, we see each other a lot."

He didn't say anything at all and, after a moment or two, she shot him a look.

"We a little much for you, Doctor Crabby?"

"I'm not crabby," he muttered, more as a reflex than anything else.

"Okay, you haven't been this morning, but the day is young."

"Thanks," he said wryly and leaned one hip against the counter.

Even from a foot away, she smelled like flowers dusted with vanilla and cinnamon. Her skin was creamy and smooth and looked like coffee with too much milk in it. Just a soft, pale brown that told him she liked being outside, but didn't bake herself just for the sake of being tanned. Her hands were constantly in motion, working on her cookies with a capable, practiced touch. Her fingers were long, her nails short and neat. She wore no rings, but she did have huge, gypsy-like silver hoops dangling from her ears.

Her full lips seemed permanently curved into a half smile, as if she knew…

And he was getting entirely too focused on the Cookie Lady.

Moving back to his chair, hoping somehow that a little distance would ease the surprising ache that had erupted inside him, Sam sat down and focused on his coffee.

"Your arm feeling better?" She glanced at his now unwrapped forearm.

"Yeah," he said, flexing as if testing his own strength. "It's fine. Always was."

"That's good. So you're all set to help with the barbecue?"

"What?" Her ability to shift conversational gears left him constantly feeling as though he were running to catch up.

"At Debbie's. She's having a barbecue for the family and for the almost in-laws at her place. We'll have to go in about an hour. Help set up the tables and chairs and stuff."

"Sure." More family, he thought, acknowledging, at least to himself, that he couldn't remember the Wright family members he'd met already.

"Don't worry," she said, as if looking into his mind—which she had a habit of doing far too often. "They don't bite." Then she paused, cocked her head and seemed to consider that statement. "Well, Katie bites sometimes," she said thoughtfully. "That's Debbie's youngest. But don't worry, she's had her shots."

"Great."

* * *

Katie didn't bite, but she did cling.

The way a dog gravitates toward the one person in the crowd who doesn't like animals, Katie decided within the first fifteen minutes that Sam was her new favorite person. To be fair, though, it wasn't as though Sam didn't like kids. He did. He just didn't have much experience with them outside his professional life.

The little girl was almost elfin. Her long dark hair swung in pigtails hanging from either side of her head. Big blue eyes looked up at Sam with a coy flirtatiousness that told him she was going to be a heartbreaker when she grew up. At four, she was two years younger than her big brother Kevin, and obviously used to being indulged. But Sam was a sucker for the kid for a whole different reason than her loving family was.

The only children Sam saw regularly were his patients. And none of them were happy to see him, thanks to booster shots, inoculations and throat swabs. To have a child actually seem to *like* him was so novel, he really enjoyed it.

Perched on his knee, Katie leaned against his chest and opened her favorite book for the third time. Tipping her head back, she stared up at him and smiled. A powerful weapon. And the tiny girl knew it. Sam couldn't stop his own smile as he reached for the first page.

"You should do that more often," a female voice— Tricia's—said from close by.

He glanced at her as she came up alongside him. "Do what?"

"Smile," she said, apparently unmoved by the irritation in his tone. It was one thing reading to a child, another altogether reading for an audience. Plopping down on the picnic bench beside him, she reached across him to poke a finger into Katie's side and release a giggle, like air escaping a balloon.

"I smile," he said and turned back to the book and a more-impatient-by-the-minute Katie.

"Now, see," Tricia countered, stretching her long legs out in front of her. "Not so much."

"You just met me yesterday," he pointed out tightly. "And I smiled just this morning."

"Yeah, but you just don't look like you do it often enough. You don't have the 'smiler' vibe."

"And a smiler looks...how?"

"Happy," she said and grinned into his best withering glare.

The woman was as much a mystery to Sam as the books she so loved to read. Every time he turned around, she was right there. Even when they'd been hanging streamers and hauling chairs, she'd somehow managed to be within arm's reach of him. Not that he'd reached or anything. But he could have if he'd been so inclined.

Ever since their conversation that morning, when things had suddenly felt too...cozy for comfort, Sam had tried to keep his distance. But it seemed that Tricia was just as determined to close that distance.

She leaned her elbows on the tabletop behind her and tilted her head to one side as she watched him. Her blond hair shone in the late morning sun and the spatter of freckles across her nose looked like someone had sprayed her with gold dust. Her mouth was curved, naturally, and her expression was one of practiced innocence. He didn't believe it for a minute. She knew damn well that he'd been trying to stay away from her, so she'd done everything she could to keep him from succeeding.

Katie, sensing that the attention had somehow drifted away from *her*, made her displeasure known.

She grabbed a handful of Sam's dark green polo shirt and yanked. "Read a book!"

Since she'd also snatched a few chest hairs, Sam winced, patted her little hand and said, "Right. No more interruptions." That was said with a telling look at Tricia. "Back to the man in the moon."

"Good."

"Good," Tricia repeated.

"Don't you have somewhere else to be?" Sam asked, sliding her a glance.

She grinned at him and her big blue eyes actually sparkled. "I'm on a break."

"And you have to stay here?" Clearly, though, she was settling in, making herself comfortable. And making him as *un*comfortable as possible.

"Katie wants me here, don't you sweetie?"

"Aunt Trish likes a book."

"See?" Tricia grinned at the girl as though they'd rehearsed the whole scene.

He gave it one more shot. "No blood and guts in this story."

"Hey," Tricia said, still aiming that potent smile of hers at him, "variety *is* the spice of life."

And there were all kinds of variety, Sam thought, tearing his gaze from Tricia's. The trouble was, when the woman who smelled like a flower garden was too close to him, his brain was unwillingly filled with amazingly in-depth and Technicolor visions of just what kind of variety there was for two people to discover.

# Four

Eric sat in a green resin lawn chair beneath the shade of a fifty-year-old elm tree. A breeze rustled through the feathery light leaves overhead, sending dappled patches of shade into a weird dance on the sun-warmed grass.

His right leg ached, and he was so tired, it was an effort to keep his eyes open. But despite everything, he felt lucky and grateful to be alive.

Whether Sam wanted to admit it or not, Eric owed him more than he could ever repay. The fact that he was sitting here, enjoying the confusion only his family could create, was a gift he'd never really thought about until today. But that debt didn't mean he wasn't worried about what was going on between Sam and Tricia.

Eric's gaze settled on his sister, his friend and his niece, all sitting on a picnic bench across the yard from him. There was too much noise from everyone else for him to catch any of what they were saying. But judging from the way Tricia was smiling up at Sam, something was definitely up.

He just didn't know what.

He hadn't said much about Tricia to Sam, knowing that his friend had been too wrapped up in his own grief and pain to be interested. But now that he saw them together, Eric had to wonder if it had been such a great idea to drag Sam upstate for a vacation. Tricia was just coming off a bad breakup and, even if she wouldn't admit it under threat of torture, Eric knew she was still vulnerable.

Tricia'd always had a hard head and a tender heart. She went her own way, wasn't afraid of speaking her mind and was usually left regretting it. She'd dated a string of guys who weren't good enough for her, and always ended up getting her heart slapped. And God help you if you tried to tell her so. She was contrary enough to date a guy you warned her away from, just to prove that she was her own woman.

So, if Eric were to take his life in his hands and tell Tricia to stay away from Sam, she'd be more than likely to find the man even more fascinating. And he'd been the one to present her with Sam. It was like dangling a candy bar in front of a chocoholic.

But even as he thought it, Eric reconsidered.

Maybe this time, Tricia wouldn't leap without looking. And even if she did, Sam at least was a good guy. He was just a man who'd been lost so long he didn't even remember how he'd gotten that way. In the last two years, Eric had watched Sam pull further and further away from everything he used to care about.

Most of the man's few friends had drifted away, but Eric had stuck. He'd tried to pull Sam back into the world of the living, but it hadn't worked. Sam had been determined to suffer. Determined to wallow in the rubble of his world.

Now, though Sam looked uncomfortable as hell, he was at least *at* the party. Surrounded by people. Sitting beside a woman who was the perfect "glass half-full" to his "glass half-empty."

Eric leaned to one side and reached down to the grass for his bottle of beer. Straightening up again, he focused his gaze on Tricia, noting her smile and the way she leaned in toward Sam. Worry snaked through him for a minute as he tried to decide who he was more concerned for—his sister, or his friend.

But the truth of the matter was, if Tricia decided to fall for Sam, there wasn't a damn thing any of them could do about it. And would he if he could? He didn't know. Tricia's heart was still bruised, but it had been bruised before and she'd survived. Plus, she had a way of enjoying life that might be just the medicine Sam needed.

So what was a brother supposed to do? he asked

himself. Just sit back and watch—wait to see if there would be fireworks?

"What do we know about him?"

"Geez!" Eric jolted in his chair. He hadn't heard his older brother Jake's approach. The man moved like a ghost. "Tryin' to kill me?"

Jake gave him a fast grin and shook his head. "Too easy a target. No challenge."

"Well, thanks, that makes me feel manly." Eric scowled at him. "What'd you say before?"

"Sam," Jake said as he went down on one knee beside Eric's chair. "What do we know about him?"

"He's a friend."

"Anything else?"

Apparently Jake's radar was on red alert, too. Hell of a thing to be a member of a close family—too many people to look out for. "Doctor. Widower. Good guy."

"Uh-huh." Jake nodded toward their sister. "Good enough for Trish?"

"Is anybody?"

Jake laughed shortly. "No. Hell, Bill's not good enough for Debbie and they're working on number three."

Eric took another sip of his beer and enjoyed the rush of cold frothy liquid before speaking again. "True. But I don't think you have to worry about Sam that way. He's…"

"Gay?"

"No way," Eric said on a short laugh.

"Blind, then?"

"No."

"He'd have to be to not see Tricia."

Blind or too far removed from life, Eric thought. He didn't say so, though. Jake was his brother, but he owed a loyalty to his friend, too. And that included not talking about Sam's problems.

"He's only gonna be here two weeks," Eric said instead, and wasn't sure who he was trying to convince—himself, or his brother. "What can happen in two weeks?"

Jake stared at him for a long minute, then laughed and stood up again. "You're kidding, right?"

Eric frowned thoughtfully. Jake had him thinking now, and even he had to admit that two weeks was plenty of time for hearts to connect...or break.

"What're you two planning?"

He shifted his gaze from his brother to his fiancée, and grinned as Jen sank to the grass and leaned back against his chair.

"Me?" Jake said, already walking back toward his father and the clutch of cousins hanging around the barbecue. "Not a thing, Jen. Not a thing."

"What was that about?" she asked, glancing after Jake.

"Just brother stuff." Eric threaded his fingers through her long, red hair. A quiet ping of guilt sounded out inside him. He should probably talk about all this with the woman he was planning to marry. But on the other hand, she'd probably think he was crazy for worrying in the first place. So instead, he hedged. "What makes you think I'm planning something?"

Jen tipped her head back and pinned him with a steady gaze. "I know you too well. Right now," she said, "you're wondering if you should rescue Tricia from Sam or Sam from Tricia."

He shouldn't have been surprised, he thought. He'd known Jen since they were kids. They'd been close since high school and had kept their relationship going even when he'd moved down to L.A. She'd been his heart for as long as he could remember. Was it any wonder she could read him as easily as she did?

"You're good," he admitted with a nod.

"Just remember that," she said and crossed her arms atop his left knee, resting her chin on her joined hands. "Wives know all and see all."

"You're not a wife yet," he teased.

"Will be in two weeks," she said, reaching for his hand.

His fingers curled around hers and held on. She was everything to him. Staring into her wide green eyes, he saw the promise of a lifetime shining back at him. He saw his future—*their* future—stretch out in front of him, and it looked great. He took a deep breath and released it on a sigh. If Sam hadn't been with him at the accident, if he hadn't been able to get

Eric out of the wreck… God, he would have missed so much.

Emotions filled him, nearly choking him with their intensity. "I love you," he blurted.

"Right back at ya," Jen said playfully, but her fingers tightened on his and he knew that she, too, was realizing just how close they'd come to losing what they had together.

Then she turned her head and looked at the three people sitting on a bench in a splash of sunshine. "So," she said, a moment later, "what did you and Jake decide about your sister and your pal?"

Eric gave them a brief glance before turning his gaze back to the woman sitting in front of him. "Jake's not talking. But I think, I'm going to remain neutral. At least for now."

"Good call."

"You think?"

Jen sighed and shook her head. "You Wrights are terrific, the way it's one for all and all for one," she said, "but you've got Tricia all wrong."

He straightened up in his chair and winced a little at the pressure on his leg. "Oh yeah?"

Jen gave him a patient, understanding smile. "She's not a fragile little woman who needs your protection, Eric. She knows what she's doing."

"In most things, sure. But about guys?"

She laughed and shook her head. "Tricia's not a wounded bird, you know."

Eric looked at his sister again and couldn't help the flicker of concern that flashed through him. "I hope you're right."

"Once we're married," Jen promised, "you'll see I'm *always* right."


An hour later, Sam realized he was actually having a good time. He hadn't expected to. Had, in fact, expected to be on the point of pulling his hair out by now. Instead, he felt himself being sucked into the crazed vortex that was the Wright family.

They were loud, funny, and almost impossible to stand against. A solitary man didn't have a chance with this group. They refused to allow anyone to be alone. Their hospitality simply wrapped around an outsider like a warm blanket on a cold night.

The scene in Debbie's backyard was one of complete confusion with a weird sense of order. Children ran and played with the old dog who looked like he wanted nothing more than to find a shady spot to collapse in. Adults dotted the yard in small conversational groups and the sun beat down on everyone, reminding them that summer was in high gear.

Sam let his gaze drift across the faces of the people who were becoming so familiar to him. The newest arrival was cousin Nora, a woman with short, dark hair, shadows under her eyes and a ready smile. A harried single mother, Nora doted on her son, Tommy. Sam kept a wary eye on the child Tricia'd told him was an arsonist in training, especially when the boy was off playing with Katie and Kevin. Surprised by the protective instincts rising inside him, Sam was *more* surprised that none of the other adults seemed concerned enough to ride herd on the kid. Even Tricia, who'd warned him in the first place, was sitting on a blanket between her pregnant sister and her mother, apparently blissfully unconcerned about potential disaster.

He had to admit that Tommy didn't look like a potential firebug. The kid had a shock of unruly brown hair, a face full of freckles and a missing front tooth. He looked like a Rockwell portrait as he ran around the backyard just like any other normal boy.

Sam frowned and glanced at the cluster of Wright men surrounding him. All of them hovered near the still-cold barbecue as the patriarch stacked charcoal in a precise pattern. While their father worked, conversations rippled like rings in a pond after a stone had been tossed in. Sam only half listened to snatches of everything.

"Football? How can you care about football in the middle of baseball season?"

"Hockey's a man's game."

"And tennis."

That statement from yet another cousin, this time a teenager, shut everyone up for a moment. Until the kid grinned and said, "Just kidding."

Jake shoved the skinny adolescent, then turned

back to trying to convince his brother that baseball was the *true* American sport. As Eric debated the issue, he swung his crutch occasionally to make a point.

"Pay no attention to them," Dan Wright said with a glance at his sons. "They've always done that. Argue over nothing just for the sake of hearing themselves talk."

Sam shook his head. "I don't think Eric even likes football."

"Probably not, but it's the argument that counts," the older man said with an understanding chuckle.

"If you say so." Sam gripped the long neck of his beer bottle, and lifted it to take a sip. The sun was warm, the breeze cool and the sounds of people enjoying themselves was almost hypnotic. It had been a long time since he'd spent a day doing nothing. Hell, he couldn't even remember when he'd last taken a day off. He frowned and sipped at the beer again.

"We appreciate you driving Eric back home," Dan said.

"No problem."

"Of course, we wanted to drive down right after the accident, but Eric wouldn't hear of it. Didn't want his mother and Jen to see him in the hospital."

Sam nodded and took a step closer to the hand-crafted brick barbecue. "He looked pretty bad right after."

"Not looking real sharp yet," Dan said, sliding his younger son a concerned glance.

"Bruises fade, bones heal." Sam saw the worry in the man's eyes and understood it. Just as he understood Eric's need to keep from having people watch over him every minute. God knew, he'd experienced the same thing himself two years ago and it hadn't been pleasant.

Basically, when you felt like garbage, you just wanted to be left alone to deal with it. The last thing you needed was a group of people continually asking if you were all right. And, as a doctor, he'd been able to assure the Wrights that Eric was going to be fine. Which had kept them at a distance and given Eric a chance to heal.

"I know," Dan said, his big, work-roughened hands stacking charcoal briquettes with as light a touch as a pickpocket. "But it's never easy worrying about someone you love."

"He's fine."

Dan shot him a quick look, studied his face for a second or two, then nodded, the anxiousness in his gaze softening. "I'll take your word for it, then. And thanks."

"You're welcome." Sam pulled in a deep breath and let it slide slowly from his lungs.

"Family gatherings not your kind of party, huh?"

"I'm sorry?" Sam watched the man finish off the black pyramid of coals.

"You just seemed a little skittish earlier is all. Guess we're a bit overwhelming at first."

"I don't—"

"Not saying I blame you any," Dan said, interrupting before Sam could apologize for letting his own discomfort show. "Just said I noticed."

"I didn't mean for you to." He stared down at the beer in his hand, studying the brown bottle as if looking for just the right thing to say. Frowning again, he realized that his "poker face" was sadly lacking. Not only could Tricia read him like a book, but it seemed the rest of her family could, as well. And that told him it really had been too long since he'd spent time with people. He'd forgotten how to relax. Forgotten what it was like to stand in the sunlight and simply enjoy being alive.

The realization hit him hard. He hadn't meant to become a hermit. Hadn't intended to become the odd man out. But somehow, without him even noticing, it had happened.

Dan slapped Sam's shoulder with one beefy hand, leaving five black streaks against his green shirt. "Don't you worry," the man said. "You're getting used to us. You've eased up a lot, seem to be less on edge. Tricia'll help you through the rough spots."

Before Sam could ask what he meant by that, Dan had already turned, letting his gaze drift across the crowd dotting the lawn. Finally, he spotted who he was looking for and smiled. "Tommy!"

Sam watched the kid skid to a stop on the grass and turn to look.

"It's time, boy. Get on over here if you want to be in charge again!"

Instantly, the boy's eyes lit up and his gap-toothed grin widened in expectation.

"What's going on?" Sam asked as he watched the kid hurtle across the grass toward the barbecue.

"Oh, just our little tradition," Dan said, taking out a long-handled match from its box. "Tommy likes to be the one to start the barbecue fire." When the child stopped alongside him, Dan ruffled his hair until it stood on end. "Our little chef, aren't you kiddo?"

"You bet, Uncle Dan," Tommy said and carefully, under the watchful gaze of Tricia's father, struck the matchhead and threw it atop the charcoal pyre.

As the flames leaped, everyone applauded and Tommy beamed proudly over a job well done. Then, in seconds, he was running back to join his cousins and the dog in their continuing race around the yard.

A budding arsonist.

Right.

Sam felt like an idiot.

He'd been keeping an eye on the boy, expecting him to set the house on fire.

Shifting his gaze to where the three women sat beneath the shade tree, Sam ignored two of them and concentrated—as he had most of the day—on Tricia. She must have sensed his gaze because she turned her head to look at him.

Their gazes collided and Sam felt the power of

that collision slam into him. Embarrassment and irritation faded. It was as if they were all alone, just the two of them, linked by an invisible thread that stretched the length of the lawn and hummed with something almost electric in its power and strength.

Sam shook his head as if to clear it of the wild thoughts crowding his brain. He didn't need this, he thought, even while silently acknowledging that there didn't seem to be anything he could do about it.

# Five

Sam watched Tricia walk into her house ahead of him and told himself to avert his gaze from the curve of her behind. Not an easy task. She wore a bright yellow tank top and dark green shorts that made her legs look even longer than they were. Her blond hair, freed from the braid she'd worn earlier, lay in a fall of rippled waves that looked like spilled honey and made his hands itch to touch.

Man, he'd been in the sun too long.

Getting a grip on both his hormones and his thoughts, he scraped one hand across his face and said, "An arsonist, huh?"

He hadn't had a minute alone with her to talk about little Tommy and how she'd set him up. Now that they were back at her house, with no audience listening in, he wanted a few answers.

Tricia half turned to look at him and gave him a broad grin and a wink. Then she lifted both hands into a *what do you want me to say?* shrug of innocence as she continued on into the house.

Sam followed. She'd lied to him about the kid. Worked him. All to get him to stay in her house.

He had to wonder why.

"If you could have seen your face," Tricia said with a laugh as she dropped onto one of the overstuffed chairs in her living room. "When Dad handed Tommy the match, I thought your eyes were going to bug out."

"Yeah, bet it was funny," he said and took a seat in the chair opposite her. He crossed his right foot on his left knee, drummed his fingers against the soft, faded upholstery and watched her.

Her eyes were dancing and her grin couldn't have been any bigger. She'd been chuckling since they left her parents' place for the short walk back to her house. And instead of resenting it, Sam had found himself enjoying the sound. But she didn't need to know that. His scowl deepened and she made a melodramatic attempt to sober up. She screwed her mouth into a razor-straight line and clapped one hand across her lips for good measure.

That lasted about ten seconds.

When her laughter erupted again, Sam shook his

head at her, gave up and reluctantly smiled himself. "So what was the point of all that? Making me think the kid's a firebug?"

"Fun?"

"Oh, yeah." He uncrossed his legs and stretched them out in front of him, alongside the wide, oak coffee table. "Me watching the boy all day, half expecting him to whip out a lighter and torch the yard." He nodded. "A laugh riot."

Tricia sighed and her grin faded into a soft smile. "I'm sorry. Seriously. But you do have to admit it was funny. I mean, did you really think we were harboring a psycho child?"

"Why'd you do it?" he asked, really curious. He'd forgotten about being angry that she'd lied to him and now just wanted a few answers. "Why'd you trick me into staying here?"

She studied him for a quiet minute. Her fingers smoothed the arm of the chair with long, sensuous strokes that caught his attention and held it. He shifted a little in the chair, trying not to think about those fingers caressing his skin, sliding along his body.

He scowled to himself at the wayward notion. He hadn't felt anything like this in years. It was as if his body were waking up from a deep sleep, and the first stirrings felt damn near painful. His jaw clenched and his fingers curled tight over the arms of the chair.

Outside, the afternoon sun slanted across the yard, stretching shadows as twilight crept closer. From down the block came the sounds of kids playing ball and, just across the street, someone was mowing a lawn. Just another day in suburbia.

"Okay," she said, squirming around in her chair until her legs were curled up under her and she looked like a contented cat. "Maybe I did color the truth a little."

"A little?"

She shrugged. "A lot."

"Why?" The light in the room was dimming, shrinking around them like a dying spotlight on a silent stage. In the shadows, her features looked as if they'd been sculpted from fine porcelain. A half-smile lingered on her mouth, and the slight curve of her lips was tempting. Especially to a man who'd been as good as dead and buried for two years.

"I don't know," she said finally, trying to answer his question. Her gaze met his. She stared at him for what felt like hours but couldn't have been more than seconds. He tried to figure out what she was thinking, but the workings of Tricia's mind were as much a mystery to him as ever.

Her eyes were a deep, vivid blue. Bluer than a lake, darker than the ocean. There was something compelling in her gaze. Something that caught him, held him, and Sam knew he was sliding into dangerous territory—but for the life of him, he couldn't look away.

"It's just," she said, continuing in a silky, thready voice that was almost lost in the drone of the power head at her, gave up and reluctantly smiled himself. "So what was the point of all that? Making me think the kid's a firebug?"

"Fun?"

"Oh, yeah." He uncrossed his legs and stretched them out in front of him, alongside the wide, oak coffee table. "Me watching the boy all day, half expecting him to whip out a lighter and torch the yard." He nodded. "A laugh riot."

Tricia sighed and her grin faded into a soft smile. "I'm sorry. Seriously. But you do have to admit it was funny. I mean, did you really think we were harboring a psycho child?"

"Why'd you do it?" he asked, really curious. He'd forgotten about being angry that she'd lied to him and now just wanted a few answers. "Why'd you trick me into staying here?"

She studied him for a quiet minute. Her fingers smoothed the arm of the chair with long, sensuous strokes that caught his attention and held it. He shifted a little in the chair, trying not to think about those fingers caressing his skin, sliding along his body.

He scowled to himself at the wayward notion. He hadn't felt anything like this in years. It was as if his body were waking up from a deep sleep, and the first stirrings felt damn near painful. His jaw clenched and his fingers curled tight over the arms of the chair.

Outside, the afternoon sun slanted across the yard, stretching shadows as twilight crept closer. From down the block came the sounds of kids playing ball and, just across the street, someone was mowing a lawn. Just another day in suburbia.

"Okay," she said, squirming around in her chair until her legs were curled up under her and she looked like a contented cat. "Maybe I did color the truth a little."

"A little?"

She shrugged. "A lot."

"Why?" The light in the room was dimming, shrinking around them like a dying spotlight on a silent stage. In the shadows, her features looked as if they'd been sculpted from fine porcelain. A half-smile lingered on her mouth, and the slight curve of her lips was tempting. Especially to a man who'd been as good as dead and buried for two years.

"I don't know," she said finally, trying to answer his question. Her gaze met his. She stared at him for what felt like hours but couldn't have been more than seconds. He tried to figure out what she was thinking, but the workings of Tricia's mind were as much a mystery to him as ever.

Her eyes were a deep, vivid blue. Bluer than a lake, darker than the ocean. There was something compelling in her gaze. Something that caught him, held him, and Sam knew he was sliding into dangerous territory—but for the life of him, he couldn't look away.

"It's just," she said, continuing in a silky, thready voice that was almost lost in the drone of the power

Rarely alone, Sam had become a member of the family team that met in the "war room" of the elder Wrights' kitchen every day. He wasn't sure exactly when it had happened, but somehow he'd been adopted into the family when he wasn't looking.

What was more surprising, he didn't mind a bit.

They were all still loud and overwhelming to the inexperienced, but he'd found something with these people that he'd never really known before. A sense of solidarity. Strength in numbers. And a feeling of loyalty that was so thick, so rich, it connected every family member to the next, like they were links in a solid chain—where every person was an individual, and yet an integral part of the whole.

He steered his car into Tricia's driveway and then put it in park, set the brake and turned off the engine. After a day spent helping to paint the gazebo where Eric and Jen would be married, Sam was looking forward to a little down time.

Funny, but life had slipped into a routine of sorts, and Sam appreciated it even while recognizing just how different this new routine was from his everyday world.

At home, his mornings were hurried. A quick cup of coffee, then jump into the car and head to work. Every night, he'd reverse directions on the freeway, head back to the condo and a solitary dinner, go to sleep and repeat the whole thing the next day.

Here, things were different. Morning was a leisurely time, when he and Tricia would sit at her kitchen table just before dawn and talk about what was on that day's schedule. The evenings were just as different. After that first night in her house, Sam'd given up trying to hide in his room, looking for the solitude that had been so important to him for so long. Tricia had insisted that since he was a guest, the least he could do was talk to her. She was a force of nature. She couldn't be ignored and wouldn't be denied.

Now his nights were spent here, at Tricia's house, watching old movies, listening to music or just talking.

Or rather, Sam thought, smiling, as he climbed out of his car and headed for her house, *Tricia* would talk, he would listen. The woman could talk for hours on any subject and never get tired. He shook his head as he realized just how well he'd gotten to know her in the last few days. She had opinions on everything and didn't hesitate to share them. He'd heard about her siblings, her parents, her old high school and her plans for her business.

She made him think, made him laugh…made him *feel*.

He stopped short of the front porch, stuffed his hands in his jeans pockets and stared at the pale light shining behind the living room curtains. She'd be inside, either baking more cookies or wrapping ones she'd already decorated. The kitchen table would be piled high with her labors and the air would smell of cinnamon and that other spice he still hadn't been able to recognize.

He'd walk through the house, step into the kitchen and she'd look up, meet his gaze and smile. In his mind's eye, he saw her amazing mouth curve into a welcome that had just recently become way too important to him. A warm knot of anticipation settled in his chest.

And he felt guilty as hell.

Pulling his hands free of his pockets, Sam reached up and pushed his fingers roughly through his hair. Then, just as harshly, he let his hands fall to his sides again. This small house with the tiny bathroom and the scent of perpetual baking had become…familiar. Cozy. Comforting. And he wasn't sure what to do about it.

He shouldn't even be here.

Shouldn't be enjoying himself.

Shouldn't be *eager* to see Tricia.

"Too late to stop now," he muttered thickly, nearly choking on the guilt that rushed through his body like high tide reclaiming the shore.

Even now, he felt his blood pump a little faster, his heart beat a little harder, knowing that Tricia was just inside. He hadn't felt this sort of…expectation in too many years to count.

Had *never* expected to feel it again.

He'd had his shot at happiness. With Mary.

And then he'd lost her. Regret crawled through him. In a heartbeat—everything changed forever.

Sam shook his head. "Too many ifs." Too many

lost chances and too many nights spent poring over what he had and hadn't done. And nothing ever changed.

Mary was still gone.

And he couldn't claim a life for himself, when he hadn't been able to save hers.

This time with the Wrights, with Tricia, was just temporary. A blip in his ordinary world. He should remember that. Remember that when the two weeks were up, he'd be headed back to L.A. Back to where memories of Mary still lived.

Back where he belonged.

"Is that you, Sam?"

"Yeah," he called as he walked through the quiet house, "it's me."

"I'm out ba-ack," she shouted in response, making that one-syllable word into at least two, and almost three.

He followed her voice, moving through the kitchen, slowing for a glance at the mountain of cookies displayed on the table. She'd been even busier than usual. Today's offerings were already wrapped in cellophane and tied with pale lavender ribbons. Sam picked one up and studied it. The cookie was in the shape of a bridal bouquet and the flowers were all outlined with bright piped icing. Looks too good to eat, he thought, as he set the cookie back with the others and headed for the back door.

Through the screen he saw her, sitting on the top step of the back porch. There was a plate of broken, frosted cookies beside her and a half-empty blender of something slushy. Opening the door, he stepped outside and looked down at her.

She leaned her head back, letting her golden hair spill down over her shoulders and hang in a swaying curtain of honey. She grinned up at him. "Hi. Want a margarita?"

Sam's lips twitched. Sounded to him like she'd already had several, but apparently she wasn't counting.

"Brought out a glass for you, too," she said and straightened her head so quickly, she gasped. "Whoa. Head rush."

"You okay?" he asked as he took a seat beside her. Only the tray of cookies lay between them as she handed him a now-full margarita glass.

"Oh, I'm great," she said and took a sip of her own drink before reaching for a cookie and taking a bite. "Have a cookie."

"Cookies and margaritas?"

"Cookies go with everything," Tricia said. "Trust me. I'm the Cookie Lady."

"That's right," he said, picking up one of the broken cookies and taking a bite. "Forgot I was dealing with a professional."

Tricia took another sip of her drink.

"How long have you been out here?" Sam asked, studying her profile in the wash of lamplight pouring out of the kitchen behind them. "And how many of those have you had?"

"'Bout an hour," she said softly, stretching her legs out down the steps. "Only a couple of drinks. Don't worry, you won't be dealing with a sloppy drunk."

"Good to know."

"Thought you might appreciate it."

"Any particular reason why you're sitting on the back porch drinking?"

"Do we really *need* a reason for margaritas?"

"I guess not," he said, though he did believe the frothy concoction was helping to wash the bitter taste of guilt from his throat.

"Have you ever been in love?" she demanded suddenly, turning to face him squarely. "I mean seriously, deeply in love?"

That guilt was back in a flash, slamming into his head and his heart with the force of a jackhammer. Mary's features flashed across his mind and it stunned him to realize that her image was hazy, indistinct, as though he were staring at her through a thick fog. His chest tightened as he said simply, "Yes."

"You have?" Tricia looked at him with questions gathering in her eyes and he hoped to hell she wouldn't ask them.

A moment or two ticked past before she said, "At least you've had that. I haven't. I mean, I'm twenty-eight years old and I've never seen fireworks."

Confusion grappled with relief that she hadn't asked for more information. "What?"

"You know," she prodded, "those metaphorical fireworks."

He nodded, lost.

She shook her head. "After sex? When it's all roses and puppies and bells are ringing…"

"Ah…" Sam smiled to himself, then listened up, since he'd already learned that it took all of a man's concentration to keep up with Tricia's racing train of thought.

"I've never seen 'em. Or felt 'em. Or even heard 'em, for that matter." She waved her margarita glass for emphasis and some of the frozen green liquid sloshed over the rim. "Oops." She pulled the glass close and licked up the spillage.

Sam's guts twisted as he watched her tongue slide along the edge of the glass and then across the back of her hand. A hunger ripped through him with an intensity that startled the hell out of him.

"I mean, my folks think I'm broken-hearted," she continued, oblivious to the havoc she was creating. "My sister tells me I'm too picky and my brothers want to interrogate the *next* guy I date—" She stopped and waved her glass at him again. More carefully this time. "—and that's not going to happen, because like I told you, the only relationship I'm interested in is me and sugar."

"So what's the problem?" he asked.

She sighed, tipped her head back and stared at the brilliant spread of stars across the sky. While she watched the heavens, Sam watched *her*. Her blond hair lay against her back and swung gently with every movement of her head. It was nearly hypnotic. And when her voice came again, she spoke so softly, she didn't break the spell that held him.

"The problem is," she said wistfully, "as great as sugar is," she blew out a breath, "I don't think I'll be finding the fireworks there, either."

Hell, there were a few sparklers dazzling in the air between them now, Sam thought, though he didn't dare mention it.

"And you're worried about this tonight because…"

"Not worried." She turned her head to look at him. "Just thinking," she admitted. "I was over at my folks' and they started walking really gently around me about Daly, my last boyfriend."

"Yeah?" He didn't want to think about her last boyfriend. And how strange was that?

"For some reason, they think I'm heartbroken. But I'm not and I think that's just so sad."

"That you're *not* heartbroken?" He was confused again, but that was no surprise.

"Exactly. I mean I obviously didn't love him…I don't even miss him," she said. "So, what if for some weird reason, Daly had proposed or something? God, what if I'd said *yes*?" She set her glass down beside her, then practically leaped off the porch, taking the steps down to the grass in a couple quick strides. A few more steps and she was in darkness, and he could only hear her. "I mean, I might have. You never know."

Sam set his own drink aside, stood up and followed her into the yard. She was walking the perimeter of her lot, wandering through the moonlight with a steady step that told him she hadn't had nearly as many margaritas as he'd first thought.

"But you wouldn't have said yes," he said.

"How do you know?" She whirled around and looked at him and suddenly there were only a couple of feet separating them. Her eyes looked huge and luminous in the moonlight. Her skin was pale and her lips, usually curved in a smile, or the promise of one, were straight now, and trembling.

"Because you didn't love him. You just said so."

"But I might have convinced myself I did. Is a person supposed to wait around forever…waiting for the fireworks? Or do you just settle for the flaring match when it comes along?"

She took a step closer and her perfume reached out for him.

Sam knew he should back up. Knew he should head into the house *now*. Hell, the *house*? What he ought to do was hop into his car, hit the freeway and punch it until he made it back to L.A. Back to where he knew how to act and what to do. Back to where Tricia Wright wasn't within arm's reach.

But he wasn't leaving.

Wouldn't even if he could have.

The moonlight, her perfume, and the warm summer air combined to fill him with wants and needs that were nearly strangling him.

"You should wait," he said, and heard the rough scrape of his own voice, "for the fireworks."

"Yeah?" She swallowed hard and took another step closer. "Want to help me look for them?"

# Six

Sam reached for her.

She moved closer.

In the next instant, she was in his arms, pressed tightly to him, and Sam's whole body lit up like a neon sign in Vegas. Every cell came alive. Blood rushed in his veins, his head pounded and his heartbeat thundered in his ears like the roar of dozens of hungry lions.

She looked up at him and, not for the first time, Sam wondered what she was thinking, feeling. But an instant later, she went up on her toes and brushed her mouth against his. Sam pulled her tightly to him, wrapping his arms around her and holding on with every ounce of his strength. Her lips parted for him and he claimed her mouth with a fierceness he hadn't known he possessed. She sighed and he swallowed her breath, taking all of her into him. His tongue tangled with hers in a wild dance of need.

She clung to him, her fingers digging into his shoulders until he could have sworn he felt the heat of her touch branding his skin right through the fabric of his shirt. And it wasn't enough. Wasn't nearly enough.

He wanted all of her. Wanted to feel her smooth, soft skin beneath his palms, hear her sighs, watch her eyes glaze over as he slid his body into hers.

God, he wanted to feel this rush of sensation grow until it overtook him.

He wanted her more than his next breath.

Tearing his mouth from hers, Sam dipped his head and kissed her neck, running the tip of his tongue along her flesh while she shivered and whispered his name.

That broken hush of sound sent new ribbons of heat snaking through him until he felt as though the flames would simply engulf him. And still it wasn't enough.

"Tricia," he murmured, his breath dusting her skin. She tipped her head to one side, to give him easier access, and then leaned into him completely, silently offering him everything that had suddenly become so desperately necessary.

"Sam," she said quietly, "I see 'em."

"Hmm…?" Taste her, his brain screamed. Touch her. *Take* her.

"The fireworks," she whispered, and the dazed wonder in her voice caught him, held him in a grip that squeezed the air from his lungs. "They're there," she continued, her voice filled with a raw wonder, "just waiting for me. Show me, Sam. Show them to me."

He lifted his head and stared down at her through eyes hazy with passion. His breath shuddered in his lungs and an inner battle raged between what he *should* do and what he so *wanted* to do.

Sam shook his head, reached up and disentangled her arms from around his neck. His hands slid down their length until he was holding her hands in his. His thumbs stroked her palms, torturing them both...yet, he couldn't quite bring himself to let her go all at once.

"I can't."

"What?" Dazed herself, Tricia shook her head. She squeezed his hands and asked, "Why not, for heaven's sake?"

"Because I'm not the one you've been waiting for, Tricia."

She laughed shortly and looked away from him briefly. Then she dropped his hands and took a shaky step back. "I didn't *propose,* Sam."

"I know that," he said, feeling completely unprepared for the task of explaining what he was feeling— why he was turning down what any red-blooded man in his right mind would make a greedy grab at. He shoved one hand through his hair, then viciously rubbed the back of his neck. "It's just not that simple."

Her lips trembled, then firmed up again. Her features tightened as she wrapped her arms around herself and hung on. "Fine. But you can't stand there and tell me you don't want me, because I won't buy it. I *felt* just how much you *do* want me."

His back teeth ground together. Of course she'd felt his arousal. Hell, he'd held her close enough that she should, by all rights, be carrying an imprint of his body on her skin. "Has nothing to do with it," he muttered and turned, heading for the house.

He didn't think of it as running, he thought of it more as a strategic retreat. At top speed.

But Sam should have known that Tricia wasn't a woman who gave up easily. She was right behind him. He moved through the kitchen like a man on a mission. His steps were fast, but sure. He was doing the right thing.

Tricia deserved better than getting involved with him. She deserved a man who was *whole*. A man who was looking for the same things she wanted. A man who could *love* her. That wasn't him.

He hit the stairs at a fast walk and heard her bare feet on the creaky treads just behind him. At the top of the stairs, he gave it up, spun around and stopped dead. She slammed right into him and he grabbed her upper arms to keep her from tumbling back down the stairs.

She took advantage of the move by wrapping her arms around his neck again and clinging like a limpet. Her eyes were clear and deep, and the tiniest of smiles curved her amazing mouth.

"Tricia…"

"Sam…" The smile deepened just enough to make him want to see more. To see the small dimple that hid at the right corner of her mouth unless she was laughing full out.

He reached up for her arms again, determined to be strong despite the fact that every inch of his body was screaming at him to hold onto her.

"I want to know why you're so determined to stay away from me," she said with a slight shake of her head. Her hair swung gently in a soft wave of scent and color.

Sam pulled in a tight breath that barely filled his lungs. He couldn't risk inhaling that scent of hers. Right now, it would be enough to push him over the slippery edge of control.

"This shouldn't happen."

She sobered and looked him dead in the eye, as if she could read his thoughts by looking deep enough. And who knew? Maybe she could.

"Are you married?" she asked.

"No." *Not anymore.*

"Engaged?"

"No," he blurted, "but that's not the point."

"It's the *only* point," Tricia said and moved in even closer to him, pressing her body along his. "Sam, we're two adults. Neither one of us is committed to anyone else. We want each other...don't we?"

Since she could no doubt *feel* once again just how much he wanted her, it would have been pointless to try to deny it.

"You deserve better than a one-night-stand," he said tightly. "And that's all I can offer you."

"Maybe one night's all I need," she said, and he wished he could read *her* mind. What was going on in that head of hers? Did she think that maybe this, whatever it was between them, would turn into something bigger? Something permanent?

Because if she did, then he was lining up to be the next guy to hurt her. He didn't want to, damn it. He *liked* Tricia. But he wasn't the man she wanted—or needed.

"Stop thinking," Tricia urged and skimmed her fingertips down the side of his face, temple to jawline. Her touch electrified him. Damned if he couldn't actually *feel* his blood boil, hear his own breath quicken.

"Tricia—"

"Just feel, Sam," she said and went up on her toes again. Tipping her head to one side, she brushed her mouth over his. Once, and he held perfectly still. Twice, his heart crashed against his ribs. Three times, and he knew he was lost.

Surrendering to the inevitable, Sam grabbed her hard, using his arms to pin her to him. His hands slid up and down her back, possessively exploring every line, every curve. He had to feel her. Now.

His mouth took hers in a kiss designed to sweep them both over the edge of reason. His tongue stroked hers in a wild imitation of what he needed to do to her, *with* her.

She groaned and he tensed.

She leaned into him and he took more of her weight, lifting her off her feet. Tricia moaned and went with him, lifting her legs to lock them around his waist, and suddenly, she was all around him, surrounding him with sensation and a pulse-pounding desire he'd never known before. *Ever.*

This was different.

This was *more* than anything he'd ever experienced.

And as that thought flashed through his mind, he set it resolutely aside.

Sam shoved both hands beneath the hem of her tank top and luxuriated in the silkiness of her skin. Smooth, so soft and warm.

She writhed against him, burrowing closer, tighter, keeping her mouth fused with his, giving as much as she took. Sliding her hands to his face, she cupped his cheeks in her palms and pulled her head back long enough to look at him through dazzled eyes.

"Bedroom. Now."

"Right there with you," he muttered, and headed for her room. There were only four doors off the small hallway. His room, the bathroom, a tiny linen closet and Tricia's bedroom. He grabbed the door-knob, gave it a twist, then shoved the door wide.

The walls were blue. Almost as blue as her eyes. And that's all he noticed as he walked into the room he somehow knew they'd been headed for since the first time he saw her. From the moment she'd plopped down into the front seat of his car and started irritating him.

The first time she'd smiled at him.

He headed for the big bed shoved against the wall in the center of the room. Another flowered quilt lay across the wide mattress and he didn't even bother to try to pull it down. Instead, he sat down, leaned back and pulled her down on top of him.

Tricia stared down at him and he read his own hunger mirrored in her eyes. Moonlight slanted through the open curtains hanging in front of the window that faced the backyard. Its pale light suffused the room with a soft glow that seemed to shimmer all around her as she levered herself up into a sitting position.

Sam's breath caught in his throat as she straddled him. But she damn near killed him when she grabbed the hem of her tank top and slowly pulled it up and over her head. Her bare breasts were full, nipples peaked and rigid, and he could practically taste them already. All the air left him in a rush and he quickly sucked in another greedy breath. "Tricia…"

She smiled, slow and lazy, eyes glinting with a

feminine pride and confidence that slammed into him. She knew exactly what effect she was having on him and she was enjoying it.

He reached up and tweaked her nipples between his thumbs and forefingers. She groaned and rocked into his touch. Lifting both hands, she covered his, holding his palms to her breasts for one long moment.

Then she whispered on a sigh, "Now you." Reaching down, she grabbed fistfuls of his shirt and tugged the hem free of the waistband of his jeans. Suddenly hungry to feel flesh against flesh, Sam shifted slightly to help her yank his shirt up and off.

She ran the flat of her palms over his chest, sculpting him, defining every muscle, and his body lit up like a flashing neon sign. Everything in him tightened expectantly. Damn it, if he didn't have her, he just might die.

She was so unexpected.

So fascinating.

So damn…*necessary*.

"You amaze me," he said, staring up into the eyes that had captivated him from the start. His hands continued to work her breasts, his fingers teasing and toying with her nipples.

"Why?" She sucked in a gulp of air, then gave him that slow, seductive smile again.

"Lots of reasons," he murmured, his gaze sweeping over her, from the tousled blond halo of her hair to the tanned, firm thighs gripping his hips. Beneath her, he felt himself tighten further until he was hard as a rock and aching to bury himself inside her.

He skimmed his hands down her ribcage to her waist, loving the feel of her skin against his palms. She sighed and he let his hands slide across the front of her body, her abdomen and then dusting along the waistband of her shorts. He watched gooseflesh bristle along her skin and smiled to himself, knowing that he was affecting her every bit as much as she was him.

"Amazing," he repeated, deftly undoing the top button of her shorts.

She sucked in a breath of air, held it for a long moment, then let it slide from her lungs on a sigh. "You're pretty amazing yourself," she said, her voice just a tightly stretched thread.

Sam smiled to himself even as his body screamed beneath her. She squirmed, rubbing her bottom against him until he felt beads of sweat break out on his forehead and jagged spears of need slice through his body. He groaned, and she smiled, tossed her hair back in a wild cloud of blond and began to rock her hips atop him as though she were a bareback rider at a rodeo.

And damned if Sam didn't feel like a bucking bronco. He wanted to plunge into her, drive himself home and feel her body surround his. He wanted to be so deep inside her heat that some of her warmth would just naturally seep into him. He wanted to watch her eyes glaze, feel her muscles bunch and hear her sighs as he drove her over the edge of madness.

He had to have that. But first he was going to make sure that Tricia needed it as badly as he did. Patience would have its own rewards…if he didn't explode first.

As she moved atop him, he felt her heat through the fabric of his jeans and knew that he wouldn't be able to wait much longer. She must have sensed his impatience, because she did all she could to feed it.

Moving slowly, she reached for her own breasts and as he watched, she cupped them, then stroked them with long, deliberate caresses. Her fingers toyed with her own nipples and Sam's mouth went dry as his gaze locked on her sensuous movements.

And still, his brain rose up and shouted at him to be fair. To give her the chance to change her mind. To let her know that he wasn't the kind of man she needed. He had to give her the opportunity to leave him aching before he inevitably left *her* broken.

Despite the fact that if he didn't have her in the next few minutes, he was pretty sure his heart would simply explode.

"Tricia…" he said, trying to keep his voice from choking on the desire clamped around his throat.

Her hands dropped to his chest. Then she leaned toward him and laid her fingertips across his mouth. "Don't." Her mouth replaced her fingers and she kissed him, nipping gently at his bottom lip and driving his control to the ragged edge. "If you're about to say we don't have to do this," she whispered—her

breath puffing against his mouth, his cheeks, his
neck, as she shifted, kissing, licking, nibbling—"then
you're oh so wrong."

She pushed herself into a sitting position again and
made sure she was perched right over his throbbing
erection. She stared directly into his eyes so that he
could read the shattering passion in hers. So he would
*know* without a doubt, that she was as eager as he.

*Thank whatever gods were paying attention.*

"I'm glad you think so," he managed to say
through gritted teeth.

"Oh, I do," she whispered and ground her body
against his. "I definitely do. We *so* need to do this,
Sam. Right now."

"I'm convinced."

"Thank heaven."

And with the last of his doubts eased, Sam cleared
his mind, banishing all thoughts that weren't directly
related to this moment. Until he'd had his fill of the
woman currently torturing him.

Which could effectively shut his brain down for
years.

In one fluid move, he rolled her over, flipping her
onto her back and covering her with the upper half
of his body. His hands shifted over her, exploring,
discovering, mapping her thoroughly enough that
every line and curve of her body would be etched into
his mind forever.

"We need to get rid of these," he said, slowly sliding the zipper of her shorts down. She lifted her hips eagerly as he peeled the fabric back, displaying a pair of pale peach lace panties. His heart almost stopped.

Sam bent his head to kiss her flat sun-tanned abdomen, just above the thin elastic strap. She shivered beneath him and sighed his name on a whisper of sound that shook him to the bone and seemed to echo inside him. He smiled against her skin as he moved further and further down her body. He pulled her shorts down her legs, then tossed them to the floor before moving again to the tiny scrap of lace guarding her center. Tan lines, creamy against her warm honey skin, told him that her bathing suit was even tinier than the panties she now wore, and he suddenly hungered to see her in a bikini, kissed by sunlight.

He touched the tip of his tongue to her belly and she jumped, moaning softly as she moved into him. "Sam…"

His name, said on a sigh of desire and passion, sent shock waves pulsing within and he gave himself up to the wonder of this moment. It had been so long, so very long, since he'd felt *anything*. Now, he was swamped with so many overwhelming emotions, he couldn't sort them out. Couldn't even identify them all.

So he quit trying.

He hooked his fingers beneath the edge of the lacy panties and in a heartbeat, he had them down and off of her. She opened her eyes and looked at him. Her tongue swept across her bottom lip and he groaned tightly. In seconds, he yanked off the rest of his own clothes, tossed them to the floor beside hers and then knelt on the mattress in front of her.

"Sam," she called his name again, insistently this time. Holding her arms out for him, she arched up, lifting her shoulders from the bed in an attempt to reach him, to pull him to her.

But Sam had other ideas.

Running his palms up and down the length of her legs, he watched her eyes roll back and her hands drop helplessly to the pale blue sheets. He stroked her slowly, then faster, each time sliding his hands higher up her thighs until his fingertips were only inches from her center. She twisted under his ministrations and tried to maneuver her body so that he would touch her core, her heat, to give her ease from the pulsing demands throbbing within.

Instead he tortured her more thoroughly.

He moved in closer, lifted her legs and rested them across his shoulders. Her eyes widened as she stared up at him. His big hands cupped her bottom, holding her firmly, despite how she twisted in his grasp.

"Sam—"

"Tricia—" he interrupted her quickly. "Shut up."

She licked her lips again, grabbed hold of the sheet with both hands as though preparing to have her world rocked, then said, "Right."

Her flesh warm and soft in his grip, he lifted her body and bent his head to claim her. His mouth covered her heat and his tongue darted out to streak across intimate flesh already sensitized.

She gasped and arched higher into him, rocking her hips helplessly as she lay in his grip.

His fingers kneaded her body as he used his mouth to conquer her. He felt the first tremors building and felt a jolt of pleasure so pure, so sharp, it nearly stole his breath. He knew what he was doing to her. Felt her response quivering inside him. Felt the heat of her, tasted her secrets and gave her more so that he, too, would feel more.

She whimpered and twisted her head from side to side on the bed. Her hands fisted the sheets, scrabbling for purchase. His tongue stroked her center over and over again and when he found the tiny nub of flesh at the very heart of her, he sucked her gently, sending her into a wild, frenzied abandon that rocketed around his insides.

When her climax erupted, he felt the tension in her body as she stiffened in his grasp. She reached up and threaded her fingers in his hair, holding his mouth to her as if half-afraid he would stop and leave her unsatisfied.

But he didn't want to stop. Sam wanted more. He wanted to taste all of her. Explore every inch of her. Claim her body as his and brand her with his touch.

When her body finally stopped trembling and she lay weak and limp in his hands, he eased her back down to the mattress and leaned over her.

"Oh, boy," she whispered, a small smile tugging at one corner of her mouth. "That was…"

"Yeah?" he whispered, slowly kissing his way up her length.

She shook her head. "I'm speechless."

He laughed shortly. "It's a miracle."

Tricia blew out a breath and stroked his hair. "Boy howdy."

"That's just the beginning," he whispered, and paused long enough to take one of her nipples into his mouth.

"Promises, promises," she teased.

He lifted his head and waited for her to meet his gaze. "Do I look like I'm kidding?"

"No," she said brokenly, struggling for air. "You sure don't." Her hands reached for him and he felt the soft scrape of her fingernails against his back, across his shoulders. Heat shot through him like a flash of lightning, and the resulting thunder pounded inside him.

Staring down into her impossibly blue eyes, he saw magic and need and knew his own eyes mirrored hers. "Good," he said. "Just so we're clear."

"Oh, rarin' to go, here."

"Glad to hear it." Sam dipped his head to her breasts again and indulged himself by taking first one nipple and then the other into his mouth.

She groaned.

His lips and tongue and teeth tormented her in a

gentle assault that had her writhing beneath him. She muttered his name on a moan that ripped through him. He sucked her and she arched her body into his, silently demanding more. Her nails scraped down his shoulders, along his arms and back up again to tangle in his hair. She held his head to her breast, then tugged him up, pulling his mouth up to hers. Hungrily, he kissed her, his tongue tangling with hers in a wild dance that fed the need erupting inside.

*Now.*

One thought rattling through his mind, over and over.

*Now.*

Sam broke the kiss, lifted his head. "Protection," he muttered thickly, cursing himself for not thinking of it sooner. For not preparing for the eventuality. But he didn't exactly travel with condoms hoping to get lucky. Hell, he hadn't planned on sex.

Hadn't planned on Tricia.

But then, how could he ever have planned on *her*?

"In the drawer," she whispered, her voice a broken shard of sound. "Over there. Bedside table. Move fast, okay?"

There was a pleading in her voice that hit his ego and pumped it higher than a helium balloon floating skyward. Knowing he'd pushed her into a torrent of emotion, of cravings, was almost as heady as hearing her sigh his name.

He shifted to one side, pulled the drawer of the

tiny nightstand table open and fumbled in its depths for a small foil package. He grabbed one, ripped it open and in seconds had sheathed himself and protected both of them.

Going up on her elbows, Tricia smiled at him again and reached down between them. Molding his length with her hand, she squeezed him gently and rubbed his hardness until Sam wanted to cry out in a guttural demand for release.

"I want you in me now," she whispered.

Sam's gaze focused on hers.

"Don't make me wait any longer, Sam," she said, closing her hand around him tightly in an imitation of the close heat he wanted so badly.

"No more waiting." The words came in a low-pitched growl as he moved to tip her flat on her back again. She opened her legs for him, welcoming him within.

As he entered her, he coaxed himself to go slow, to luxuriate, to take the extra moments and enjoy the sweet sensation of sliding into liquid heat. But the need was too much and her welcome too warm.

She lifted her hips, taking him deeper, more fully, until he felt captured by her. She held him inside a tight, hot glove of sensation and it took every ounce of his will to keep from ending it all too soon. He wanted this moment, this night, to last forever. He wanted this…*connection* to remain unbroken.

He rocked into her depths and she met him stroke

for stroke, touch for touch. They shifted into an instinctive rhythm, moving together as if they'd danced this way before.

Hunger raged, passion blossomed. And in the moonlit night, they raced in tandem toward oblivion and together, fell into the magic awaiting them.

# Seven

**W**hen the madness lifted, Sam groaned and rolled to one side. His body humming, his mind racing, he fought for breath and stared up at the moonlit patterns on the ceiling. Heartbeat thundering in his ears, Sam listened to Tricia's uneven breathing and almost flinched when her leg rubbed against his.

Throwing one arm across his eyes, he blocked out the room, her, what had just happened, and retreated into the darkness. Guilt nibbled at him, gnawed at the edges of his soul and taunted him with the knowledge that he'd forgotten all about Mary in those moments with Tricia.

He winced, squeezing his eyes shut against the

pain and misery arcing through him. How could he have forgotten? Even for a moment?

And how could he *not*?

Hell, he'd never experienced anything like this before. Sex with Mary—more guilt churned inside and took a shark-sized bite out of him—was, he had to admit to himself, less exciting. Their lovemaking had been quiet. Tender. Loving.

With Tricia, he'd found hunger and passion and a need so all-consuming, his whole body ached with it anew, despite the climax still rippling through his bloodstream. Mary had been quiet fires. Tricia was explosions.

And he was surely damned for lying in one woman's bed thinking about another.

"Wow."

Naturally, Tricia wouldn't be able to be silent for long. If there was one thing he'd learned about this woman over the last several days, it was that she, like nature, abhorred a vacuum. Silence was merely the pause between conversations. The beat before the noise began. The buildup to takeoff.

Turning his head on the pillow, he lowered his arm and looked at her, not surprised at all to find her staring at him.

"That was…" She blew out a breath that ruffled her blond hair. "Wow."

He fought against the rising tide of want already reaching up to choke him again. Her lips were puffy and red from his kisses. Her hair lay like a blond halo around her head as she lay flat on her back, arms and legs splayed, as though she'd dropped from exhaustion and had no intention of moving.

Sam smiled to himself. With Tricia there was no coy grabbing of the sheet to clutch to her breasts. Another jab of guilt poked at him for yet another unfair comparison to Mary. His late wife had been shy, even when they were alone together. And, Sam recalled, he'd loved that about her even while at times wishing she'd been more open, more free to explore a deeper, richer sex life.

"You're thinking."

He stopped thinking immediately. "What?"

"I said, you're thinking," Tricia repeated. "Thinking is not allowed during sex."

"Sex is finished."

"That's what you think." She rolled to her side and reached one hand out to him. Her fingertips skimmed along his chest, trailing across his flesh, starting tiny fires just beneath his skin. Sam sucked in a quick gulp of air and grabbed her hand, holding it tightly in his.

Tricia went up on one elbow and looked down at him. Her eyes looked even bluer than usual and glittered with confusion and something else he didn't even attempt to identify.

"Okay," she said, her voice coming as soft as the moonlight shining in the room, "not exactly the response I was expecting."

"Tricia…"

Her fingers curled around his, turning his attempt to put distance between them into an intimate act, linking them together.

"Sam," she said, meeting his gaze and holding it, "what's going on? One minute you're here with me and everything's terrific and the next—"

Sam gritted his back teeth and stared up at her. He felt like an idiot. Like a cheating husband in a cheap motel. And even he knew that was ridiculous.

Untangling his hand from hers, he pulled away, swung his legs off the bed and stood up. Walking naked to the window overlooking the backyard, he stared down at the place where this had all begun and wondered why he hadn't tried harder to stop it. But then, if he had, he would never have had this time with Tricia. And even as terrible as he was feeling now, he wouldn't want to have missed it.

Bracing one hand on the wall, he kept his gaze on the shifting shadows outside as he said, "It's nothing to do with you, Tricia."

"Funny. It feels like it does."

He risked a quick glance at her over his shoulder. She was sitting up on the bed, the rumpled quilt and sheets a puddle around her. Moonlight played over her skin and danced in her eyes. She shoved one hand through her hair, pushing the thick blond mass back from her face before letting it fall again.

Turning from the window, he walked toward the

bed—toward her—and stopped just short of being close enough to reach for her. "It's me."

"Ah," she said, with a slow nod. "The old 'it's not you, it's me' routine." She went up on her knees. "Can't you do better than that?"

"What?"

Apparently unable to sit still, she scooted off the edge of the bed, stood up and faced him. The top of her head just hit his chin, but the fire in her eyes made her look ten feet tall.

"I told you, I wasn't proposing, Sam. This was sex. Great sex, but sex." She waved one hand at the bed behind her. "We're not betrothed or anything so you can relax and quit mentally racing away in your getaway car."

He stared at her for a long minute. Couldn't really blame her for taking all of this the wrong way. Reaching up, he scrubbed his palms over his face, then folded his arms across his chest. Defensive. He knew that. Couldn't seem to help it, though.

Sam pulled in a deep breath and mentally searched for the right words. When they didn't come, he settled for anything that happened to fall out of his mouth. Meeting her eyes, he blurted, "Look. Believe it or not, it really *is* me. It's the first time—"

She laughed. Shortly, sharply. Stalking past him, Tricia snatched a T-shirt off a chair near the window and yanked it over her head. The neck of the shirt wasn't even all the way down when she started talking again, her voice muffled against the fabric. "A *virgin*? You're trying to tell me I seduced a *virgin*?" She shoved her arms through the sleeves and laughed again. "If that's the case, then I hope you don't mind me saying you're an exceptionally gifted newbie."

Shaking his head, he muttered, "I'm not saying that, I'm—"

"What exactly are you trying to say, then, Sam?" She plopped both hands on her hips and tapped the bare toes of one foot against the braided rug on the floor.

Still naked, he felt decidedly at a disadvantage. If they were going to go to war, then he at least wanted some pants on. Walking around the end of the bed, he found his pants lying just where he'd tossed them. Grabbing them up, he pulled them on and didn't speak again until he had the buttons on his jeans done up.

"It's the first time I've been with anyone since my wife died." He'd half expected to choke on the words "wife" and "died." But he hadn't. They'd come out easily. And what the hell did that mean?

"Your *wife*?"

The stunned surprise in her eyes was clear, even from across the room. He nodded. "Mary."

"Mary." She repeated the name slowly, almost as if it were in a foreign language.

"Yeah."

"And she died."

"Two years ago." Yesterday. A lifetime.

Tricia pushed her hair back, smoothed her T-shirt, then folded her hands at her waist before unlocking her fingers and letting her hands hang at her sides again. "You should have told me."

"Yeah, I know."

"Well," she snapped. "As long as you know."

"Tricia—"

"No." She shook her head and pointed a finger at him. "Sam, I told you all about the losers I've dated. About how my family thinks I'm a bum-magnet. About how I've given up on men and taken up with sugar—"

"Until tonight," he pointed out.

"Okay, until tonight. Granted," she said, nodding fiercely, "as good as sugar is, it can't do for me what you just did."

"Thanks, and same to you."

A tight smile touched her lips briefly then disappeared. "Okay. We agree the sex was great. Now we just have to get past the whole why-didn't-you-tell-me-you-were-married-and-that-she-died?"

"I don't know."

"Gee, good answer."

"The only one I've got." Which was stupid, he admitted. Of course he should have told her about Mary. Should have told her when she'd asked him if he'd ever been in love. But he hadn't wanted to talk about it. Hadn't wanted to be on the receiving end of more sympathy or understanding.

Mission accomplished.

"I'm not saying it would have changed my mind about…" She nodded toward the bed. "But you should have told me—"

"Probably."

"Can't believe Eric didn't tell me," she muttered, starting her meandering again. "My brother usually has much looser lips."

Sam sat down on the foot of the bed and watched her as she walked. Her long legs looked silky, smooth, and he had reason to know just how smooth they were. Just a few minutes ago, those leanly muscled legs had been locked around his hips, holding him to her.

His body tightened and his heartbeat skipped unsteadily. Damn it, he wanted to be back inside her. Wanted to feel her warmth surrounding him again.

"I should have told you," he admitted and she stopped dead to look at him. He really wished he could tell what she was thinking. "But I hadn't planned on us ending up in bed together."

"I did."

He blinked. "What?"

"I planned it." She lifted both hands and let them drop to her sides. Shrugging, she walked to the end of the bed and dropped down beside him. She rocked her shoulder against him briefly and admitted on a sigh, "I've been thinking about doing this for the last few days. Figured hey, maybe he's crabby because he's single." Before he could open his mouth, Tricia lifted one hand and said, "No, I wasn't planning on a quote 'relationship.' I just figured, you were single, I'm single, why shouldn't we be single as a couple?"

"Be single as a couple?" Sam shook his head as if the action could make sense of that last sentence. It didn't help. "You deliberately try to confuse me, don't you?"

Tricia sighed, reached around him and draped one arm around his shoulders companionably. "Nope, it's just a gift."

"You're good at it."

"Thanks." Sliding her hand along his back and then down his spine, she let her fingertips blaze a trail that dipped just below the waistband of his jeans. "But my point here is…I don't know that I'd have done this any differently had I known about your wife."

He tensed.

"But it would have been nice of you to tell me."

"Granted."

"Anything else you'd like to confess?"

He snorted. "Now you're a priest?"

She slapped her free hand to her chest and blinked up at him in innocence. "Hey, what's said to the Cookie Lady is kept in strictest confidence."

One corner of his mouth lifted at the same time as the burden of guilt began to trickle off his shoulders. Was it the look in Tricia's eyes that did it? Was it the feel of her hand sliding beneath the fabric of his jeans? Was it the knowledge that for the first time in way too long, Sam wasn't feeling desperately *alone*?

He didn't know.

Cared less.

All he was sure of was that he needed her again. And if that made his eventual departure harder…then he'd just have to deal with that when the time came.

"I do have one confession," he said, squeezing each word past the tight knot in his throat.

Her gaze dropped to his mouth, then up again to his eyes. "Yes…"

"I found more than one condom in your drawer."

"Really?" She smiled and crawled across him to straddle his lap, wrapping her arms around his neck and bringing his mouth just a breath away from hers. "Imagine that."

He skimmed his hands up beneath the hem of her T-shirt and along her warm, soft body until he cupped her breasts in his palms.

She sighed heavily and arched into him.

His body went rock hard and ready.

She squirmed atop him and blew the top of his head off.

"How many did you find?" she asked, scraping her fingernails down his chest to slide across his flat nipples.

He sucked in air through gritted teeth. "Enough to keep us busy for the night."

"Then stop talking, Doc." She brought her mouth to his and whispered, "You're wasting moonlight."

Wrapping his arms around her, Sam fell back onto the mattress and let himself get lost in the glory of Tricia.

The next morning, Sam woke up in Tricia's bed. A spear of sunlight poked through a part in the curtains and jabbed him in the eye. He groaned and slammed an arm across his eyes, taking a minute or two to remember exactly where he was, and why.

Naturally, it all came back in a roaring flood of sound and color. He sat up, avoiding that particular spear of light, and rolled off the bed. A soft breeze drifted through the partially opened window and from outside, he heard a dog barking, kids laughing and in the distance, a growling lawn mower.

Just another day in suburbia.

Except, he told himself as he stalked around the room grabbing up his clothes, *today* was the day after he'd slept with his best friend's sister.

"Correction," he muttered as he left her room and cautiously moved across the narrow hall to the guest room, "you didn't do much sleeping."

He paused at the door to his bedroom and listened to Tricia's off-key singing coming from downstairs. He smiled to himself despite the churning emotions jangling around inside him like wind chimes in a hurricane. The woman couldn't carry a tune with both hands, but it didn't stop her from singing.

Was there a lesson there somewhere? Hell, it was too early to be looking for hidden messages. With his lover's voice still scraping his ears, he grabbed a change of clothes and headed for the shower.

A half-hour later, he was clean, shaved and nursing a knot on top of his head. Her shower had been built for pygmies.

But a headache was the least of his problems, Sam thought as he headed downstairs to face the music. Appropriately enough, an old girl-group was singing a song about begging someone to *rescue me*. He knew just how they felt. He could have used a good rescue about now.

But the plain fact was, no cavalry was on the way.

He'd have to face the woman he'd made love to all night and tell her it was going no further. And despite her claims to the contrary, he knew damn well that Tricia Wright was the kind of woman who would expect what they'd shared to lead somewhere.

In a way, she was right about that.

It had led *somewhere*.

Right to a skating rink in hell, and he was about to strap on his skates.

# Eight

**T**ricia'd been busy.

A teetering mountain of cookies lay frosted and wrapped on one end of the kitchen table, and the countertop was lined with even more cookies, cooling on trays.

"Want some coffee?"

He snapped her a look. She hadn't turned around. Her blond hair hung in a cheerful ponytail. Her long, honey-colored legs were bare beneath a pair of denim shorts with a frayed hem and her bright red tank top displayed every inch of her smooth shoulders.

Sam's insides jumped and his hands itched to stroke that satiny skin again.

She glanced back at him and offered a smile. "Coffee's hot. I've been up for hours."

"So I see." He walked into the room and reached into the cupboard for a mug. Her place was familiar now. He felt…at home here. Or he had, until this morning. Today was different. *Everything* had changed. Today, they'd crossed a line and nothing would be the same. They'd shifted into a different…he didn't want to use the word "relationship." But what the hell other word would do the job?

He poured a cup of coffee and inhaled the rich, fragrant steam gratefully. Taking a sip, he nearly groaned when the hot liquid hit his stomach like a gift from God. And he'd need all the help he could get.

"Sleep well?"

He shot her a look from the corner of his eye and caught the faint smile tugging at one corner of her mouth. A like response hovered at the edges of his mind, but he couldn't quite pull it off. Not until they'd talked. Not until she understood that despite what had happened the night before there couldn't be anything between them.

"I usually require more than twenty minutes' sleep a night," he admitted.

"Yeah, me too." She scooped up the cool cookies from the wire rack and slid them onto a wide, stainless steel tray. Stepping around him, she carried them to the far end of the table and set the tray down near several bowls of frosting. She took a seat in a splash of sunlight and got right to work. "But despite the lack of sleep, I'm feeling surprisingly perky today." She looked over at him. "Unlike *some* people I might mention."

"You want perky, I'll need more caffeine."

"As a doctor, aren't you supposed to be careful about that stuff?"

"As a doctor, sure. As a person—not a chance."

"So doctors are people, too?" In just a few minutes, she whipped a coating of bright yellow frosting over a third of the balloon-shaped cookies. "Wow. Who knew?"

He walked around the table and took a seat opposite her. "It's a closely guarded secret." Another sip, and another marginal inch of wakefulness skipped gleefully through his system.

"You know, I think we're doing a good job," Tricia said, starting on another cookie, this time with fire-engine red frosting.

"You're doing fine. I'm just sitting here."

"Not what I'm talking about."

"What then?" He knew. He just didn't want to be the one to start the ball rolling. Cowardice? He didn't want to call it that. Better to think of it as cautious trepidation.

She paused in her work, one hand holding a cookie, the other holding a pastry brush dripping red frosting. Her eyes danced with wry humor. "You know what I'm talking about. We're doing the 'morning after' dance very neatly."

"Are we?"

She shrugged and lowered her gaze to the cookie again. "We're skirting all around the subject. Not talking about it, as if not talking about it will make it go away. It's the elephant in the kitchen."

He shook his head. "Elephant?"

"A metaphorical elephant. You know, a figure of speech," she said, setting down the first cookie and reaching for another. "The one subject we don't want to talk about."

"You're right there."

"So naturally…"

"…You're going to talk about it."

"Got it in one." She flashed him a smile that sent alarm bells ringing in his brain and shouts of hallelujah echoing through his body.

Sam sucked down another greedy gulp of coffee, hoping the caffeine would kick in real soon. She'd been up for hours already, no doubt thinking about just what she was going to say. What she expected *him* to say in return. He'd been up fifteen minutes and all he was sure of was, he wasn't ready to have this conversation. But knowing Tricia, "There's no way to stop you either, I'm guessing."

"Unlikely."

"Fine." Sam set the mug on the table in front of

him and cupped both hands around the warm ceramic. Inhaling deeply, he said, "Shoot."

She laughed. "Well, that's an optimistic start."

"I didn't mean that literally."

"Just as well, I'm a lousy shot. Jake took me shooting once. He was humiliated."

"You're sliding off target now, too."

"I know." She gave him another quick look. "Just giving you time to settle into it, I guess."

"Thanks." *A year ought to be about right.*

"Oh, no problem." She picked up the next cookie and washed it with red color. "But now that you're all relaxed, why don't we jump right into it?"

Sam bit down hard, clenching his teeth. Relaxed? He wouldn't go that far.

"You want to tell me about your wife?" she asked quietly.

And so it began.

"Not particularly." Talking about Mary would only make the guilt gnawing at him more tangible. It would give it life, bring it into the sunshine-filled room and plop it down onto the table between him and his lover. Damn it. His lover. This shouldn't have happened. He should have kept his distance.

He'd had no trouble avoiding women for the last two years. What was it about Tricia Wright that had enabled her to slide beneath his radar so damn fast? Why had he been so drawn to her that he'd turned his back on memories of his late wife? And why did he want her so badly again now?

His hands tightened on the coffee cup until he wouldn't have been surprised to find the damn thing shattering in his grasp. Good thing it didn't though. He needed that coffee. He took another sip.

"Too bad." Tricia set the last red cookie down and pushed the red frosting to one side. Drawing up a bowl filled with grass-green frosting, she dipped a clean brush into the mixture and started her task again. "See, I told you about the guys littering my so-sad past. Now I want to hear about the woman you were thinking about while you were having sex with me."

That got his attention. His gaze snapped up to hers. In those blue depths, he saw pain and he winced to know that he'd caused it. Damn it. His own stupid fault. He should have fought the force of nature that was the Wright family. Should have stayed in a hotel. Should have stayed *far* away from Tricia. But it was way too late for should haves, wasn't it?

"I wasn't," he said tightly, wanting, *needing* her to believe him. "I wasn't thinking about Mary when I was with you."

After, certainly, but not during.

"That's something, I guess." Another green cookie joined its comrades.

"No, that's the problem," he said and pushed up from the table. Carrying his cup to the counter, he re-filled it and stalled by taking a long sip of coffee.

She'd stopped working, turned on her chair to face him, and was now watching him with open curiosity. There wasn't enough stall time in the world to buy him a reprieve.

"Explain."

One word, but a world of questions in her eyes.

Setting the cup down, Sam leaned back against the counter and braced his hands on either side of him, fingers curled tightly around the sharp edge. "You're the first woman I've been with since—"

"Yeah," she interrupted. "I got that last night."

"And I didn't think about Mary," he blurted. "Not once."

"That's a good thing."

"Depends on your point of view."

"Whatever the point of view, it's not a crime." Her voice was soft, but firm.

He stared at her, backlit by the sunlight pouring in through the wide window. Her hair was golden, her eyes in shadow. He knew every inch of her body. Learned it during the long night they'd snatched for themselves. He knew what made her moan, what made her gasp, what made her shiver. He'd touched her and found, for a while, *life*. And she, in turn, had touched him more deeply than anyone ever had before.

Acknowledging that, Sam knew, was like a slap in the face to the woman he'd once loved and married.

"Yeah, it is. For me, it is. She was my wife. We were married for three years, together for five."

"And…"

"*And*," he repeated, still stalling. "She was sweet and quiet and kind and—she died." He paused, took a breath and said the rest. "She died and it was my fault."

Tricia blinked.

He saw it and knew what she must be thinking. The same thing he was. Bastard. He was alive, Mary was dead—because of him. And instead of remembering her, he'd spent the night bouncing on a gorgeous blonde, losing himself in her.

"I don't believe that." Tricia stood up and walked toward him.

He thought about moving away, but didn't. Instead he stood perfectly still, tightening his grip on the counter so fiercely, he felt the cold tiles biting into his flesh. "Believe it."

"Tell me what happened."

Memories rushed through his mind like water escaping a dam after the floodgates were opened. Mary's face, her shy smile, her soft, dark eyes. Her broken body. Her last quiet sigh of breath.

Sam lifted one hand and rubbed his eyes viciously as though if he scrubbed hard enough, he could erase at least that *one* memory. Though he knew it was useless. That moment was burned on his brain.

"Sam?"

He heard her, but didn't open his eyes to look at her. If that made him a coward, then he'd just have to live with the knowledge. Retreating into memory, he started talking, describing the scene that replayed through his mind at least once a day. "We'd just picked up her new car. Driving back home." To the empty condo where misery now lived as his only company. "I was ahead of her, driving slowly, since Mary never liked to go more than forty-five. Scared her."

Everything had scared her, he thought now and tasted the bitterness of disloyalty. But she'd been so delicate, so fragile. He'd had to take care of her. She'd needed it. Needed him. And he hadn't been able to do it. Hadn't been able to save her when she'd needed him most.

"Tell me."

Tricia's voice, grounding him to the moment, keeping him in the present despite his brain's attempt to drag him back into the past.

He swallowed hard. "A drunk. Crossed the yellow line, coming right at me. I swerved. Instinct, I guess. Yanked the wheel to the right. He missed me. I checked the rearview mirror…"

"And?" Her voice was tight now, as if she were afraid to ask the question and afraid not to. He still couldn't look at her.

He blew out a breath. "I watched the guy plow head-on into Mary. She didn't even turn the wheel. Didn't even try to avoid him. But it happened so fast. She couldn't get out of the way. Even if she *had* tried—" Why hadn't she tried? Why hadn't she made an effort? He didn't know. Would never know. That haunted him, too.

"Oh God, Sam."

He opened his eyes then and read the sympathy he'd seen so often in others, glittering now in her gaze. Sam stiffened against it. He didn't deserve it. "Don't feel bad for me. It's Mary who deserves your pity. Not me. Not me, because I couldn't save her. I wasn't good enough."

"Sam, that's crazy."

He pushed away from the counter, suddenly too tense, too wound up to stand still. Stalking the circumference of the kitchen, he talked, avoiding her gaze as he relived those last agonizing moments. "No, it's not. I'm a doctor. That's what I do. I save people. Hell, I saved Eric. Saved my best friend, couldn't save my wife."

She'd moved too. She stood at the head of the table and looked at him. "We were lucky that you were there for Eric. But it wasn't the same. Wasn't the same at all."

"Close enough," he snapped. "I stopped the car and I ran back to her. The front of her car was like a closed accordion. The drunk was moaning, crawling out of his car, but I didn't even look at him. All I could think of was getting to Mary."

"Of course—"

He wasn't listening. Instead, he was back on the side of the highway, rushing toward his wife in the wreckage of her car. "The airbags had opened and were already deflating. She was alive though." He remembered it all. The blood. The agony shining in her eyes. The strangled groan ripping from her throat as he tried to help her. "I got her out of the car. Shouldn't have moved her, but didn't have a choice. Had to try. Had my bag with me. Doctors always have their bags."

"Sam…"

"But I couldn't fix her. She was…broken. Inside. Internal bleeding. Someone called 9-1-1, I tried, kept trying until the paramedics got there, then *they* tried. But Mary died anyway. Because I wasn't good enough."

"It wasn't your fault."

He snapped her a look filled with the rage pulsing inside him. "Of course it was my fault. If I hadn't swerved, the drunk would have hit *me*. Mary would have been all right."

"Maybe. And maybe he would have killed both of you."

"No." He shook his head. He'd relived those few moments too many times to believe her rendition. He *knew*. He knew it in his bones. If he had just taken the hit, he could have saved Mary.

"Sam, you can't believe that."

"Yes, I do."

"That's crazy." She took a step. "It was an accident."

"That should have happened to me."

"It shouldn't have happened to *anyone*."

"True. But it did. To Mary. And I couldn't save her."

"Neither could the paramedics."

"They're not doctors. I am. I should have been able to keep her alive." He shoved both hands through his hair, yanking at it as if that small pain could ease the larger one raging within. It didn't help, though. Nothing did. Nothing could. The guilt lived and breathed inside him. Like a dragon, crouched in the shadows, it erupted now and again to flame his insides with the burning knowledge that he'd failed. And nothing would change that. Ever.

Sam stood at the window, staring out at her driveway and the trees beyond the fence separating her house from the one next door. Wind played in the leaves, dancing along the fencetop.

"I had no idea."

He flinched at the stiffness in her tone. "Now you do."

"Oh, yeah."

She walked toward him. He heard her bare feet on the linoleum and braced himself for whatever it was she was going to say.

She turned her back on the window and perched her hip on the window ledge. Staring up at him, she shook her head and said, "If I'd known, I would have treated you totally differently."

He winced inwardly, but didn't let the pain show on his features. He'd expected her to feel this way. To be as disgusted with him as he was with himself.

But hearing it was harder than he would have thought.

"I'm not surprised."

"Well I am," she said, her voice rising slightly. "I mean I knew you were a doctor. But I had no idea you were God, too."

"What?" He snapped his gaze to hers and was startled at the flare of emotion glittering in her blue eyes.

"You heard me."

"Don't you get it? Don't you understand what I'm telling you?"

"Better than you do, I think."

"Apparently not."

"Is this how Mary would have wanted you to feel?" she asked hotly. "Would she want you drowning in guilt for something you couldn't have changed?"

"No, but—"

"But nothing. For heaven's sake, Sam. You don't control the universe."

"I never said I did."

"Might as well have," she said and stood up. "You're taking the blame for what was clearly a tragic accident. Why is it your fault and not the drunk driver's?"

He scrubbed one hand over his mouth. "He was the cause, but I—"

"—couldn't work miracles?" she countered.

Sam blew out an angry breath and forgot about

trying to argue with her. What would be the point? She wasn't going to understand this. Wasn't going to see that day as he did.

He shook his head, refusing to believe, refusing to grab hold of the life preserver she was trying to throw him. How could he let go of the guilt? Let go of the pain?

They were only inches apart now. The scent of her perfume mingled with the fragrant aroma of her morning's baking and filled him, whether he wanted it to or not.

"You don't understand."

"Oh, sure I do," she countered, cutting him off before he could even finish his sentence. "You're so busy punishing yourself, you don't have to worry about actually living anymore."

Irritation flashed inside him.

"You're a doctor," Tricia said, her voice a low-pitched thread of steel that couldn't be ignored. "You did your best to save her and Mary died anyway."

"Exactly."

"Have you lost other patients?"

"Of course, but—"

"This is different?"

"Yes."

"How?"

He opened his mouth, then snapped it shut again.

"Lost for words?" she coaxed.

"She was my wife," he said.

"And she died."

"Because of me."

"Because she *died*." Tricia laid one hand on his forearm and Sam felt the warmth of her touch right down to the bone. "Not because of anything you did or didn't do, Sam."

He looked at her, staring hard, trying to read everything he saw in her eyes. There was no pity there. No censure. But he couldn't accept her words. Couldn't make himself believe it. He'd clung to his own guilt and sense of failure for too long now to be able to go on without them. And if he *did* somehow let them go…wouldn't he be letting Mary go, too?

She reached up, laying both hands on his shoulders. The warmth of her skin seeped into him, easing back the chill still coating his insides. And everything in him yearned for that warmth.

"Don't be a dope, Doc," Tricia said, with a slow shake of her head. "The accident wasn't your fault. Mary dying wasn't your fault."

"You don't know that—"

"I know that you clearly loved her. If you could have saved her, you would have." She squeezed his shoulders tightly as if trying to give him a good shake.

"Fine. Then if I'm not to blame, who is? God?"

"It was an *accident*." Tricia let her hands drop from his shoulders as she frowned up at him. "God wasn't driving that car."

"Clever. But it doesn't help."

"What does?" she demanded, slapping both hands to her hips and giving him a look so hot it could have fried an egg on his forehead. "Locking yourself away? Shutting out the world? Refusing to live because someone you loved died?"

"You don't—"

"Fine. I grant you, it didn't happen to me, so maybe I don't get a vote in how you handle it." She reached up again and grabbed two handfuls of his dark blue T-shirt. "One thing I do know though. If all you learned from loving Mary was to close yourself off, then you missed the whole point."

She went up on her toes and planted a long, deep kiss on him that left his brain spinning. When she let him go, he had to fight for balance. Shaking her head until her ponytail danced behind her, she said, "That's not what love's supposed to teach us, Doc."

# Nine

The Wright family swallowed the day in one noisy gulp. Sam found himself making liquor runs, dropping by a local craft store for more decorating supplies and loading rented chairs into the back of Jake's truck. He'd ridden herd on Debbie's kids for an hour while she grabbed a quick nap and everyone else was busy with more wedding stuff. He'd helped mow the lawn and trim the flowering bushes in the backyard and was so tired at the moment, he just wanted a place to sit down and quietly die.

But at least he'd been busy.

Too busy to think about the conversation he'd had with Tricia that morning. Just as well, he thought. There was no point in going over it again and again.

He groaned tightly and scraped one hand across his face. No point in telling himself that maybe, just maybe, Tricia was right. Because he couldn't make himself believe it. And when this two-week span was up, he'd be back in L.A. Back to the world where his only companions would be memories of Mary and his own failure.

A cold stone of dread dropped to the pit of his stomach and shook him to the core. When he'd arrived here, all he'd been able to think about was escape. Now, it was just the opposite.

Sam walked out to the middle of the backyard and let the cool, ocean breeze ruffle past him. From inside the house behind him came the voices of too many Wrights, with children's laughter ringing out above the rest. It was all so…ordinary—and yet, special, too. And maybe, he told himself, that's what the extraordinary really was—taking the time to realize that the ordinary was a small miracle in itself. And families loving each other, most of all.

"Man, I've been here too long." He shook his head, then lifted his gaze to the wide sweep of summer sky. A few stray white clouds scuttled across the broad sweep of blue, blown by the same wind rushing past him. For one brief moment, he wished that wind was strong enough to blow him the hell out of there. To get him back to where he knew how to behave. Knew what was expected of him. Knew what the rules were. But even as he stood there, he realized that he wasn't sure where that was anymore.

The back door flew open, slamming into the side of the house. He spun around. Tricia was framed in the doorway and something in Sam's chest turned over.

It couldn't have been his heart.

"Hey," Tricia called out, a wide, impossibly attractive smile on her face. She hadn't brought up their earlier conversation once during the long day. Hadn't prodded or probed or tried to resuscitate their argument—as, he admitted silently, Mary would have.

Thoughts raced randomly through his mind as time seemed to stand still. Staring at Tricia's open grin, he saw instead, Mary, her eyes wounded, biting her bottom lip as silent tears coursed her cheeks. He vividly remembered the guilt along with the sense of resentment that had crowded him every time an argument had become a cold war. Mary hadn't liked dissension, as she called it, and had simply retreated whenever they'd had a disagreement. It had been infuriating and frustrating to watch the woman he loved pull away from him rather than talk to him.

Instantly, though, he gave himself a mental shake. *Resentment? Frustration?* Mary had been fragile and tender. She hadn't been the kind of woman—as Tricia was—to go head to head with a man. She'd needed care. She'd needed…oh God, so much.

Where had that come from?

What the hell was wrong with him?

"Yo, Sam!"

He snapped out of his self-induced coma and focused again on the woman now standing on her parents' back porch. Hands at her hips, she stood in a slice of late afternoon sunlight, blond hair shining, tanned limbs gleaming—and she made his mouth water. Even at a distance she reached him as no one else ever had. He shook his head again. "Yeah?"

"Good." She jumped off the porch, hit the sun-warmed grass with both sneaker-clad feet and walked toward him with a sway in her hips that spiked his temperature and fired his imagination. "Thought maybe you were sleep walking."

"Wide awake," he snapped, *and dreaming anyway.*

She stopped just an inch or two from him and tilted her head to one side as she looked up at him. "Wide awake and just a little on the crabby side?"

He inhaled sharply and glared at her.

She ignored it. "Well, that doesn't matter. You've been elected, and I volunteered to go along for the ride." She hooked her arm through his and started for the driveway.

His skin tingled at her touch. But that was nothing new. She seemed to electrify him on a continual basis. Tricia was a toucher. She was forever reaching out, patting his hand, stroking his forearm, leaning into his chest to laugh. He wasn't used to it, but he was getting there. Mary had never been very affectionate. At least not publicly. Her own innate shyness had kept her from it.

And damn it, why was he comparing the two women again?

"Go where?" he demanded, slipping his arm from her grasp. "For what?"

"Questions," she said, laughing. Apparently, it hadn't bothered her a bit that he'd deliberately uncoupled them. "Don't you trust me?"

The problem was, he didn't trust himself around her. But how the hell could he admit that? "Should I?"

"Oh, absolutely, Doc." She kept walking and, naturally for Tricia, *talking*. "See, I'm the one who's not afraid to look you dead in the eye and call a crab, a crab. So you should always trust the person who's not afraid to—"

"—insult you?" he finished for her.

She grinned at him. "Exactly." Rising on her toes, she dusted a quick kiss at the corner of his mouth, then headed around to the passenger side of his car. When he didn't move, she urged, "Hello? Dinner not going to walk here on its own."

He just looked at her, his mouth still on fire from the quick press of her lips. "You're not mad, are you?"

She opened the car door and paused, one hand on the door, one hand on the roof of the car. She stared at him for a long minute, then blew out a breath and shook her head. "You mean about this morning?"

"Yeah."

"What's to be mad about? We both had our say. It's over."

Amazing, he thought. "Just like that."

"Well," she said, her smile spreading, "I didn't say there wouldn't be Argument II: The Return. But, yeah, it's over."

"You're an unusual woman," he said, opening his side of the car.

Tricia grinned at him and her eyes actually seemed to sparkle. "You know," she said, "I think that was a compliment."

"It was."

"Well keep 'em coming, Doc," she said and slid onto the passenger seat. "A girl could get used to it."

Getting used to it was the problem though, wasn't it? He was getting used to Tricia, to her family, to the world he'd discovered outside his own small circle. But in less than a week, it wouldn't matter because he'd be gone and in no time at all, Tricia would be arguing with someone else.

He fastened his seat belt, fired up the engine and tried to tell himself that he didn't care.

But even *he* wasn't believing him anymore.


"It hurts!" Katie wailed, and her voice hit notes that surely only dogs should be able to hear.

Sam winced and tried to take hold of the little girl's knee. But she was so busy kicking and wailing, it was like trying to catch a live electrical wire.

Not as easy as it looked and downright dangerous to boot.

The child's wildly kicking foot narrowly missed his groin and Sam did a quick two-step to stay out of range. As a doctor, he was more than used to having to deal with frightened children. But doing so in a crowded bathroom with not only the crying child but her pregnant mother, older brother, grandparents, aunt and uncles crouched and perched around him was something else again.

And that wasn't even counting all of the advice flying around him.

"Does she need stitches?" Debbie asked.

"Should have just taken her to the emergency room," Jake muttered.

"Sam can do the job right here," Tricia said and leaned over Sam's right shoulder until her face was alongside his and all he could smell was her perfume. She turned her face at him and smiled encouragingly.

"Is she gonna bleed some more?" Kevin demanded, inspecting the bloody washcloth with incredible relish.

"No and put that down," his mother said, and clapped one hand to her mouth and the other to her distended belly. "Think I'm gonna be sick."

"Can't," Eric piped up from the hallway. "No room."

"Put your head between your knees, honey," Tricia's mother shouted to her pregnant daughter.

"I haven't seen my knees in two months," Debbie moaned.

"Well if Doctor Parker was still working we could go there." This from Tricia's father.

"He's not though, and isn't it a shame, that nice office and his practice going to waste." Tricia's mother said again. The woman leaned in and patted Sam's shoulder companionably. "It's just the right sort of practice for a young married doctor. Family close by and all…"

"Geeezzz, Mom, show a little subtlety," Eric complained, and a moment later a sharp slap sounded out, followed by an outraged, "Ow!"

"When's she gonna bleed some more?" Kevin's indignant voice rose up to rival even Katie's wailing.

"Will everyone please shut up?"

Stunned silence dropped onto the group and Sam paused to enjoy the quiet. He hadn't meant to yell, but it seemed there was no other way to get the Wright family's attention. You had two choices with them—either be overlooked or shout them down. Well, it appeared he'd warmed up to them all enough that it didn't bother him a bit to tell them to put a collective sock in it.

"Way to go, Doc," Tricia whispered in his ear. "My hero." Her breath dusted his skin and he had to fight to shrug off the sensation. After all, four-year-old Katie was the star of this show.

And the only one currently paying no attention at all to his demand for silence.

He stared into the little girl's watery eyes and felt

his heart twist. What was it about a child's pain that could slice right through a man?

"Do I hafta get a shot?" she wailed the last word, making it almost four syllables long.

He thought about it, then glanced at the girl's mother, still looking a little green around the gills. "Has she had a tetanus shot lately?"

"Yeah," Debbie said, keeping her hand firmly against her mouth and avoiding looking anywhere near the bloody washcloth or her child's scraped knee. "Last year."

"No shot then," he announced and won Katie's love forever.

"But there's gonna be more blood, right?" Kevin again.

"Oh, God," Debbie moaned again.

"That's it," her mother said and snatched her out of the bathroom as though she were a child again. "Come on, you're not being the least bit of help, here."

"How come Mom doesn't like blood?" Kevin demanded. "It's really cool and stuff and—"

"That's enough from you," his grandfather said, scooping the boy up and pushing his way out of the bathroom. "What're you, a vampire?" He tickled the boy and a trail of giggles floated like soap bubbles behind them as they went downstairs.

"Keep your chin up, kid," Jake said. "Never let 'em see you cry."

"Girls can cry," Katie argued.

"The ones I know do it all the time," Eric quipped and got another slap, this time from his fiancée. "Man. Guy can't say anything around here."

"You know," Sam said loudly, pitching his voice to cover the remaining Wrights and all of their conflicting opinions, "why don't all of you go on downstairs and Katie and I will be along in a minute."

With a lot of muttering and more than a few grumbles, the remaining Wrights finally trickled out of the bathroom. All except Tricia. But then, Sam thought with a sigh, he hadn't really expected her to leave and was rather grateful she'd stayed. She could distract Katie while he washed and bandaged the scrape on her knee.

"She's all yours, Doc," Tricia said and perched on the edge of the bathtub to watch.

"I'm a brave girl," Katie said stiffly, her bottom lip trembling with the strength of an 8.5 earthquake.

"Sure you are," Sam said, falling into his routine for dealing with scared kids. He fumbled in the leather bag Jake had retrieved from Tricia's house and came up with a grape sucker. Well, he wasn't a dentist. Why should he worry about kids' cavities? "But even brave girls like candy, don't they?"

"Uh-huh." Katie snatched it and tore at the cellophane while Sam worked quickly, quietly. She took one lick, then winced and pulled her leg back. "That hurts."

"Not a lot, though."

"Uh-huh."

"Katie," Tricia said, drawing the girl's attention from Sam's ministrations. "When Sam gets you all fixed up, you know what?"

"What?"

"It's time for me to go and pick up Sheba."

"For real?" Katie's face lit up.

"Sheba?" Sam asked, one eyebrow lifting. "As in, Queen of the Jungle?"

"That would be Shee*na*," Tricia corrected, still smiling at him.

"My mistake."

"Sheba's not a queen," Katie said, reaching out to tug at Sam's shirt to regain his attention. "She's a puppy. Aunt Tricia's puppy."

Tricia shrugged and lifted both hands as she looked fondly at her niece. "Loose lips."

"A puppy?" Sam echoed, trying to keep Katie still despite the fact that she was practically vibrating with excitement.

"We've been waiting and waiting for the puppy to be big enough to leave her mommy," Katie burbled.

"And now it's time."

"And we can go get her?" The little girl nearly hopped off her perch on the toilet seat.

"You bet." Tricia went down on one knee beside Sam and caught one of Katie's hands in hers. "So, you want to go with me to get her?"

"Oh," a brilliant, teary smile lit the little girl's face. "Just me and not Kevin?"

Sam laughed. Nothing like a little sibling rivalry to get a girl's mind off her pain.

Tricia laughed, too, and the music of it seemed to settle over Sam like a warm blanket. His fingers fumbled at his task as he shot a quick look at her. Her nose was sunburned, her hair a mess, and a splotch of something that looked suspiciously like ketchup stained one shoulder of her T-shirt. He'd never seen anyone more beautiful.

"Sure," she was saying to Katie. "It'll be just you, me and Doc."

"Me?"

She looked at him and grinned. "Don't you want to come along?"

If she kept smiling at him like that, Sam thought, he'd probably be willing to go anywhere with her. And that realization shook him right down to the bone. It took everything in him to keep from grabbing her and pulling her close. A damn good thing that Katie was there. And wasn't that a hell of a thing, a grown man grateful to be hiding behind a four-year-old girl.

"What do you say?" Tricia asked, cocking her head to one side, keeping her gaze fixed on him.

He swallowed hard, and shifted his gaze to Katie's scraped knee as he applied ointment and a bandage. Much safer that way. "I don't—"

"Don't you like puppies?" Katie asked.

"Sure, but—"

"Don't you like *us*?" Tricia asked.

He shot her a frustrated glance. "Yes, but—"

"I like *you*," Katie said, crooning the words. Then she pouted, her bottom lip thrusting out in a way that told Sam females were obviously *born* knowing how to do that.

"Me, too."

Sam looked over at Tricia and caught the sparkle of humor in her eye along with the deliberately pouty lip. Like any smart man, Sam knew when he was beaten.

"Okay," he said. "I'll come."

"Good." Tricia grinned and winked at Katie conspiratorially.

"But first, my doll fell down, too," the little girl said, thrusting a beat-up, nearly bald baby doll at him. "Fix her."

Tricia just smiled.

Katie waited impatiently.

Indulgently, Sam wrapped the same kind of bright, neon-colored bandage on the doll's knee and when he was finished, Katie scooted off the edge of the toilet seat and threw her arms around him. Holding on tight, she gave him a smacking kiss on his neck and squeezed with every ounce of her little-girl strength.

Over the child's head, his gaze met Tricia's. Warmth shone in her eyes and for a long moment, he simply basked in it as a man starved for the sun would seek out a beach. Everything in him yearned for her. Her scent reached for him. Her steady gaze warmed him.

And as the moments slipped quietly past, Sam felt himself fall a little deeper into the vortex that was Tricia Wright.

# Ten

Sam lay in his bed, staring up at the moonlit ceiling. A soft breeze ruffled the curtains at the window and threw dancing patterns of light and shadow across the pale blue walls. He'd been watching those shadows for what felt like hours. He couldn't sleep. Every time he closed his eyes, Tricia's features rose up in his mind, making it impossible for him to relax enough to fall asleep.

He threw the sheet back with a grumble and swung his feet to the floor. Naked, he paced the room for a few minutes before stopping at the window. He stared briefly into the shadows below, his brain racing, his thoughts churning. A muffled whimpering reached him and he glanced over his shoulder at his closed bedroom door. Tricia's new puppy was making herself heard from the bathroom. Apparently Sheba was unhappy with her new bedroom.

A moment later, Sam heard Tricia's whispered voice, crooning sympathetic, nonsensical words. He smiled to himself, imagining her cuddled up on the bathroom floor, soothing the puppy. He wished he could join her. Wished he had the right to go to her, to help her with the puppy that he wouldn't be around long enough to watch grow.

The new puppy was just one more addition to the Wright family circus and she'd already made herself at home. Tricia and Katie had smothered the little dog with affection from the moment they'd picked her up. Sam had kept his distance, not wanting to involve himself any further than he already had.

Naturally, the midnight-black pup had unerringly attached herself to Sam, the one person *not* trying to bond with her. Tricia had even resorted to bribery, pulling out dog treats and toys—but Sheba had chosen her favorite human. And damn it, he'd had no better luck steering clear of the puppy than he had keeping his distance from Tricia. Sheba was as stealthy as her new owner. She'd slipped past Sam's defenses as easily as Tricia had.

It hadn't taken more than curling up in his lap. He'd never had pets. His parents hadn't approved of animals in the home, calling them, as he remembered it, "germ factories with legs." And Mary'd been allergic, or so she claimed, though Sam used to think that it was just her way of avoiding a discussion she wanted no part of.

He winced slightly as he realized that more and more lately, he was looking at Mary's memory without the sweet, soft-focus lens of distance. And why was that? he wondered. Why now? Why here?

But the answer was clear. Kids, dogs, Tricia…it was all crowding him.

*Life* seemed to pulse all around him and it was impossible to be oblivious to it when every glance at Tricia only reminded him how alive and…*alone* he really was.

He wasn't spending all his time revisiting old memories here. He was building new ones, whether he wanted to or not.

And Sam knew damn well that once he'd left town, once he'd gone back to his old life, the memories of Tricia and the puppy and the kids, and the whole damn Wright family, would haunt him every bit as much as Mary had. No, damn it—still did now.

He'd been alone for two years, shutting himself off from everyone and everything that used to matter to him. He'd sought to punish himself and he'd done a hell of a job. But in the last ten days or so, he'd been dragged kicking and screaming back into the world.

With the wedding only a few days away, all too soon he'd be going back into the cold silence of his own world, and the very thought of it nearly strangled him. How could he go back to that life? After being here, being with Tricia, how could he blindly return to the solitude that suddenly looked so empty? So depressing?

And how could he not?

"Sam?"

He whirled around and stared at the closed door for a heartbeat or two. Then a gentle knock sounded and Tricia's voice came again.

"Sam? You awake?"

His heart jumped into high gear, slamming against his ribcage like a sledgehammer on an anvil. Snatching his jeans off a nearby chair, he dragged them on but didn't bother buttoning them closed as he walked across the room in three long strides. Grabbing the doorknob, he turned it and pulled.

Tricia was right there, hand lifted to knock again.

The hallway light spilled down over her, highlighting her hair, soft and loose. She wore a pale peach-colored nightgown with thin straps over her shoulders and a lace-trimmed bodice that dipped low over her breasts. It looked silky and cool and eminently touchable.

Just like Tricia herself. Damn, why did she come to him now? When his resistance was at its lowest?

"You *are* awake." She smiled up at him.

"Or sleepwalking."

"With your eyes open?"

One corner of his mouth lifted. "Easier to see that way."

She walked past him, into his room and when she'd taken a few steps, she stopped, turned around and looked at him. "Are you really seeing me?"

"Oh yeah," he muttered, voice thick, heart now rising high enough to lodge in his throat and threaten to choke him.

"What do you see when you look at me?"

He saw images of what might have been. A life he could have had if things had been different. He saw everything that he hadn't known he'd always wanted. And so much more. "Tricia…"

"Tell me."

He couldn't. Couldn't tell her all of that because he didn't have the right. He'd long ago given up on life and now, even if he'd wanted to rejoin the land of the living, he wasn't entirely sure he could pull it off. So instead, he gave her the much shorter answer. "A beautiful woman."

"Is that all?"

He smiled tightly. "Not enough?"

"Nope."

"What do you want to hear?"

She tipped her head to one side and looked up at him. "I *want* to hear that when you look at me, you want to make love to me. That I'm the reason you're not asleep."

"I do," he ground out tightly, against his better judgment. "You are."

Tricia smiled briefly. "You weren't going to say so, though."

"No."

"Interesting."

"Glad you think so." He could hardly think himself. Moonlight speared through the lace curtains at the window and backlit Tricia as though she were the lead actress on an empty stage. She looked like a dream. A vision come to taunt a lonely man.

And God, he hoped she wouldn't leave.

"You were good with Katie today," she said.

"What?" Katie? They were going to talk about kids, now?

"Katie. She really likes you."

"Uh-huh." Confusion rattled through him. The woman's conversations were like mental Ping-Pong games. It took all a man's concentration to keep his eye on the ball and remember where he was.

"I really like you, too."

Sam groaned inwardly, but kept the sound wrapped tightly inside him. Folding his arms across his chest, he braced his feet in a wide apart stance and fought for balance. What was it about this woman that could so tilt the world? "Good." A safe answer, right?

She turned away and walked toward the window. Her bare feet didn't make a sound. The breeze ruffling the curtains danced around the hem of her nightgown and lifted it against her tanned legs. Sam swallowed hard and hoped to God he could keep from grabbing her, throwing her onto the bed and forgetting all about being rational.

"The puppy was crying a minute ago."

"I heard." There went the Ping-Pong ball again. New direction.

She turned around to look at him, silhouetting herself against the moon-washed window. "She's quiet now, though. She was just lonely. I gave her a stuffed animal and she snuggled right in and went to sleep."

"Yeah?"

"And I was thinking…" She bent forward slightly and lifted the hem of her nightgown. Drawing it up by slow, incremental inches, she tantalized him with an ever-growing peek at her legs.

"What?" One word. The best he could do. His gaze was locked on the lacy edge of satin and the ever-increasing expanse of lean, tanned thighs.

"That maybe that's all any of us need," she said, pausing long enough in her undressing to cause Sam's heart to stutter to a stop. "Not to be alone. To have someone to snuggle up to when the night gets lonely."

He shook his head and fought for clarity…and lost. "You want a stuffed animal?"

She laughed that low, luscious, music-filled laugh that reverberated inside him.

"Not exactly," she said, a moment later. "What I want is *you*."

She pulled the nightgown up and over her head, then tossed it to the side in a wide arc that had it fluttering like a half-open parachute before landing on the floor.

Beautifully, gloriously naked, her soft, smooth skin seemed to absorb the moonlight. She damn near glowed.

Sam sucked in air and knew it wouldn't be enough. His lungs felt as though they were being squeezed by a giant, uncaring hand. His heart erupted into a wild beat and his temperature shot up about twenty degrees. His mouth went dry, his hands went damp and his groin tightened eagerly.

"Tricia…"

She walked toward him with no hesitation, no coy smiles, no pretense of embarrassment. When she reached him, she stopped, lifted both hands to his shoulders and held on. The warmth of her fingers on his skin slid down inside him and filled the last few crevices of cold.

"If you don't want me," she said, going up on her toes, "just say so. Otherwise, kiss me."

Trembling with need, Sam forgot about everything but the moment. She was back in his arms when he'd thought he'd never hold her again. She was warmth and light and laughter and *life* and he wanted her more than his next breath.

Grabbing her close, he bent his head and kissed her, laying siege to her mouth in a frenzy of need that swamped them both. Tricia clung to him, turning into his kiss, pressing her body along his, rubbing herself against his chest. Heat, delicious, mind-numbing, soul-searing heat rushed through him.

He half carried, half dragged her to the bed and tossed her down onto the mattress. Yanking his jeans off, he knelt on the bed beside her and filled his hands with her. He touched her again and again, stroking, caressing, exploring every inch of her sweetly curved form.

Her breasts became a feast. One after the other, he kissed them, tasted them, taking first one nipple and then the other into his mouth. His lips and tongue tortured her gently. As he sucked her, she lifted into his grasp, arching toward him, demanding and taking more.

Her hands moved over his back, his shoulders and down along his spine. She nibbled at his shoulders, swept her tongue along the side of his neck and shifted until she could teasingly bite his earlobe. Jolts of white-hot heat splintered inside him and Sam clung to it all. He memorized the very feel of her. The way she bent into his grasp. The way her leg slid up his and hooked around his waist. The damp warmth at her center when he dipped first one finger and then another within her.

She sighed and it was music as sweet as her laughter. She gasped and whispered his name and it was a gift that swept inside him, settling in one corner of his heart.

"Sam," she called his name again as his fingers continued to tease her, push her higher along the frantic edge of urgency. "Sam, I need you inside me, now."

"Oh yeah," he murmured, inhaling her scent as he kissed and licked his way along her throat and down, down to the tips of her breasts again. He couldn't taste her enough. He couldn't feel her enough. He wanted more. Wanted *all*.

She rocked her hips into his hand as his thumb slid across a small nubbin of flesh.

"Oh!" Her eyes wide, she looked up at him with the same need pulsing inside him. "Now, Sam. Seriously, I mean *now*."

He needed her, too, but he didn't want to rush it. Wanted, in fact, to prolong it. He made no move to claim her body, to push his own into her depths. Instead, he only pressed another finger into her center, stroking, rubbing, pushing her higher, faster, until her breath exploded from her lungs and her hips rocked feverishly.

"Take this first," he whispered brokenly, caught by the passion glazing her eyes, by the parting of her lips, by the desperate grasp of her fingertips on his shoulders. "First you, then *us*."

"Not fair," she whispered, licking her lips, tossing her head from side to side. "This was my idea. Not fair to change the rules."

"No rules," he said and deliberately stroked that most sensitive spot at her core again, just to watch the tremors take her. "Not tonight."

She smiled briefly, brightly, then gave herself into his hands. "Oh, Sam…so…good. So…amazing."

"Let go, Tricia." His words came softly, gently beneath the frantic rush of her breath and the staccato pound of her heart. "Let me see you go over."

"Can't…wait…can't…stop…"

He took her mouth when the first ripple of sensation caught her and shook her in his grasp. His tongue swept past her lips to taste her sighs, swallow her cries as she erupted beneath him, straining and reaching for the release shuddering through her.

And before the last tremor died away, Sam shifted, knelt between her raised thighs and pushed himself home. She was more than ready for him and she took him into her depths, surrounding him with a heat that branded him.

She reached for him, wrapping her arms around his neck. He moved and she echoed it. The dance was as old as time and as new as a morning. Together, they found the rhythm that sent their bodies into urgent tandem.

Sam had never known such completion. Such intimacy. He didn't want it to end. He could have stayed locked together with her forever. But as the need pulsed within, he knew his control was slipping.

That's when he remembered. "Condom."

Her eyes flew open. "Damn. My room."

He groaned tightly and moved to pull free of her.

"No, don't. Don't leave me."

The fine thread of control was frayed, and inches from snapping entirely. "Need to."

"Take me with you."

He choked out a half laugh, then grinned. "Never cease to surprise me."

She smiled back at him even as she wrapped her arms and legs tightly around him. Sam eased off the bed, bringing her with him. And holding her to him, still locked within her, he hurried from his room, across the short hall, to hers. There, he made a wild grab at the bedside table and blindly scrabbled inside the top drawer. Finding one of the dozen or more condoms there, he frantically tore it open, then lay down on the bed.

"Hurry," she whispered, and she twisted and writhed beneath him as he was forced to withdraw from her long enough to sheathe himself.

"Trust me, I am." Only seconds, but it felt like lifetimes. And then he was inside her again, pushing home, delving deep, surrounding himself with her.

"Welcome back," she said, smiling up at him. Taking his face between her palms, she drew his head down for a kiss.

"Glad to be here," he murmured.

Then their bodies took over and the flames rising

within consumed them both. And, locked together, they found the fireworks.

Later, when they could separate without shattering, Sam lay across the mattress with Tricia beside him. She flung one leg across his, one arm across his chest and breathed out a long, deep sigh. He turned his head to look at her, to simply admire her, as she lay sated in a splash of moonlight.

Emotions churned in her blue eyes, shifting, flashing across their surfaces so quickly, he couldn't identify them all. And not for the first time, Sam wished to hell he knew what she was thinking, what she was feeling. A moment later, though, he realized that he would never have to wonder what Tricia was thinking. If he simply waited her out, she'd say it.

"Doc…" She stretched languidly. "For a crabby man, you sure have a way about you."

He laughed, in spite of the situation, and damned if he could remember a time before Tricia when he'd ever laughed during or after sex. "My pleasure."

"Good to know." She pushed herself up onto one elbow and looked at him. Her hair stood up in a tangled halo around her head and her eyes were still foggy with satisfaction.  She was breathtaking.

"But, the thing is…"

He cocked an eyebrow and narrowed his gaze on her. Something was bothering her. Hell, how was a man supposed to think after experiencing what they'd just shared? His body was still on fire, but his brain now raced to catch up and pay attention. The concern suddenly etched on her features worried him. "Problem?"

"Sort of."

Sam groaned.

She ignored him. "It's just that…well, I don't want you to get the wrong idea here or anything—"

"About what?"

"About *me*."

"Like?" He pushed himself up until he was braced on both elbows. Totally confused now, he watched her, and noticed the way her fabulous mouth twisted with whatever was worrying her. Then he noted her gaze shift to one side of him so she didn't actually have to meet his eyes. The last of the fire in his blood fizzled out. "What's going on, Tricia?"

She huffed out a breath and let herself flop back onto the mattress. "Stupid. But I don't want you thinking that I act like this with just anybody."

"Huh?" This was making no sense at all and he had a feeling it was about to get worse.

"This, you know…" She blew out another breath and glanced at him. "Coming in here, seducing you and everything and—"

"Seducing me?" He grinned. Couldn't help it.

"Well, yeah."

He grabbed hold of the foot she had draped across his thigh and began to rub it. "Do you really think that if I hadn't wanted this to happen, it would have, just because you'd decided it would?"

Her features screwed up as she tried to work that one out.

Sam chuckled. "Man, I have been here too long. I'm starting to sound as confusing as you do half the time."

"Gee, thanks." She pulled her foot free of his grasp and sat up on the bed, wonderfully uninhibited about her own nudity. "But you know, some guys don't like a 'pushy' woman and—"

Laughter faded as he watched her. "What man wouldn't like what just happened?"

"Well, for instance," Tricia said, "my ex-boy-friend. He didn't really like it when I made the first move and—"

Sam squeezed her bare foot gently. "He was an idiot. Don't change, Tricia. You're...*refreshing*."

She snorted. "Sounds like a soda commercial."

He smiled and shook his head. "Being with you is—"

He paused and the silence stretched on so long, she rushed to finish his sentence for him.

"Amazing? Wonderful? Inspiring?"

"Yeah," he said, nodding, wondering how it had happened that this incredible woman had come to him. What had she seen in him that had made her want to reach out? And how would he get by without her in his life? "All of those." Then, without thinking, he blurted, "Your ex-boyfriend sounds like he would have been perfect for Mary."

"What?"

"I can't believe I said that," he muttered, shoving one hand through his hair. Staring blankly up at the ceiling, he muttered, "I didn't mean to, I just—"

"Hey, I talked about my past—no reason why you can't talk about yours."

He looked at her. He'd just dropped his late wife into the bed between them and Tricia wasn't even angry. Would he ever understand how her mind worked? And did that matter? Shaking his head slightly, he started talking again, "It's just that Mary was…shy. And fragile, somehow."

"Really." Not a question. Just a statement.

He looked around the moonlit room, then back to where she lay naked and completely at ease, and smiled to himself. "Mary never wanted a light on when we made love. She even put blackout shades on the windows to block moonlight."

"Wow."

Sam winced. "I shouldn't—"

"Hey," she said with a shrug, "lots of people like the dark."

"Mary did. Until the night I couldn't see her and moved the wrong way and she ended up with a black eye."

"What?" A muffled snort of laughter shot from her throat.

Sam glared at her, instantly defensive, and irritated with himself for even starting this. "It wasn't funny," he snapped. "She—"

"I'm sorry, of course not." Tricia clapped one hand over her mouth and didn't look at him. She held up one hand, breathed through her nose, then gave up. Her laughter helplessly spilled out.

"You shouldn't laugh and—"

Still shaking her head and trying to get a grip on the giggles rolling from her throat in long waves, she struggled to breathe. "I know," she said in between fresh bursts of laughter. "I know, it's just…a black eye? Oh God, Sam, you must have felt awful."

"Hell yes," he snapped, remembering just how badly he'd felt and how much Mary had added to his guilt. She'd made him pay for that mistake in dozens of different ways, for weeks. Why hadn't he remembered that before now? he wondered. Why had he allowed himself to forget that Mary hadn't been perfect? That their marriage hadn't been an amusement park?

Tricia's laughter had faded into an occasional eruption of chuckles when he finally smiled, too. It really was funny if you looked at it objectively. And Mary hadn't been hurt, really. More embarrassed than anything. And he had the distinct feeling that if the same accident had happened between him and Tricia, Tricia would have worn the black eye like a badge of honor.

Oh yes.

Two very different women.

"Poor Mary," Tricia finally said. "I shouldn't have laughed, but Sam, dumb stuff happens to me all the time. One night, I almost knocked my boyfriend out when I turned over suddenly just as he was sitting up, and my elbow caught him right between the eyes."

"No way," he said, watching her with a smile on his face.

"Oh yeah." Tricia grinned. "He went down like a redwood."

Now it was his turn to laugh and it felt good. It felt damn good to be with a woman who could turn his insides into a molten mess one moment and make him laugh like a loon the next.

"Anyway," Tricia said, "it's sort of nice to know that I am not alone in the world of quirky happenings."

"No, you're not."

"And now that we're in the 'share' mode," she said softly, her expression shifting from amusement to serious.

*Uh-oh.*

"I wanted to tell you that I'm a very picky woman, Sam." She watched him through steady eyes filled with raw emotion. "I've only been with two other men and each of them meant something to me. I don't take this kind of thing lightly."

He'd known that about her from the first. Which was why he'd tried so hard to keep his distance. For all the good it had done him.

"I know." He stared at her in the moonlight and knew that this image of her would always remain with him. Twenty years from now, he'd be able to reach into a corner of his mind and pull out this one moment and relive it. The scent of her, the look of her, the very real temptation of her. But he forced himself to meet her gaze squarely and say again, "I know exactly what kind of woman you are, Tricia."

She studied his gaze for a long minute before, apparently reassured, she nodded. "I'm glad," she said finally as she shifted position, then leaned in, bracing one forearm on his chest as she rested against him. "And there's something else you should know."

It wasn't easy to concentrate when he had a warm, wonderful woman draped across him. But he did his best, trying to ignore the brush of her breasts against his chest.

"What's that?" He forced himself to ask, even though he was half afraid of what she might say.

"I found them tonight."

His guts twisted. ESP? Foreboding? He didn't know how he knew, but damn it, he *did* know what she was going to say. And he didn't have a clue as to how to respond to her. Naturally enough, Tricia didn't give him much of a chance to consider it before she started talking again.

"The fireworks I told you I was looking for? Well, I found 'em tonight."

# Eleven

Everything in Sam ached.

His whole body prickled and tingled, like a long-asleep limb just waking up. Painful, irritating, impossible to ignore. Then his heart twisted in his chest and he felt a new kind of pain. He knew what she wanted him to say. And he couldn't give it to her. "Tricia, I—"

"It's funny," she said, her voice wistful as she cut him off neatly, "you spend your whole life waiting for something and then, when it finally comes along, you can't have it."

Sam sucked in a gulp of air and trapped it in his lungs, afraid that if he let it go, he might not be able to draw in another.

She was telling him that she loved him.

He knew it.

Felt it.

And there wasn't a damn thing he could say to her to make this easier.

He couldn't be the man she wanted. The man to be her husband and the father of the children he already saw shining in her eyes. She deserved better. She deserved a man who hadn't already given up on the very things she was still dreaming about.

No. He'd failed once. He couldn't live through another failure.

"It's okay, Sam." Tricia smiled and stroked her fingertips along his jaw and then across his lips. "I don't expect anything from you."

"You should, though," he said, suddenly tired right down to the bone. "Damn it, Tricia, you have a right to expect a lot from a man." He only wished he were the man to give it to her. "You have a right to expect *everything*."

"Sam—"

He slid one hand along her arm, lulling himself with the silky smooth feel of her beneath his fingertips. "It's just that—"

"Relax, Sam." She smiled slowly, intimately, and shook her head. "If you're lying there worried that I'm about to propose, don't."

He started. "I didn't think—"

"Sure you did." Her smile widened briefly. "I saw the momentary flash of panic in your eyes."

He grabbed her hand and swallowed the bitter tasting, fresh serving of guilt. He'd lost Mary. Hadn't had the ability to save her. And now, he was hurting Tricia, losing her. Yeah, he was a real prize. All he could do now was try to lessen her pain. Help her to see that she was better off without him. "I wish…"

"I'm not asking you to love me, Sam," she interrupted him, her voice a soft hush of sound. "But I *am* asking you to love *someone*."

He went completely still. He would have sworn that even his heart stopped for one hideously long moment. Then Tricia spoke again and her quiet voice shattered the stillness.

"It's not going to be me," she said. "I get that. I knew going into this that you'd be leaving. In fact, even as close as we are right now, I can feel you mentally backing away."

"No, I'm not." Yes, he was. And she knew it, damn it. What was it about this woman, that she understood him better than he did himself? How could she look at him and see beyond the face he presented to everyone else? How did she look deeply enough to see the real him and want him anyway?

She only gave him a patient smile.

"Tricia." He forced himself to look up into her eyes, to read the patience and yes, the love, written there. "I can't be the man you want."

She tipped her head to one side to study him. "How do you know what I want?"

Sam wished he could pretend he didn't know. But how could he? It would be lying to them both. "I knew what kind of woman you were the first moment I saw you." He smiled sadly. "You're picket fences and kids and a dog. You're the PTA and cookies and barbecues on Sundays. That's who you are, Tricia." Everything he ached to have and couldn't claim.

"I *do* know."

She lifted one shoulder in a half-shrug. "Maybe. But I know something about you, too, Sam." Her gaze locked on his and he felt the power of it slide right down to what used to be his soul. "You gave up too soon. You walked away from life when you should have stayed and tried harder. And now, you don't have anything left." She bent her head and kissed him briefly, gently. "Until you love again, you'll stay just a little bit dead inside."

He flinched, but she wasn't finished.

"And if that's all you want out of life, Sam," she said quietly, "then you should have crawled into that grave with Mary."

Fury still clouded the edges of Sam's mind three days later. He clung to it like a child to the string of a balloon. But the tighter he held on, the more that string seemed to slip from his grasp. Hard to keep righteous indignation going when you suspected that the person who'd made you so damn mad was partially right.

Naturally, Tricia had been acting as though nothing had happened. As though she hadn't forced him to take a hard look at himself. As though they were nothing more than casual acquaintances.

They'd continued sharing her small house. They'd worked together on the reception plans, the last-minute wedding details and he'd even helped make several cookie deliveries. He'd seen the new shop she'd be moving her business into and had even helped with some of the clean-up. He'd watched her play with the puppy, laugh with her family, and he knew he'd be imagining her doing all of those things once he was back in his own house in L.A.

And late at night, he'd ached for her when he lay in his bed alone.

She treated him as politely and warmly as she would any guest, and Sam hated it. It would have been easier on him if she'd fought about it. If she'd been as furious as he'd been that night. If she'd thrown him out and sent him to a hotel. But in typical Tricia fashion, she never did what he expected— or hoped—she would do.

She was giving him too much time to think and damn it, he didn't like the thoughts he was coming up with.

He couldn't really bring himself to admit that Tricia was totally right. That was asking too much. But

at the same time, a small, rational voice in the back
of his mind taunted him with reality.

He had been as good as dead for two years. He'd
hidden behind the failure of losing Mary and let himself be buried in thoughts of what "might have been."
Easier, safer than having to try. To face the world and
pretend to care about anything other than his work.
Guilt and misery had become second nature to him.
At this late date, he didn't even know if he *could*
change. Or even if he should try.

Say he did, Sam thought, arguing silently with
himself. Say he gave it a shot, and failed. What then?
Then his guilt would be doubled and he'd have
screwed up Tricia's life on top of it. Did he really
have the right to risk that?

The last two weeks had only been a blip on his oth-
erwise straight and narrow highway of solitude. The
Wright family had brought him out of the shadows.
They'd welcomed him and made him one of them.

Tricia had made him want to really *live* again.

But he just didn't believe he deserved to.

He scraped one hand across his face, trying, un-
successfully, to wipe away his thoughts. But nothing
would be that easy ever again. He picked up the cup
of coffee sitting on the table in front of him and, almost desperate for distraction, turned his attention to
the rush of activity surrounding him.

The wedding had been everything a wedding
should be.

Nothing fancy. Nothing over the top.

Just family and friends and a reception that looked as though it was going to rock on long into the night.

Sam sat at a table in the far corner of the Wrights' backyard, hidden by the shadows thrown from the strings of white lights stretched across the property. From beneath the overhang of one of the trees, he watched the party happening around him and, not for the first time, realized that he was already becoming the outsider again.

And he was doing it voluntarily.

Dance music poured from the stereo speakers and smiling couples whirled across the neatly trimmed grass as smoothly as if they were on a polished dance floor. The kids raced through the crowd, laughing and eating handfuls of cake. Tables rented for the occasion groaned under the mountains of food brought in by the local Mexican restaurant, and the margarita bar was standing room only.

Sam was clearly the only one *not* having a good time.

"Having fun?"

Startled to hear his own thoughts spoken out loud, Sam shifted in his seat and looked up at the groom. He forced a smile and lied through his teeth. "Sure. Great party."

"Oh yeah, I believe you," Eric said, setting his crutches aside and lowering himself into a chair beside his friend. "I came to tell you the other guests

were complaining. You're having too much fun—
getting a little too loud. Want to dial it down a
notch?"

"Funny." Sam's gaze slid away from his friend.
Hell, he was here, wasn't he? He'd stayed through the
wedding when all he'd really been thinking about the
last few days was escape. He was living in Tricia's
house and keeping his hands off her. Torturing himself so he wouldn't let Eric down by leaving early.
Talk about the mark of friendship.

"I'm a funny guy."

"Not really," Sam said, shifting Eric a quick look.

"Uh-huh. So, do you love my sister or what?"

"Huh?" Sam tensed, straightening slowly. Hell, he
hadn't expected this. Should have known by now
that the Wrights, every damn one of them, excelled
at the unexpected. But he couldn't tell Eric the truth.
Not when he hadn't had the guts to tell Tricia. His
gaze met Eric's and he heard himself say, "No."

Knee-jerk. Even as the single word shot from his
throat, his mind and heart argued the lie. Love. Dear
God, did he really love her? And if he did…did it
change anything?

No.

"Then you're an idiot."

Sam's gaze narrowed as he lifted his coffee, took
a sip and stared at his friend over the rim. Once he
swallowed, he said, "Stay out of this, Eric."

"Not gonna happen."

"I'm leaving tomorrow," Sam pointed out. "Problem solved."

"Think so, huh?" Eric glanced over his shoulder at the crowd behind them.

Sam followed the man's gaze until he spotted Tricia. Dancing with a man old enough to be her grandfather, she was laughing and clumsily trying out a half-hearted jitterbug, just to please the guy. Sam smiled to himself and indulged in one good stare. Her soft blond hair was loose and wild, shining in the glow of the lights. Her dark green bridesmaid dress clung to her figure, making Sam grateful for talented dressmakers.

Her laughter bubbled up again and Sam had no trouble hearing it over the crush of noise in the backyard. Something told him that for the rest of his life, he'd be half listening for that laugh—just as he'd be looking into crowds, hoping to find her.

Regret pooled in the pit of his stomach and spilled through his veins. Darkness crouched inside him and his heart ached with the numbing throb of a toothache.

"Oh yeah," Eric said, looking at him again. "An idiot."

"Go away." God, he wanted a drink. But he settled for another gulp of coffee. He'd already decided to drive home to L.A. right after the reception, so he couldn't afford to drown his sorrows in a bucket of margaritas—despite how good that sounded to him.

"I'm going." Eric pushed himself to his feet, then

settled his crutches into position beneath his arms. Staring down at Sam, he said, "I should have warned you before not to hurt my sister. Now it's too late."

Guilt, his old friend, reared up inside him. Sam stared up at Eric, backlit with the tiny fairylights strung out behind him. A summer wind shifted through the party and those lights danced as if they had wings.

Jaw clenched, Sam forced himself to meet his friend's gaze. "I didn't want to hurt her—and once I'm gone, she'll be fine."

Eric snorted and shook his head. "God, Sam. You really *are* an idiot."

Another hour or two passed before the crowd started thinning out. Eric and Jen had left for a honeymoon that would be only slightly hampered by the groom's cast. The caterers were slowly cleaning up, the music had changed from blistering rock and roll to quiet love songs and the remaining guests had splintered into small groups clustered around the rented tables.

Sam's gaze fixed on Tricia and after a few moments, she seemed to sense his attention. Turning away from the friends she'd been chatting with, she started a slow walk across the yard toward him. Like the pull of a magnet on metal, Sam couldn't resist her. He stepped out of the shadows and met her in the middle of the grassy dance floor.

Her scent reached out to him and Sam inhaled it deeply, knowing that soon, this would be all he would have of her. This night. This memory. This fragile scent that wrapped itself around his heart and held on with a tenacious grip.

"Wasn't it a wonderful wedding?" Tricia smiled, her eyes shining with happiness.

"Yeah, it was."

She sighed tiredly and glanced around at the remnants of the reception. "And a great party."

"Yeah, it was."

Tricia's lips twitched as she looked up at him again. "Jen looked beautiful, didn't she?"

"Did she? Hardly noticed her. Too busy looking at you." Stupid, he told himself. Don't dig yourself in deeper. Don't make this harder on both yourself *and* her. But he couldn't seem to help it. Just being near her was far more intoxicating than anything he could have gotten out of the margarita bar.

Her smile slowly faded, dying away as completely as the stars in her eyes. "You're leaving, aren't you?"

He nodded tightly. "Tonight."

She took a deep breath then blew it out in a rush. "Well, that's eager."

Eager? No. Safer? Oh, yeah. "I have to get back to my practice, Tricia."

She studied him. "Doctor Parker's practice is for sale, right here in town. You could work here. Be needed here."

"I know," he said. "Your mother already gave me his phone number."

Tricia smiled sadly. "Then you know you'll be missed."

No one since Mary had missed him. And knowing that these people would—that Tricia would—made leaving even harder.

She sighed. "But you're still leaving."

"It's better for both of us if I just go. Soon."

She shook her head, then lifted one hand to push her hair back from her face. "You know what's really sad? I actually think you believe that."

Another slow song started up from the CD player in the corner of the yard. The melody swam on the summer breeze and swirled around them both, drawing them inexorably closer.

"I do," he said, his voice ringing with the regret churning inside him.

"Sam—"

"Dance with me," he murmured before he could stop himself. Hell, if he had to leave, the least he wanted was to hold her in his arms one more time. Was that too much to ask? Too much to want?

She stepped in close, sliding her left hand up high on his shoulder and allowing him to fold his fingers around her right hand. They barely moved. It was more swaying than dancing, but neither of them cared.

Sam looked his fill of her, letting himself get lost in her eyes. She felt right, nestled close to him. He could almost feel her heart beating in time with his. And he knew he would miss her for the rest of his life.

"You're thinking again," she whispered.

"Yeah, guess I am."

Tricia pulled her head back and looked up at him. Her gaze met his. "You're going to miss me."

"Guess I am."

"You're going to regret leaving."

Something in his chest tightened, squeezing until he was sure his lungs were exploding. And still, he forced a smile and played their last game. "Guess I am."

"You love me."

He stopped the dance, but didn't let her go. He didn't speak. Didn't think he'd be able to if he tried.

One corner of her delectable mouth tilted slightly. "Ah, no quick answer that time."

"Tricia, I wish it could be different."

"It could be. If you wanted it badly enough."

Everything in him ached to believe her. But it had been too long. Two weeks of happiness wasn't enough to ease two years of misery. And how could he possibly believe in a future when he was still tied to the past?

She stepped back, out of his arms, but stayed close enough that she could speak softly and still have him alone hear her. "I lied before, Sam."

"What?"

"When I told you I didn't expect you to love me, but you had to love *someone*." She reached up and cupped his cheek in her palm. "I want that someone to be me."

"Tricia…"

Shaking her head again, she spoke up quickly, before he could finish. "I'm not asking you to *stop* loving Mary. You'll always love her. And you should. I just want you to love me, too."

God, she made it sound so simple. Yet, he knew it wasn't. It couldn't be that easy to put aside one life and pick up another. Could it?

Her eyes swam with emotion and he hoped to God she didn't cry. Because he was pretty sure that would kill him. "I'm sorry, Tricia."

"I know," she said. "I love you anyway."

"I know," he said and forced himself to walk away.

# Twelve

The condo felt as empty as a tomb.

Sam had thought the sense of isolation would pass once he got used to being back where he belonged. But it had been a little more than a week since he'd left Tricia and nothing had changed. Every time he walked into the place, silence dropped onto him like a sack of bricks. He felt suffocated by the very stillness he'd once craved.

Before, there had been a sort of comfort in the silence. Now, there was only a profound loneliness that gnawed at him relentlessly. Reminding him that he'd had a chance to change his life and had turned his back on it. He'd walked away from the only woman who'd been able to touch his heart…his soul.

When he slept, his dreams were haunted by images of Tricia. When insomnia struck, his mind filled with thoughts of her.

There was no escape.

Waking or sleeping.

Worse, he didn't *want* an escape.

So what kind of fool did that make him?

Sam stood on the narrow balcony off his living room and stared up at the night sky. Below him, the lights of the city shone in the blackness, but he didn't notice. Didn't care. The city held nothing for him because his heart was still in a small town in northern California.

He grabbed hold of the iron railing, his fingers tightening around the cold metal until his knuckles whitened. A slight breeze whipped past him, but it was hot and airless. There was no scent of the sea, no hint of Tricia's perfume. No life in it at all.

"You're in bad shape," he muttered, just to hear the sound of a voice in the numbing quiet.

And when a man started talking to himself, things were going downhill, fast.

He pushed away from the railing before he started answering himself and stalked the narrow perimeter of the balcony. Here, he was safe. Here, no one expected him to live. To love. To be involved in anything beyond his own pain.

So why wasn't that comforting anymore?

"Why can't I stop thinking about her?" He

dropped into one of the two chairs pulled up to a small, round table. Bracing his elbows on the glass tabletop, he cupped his chin in his hands and stared off into the darkness as if half expecting to find the answers he sought.

But all he found were more questions.

His mind filled with thoughts of the Wright family and all he'd left behind. And he wondered...

*Was Tricia's business settled into the new shop?*

*Were Eric and Jen home from their honeymoon?*

*Did Kevin get the stethoscope he'd sent him, as promised?*

*Did they miss him as much as he missed them?*

*Was Tricia as lonely as he was?*

His heart tightened as though it were in the grasp of a huge, cold fist. Sam jumped to his feet, shoved both hands through his hair, then scrubbed his palms across his face. There was only one way to find out.

Tricia opened her front door and immediately spotted the large, pink pastry box on the porch. Sam quietly stood to one side and watched as she opened the box and gasped at the contents.

He knew all too well what she'd found.

Nine cookies. Each of them frosted and boasting a single word that, together, spelled out a simple, yet heartfelt question.

*Tricia I love you. Will you marry me? Sam*

Stunned, she looked up and met his gaze as he stepped out of the shadows to stand in front of her.

"Sam?"

"You look wonderful," he said, not trusting himself yet to reach out and grab her. First he had to know. Had to know if he'd ruined what they'd had. If, in his own stupidity, he'd thrown away his last best chance at happiness.

His gaze swept up and down her quickly, thoroughly. Her blond hair was pulled into a high ponytail at the back of her head. Flour dusted her nose and forehead and her blue eyes looked impossibly beautiful. She wore an old T-shirt and the denim shorts with the frayed hem that showed off her legs to perfection.

Sam's heart jolted and his blood pumped in a fury of want and need. One look at her again and he knew without a doubt.

She was his future, his present, and everything in between.

Through some incredible stroke of good fortune, he'd not only found love again…he'd found *life*.

Now he could only hope that he wasn't too late to claim it.

"Don't say anything yet," he blurted before Tricia was able to launch into one of her rambling conversational threads.

She inhaled sharply. "Okay."

He nodded, shoved both hands into his pants pockets, then pulled them out again. Pushing one palm along the side of his head, he then let it drop to his side and gave up trying to find the perfect words. Instead, he settled for speaking from the heart and hoping it was good enough.

"I love you."

"Oh, Sam…"

"Still talking," he said quickly.

She grinned. "Right."

Okay, smiling. That was a good sign, right? He kept talking, half afraid to stop now that he'd started. "I did love Mary and she'll always be a part of my heart—but," he said, swallowing hard as he said the words it had been so hard for him to accept, "she's my past. You're my future."

Her eyes filled with a sheen of tears and she blinked frantically, trying to clear them.

Taking one step forward, Sam reached out and grabbed her upper arms as if to reassure himself that she was really there. Really standing there smiling at him.

"I want to be your future, Tricia. I want to build a life with you. Have lots of babies with you. I want us to live in the middle of the Wright whirlwind, because outside it, life is just too damn lonely. Too empty. And without you, it's unbearable." He shifted his grip on her, sliding one hand up to stroke her cheek. "*I'm* too empty without you. I *love* you, Tricia. I think I have from that first moment."

"Well, *duh*."

Sam blinked and stared down at Tricia's wide grin. But he only had a moment. She dropped the pastry box and leaped at him. Wrapping her arms around his neck, she laughed and buried her face in the curve of his throat.

His arms came around her tightly and he bent his head to hers, dragging her scent into his lungs with a silent prayer of gratitude. She leaned into him and Sam held her tighter, closer, and knew there was a part of him that would never want to let her go.

"Took you long enough," she whispered brokenly, and finally pulled her head back just far enough to look up at him.

He smiled, feeling the old guilt and misery slide off his soul, leaving him feeling lighter than he had in years. "I'm a slow learner."

"Apparently." She didn't let him go, just held on as though she had no intention of ever releasing him. Rising up on her toes, she planted a quick kiss at the corner of his mouth and confessed, "If you'd taken much longer, I was going to L.A. to drag you back here myself."

"Is that right?"

"You bet, Doc." Her fingers tangled in his hair. "This is home. This is *your* home. *Our* home."

"I know that now."

"Good."

"Oh, better than good," he assured her. "I sold my

half of the practice to my partner and as soon as I contact Doctor Parker, I'll get set up here in town and—"

Tricia laughed. "Won't take long. Mom already talked to Doctor Parker and told him you'd be back to take over his practice."

"Of course she did." Sam laughed, too, and then lifted Tricia off her feet, swinging her up into his arms, close to his heart. Where she'd always been. Where she would always belong.

Her smile warmed him down to the bone and chased away any last traces of the shadows that had held him in their grasp for too many years. Sam stared down into her eyes and saw the future stretch out in front of them. He saw his heart. His life. His love.

"Welcome home, Doctor Crabby."

"Not feeling so crabby right now," he said and seriously doubted he ever would again.

"I really do love you so much, Sam," Tricia said, cupping his cheek in her palm.

"Don't ever stop," he whispered.

"Not a chance."

From inside the house, the kitchen timer rang out, its shrill tone sparking a loud, yapping response from the puppy in the backyard. Next door, at her parents' house, the old black Lab added his deeper bark to the fray and the noise hit amazing proportions.

"Cookies burning?" He shouted the question over the din.

"Whoops! It's a double batch, too!" She clambered out of his arms, then stopped long enough to grab her proposal-in-a-box off the porch. Clasping it to her chest with one arm, she grabbed Sam's hand and tugged him inside. "C'mon, Doc. Once the cookies are safe, we've got some celebrating to do!"

"Home, sweet home." Sam grinned and jumped into the whirlwind, enjoying the rush and pull of a rich, full life so unlike the silence he'd left behind forever.

* * * * *

# Critical acclaim for Theresa Michaels

"Readers often complain that there is no depth to romance novels, but they have obviously never read a Theresa Michaels...."

—*Popular Fiction News*

"...a stunning rendition of *Romeo and Juliet*... *Fire and Sword* has classic written all over it...."

—*Booklovers* ★★★★★

"Like the great bards of old, Theresa Michaels enthralls readers with a dramatic and action packed story...."

—*Affaire de Coeur* ★★★★★

"...FIRE AND SWORD takes you on an adventure you won't long forget."

—*The Medieval Chronicle*

"...the name Theresa Michaels brings solid GOLD 5 ★★★★★ writing. Another star in the romantic galaxy!"

—*Heartland Critiques*

"...a tender evolution from fierce hate to deep love.... Well researched and brilliantly laid before the reader, it is a banquet for the heart."

—*The Paperback Trader*

# Micheil's laugh was cruel and mocking

"You once warned me, wee bairn though you were, that when you had grown to your promise I'd want no other woman. Witch that you are, it's come to pass. And as you lay claim to my heart, so I claim yours. As my body hungers to find the passion and peace you alone give me, so will you hunger. If you deny me again in this life, Seana, I swear by all I hold dear, I will follow you into hell itself."

He released her and had already turned away when she called out, "Micheil, do not—"

"Do you beg, witch? Will you recant your words that any man but me can have you?"

"I cannot beg you, Micheil," she whispered as sorrow tore at her. "You cannot trust me. On the day you do, I will give you the love I hold...."

# Theresa Michaels

# Fire and Sword

## Harlequin Books

TORONTO • NEW YORK • LONDON
AMSTERDAM • PARIS • SYDNEY • HAMBURG
STOCKHOLM • ATHENS • TOKYO • MILAN
MADRID • WARSAW • BUDAPEST • AUCKLAND

ISBN 0-373-28843-3

FIRE AND SWORD

**Books by Theresa Michaels**

Harlequin Historicals

*A Corner of Heaven* #104
*Gifts of Love* #145
*Fire and Sword* #243

---

## THERESA MICHAELS

is a former New Yorker who resides in South Florida with her husband and daughter—the last of eight children—and three "rescued" cats. Her avid interest in history and her belief in the power of love are combined in her writing. She has received the *Romantic Times* Reviewers' Choice Award for Best Civil War Romance, the National Readers' Choice Award for Best Selling Series Historical and the B. Dalton Bookseller Award for Best Series Historical. When not writing, she enjoys traveling, adding to her collection of Victorian perfume bottles and searching for the elf to master her computer.

To Joelle for the title, to Elizabeth for tenacity,
and to Tracy for giving me the opportunity to write
this long-dreamed-about story.

# Prologue

Seana had known the challenge would come. At dawn, when the mist lifted, she was forced to watch the personal combat between her brother, Liam, and Micheil Gunn.

Her brother fell to one knee, wounded. The Gunn chieftain raised his broadsword for the mortal blow.

"Spare him!" Seana cried, rushing through the open gate to plead for her brother's life. "For eleven years you've wreaked your vengeance upon us. Cease now. Micheil, I beg you." The words were themselves bitter gall, for she had sworn never to beg him. Calling upon the remnants of her pride, she stood tall until her gaze met his.

The highland warrior's eyes were bleak, targeting her now-slender form.

"The bairn?" he mouthed across the distance that separated them. His features hardened when she did not answer, but before he could move, before he fathomed their thoughts, his two brothers rushed forward on their steeds and caught Seana up between them.

Her cry was cut off, her struggle immediately stilled. Horrified, Micheil saw Jamie press his dirk to her bared throat.

Without a thought to what he was doing, Micheil dropped his sword, turned his back on his enemy, Liam, and started forward.

"Hold, brother," Davey, the youngest Gunn, ordered. "The bitch's whelped your bairn. Now Jamie and me'll have an end to your torment." Davey held tight with one hand to Seana's arm and controlled his mighty horse with his knees. With his free hand, he gripped a length of her honey-blond hair, forcing her head back until she had to look up at him.

"For your life and that of your worthless brother, give the bairn over to us."

Seana felt the pinprick of the dirk's point at her throat and lost what little breath she had left. There was no moisture in her mouth to allow her to speak. Her eyes closed in defeat and despair. Was this to be the final revenge? She longed to curse Bridget Gunn MacKay. For their sister, the Gunns had raised their clan and destroyed hers. So much blood. And now they demanded her child.

"She'll not tell us, Micheil," Jamie declared. "She leaves us no choice. And will you not be thanking me, brother, for ridding you of the witch that haunts you?" His jeer brought forth no response. "'Tis not the fitting end our father decreed, but 'tis well served." Jamie glanced once more at his older brother. "Micheil?"

"Are you blind, Jamie? He cannot speak." Davey's laugh was mocking. "He'll thank us once the deed's done. Wait no longer, Jamie. Slit her lying throat. Rid Micheil of the MacKay witch."

# Chapter One

*The Beginning*
*Halberry Castle, 1372*

The smoke-blackened rafters resounded with the high keening of the bagpipes in the great hall of the Gunn stronghold. Halberry Castle occupied the headland jutting into the sea at Mid Clyth, on the northern coast of Caithness. Ingram, chief of the Gunn clan and hereditary Crowner of Caithness ruled here.

Servants were hard-pressed to keep filled the gem-encrusted gold and silver goblets at the high table. Urged on by his love for his only daughter, Bridget, Ingram offered the first congratulatory toast to the bridal pair. It galled him to drink to Liam of clan MacKay, groom and enemy, but he bitterly resented his clansmen's reluctance to celebrate this marriage with joy.

He thought them fools not to see that wedding his Bridget to the heir of the MacKays secured an immediate peace between the clans. The constant warring depleted stock and men. The additional betrothal of

his eldest son, Micheil, to Seana, the only daughter of the Mackay, would ensure a lasting peace.

Within Ingram was the regret of a seasoned warrior that the call to arms against the MacKays would no longer be cried in his hall. Bridget and Liam, two headstrong young people, as wild and as passionate as the mountainous crags of the highland tracts of Caithness and Strathnaver that were their birthrights. These were the two who had brought together the powerful clans and their related allies.

Ingram's gaze narrowed. Despite the somewhat forced gaiety, there were those, he knew, who would bear careful watch to ensure that this peace was kept. Many were the same men who had voiced their displeasure when Robert II, of the house of Stewart, celebrated his first year as king of Scotland.

Seated as he was to the right of the bridal pair, Ingram sensed the undercurrents that shimmered like the mist over the loch. The hot blood and long memories of the highlanders were immersed in feuds. Few of these men, here tonight by his order, would ever forget those of their clans who had died by the dirks and swords of their sworn enemies.

His craggy brows lifted over eyes some called a piercing blue and glanced down the length of the crowded tables. He paid no heed to the richness of the fine linen covering his tables, nor to the bold tapestries hung upon his stone walls. For once, he discounted the cost of the abundance of foods served upon plate worth a king's ransom. His wealth had come in part from Malcolm, Earl of Caithness and Angus, whose daughter Maud had married Sir Gil-

bert de Umfraville, of that great Norman baronial
house. He had added to the wealth, so he did not
weigh the cost of the unending flow of drink, which
would have beggared another man's purse.

Fingering the large silver brooch he wore—a brooch
local legend called *am Braisd Mor*, "Big Broochy," for
this was the insignia worn by the Gunn chiefs as
Crowners of Caithness—Ingram fastened his gaze
upon those he knew had vocally opposed this marriage and counted them well.

Sipping at the potent dram of his own homemade
brew, a malt Scotch so thick a man could float an egg
upon it, he marked the number of MacKays and al-
lied Keiths, lining one length of the great trestle tables. To a man, he knew the number of Gunns in
attendance. Ingram smiled with deep satisfaction. His
clan yet outnumbered them.

His roving gaze was snagged by that of Heth, chief
of the MacKays, who believed himself the stronger
man. The MacKays held Strathnaver, the whole
northwestern corner of the mainland. In honor of his
daughter, Ingram hid his smile when Heth touched his
butcher's-broom-plant badge. His memory drew him
to recall the days of his youth, when he had set fire to
the MacKay lands as a taunting reminder that their
name was the ancient Gaelic *Aed*, meaning *fire*.

But fire had only tempered and forged the steel of
his sword. Fire could never conquer it.

Perhaps fire had not, but as the silvery peal of
Bridget's laughter drew his prideful gaze, Ingram
knew that for her he had sheathed his sword.

Bonny Bridget, born first, before three braw sons. His chest expanded when she turned to him and lavished praise for the wondrous feast. "Are ye then pleased, lass?"

"Aye, that I am. You've given me my heart's desire this night."

"Would that I always could." Ingram patted her slender-boned hand and sipped again from his goblet, motioning to have it refilled. Aye, he thought, I've given her what she wanted. As if there had been a choice.

There had been no peace until he relented and gave his consent for the marriage. Not that either Bridget or Liam needed his consent, or that of Heth. But he knew his daughter well. She would have run off with the MacKay heir. Liam, to his credit, had insisted they would wed with their families present or not at all. Ingram had grudgingly conceded the point in Liam's favor. Privately, Ingram still held the opinion that quartering was too good for Liam. Never had a MacKay been considered as a possible mate for his Bridget. And never had the thought crossed his mind to bind Micheil to one.

His sigh expressed the weariness of a man who had been beset and bested by the fairer sex. Bridget, for all her delicate form, was not a gentle flower. She was of his own blood, blood that had flowed in the veins of Norse sea kings, and like himself, she would not be deterred from a course once it was set.

His lady wife, Onora, offered him a serene look and he raised his goblet in tribute to her. Theirs had not been a love match, but over the years they had worked

to ripen affection into a stronger bond. She appeared pleased with their daughter's joy, and had prepared her well for her role as a laird's wife.

Would that his eldest son, Micheil, had offered him a sign that he no longer held a grudge over this night's work.

A frown creased his brow, and Ingram looked upon his son briefly before he settled his gaze upon the bonny young Seana. His frown disappeared, his smile deepened, and he chuckled softly to himself. The lass yet stared wide-eyed at Micheil. Not that she was alone in admiring him. Grown women were casting lures his way this eve.

The small lass was a delight to watch, despite her being a MacKay. If she kept her promise when grown, she would set men to dreaming of faeries and kelpies, the kind highland legends were fashioned upon. But, young as she was, she, too, was as headstrong as his Bridget. No bairn of eight winters should be witness to the ribald talk that was making its way to the high table as tongues loosened with drink at this late hour.

But Ingram would not deny it boded well to know that Heth could not deny his daughter her wishes. He would tuck that bit away and pass it along to Micheil. When the time came for them to marry, Micheil would use that knowledge as he saw fit. There was no doubt in his mind that his son would do as he was bid to uphold the honor of their clan.

*For the honor of the clan.* Micheil's thought paralleled his father's. He answered a toast far down the table acknowledging his own betrothal. The clan—all was for its survival. The words echoed in his mind, but

none could have discerned that beyond his cool smile and glacial blue eyes there hid a raging anger.

His gaze meshed with that of George, a Keith ally. Micheil knew he was another not pleased with this night's work. George had wanted Bridget for his own bride. Micheil knew Bridget was no docile female to be led where she refused to go. She was their petted and spoiled darling, loved too much to be denied what she wanted, but fiercely loyal and loving in return.

He feared for his sister that she ignored the risk to the clan, and because he knew the temper of the MacKay heir. With Liam older by two years, Micheil, just turned fifteen, had fought him more than once. The bloody feuds that raged and ebbed in the highlands left little time for childhood. Micheil had been called a man for three years. It was as a man that he thought he knew his sister. Her own too-hot temper and passion for living would challenge Liam's pride and temper at every turn if he tried to control her.

Bridget was obsessed with Liam. There was no other way to describe her feelings for him. Seven months had passed since she first met the MacKay in Wick. It had galled him to admit that they owed Liam a debt for having saved Bridget's purse from a thief. And, from that day, his sister would not rest until she saw him again.

Micheil alone knew of the times she had daringly crossed the Halladale and Helmsdale rivers in hope of seeing Liam. His adoration for Bridget had kept him silent. And when his sister finally succeeded in finding Liam, only Micheil knew that her claim of Liam's

having dishonored her rang false. She was as virgin as the bairn he'd been betrothed to this night.

His father had sworn revenge, promising Bridget he bring her Liam's heart, cut out with his own dirk, but she had suddenly pleaded for marriage.

Exchanging a bitter look with Liam, Micheil, with a dark scowl so like his father's, reached for his brew. They were all to blame for allowing Bridget to run wild. Whatever she wanted, or thought she wanted, his sister allowed no peace or rest until she had it. Liam had best beware. Bridget had already used her wiles on him until he too had demanded they be allowed to marry.

Pray the saints, he thought, that Liam was strong enough to temper Bridget's reckless nature, and gentle enough to understand her consuming need to be loved.

The prayer gave him no comfort and he was filled with an unnamed dread as he tossed down the last of his drink.

"You'll be tipsy if you drink more, Micheil," Seana whispered at his side. It was the second time she had dared to talk to him. Seated with honor beside him, Seana was hurt that he would not look at her, nor acknowledge her as he motioned to have his cup refilled.

Impatience sent her squirming in her seat. She had spent the better part of the eve staring at Micheil, thinking him the most handsome boy. Well, not a boy any longer, she amended. He stood taller than her only brother, Liam. She had heard the tales of his fierce fighting skills, and she buried a quick stab of fear.

After sneaking a look at his scowling face, she lowered her gaze over his angled body. Where Liam was broad and thickly muscled, Micheil had a catlike grace that belied the lean hardness of his frame. That was how her mother had described him.

Seana sat up straight in her overly large chair. She knew Micheil did not like her. He had brushed aside her timidly asked request that he take her for a ride on the morrow. She had been disappointed, for the Gunns raised fine horseflesh and she had prayed to be allowed to ride one, racing madly with the wind off the sea.

But there would be no rides, no tumbling down a hillside to a burn that ran mountain-cold, a burn where the sweetest of berries could be found.

Micheil would not spend time with her now, or later. He would not court her. Her mother had carefully explained that she must wed him to ensure the peace, and that Micheil was ordered to do the same. Love, such as her parents shared, would have to wait, if it came at all.

Still, she knew his coldness to her was wrong. It pained her that he had not once smiled at her, but had smiles aplenty to offer others.

Her small, rose-hued lips formed a pout, and once more her gaze swept over his scowling face. Micheil's dark, hawklike features seemed to have been carved from the very stone of the Highlands themselves.

Boldly, her hand came to rest on his velvet-clad forearm. "You've not said a word to me these long hours past, Micheil. I like it not. 'Tis not right to treat me so.''

With all the cruelty of his lofty years, Micheil glared at her, then ignored her. Much as he loved his father, as much as he honored him as chief, resentment flared anew at this long betrothal forced upon him. Micheil had lived with death as his shadow, and knew only the impatience to taste all of life he could. Waiting years until his bride came of age and could be claimed sat ill with him.

He sought to escape the high table, but could not without encountering his father's wrath. With a restless gaze, he searched for distraction, and found himself looking at Alura, Seana's mother. Would the lass grow to resemble her? He had no compassion to see that the lines marring Alura's face had come from the burying of bairns lost in the years between Liam's birth and Seana's, and not from age.

She was no great beauty, but there was a gentle radiance to her features when she smiled at her daughter. A smile that quickly disappeared as she intercepted the black look Micheil cast her way. She silently pleaded with him, glancing at Seana, then back to meet the cold stare of Micheil's eyes.

It was Micheil who finally looked away.

"By king and law, drink up, lad," Ingram rebuked his son. "Your bitter scowl casts a pall over the table."

"Micheil?" Bridget queried, her look stricken.

With a forced smile, Micheil did as he was bid, unwilling to answer his father. Far down the table, Fiona, a distant cousin who sat with her sister Janet, snared his gaze. If Micheil was to believe the tale his older

cousin Niall had told, Fiona had already proven herself a woman.

Finding a sultry invitation in Fiona's eyes, Micheil imagined her flaming red hair, now neatly braided, freed and crushed beneath his hands, while her luscious mouth parted for his in surrender. His young loins swelled in reaction, and he shifted in his chair, somewhat annoyed that Fiona licked her lips as if she had sensed his thoughts.

"Micheil?"

"'Tis time you were abed, Seana," he snapped without a glance at her.

Seana saw the looks they exchanged, and sensed a danger that she did not understand. Once more her hand came to rest on Micheil's arm, tightening and demanding his unwilling attention.

"Fiona's not for you. You're promised to me." His soft but harsh laughter made her eyes flash with temper. "Aye, 'tis a promise you'd best remember. I'll not share what's mine."

Seana was distracted when Bridget suddenly rose, Liam at her side, holding out his hand, as space was cleared for dancing. Eager to show off the new steps she had learned, she leaned forward. "Micheil, will you dance with me?"

"With a wee bairn? Do you think I'd have them all laugh at me? I'll say again, 'tis time you were abed."

"I won't always be a wee bairn." When he merely glanced at her with one brow quirked, her childish ire rose. "When I'm full-grown and you're wed to me, you'll not dare to seek out the likes of Fiona. I'd not

be pleased with her looks at you. She's like that great hungry cat near your mews, just waiting to pounce.''

''And I'm no sweetmeat to fight over, lass. I belong to no one but myself.''

''If I grow to my promise, I'll have you en—ensnared.'' Her earnest little face revealed nothing of the hurt his laughter once more brought.

''Where did a wee lass hear that? You're too young to know what you're saying. And that's not pleasing to me.''

''Tis your place to please me, Micheil. I'm to be your lady wife. And it was your own Bridget who said that to me, when she dressed for her wedding.'' His scowl returned. Seana gripped the arms of her chair. ''Are ye planning to tumble her?''

Seana had longed for his undivided attention all night. She had it now, as he turned his lithe body in his chair, leaned close, then closer still, so that his breath fanned her flushed cheeks.

''Your father should be laying a taste of the taws to your bottom. If any heard you—'' Her face blanched, but his anger had been goaded, and was not yet sated. His eyes were narrow slits, and his voice became chillingly soft. ''A wee bairn like you knows naught of men and their needs. You know tumbling to be play on the moor. And I'd best not find out different. Now cease your prattle, brat, or I'll use the leather strap on you myself.''

''You cannot.''

He gripped his goblet until his knuckles stood out white. No one dared to tell him what he could or could not do, but for his father.

"I cannot," he repeated in a murmur that was velvet over steel. "I'll be laird here one day, and my word will be law. If I want you kept here now, none will gainsay me, Seana. 'Tis my right to ask, since we're betrothed."

His threat finally silenced her. Micheil's remorse lasted a moment, while he examined her face for the first time. She was pale, her cheeks were undefined, but her nose, with its saucy tip, revealed nostrils flaring with temper. Her eyes, the color of mist on the moors, were fringed with the thickest of honey-silk lashes, and the faint arch of her brows was feathered in the same shade. He caught himself wondering if her hair, braided with ribbons and pinned up for the first time, would stay the color of a new fawn's coat, or darken like her brother's. He saw the flush deepen on her skin as he kept staring at her.

Silently he agreed with his sister. There was a promise of beauty here when she was grown. The small, bow-shaped lips were pursed, and the rounded chin hinted of stubbornness as she glanced away from him. But she was years away from being his.

"Remember my warning well, Seana."

"Aye. I'll remember," she whispered, vowing that he would, too, someday. Just then, with shouts, the jugglers began their performance, and merriment filled the hall. Seana clapped her hands, excited as any, and quickly forgot Micheil at her side.

"Have we found a way to make you smile, lass?" Ingram leaned forward to ask her.

Seana gave a quick look at the fierce-eyed laird. "Aye. I love them so."

"Then 'tis glad I am to hear that. I want you to believe you'll be happy here." Ingram stressed his words, both his look and his voice a warning to his son.

Seana looked to her mother for guidance when Ingram held out his large, scarred hand to her. Alura's nod made Seana hold her own, smaller hand out to him. She laughed with a return of her spirit and looked at Micheil.

"May the time be long until I am lady here. But when I am, there will always be joy in this hall."

"Aye," Micheil agreed. "May it indeed be a long time to come. Your good health, Father." He drank deeply from his cup, and wasted no more time on Seana.

Amid the cries for more from the jugglers, who were working with lit torches, Bridget claimed his attention. Her gay laugh beckoned him like a light shining in the midst of night, and love filled him for his sister.

"That's better, Micheil. I want you to be happy for me," Bridget said, gently admonishing him.

"I pray you stay so," he muttered softly. She was older than he by one year, and adored by him and their two younger brothers, Jamie, twelve, and Davey, ten. It seemed to Micheil that his brothers were of like mind with him, for their gazes were directed at Bridget, as well. As one, all three brothers shifted to glance at Liam. One look, one thought—death to the man that harmed their bonny Bridget.

Micheil understood why men were taken with his sister. She was fair, and her skin had the sheen of new-fallen snow. Her hip-length hair, a bright, rich chestnut color, gleamed in the flare of torchlights. Their

mother's hair was the same. The brothers had varying shades, from Davey's soft, light brown to Jamie's wavy dark copper color, then his own thick, near-black hair, as unruly as his father's. Onora's eyes, with their sparkling brown lights, had been passed to three of her living children—all but Micheil. He alone had his father's glacial blue eyes, rimmed with thick, dark lashes.

Those blue eyes narrowed as Liam rose from his seat once again and urged Bridget to join him. Micheil found himself tense. He didn't fully understand why his insides twisted in frustration that he couldn't prevent Liam from claiming his sister. His mother rose, and the other ladies followed her.

Liam whispered to Bridget, and with a blush staining her cheeks, she left the hall, the women trailing after her. Micheil did not rise then, nor did he attempt to join the men crowding around Liam, offering ribald comments on the night to come.

Micheil found little satisfaction in noting how few of the Gunn clansmen were with Liam. He barely managed a civil nod to Alura as she came forth to take Seana.

The tension seeped from him now that he was free to leave the high table. Fiona's bold, inviting looks had not wavered from him. His loins thickened with the heat of his blood.

Shoving back his chair, he rose, all six feet of him moving with a lithe, flowing grace that belied his tender years and set more than one woman sighing to see the hot, predatory look in his eyes.

"Walk easy, Micheil," Jamie warned as he passed behind his chair.

"Aye, do," Davey echoed, with a nod toward their watching father.

"I've done his bidding. He'll not dare to ask more of me this night." With a wink at his brothers, Micheil made his way to Fiona. He ignored the black look from his cousin Niall. Without a word, he held out his hand, and Fiona, with a sigh that said she was glad the waiting was over, placed her hand in the rough, callused palm.

"You're a bold one, Micheil," she whispered as he led her out among the dancers. She gazed up at his eyes, shivering a little to see them filled with dangerous shadows. "Your father does not like what you've done, by the fierce look of him."

"Are you afeared, lass?" He faced her as the wild, keening song of the bagpipes filled him with its haunting. Sliding one hand over the full, lush curve of her hip, Micheil smiled at her.

Fiona, remembering that some whispered his smile was the devil's temptation, and others claimed it was an angel's own, barely managed to nod. "Aye. I'm afeared. But that will not stop me. You're the most exciting man here."

"Am I? There's a thought." His smile became a challenge. "I'd wager you'd not be wanting me otherwise." He danced forward, then away from her, heightening both their aroused senses with every touch as he led her through the intricate steps.

Fiona, mesmerized by the dark attraction that had first drawn her to Micheil, knew nothing else mat-

tered. She didn't care about his betrothal. She only cared about Micheil. And the desire that made her ache.

"I want you. It seems I've always wanted you, Micheil."

"Have you?" One corner of his carnal mouth lifted. "The night's near gone. Come." He took her hand and led Fiona from the hall.

Watching Fiona leave with Micheil, Niall clenched his hands. "Bastard!"

"'Tis your dear cousin that you curse, Niall."

Niall spun around to see who taunted him. His lanky body tensed when he saw George of the clan Keith. "I'll deny—"

"No need to me. I've no liking for the bastard myself."

"Someday," Niall muttered, seeing the last of Micheil's back, "he'll be wanting something so bad that he'd be willing to kill to have it. And when that day comes, I'll be the one who walks away in possession of it."

"When that day comes, let me know."

Niall eyed him with sudden wariness. "You'd betray your clan?"

"Betray Keiths? Never. But I've no such loyalty for any MacKay."

George rocked back on his heels. His shorter stature made him tilt his head back. "Wanting the lass Seana for yourself?"

"My reasons are my own. Suffice it to say I've had too much stolen from me this night."

They both glanced around, as if suddenly aware of how their conversing in soft tones would appear. Niall found Jamie watching them. Without another word, he walked rapidly away to lose himself in the crowd. But he didn't forget what George had said. Someday he might have use of it.

Jamie turned to Davey. "Mark those two well in your mind, brother. They mean Micheil no good."

With the wisdom stamped upon a child raised in the midst of warring clans, Davey nodded. "Aye, we'll watch his back." And he closed his eyes against the sudden pounding in his head. Davey fought not to let the image form. He was helpless to stop it. He always had been. Bloodred flames turned black around the entwined lovers in their center.

For who? he cried silently. For Liam and Bridget? Or was it Micheil that held the woman?

With a cry, he fell forward, but Jamie was there to catch him. No one watched the two young boys make their way from the hall. Only Jamie knew how they both shivered after Davey told him what he saw. And Davey was never wrong.

Long into the night, Jamie stared into the dark, ignoring the twisting and turning of those who shared the room on pallets scattered over the floor.

Flames of passion? Flames of fury? Which would burn the pair of lovers in fire?

# Chapter Two

Micheil's seventeenth birthday was fast approaching, and he was anxious to be home. For almost a year he had overseen repairs to the tower at Dirlot, close to the river Thurso. It was a lonely place, on an isolated crag that faced the Orkney Islands across the Firth of Pentland.

Spital, the village where the Gunn clan had their burial place in St. Magnus's Chapel, was also the home of Fiona and her family. Her father, Uallas, paid little heed to his daughter's frequent disappearances when Micheil came to visit.

Nor did Uallas pay any mind to Fiona's temper, which was in a full-blown rage this day, when Micheil's brothers had come to fetch him home.

Fiona, up before dawn, had watched them go. She had been so sure that Micheil was on the verge of telling her that this time he would ask his father to break the betrothal to the MacKay brat.

Micheil was hers! She would never share him with another woman. Her blood was every bit as good as Seana's. It was she who would be the laird's wife. God curse her to hell! Seana would never have him.

Micheil looked back once to see Fiona's forlorn figure watching him leave. By the time they crossed the river Thurso, riding hard to make Watten, where they would spend the night and obtain fresh horses, he had set Fiona from his thoughts. He knew what she wanted from him, and he was of half a mind to do it.

Gabhan and Crisdean, clansmen and boyhood friends had accompanied Davey and Jamie. Their pace left them little time to talk. Exhaustion overcame them by nightfall, and they broke their morning fast with bread and cheese before they rode south and for home.

The full moon shone on the gray stone towers that rose in tall majesty against the night sky. The scent of the sea brought an intense sense of pride to Micheil as they neared Halberry Castle.

With an unconscious sigh, he realized anew how much he had missed being home. A trench was cut into the rock for a drawbridge on the landward side, and they all slowed their horses to a walk, for the footing here was treacherous, as the salt spray from the sea misted the rocks.

Micheil stroked away the froth lathered on his steed's neck, and listened to young Davey's excited chatter begin, now that they had slowed their pace.

"Wait till you see your mare's get, Micheil. He'll be a braw steed to carry your weight in a few years' time."

"Aye, he's a fine one," Jamie agreed. "'Tis the very gray of our walls that make his color."

"He's a beastie of the faeries," Crisdean added. Then he raised his voice over their laughter. "Wait, you'll see. He'll not be letting a man touch him."

"Da promised me the choice of mares as a gift for Bridget's name day," Jamie informed Micheil. "She'll be surprised to see the three of us visiting at one time."

"She fares well?" Micheil asked, having had little news of his sister.

"'Tis hard to say. She's not sent word often," Jamie answered. "Davey's been to visit."

Catching the quick looks his brothers exchanged, Micheil urged his horse closer between them. "Are ye telling me Ma's assurances that all's well with Bridget did not come from our sister being seen?"

His thickening brogue was a signal Micheil was upset and Davey quickly replied. "I saw her. I did, Micheil."

"When was that, Davey?"

"A while. A long while."

"Ma was angry with her for not coming home to share Twelfth Night with us. She sent no reason, Micheil," Jamie said. "Da thought she might be breeding, but MacKay sent no word of her expecting his bairn."

Fear, unexplained, unexpected, crawled up and down Micheil's spine. His hawklike features deepened into a scowl and his brothers eased their horses closer to their clansmen.

"You would hide something from me?"

Jamie thought of the night two years ago when Davey had had his first vision of flames and lovers. The image had never changed in all this time. But he couldn't tell Micheil.

"Not me. And do not bother to ask Davey. He kens less." Gripping his reins tight, Jamie added, "Ease

your mind, brother. We'd hear quick enough if naught was right between them.''

"Aye. You're right.'' Micheil sensed it would be futile to continue to press them. "Then I'm for home. Are ye lads with me?''

Hoops and shouts warned they were coming, the three brothers riding abreast, with Gabhan and Crisdean following. They passed through the stout oaken gates, massively thick, that opened in welcome to them.

There was much teasing and backslapping as Micheil dismounted first, greeting those who came forward to see him. He spied his mother running down the wide steps of the hall, and pushed his way clear until he could hug her.

To Onora's delighted shrieks, he lifted her high and swung her around. Breathlessly, Onora, between laughter and tears of joy at having her oldest son home, managed to get Micheil to set her down. "Here, stand still, my fine stallion, let me look at you.''

She eased aside the thick cloak, satisfied to see that he had put on weight, but with clucking sounds admonished him to seek a bath. "Now,'' she said, offering up her cheek, "come greet me properly.''

"You'd be as slender and bonny as the day Da wed you,'' he teased, hugging her close.

"Your da missed you sorely, Micheil. Go to him.''

He turned to find himself enveloped in a bear hold from his father, the words of welcome warm to his ears.

Later that night, the feasting done, his brothers sent off to bed and his mother retired, Micheil sat with his

father before the great hearth in the hall. They spoke easily of the crofter's yield, between sips of the malt Scotch they both favored, and of the uneasy peace maintained between the feuding clans and the Stewart king.

Micheil shared his news from England. "They say that John of Gaunt, the Duke of Lancaster, is planning to lead an English invasion of France. There's a rumor that clans will raise their banners for France."

"Gaunt's near set himself as king, with both Edwards sick and failing. Mark my words, Micheil. He's got his eye on the crown for himself. We've troubles of our own with the Sinclairs, Sutherlands and Keiths, who grow greedy for more land."

"But none have defeated us yet, Father. You'll soon have rich coffers. Uallas has done well with his trade, Da. He'll be sending you a fine share of it. I set aside furs so thick and glossy they're worthy of a king. Ma complains of the sea chill more and more."

"Davey's been talking to you. Aye, 'tis true. She finds it hard to warm herself these days." Ingram set aside his cup and studied his son. "I'd be knowing that look. You've something more to say."

"Da, Fiona's asked me again to break the betrothal."

"Ah, I thought as much. I cannot do that, Micheil. Our clan's wealth is growing. Heth has kept his word. There's been a few raids, and those I blame on the Keiths. The clan's a wily bunch, and not to be trusted. I cannot do as you ask, for the honor of our clan."

Micheil grew pensive. He wasn't sure why he mentioned it himself. Guilt, perhaps. But he had never

promised Fiona anything but the pleasure they had shared. He knew he had spared little thought to the lass who would one day be his bride. He looked across at his father, and realized that contentment had mellowed him.

"You're not fighting with me? You cannot want Fiona to wife badly. She has naught that is needed for a good wife. If she had, I would've chosen her for you." He paused, searching for a delicate way to ask, understanding how much of a man his son had become.

"Does Uallas know?"

"He's blind to all but his furs. I've made her no promises."

"You've an edge to your voice, when there's no need. 'Tis for the clan's sake that I ask."

A curt nod was all Micheil offered. Their bond had always been a strong one, and he consoled himself with the thought that his marriage was a long way off. Who was to say what would happen that could change things?

Finishing the last of his drink, Micheil rose with the intent of bidding his father good-night. The sudden shouts of challenge at their gates were faint, but demanded his attention.

"I'll go," he said to his father, reaching the doors first. He drew up the thick wooden bar, then opened the doors of the hall wide before Ingram had risen from his chair.

Hearing a wild howl of rage from Micheil, Ingram clutched his chest, stumbling, as he made his way to the doors.

Torchlights were held high by those roused from sleep and attracted by the clamor. Ingram looked down to see his son surrounded by flame and shadows. He crossed himself, for the scene was surely wrought in hell. Once, twice, he shook his head, denying what his eyes did see, believing that his mind was befuddled with drink.

But it was Micheil who rose and faced him, holding a limp Bridget in his arms.

Ingram's throat constricted, but no sound emerged. Micheil's gaze met his. Pain, unlike any he had known, filled him with a quick, hot, bursting fury when he saw his son's stricken face.

There were no words exchanged. All around them remained silent as Micheil walked between them and carried his burden into the warmth of the hall. He sat in one of the massive chairs before the fire, gently stroking his sister's head.

"Who dared this, lass?" Micheil asked over and over, his voice a crooning wail of raging grief. "Who did this outrage to you? Och, Bridget mine, by our blood, tell me who dared?"

With both brawny hands, Ingram grabbed his chest again. A knifelike pain seemed to split his chest in two. Battle-scarred warrior that he was, hardened to the worst tortures man inflicted on man, he could only stand there, helpless. He stared down at his once bonny daughter. He even tried to force his eyes to close, wanting desperately to shut out the sound of Micheil's voice, and found that his body would not obey his commands. He could not make the sights nor

the sounds disappear, and after minutes Ingram understood that he would carry this to his grave.

"You understand that you're safe, Bridget," Micheil whispered. "None will hurt you here. But, I beg you, tell me who did this to you."

Bridget, swamped with agony, her lips puffed and swollen in a face beaten beyond recognition, uttered one word.

"MacKay."

And Micheil growled, "'Tis his death she's spoken."

"Nay!" Bridget cried, then fainted.

Rousing Onora to tend their daughter, Ingram, along with his sons and the few clansmen within the castle walls, paced the length of the hall. They listened to the wails of grief falling from the women's lips in the chamber above. Time and again, their eyes met, none of them ashamed to reveal the pain they felt at the knowledge that even their strength left them helpless to stop the cries.

In the darkest hours of the night, Ingram watched his eldest son and heir. He knew the fierce demand Micheil exacted from somewhere deep inside himself not to ride out immediately after the MacKays. He knew his son's agony well, for he fought the same demon.

But the years, of war and of peace, had taught him patience, something Micheil had yet to learn. He would hear what happened from his daughter first, before he moved against the MacKays.

Onora's wails became screams.

If Bridget lived, he amended, banging his fist on the high table, fresh pain searing his body.

"The Highlands will ring with our war cries if my daughter dies. And none, I swear on the bones of Saint Magnus, none will have known their like!"

It was nearly three days before Onora pronounced Bridget able to speak to them. Micheil, his features gaunt and ravaged from the long vigil, followed his father into his sister's room.

The small chamber was lit with one candle in the far corner and Bridget lay on the bed, shrouded in shadows. Micheil came to his knees and reached for her hand.

Sweet scents rose from the crushed herbs scattered in the rushes. Micheil offered a prayer when Bridget returned a slight pressure of her fingers against his.

The darkness hid the shame in her eyes. Bridget was glad they couldn't see all of her. She clutched the fur throw with her free hand. No one spoke, but she nonetheless wanted to hide from the almost tangible feeling of her father's and Micheil's wrath. Suddenly she was afraid—deathly so—of having to tell them the truth.

That was all they wanted from her, her mother had said over and over. Just the truth.

How well she knew their ways, their intense pride in upholding the honor of the clan. Her father would be ten times harsher dealing with his own, since he maintained his position as chief.

She could not bear to have her family turn on her now. Not now, when her loss of Liam was a wrench-

ing pain that left her without peace, without even the will to live.

"You're the precious heart of me, lass," Ingram murmured. "'Tis glad I am that you're awake."

"Aye, Da." But her voice wasn't strong, and she needed strength for what she had to do. She wanted to close off her brother's voice, soft and yet so insistent, urging her to tell them.

And then her mother was adding her plea to Micheil's. She had no more time, no way to escape.

The words she spoke, at first slowly, then faster, came from the depth of her terror at being cast out from her clan.

Weeping to evade prying questions, she led them to believe that she had been beaten and cast off for her failure to conceive a child. She knew she signed Liam's death decree with every word. But she could never go back to him. She could go to no man. Her mother had been gentle, but most truthful about how badly scarred she would be.

"Swear this, Bridget?" Ingram asked one last time.

Squeezing Micheil's hand, she swore.

Micheil kissed her hand, then her bruised cheek. He glanced up at his father. They had to demand the ultimate payment for this outrageous deed. This time it was Ingram, shoulders bent, who followed his son from the room. And the door closed behind him to shut out the crying.

Filled with a black rage that gave his face a demonic cast, Micheil demanded the moment they were alone, "'Tis my right to take his life for what he's done to Bridget. Once you had promised her his heart, cut

free by your own hand. I will settle for nothing less. That he dared this! That he used his strength against—"

"Nay, Micheil, cool your rage." Ingram poured out two drams and handed one to his son. "I'll not have it so," he commanded. He bore in silence his son's recoil from him. "I'm still your laird, and your sister lives. 'Tis not his death I'd be seeking."

"Are you a weakling? Will you not—"

"Silence! The MacKays will pay for what he's dared. Never be thinking I've grown so soft that I'd forget our clan honor."

Ingram watched his son. For all his height, Micheil moved as gracefully as an animal. He knew his son was weary—they all were—yet Micheil had no desire for food or sleep. Ingram understood the blood that ran hot with the need for action. It ran in his own veins, demanding a full measure of revenge. But Micheil's way would not bring the peace he thought.

"Tell me, then. What plan have you?"

"Micheil, you're too proud by half, and the blame is mine. I've had more pride in you than I give to any. I want the MacKays stripped of everything. Not a day is to pass that their lands are not raided." Pain sliced his chest again, and he closed his eyes, struggling to control it. There was more he had to say.

"Da, are you—"

"'Tis naught," Ingram answered, waving him off. "Listen well. I will have the very stones of their miserable keep littering the Highlands when we're done with them. None shall ever recall where the tower belonging to the MacKays ever stood. Their name will be

wiped from all memory. You are my heir, Micheil. 'Tis meet that you should be in full accord with my decisions. If not, be telling me now.''

His duty to his father, his owed allegiance and instilled obedience to his laird, warred with Micheil's overpowering need to ride out against the MacKays now. For long, agonizing minutes, he kept his back turned on his father. Fists clenched at his sides, denying all that cried out for revenge within him, Micheil finally turned.

"You're still my sworn chief. Father or not, I'll stand with you."

With a last, thoughtful look, Ingram nodded. He knew the full cost of these words from his son. While it hurt him to ask so much from a son of his loins, he could not deny the pride he felt for the man's control that Micheil exhibited.

Ingram summoned those closest of his clan.

Within two days, the hall where a marriage had once brought them peace saw councils of war plan a destruction so complete none could recall its like. As for those who had arrived too late to join in the planning, they were told their roles.

At the last, Ingram motioned for Micheil, and silence overcame the hall.

"'Tis time for the message to go forth."

"Let me carry the *crois taraidh*," Davey begged. "Let me proclaim to all that the peace is broken."

"Nay, lad," Micheil answered as he worked near the great hearth's fire to char two sticks of wood. "'Tis not fitting for you to ride out."

Davey had to content himself with watching Micheil take the two charred pieces of wood and fasten them together to form a cross. Jamie handed him a rag dipped in sheep's blood, and Micheil attached it, then held the bloody cross high when he was done so that all could see it.

Jamie unfurled the Raven Banner of the old Orkney jarls who had been ancestors of the Keiths, the MacKay allies, and the Gunns alike. The raven symbolized the spirit of the mighty Woden, from their common Viking past.

At a signal from his father, Micheil took the banner staff in his other hand. The burnt and bloody cross represented the Fire and the Sword. It would be passed in relays throughout every town and clachan in Caithness. Each successive bearer would shout the news that the clan was to gather here at Halberry, and that every able-bodied clansman was to seize his weapons to answer this call to war.

Micheil knew his father had honored him by allowing him to choose who would be the first to carry it forth. His gaze skimmed over eager faces, young men of an age with himself.

At the last, he went to his cousin Niall. "You. I choose you to carry this forth."

Niall recoiled, and only the press of bodies behind him stopped him from running. Faces turned away from his show of cowardice. But he knew they were all aware of the curse that awaited the bearer of the banner. The prophecy claimed they would always have victory, but the bearer would always be killed.

Micheil leaned closer to his cousin. "Are ye daft, man? Take it, or you'll be shamed before all."

Niall roused himself to stand tall, burying the panic he felt. "Aye," he said loudly, "I'll carry it forth."

Once he was on his way, Ingram summoned his sons to him, for Jamie had reminded him that there was yet a thread to be woven tight.

"'Tis the betrothal, Da? You'd be breaking it now?" Davey asked.

"Aye! We'll damn well break it," Micheil declared before his father answered.

"You'd be speaking in my stead?" Chiding Micheil never came easy for Ingram, but he could not shirk his duty as chief. And it was as chief of their clan that he added, "I've not gone to my grave yet. I'm not setting myself aside for you, either, Micheil."

There was censure in Ingram's look, but little sting to his rebuke, for Jamie had set him thinking about another form of revenge. It would be a longer road, he knew, but one just as devastating to the MacKays as what he had already planned.

"I'm not thinking to break the betrothal at all."

They were all silent. Davey's eyes were wide with shock, Jamie turned away, and Micheil, Micheil forgot to whom he spoke. "Are you daft? Damn you to hell! You must break it. None shall dare to think I'd hold to that betrothal now."

Ingram leaned back against the table's edge and folded his massive arms over his chest. "Would you recall your own words of honor, freely given to me this

night? Are you now saying you stand against me, Micheil?"

Their gazes clashed. Micheil knew they were too much alike, both proud and hard, his father's manner tempered by age, his own tempered by his rage. Micheil boldly faced his chief with hands clenched at his sides. His jaw hurt as he ground his teeth together, fighting not to speak words in haste. He saw Davey step away from him, and caught Jamie's helpless glance from him to their father before he, too, stepped away from them.

Micheil swallowed. He forced the tension from himself. He could not go against his father. He had given his word, his very honor, to him. But his pride made gall rise, and taint his words with the bitterness of defeat.

"Nay. I'll not go against you."

"Thank you, Micheil." Ingram acknowledged his concession with a curt nod, taking no victory from it. "Bridget suffered at the MacKay's hand."

"We do not need you to remind us, Da. She'll be scarred for life."

"'Tis enough, Micheil. Hear me out. When Seana is full-grown, I'll have you swear to me now, that you will exact the same revenge upon her. I want the lass taken."

"She's a bairn!" Davey cried out, coming forward only to stop at Jamie's signal. "Da, do you mean to beat a wee lass for her brother's doings?"

Davey glanced around at the furious looks his family gave him at his outburst. He gulped, a red flush of

shame he couldn't help stealing over his fair cheeks, and he hung his head.

"I'd not touch the lass now, Davey," Ingram said, in a voice softened a bit by the love he had for his youngest son. "We'll take her and bring her to your aunt Ailis, at the abbey near Tannach Moor. The lands are ours, well protected, and none shall dare attempt to rescue her from them.

"But when she's grown," he spat out harshly, directing the full power of his edict to Micheil, "there'll be less than a handful of MacKays to stay your hand. Liam is to live," he commanded. "Mark these words well, each one of you. Guard his life as you would one of our own. Not one hair of that proud mane of his is to be touched. Be sure of that, Micheil!"

"Da—"

"Silence! I want him to know with every breath, every beat of his black blood, for every waking moment and every nightmare I wish upon him, that he'll live to see the sight of his sister shamed and beaten before him!"

He held each of his sons' gazes for long moments with the sheer power of his fierce blue eyes before he drew his dirk from his belt and his voice rose again to the very rafters of the ceiling.

"Your hands!" Ingram demanded, making quick work of cutting across his own fingers, then his sons'. "Now, swear it! By our blood on these very stones, swear you'll see my will done!"

And so it came to pass, not even two weeks later, that the deed Ingram decreed was done.

Seana, returning from a visit to Wick, where she had celebrated her ninth birthday, was torn from her mother's arms. Heth, fatally wounded, his clansmen killed or dying, heard above his wife's wild cries the fate that awaited his daughter before he died.

# Chapter Three

*Deer Abbey*
*1382*

Seana gloried in the promise of spring, picking heather-bells and tossing them high in the air. The abbey's jennet and mule were staked nearby, munching tender, sweet grasses. She plucked a delicately hued primrose that peeked out in shy splendor amid its leafy guardians. The scent of the small pink bloom held the faint memory of her mother scattering its petals among their linens before storing them in the great chests.

With a frown, she tossed it from her.

Such memories were best forgotten, for the pain they caused.

It was enough to be free of the dark, brooding walls of the abbey. Today, as with so many others past, she thought about escape, but a glance back over her shoulder revealed that one of the nuns was in the bell tower, watching her.

Knowing she would not get far before an alarm was sounded, Seana ran with a natural grace through the

tall bracken, whirling and skipping, until, with a small burst of laughter, she collapsed on the bracken. With her ankles demurely crossed, her arms flung behind her head, Seana allowed herself to dream about tomorrow. Ailis, the abbess, had promised her a visit to the fair.

It was a sour note to know that she owed the promise to the arrival of Fiona and her sister, Janet. She would be treated little better than a servant, trailing after the two Gunn clanswomen to carry whatever it took their fancy to purchase, but Seana would have trailed after the devil himself for a chance to see a fair and perhaps, just perhaps, taste a sweetly spiced ginger cake.

She licked her lips at the thought, and averted her gaze from the walls that had held her prisoner for ten years. But thoughts were harder to avert once they had been allowed to come. No matter her teachings, she could not stop the hate she bore for the laird of the clan Gunn for holding to his father's vow that here she would remain until he came to claim her.

The waiting was a torment. "When?" she often asked Ailis. And the abbess, pity in her eyes, would shake her head and answer, "When Micheil sees fit."

Seana rarely allowed thoughts of Micheil. Fiona's arrival had triggered the reminder that her youth was passing. Did any of the abbey remember that on the morrow she would be nineteen? Did Micheil, wretched savage that they called him, ever think of her wasting away all these years? The man had to be old, nearly twenty-seven, but Seana no longer hoped for word of his death at the hands of one of her clansmen.

She knew her brother was still alive, but he had offered no ransom as a way to end this feud.

Once she had ventured to ask Ailis why a ransom had not been demanded and paid, and found the hope quickly killed.

For the first time, she had been told what Ingram had decreed as revenge against her clan. And with that Ailis's added caution, despite her service to the church, that Seana should be thankful that Bridget lived, or her fate would have been sealed. Ailis's council was to hope, but there were days when fear of what would happen to her allowed no room for hope.

She was not ill-treated, but to be denied freedom was a terrible punishment. Escape was a thought that came less and less. She had braved the Gunn clan's wrath to run one time. Once had cured the notion of attempting it again.

It did not bode well to dwell upon the events of five years ago. But it had been spring then, too. She had received word of her mother's death, and Ailis had tried to ease her grief. The abbess had, in despair, sought permission from Ingram to claim a truce for a few days to allow Seana to go home.

"But the beast refused," she whispered as a breeze rose. "Refused me that comfort, refused me permission to take the veil, refused to set me free."

Tears no longer came easily to her. She sat up, amid the bracken, hugging her knees to her chest.

Fourteen winters old, and she had thought herself brave, escaping from the abbey, walking across the open moor. She had jumped and started at every shadow, hearing the frantic beat of her heart pound-

ing until dawn forced her to seek shelter in a grove of trees. Thinking herself safe from pursuit, she had finally fallen into an exhausted sleep.

"I was a woman grown, but with the foolish thoughts of a wee bairn." A shiver rode her spine as she recalled the vivid memory of that night. Of how she had awakened to find herself trapped within a man's arms.

The shivers deepened, despite the warm sunlight. Seana tried holding her ears, as if she could shut out the husky timbre of his voice.

"You are mine, Seana. Promised and bound until I claim you." It was only then that she had understood it was Micheil himself who had captured her.

And a blazing heat born of rage beset her now, as it had that night. She remembered her brazenly given challenge.

"Then take me or kill me, but be done with this!"

The sweet smells of spring disappeared. It was dark. There was a lightly misting rain, and the damp musky scent of Micheil's body. The strength of his arms catching hold of her. The capture of her mouth beneath his. The sear of a man's lips taking her breath, her will. The dizzy swirl of a darkness more potent than the night. She had not been able to see him. Even when he had flung her away from him, she had had but a shadow to burn in memory.

It had been a night born of storms, for terror had held her in its grip from the moment he lifted her up on the great ghostly gray beast that snorted and stamped with wild warnings.

Anger had ridden his voice at having been forced to ride out and search for her. Seana hugged herself tight, shaking as if she were still chilled by the rain that had sheeted down. But even as she tried to keep it buried, the remembered warmth of Micheil's body once he had unfurled his plaid and wrapped it around both of him came to her and stayed.

"You'll never be a match for me, Seana," he had taunted. "I'll be waiting till you're grown and ripe for a man's pleasure before I come back to claim you as mine."

She had never spoken a word to him on the ride back to the abbey. Fear had kept her quiet—fear of what her punishment would be.

Rubbing her arms now, she tried to remove the feeling of his hands as he had set her roughly from his horse. She heard the scrape of the abbey gates, her prison gates, opening at his command. Knew the terror of seeing men milling about the courtyard, and once more, in her mind, she fled to the safety of her small cell.

She had never once seen Micheil's face. There had been no punishment beyond the posting of someone in the bell tower whenever she left the abbey walls. But she had learned that night, from his aunt, the name her clan had given him. Dhu Micheil. His revenge against her blood clan had been savage indeed for all to call him Black Micheil.

The bell for nones pealed. Startled, Seana rose and shook her skirt free of the bracken, hurrying now so that she would not be late for prayers. Fiona would be there, with her finely woven kirtle of green wool.

Seana glanced down at the drab brown gown she wore. There was no help for it—she had only one other, as poor as this, to wear. Her pride could shield her. Setting off for the abbey, she knew it would have to do.

Pride was not enough. If anything, her pride had her rising before dawn after a sleepless night. Seana prayed for the wisdom to hold her tongue once she angrily combed the tangles from her long hair. Fiona's barbs had resulted in Seana's being sent from the table in disgrace last eve.

"And likely cost me the chance to go to the fair. It was what that witch wanted all along," she muttered, smoothing the rough linen sheet over her straw-filled mattress.

Seana took no pleasure in having angered Ailis, or in shocking the sweet nuns, who had showed her only kindness. Even without a polished steel to see herself in, she knew heat had flushed her cheeks. Just how much did anyone think she could bear?

Fiona had deliberately sat next to her for their simple meal, whispering taunts.

It was no secret what Seana's fate would be at Micheil's hands. But to hear Fiona say it, to know that she was just waiting for it to happen so that she could have Micheil for herself, had unleashed a viciousness Seana had not known she possessed.

"It could be that Dhu Micheil might have his revenge turned upon himself, Fiona. He has had use of you all this time, and a fresh lass warming his bed might prove to be his undoing. You're old, Fiona. A

man would be near blind afore he'd bind himself to the likes of you.''

She had stopped short of calling Fiona a whore. But her outburst had been enough to have her banished from the table in disgrace.

Seana knew her sharp tongue wanted curbing, for she would pay dearly for having forgotten it.

Faced with Ailis's stern countenance later that morning, Seana chose to stand, rather than take a seat on the plain wooden bench that Ailis offered. Perhaps the reason a new spark of spirit burned was that today was her birth day, with none to remark upon it—or the memories she had revived the day before. Whatever the reason, Seana refused to cower.

Patiently and silent, she waited for Ailis to finish entering her accounts.

The room was bright with sunlight that formed patterns across the uneven flagstone floor, swept clean of its winter rushes. The walls of this room were of the same rough-cut stone, bare but for the simple cross that rested over Ailis's prayer bench. Seana had spent many hours on her knees, praying after some infraction of the abbey's rules. The chest in the far corner was of plain wood. Only the ornately carved table and chair where Ailis sat hinted at the abbey's wealth.

Reed-thin, her spine straight, Ailis had the same blue eyes as her brother Ingram. Her voice, always soft, could make novices, nuns, or those of noble birth quake when delivering a reprimand. She had been educated in a French convent, like so many others, for the English king, Edward, had died trying to subdue Scotland and had left the legacy of implacable hatred

of Scot for Englishman that allowed the alliance with France these seventy-five years past.

Ailis was dressed in the same coarsely woven brown gown as Seana, only the sideless surcoat of white wool marking her office. Seana came to with a start as she realized she had been staring. Ailis had set aside her accounts, and waited with hands folded on the table, the sun glinting off her seal ring.

"Fiona is a guest here, and you caused her discomfort, Seana," Ailis began. "The years have been a sore trial to you, child. It has not gone unmarked."

"I won't take back a word of what I said."

"I have not asked you to. It is too late, for Fiona left with her sister early this morn to attend the fair."

*Please, please, Lord,* Seana prayed, *do not let her refuse permission to go.*

"I thought to keep you close today, Seana, but both Sister Edeen and Sister Anice have requested that you be allowed to accompany them to the fair."

Hope rose, and Seana was hard put to stand still as Ailis paused, appearing lost in thought.

At last she looked up. "They are both elderly, and in need of someone young. But I must have a sworn promise from you, Seana, that you will not leave them."

"It is yours."

"Then you may go." Ailis prayed she had not made a wrong choice. The treat of going to the fair was a small gift, the only one she could give Seana to mark her day. She owed too much to her brother to go against his orders, for he alone had stood in support of her taking the veil so as not to be forced into mar-

riage. Would that Micheil answered her request to allow Seana to follow in her footsteps. This was the longest he had gone without answering her over the years, for she had made the request many times in hopes that her brother's edict would not come to pass.

For all her independence of rule at the abbey, Ailis knew how dependent she was on the protection of her clan. She salved her conscience by reminding herself that she had not rewarded Seana's outburst, but had denied Fiona the satisfaction of having goaded the young woman into punishment.

Seana wasted no time reasoning why she had been given leave to go. She prodded gently at the two elderly nuns, for the warm spring air made her impatient, and the mule, for a change, seemed to share her need to get to the fair.

The open moor of the abbey's grounds were covered with bright, gaudy-colored tents and stalls. For Seana, it was almost too much for her starved senses to take in all at once.

Smells assaulted her. Hot sweet cakes hawked by bakers at the first stalls made her regret having no coin to spend. The fair was already crowded, and a roaring din played its own enticing music for Seana. The noise of traders bartering their goods mingled with the sounds of restless animals and children's gay laughter as they ran in response to the shouts of goodwives trying to maintain order among their broods.

The three of them were jostled as they walked along, and Seana found her gaze darting from one stall to another, longing to stop when she saw the linnets in their small wooden cages. She had once had a similar

tiny bird with lovely plumage. But, like her great hound, Dearg, named for his glossy red coat, the bird had been left behind, lost to her.

"Seana. Seana," Sister Edeen shouted, and grabbed her arm. Having her attention at last, she shook her head, but smiled. "The way is uphill to stake the mule. 'Tis too much for these old bones. Take the mule up, and mind you tie him carefully. We'll be buying spices, so come directly to us." Pointing across the crowded way, she added, "The stall with the bright blue banner. That is where you're to come."

"Aye, Sister." Seana lowered her head. She could hardly hide the excitement she felt. She knew they were to meet later with other nuns here to shop at the cloth merchants' tents, but for a little while she was free.

Once the mule was securely staked, Seana was drawn to join an admiring crowd that had gathered around a string of fine-blooded horses. Horses meant wealth to the highlanders. These, even to her untrained eyes, were prizes. The horses' sleek coats shone, their eyes were bright, and their ears pricked forward alertly. She slipped behind the men gathered near a roan horse, drawn to a dappled gray stallion tied off alone, restlessly pawing the ground as if he were jealous of the attentions paid to the other steed.

"A beauty you are," Seana whispered, holding out her hand for the horse to sniff. The horse snorted, still pawing the earth, but after a few minutes of Seana's soft, crooning voice, the muscled neck quivered beneath the glossy hide and his nose stretched out toward her hand.

Delighted, Seana was shocked to have her wrist roughly snagged and yanked back.

"Dinna touch him! He's a killer, lass. Only his master rides him. He'll let no other on his back."

Seana tugged her wrist free and stepped away. She faced a young man, not much older than herself. Unruly locks of brown hair tumbled over his forehead, and his eyes sparkled.

"'Tis sorry I am, but I did not know." Her gaze turned once again to the horse. "He's a fine beauty, just the same."

"Aye," he agreed, "a fine beauty." But the young man's gaze feasted on her. "You've a good eye for horseflesh, lass."

Seana felt daring talking to the first man since her imprisonment. Sneaking a look at him from beneath lowered lashes, she decided he was fair to look upon, too. It was impossible for her not to return his smile.

"Are you alone, lass?"

"I'm to meet—others. I've but come to secure our mule."

Taken by her shy manner and lovely looks, and seeing no mark of a clan badge upon her gown, he decided his luck had changed. The lads with him could finish showing their horses.

"I'll walk with you. My brothers are hereabouts. It's time I found them. Wait a moment. I'll tell the lad I'm going."

Temptation beckoned to Seana, but warnings had been ingrained in her at an early age of what could happen to a maid alone. The moment his back was turned, she hurried away. All she needed was to have

one of the nuns see her with a young man and tell Ailis. Her transgression had not been forgotten, even if she had been allowed to come to the fair.

But when Seana reached the stall where the spices blended heady scents, there was no sign of either of the elderly nuns.

Panic came swiftly. Had she been abandoned? Was this some scheme to get rid of her? She stood, letting the crowd push her to and fro, slowly dismissing the notion. Ailis, despite her loyalty to her clan, would never be a part— But she was, a small voice countered. She would allow Black Micheil to fulfill the vow he'd made to his father.

Undecided, Seana knew she had to stop thinking of it, and knew, too, that she should wait right here. But the crowd parted, and the sight of a clumsy bear cavorting on the end of a heavy chain for a widening circle of onlookers drew her attention.

She peeked through the press of bodies at the great shaggy-coated beast, sorry for the way he was being poked and prodded by his handler to make him stand. A few more shouted orders accompanied by pokes from a wooden staff made the bear roar. The handler bowed, and a few people tossed him coins.

Seana found herself caught in the crowd, unable to turn back. A few tents down, a troupe of jugglers appeared, and she pushed herself close to the front to see them. A flash of memory brought back the night of her brother's wedding, and her own foolish boast that when she was lady the Gunn hall would always be filled with joy.

But the day was too lovely, and she cast off her apprehension and enjoyed the performance. Time and again, despite the excitement rippling through those around her, Seana caught herself letting her gaze stray to study the women's dress. The visitors were not many at the abbey, coming of their own will or sent there to do penitence, and most women left off their rich gowns to wear the same cloth as the nuns.

But here was a feast for her eyes, color and cloth of bright hues. Where her gown had a high, curved neck, women here favored a new square neckline, revealing skin, and some of the wealthier ones even had a thin band of precious furs around them. Where her gown was a shapeless drape of cloth, belts, some with flashing jewels, clung to the curve of hips. Seana touched her fitted sleeve, curious about the ones she saw cut wide at the wrist, and turned back to reveal linen or silk underlinings.

Had her mother lived— No, she refused to think about her, but she couldn't help a sigh of envy for the crisp white linen headdresses and nets that covered women's hair while her braids hung free past her thighs, like a lowly serving girl's.

Lost in her thoughts, Seana paid no attention to the notice she attracted.

"I tell you I've got to find her." Dragging his brothers along in his wake, ignoring their annoyance at being taken from their drinking, the young man stopped short when he spied his quarry.

"There. That's the lass. I'd wager not one of you has seen such eyes. I told you she was the bonniest one here."

"'Tis a wonder, from the size of her, that she dared to touch my steed," the tallest mused, trying to focus eyes that were blurred from drink, gaming and lack of sleep. "But aye, she's bonny, and appears alone."

The crowd surged, and for a moment Seana found herself squeezed by a press of unwashed bodies that made her long for a breath of clean air. She felt a sharp pinch on her bottom, but couldn't even turn to see who dared.

Another set of jugglers brought a shift and turn of the crowd, and once more Seana found herself in front. She couldn't escape, for moving around the circle would incite the anger of those watching, should she block their view, and there was no way to slip between those pushing at her from behind. She gave up, and watched the tumbling.

"She claimed to be meeting others but dinna name anyone." The young man grew uncomfortable with his older brother's intent perusal. "None of your looks, now. I saw her first. I only wanted you to see her since you refuse to believe me."

The other two men laughed, but again it was the elder who spoke. "She ran from you, lad. You standing here," he teased, "while the lass is there alone, will not get you a tumble anywhere." Grinning at the flush across his brother's cheeks, he slapped his back. "Stand back, lad. I'll show you how it's done."

He gazed again at the lass his brother had found, feeling the fog of liquor clear with every passing moment. She clapped and shouted as loud as any, adding her cry for more of the tumbling tricks. Her cheeks

were flushed with a soft pink hue that made her flaw-less skin appear the color of fresh cream.

For a long moment, his gaze targeted her wide eyes, beguiled with their color and sparkle. Desire raced hot in his blood as he saw the length of her honey-colored braids moving from side to side with her glee, and he thought only of their silken ripples free and covering his skin.

A rising breeze pressed the dowdy, shapeless gown flat against her body and revealed the sleek line of a woman's flesh. His hands slowly curled as he thought of holding her slightly flaring hips to meet the surge of his thrusts. With a mouth suddenly dry as straw, he knew just how tightly she would glove him, and his loins burned with need.

"Aye, lad," he said at last, repeating himself. "I'll show you how it's done."

"Selfish beast" came from the younger. "You've already got a woman waiting for your attentions. Would you be forgetting her? Aye, 'tis a selfish oaf you are to deny your own brother the pleasure of tumbling such a sweet, tempting lass first."

"Selfish, am I? Here, then," he offered, fumbling with his leather belt pouch to pull out several gold pieces. "Buy yourself another."

"Not so fast. I'd wager you won't have her," the third brother ventured, his gaze on the maid, too. The merry smile, the flawless skin and the curve of her breasts made him ache to touch her. "She's got to be some lord's bastard get. She's far too dainty to come from common stock."

"You've a good eye, brother Jamie," Micheil Gunn agreed. "But I've a strong desire for her just the same."

Davey, intent on drawing the lass's attention to himself, found he was outclassed when he saw the lass look toward them and settle her gaze on Micheil. The moment his brother smiled at her, Davey shrugged his shoulders and inclined his head in defeat.

Seana, flustered by the bold stares, blushed when a kiss was blown her way. Her gaze skimmed the three men, and recognition of the brown-haired man who had spoken to her earlier flashed a warning as she looked again at the tallest.

There was a dangerous look about him, with his narrowed eyes and wind-ruffled dark hair. For all that he was smiling at her, the sharp cut of his features sent a nagging from the back of her mind. Not understanding why so strong a reaction was begging her to pay heed, Seana ignored it. His staring sent a warm flush of excitement through her young body, and tentatively, without thought, she returned his smile.

It was all the invitation Micheil needed.

# Chapter Four

Micheil was still smarting with anger that Fiona, upon learning that he was coming to the fair to sell off some of his horses, had dared to follow him here. It would serve her well to have yet another lesson that she could not control him. He had never had any intention of keeping the meeting she insisted upon later, and now, with his desire aroused by a honey-haired lass, thoughts of Fiona were driven from his mind.

"She looks clean enough, but poorly dressed," Jamie remarked, hooking his thumbs in his belt. "Have a care, brother. There's Keiths and Sinclairs about." And, leaning closer to Micheil, he asked, "Why not let Davey have her?"

"You bletherin' fool, he would not know what to do with her." But even as Micheil made a move toward crossing over to her, he saw her start and, with a turn, push her way into the crowd. Every male hunting instinct was aroused for the chase, and he went after her.

"He's frightened her off with his bold stares," Davey muttered. Micheil's long-legged stride had already taken him away.

"Come, Davey. When he's had his fill, he'll come looking for us."

With a last longing look to where Seana had stood, Davey turned to follow Jamie. "If I had her, I'd never be having my fill."

"There's not a lass born who keeps Micheil's attention. This one's no different."

Micheil had a similar thought as he used the advantage of his height to keep his quarry in sight. Ruefully he rubbed the thick growth of beard on his lower face. He was not at his best, but then, his pouch was heavy with gold, and he'd yet to meet a lass not in need of coin.

For a moment she was lost to view. Then Micheil spied her fingering a fine length of linen and hurried after her. It irked him that she pretended to be unaware of his presence behind her.

The merchant saw her poor dress and neatly grabbed the length of cloth from Seana. "Off with ye! I'll no have the likes of you soilin' me goods."

Micheil reached out to stop her from moving on, but was jostled, and his hand closed on air. His gaze snagged hers as she tossed a look over her shoulder. He inclined his head, moving toward her, unaware of the intense, predatory look of him.

Seana fled, shoving her way past people close to the stalls, suddenly afraid. A baker's tent sent an enticing aroma wafting on the air, and she stopped. Too late she saw that while one lad flipped a coin, attracting the baker's attention while he mulled over his choice, another was stealing buns from a tray set out to cool. The

boy was young, and the punishment for thievery se-
vere. Seana acted without thought.

She upset the tray nearest her, drawing the baker's
attention, but she was unbalanced and he caught hold
of her braid.

"Thief!" the man shouted. "I'll not let you go!" he
added as Seana tugged to free her braid.

"Unhand me. I've not stolen a thing." Seana was
frantic, and she looked up, hoping to see one of the
convent nuns. She would even welcome the sight of
Fiona and her sister, but only strangers' faces peered
down, drawn close by the continued yelling.

A powerful hand clamped over her shoulder, but
Seana couldn't see who made so bold as to touch her.
Then the man spoke, and a strange shiver of appre-
hension ran up her spine.

"Unhand my lass, or you'll not have one left to ply
your trade." But Micheil did more than merely order
the baker. His own free hand came forth to uncurl the
man's hand from the braid he held.

"She stole—"

"Nay! I took naught!"

"You err," Micheil calmly stated. "We were jostled apart by the crowd and intended to buy your
sweets. Choose what you'll have, love."

"Half a tray fell. Ruined."

"Three buns, and no more. I'll be paying for
those," Micheil told the baker, his gaze daring him to
continue with his protest. His hand tightened on
Seana's shoulder, and he leaned down to whisper in
her ear, "I came after the bold promise of your smile,

so there's no need to run from me." Then, softer still: "I'll not bargain your price."

Seana stilled. Her mouth opened, but when she twisted to look at the man who held her in his firm grip, fear receded, and anger took its place. "I meant no promise to you or any man. I laughed at the jugglers."

She tipped her head back to look at him, and once again felt a shiver crawl along her spine. He was the man who had stared at her from across the circle, but it was something deeper, something she couldn't have named, that urged her to run. She looked away as the jingle of coin in his pouch stilled the baker's tongue.

Micheil concluded his payment quickly, surprised to find a glint of tears in the lass's eyes. Her subtle scent rose, warm and sweet as sunshine, and he masked the desire that rocked through him.

"I mean you no harm, lass. You know that." But her darting glance at all but him had Micheil adding, "Do you seek your mistress?"

"I've none. Let me free."

"I'm not ready to do that." *I may never let you go.* This, too, was a surprise Micheil was forced to mask. Where had this possessiveness come from? He hadn't even tasted her lips. It was her loveliness that caused it, nothing more.

Seana refused to look at him. His grip was strong, although not hurting her, and she knew she couldn't get free. A glimpse of his dress and his full pouch told her she would have no help from the crowd against this wealthy highlander.

But why did a sense of knowing him nag at her? And it was the fear generated from this that added a frantic note to her pleading with him.

"I do not want your fear," Micheil admitted, and with some reluctance he released her. He saw her give a hasty glance full of longing to the tray of ginger cakes the baker had set in the place of the one that had been upset. The sight of the tip of her tongue licking her bottom lip sent his blood pounding.

He couldn't resist moving close to pin her in place against the stall while he purchased several of the cakes and ordered the baker to hand them to her.

"I cannot take—"

"But you want them," he countered. "Have you no coin to spend?"

"Not a one," Seana admitted, eyeing the cakes.

"I saw what you did. You risked yourself for those lads. 'Twas a foolish—"

"Nay! They likely had no coin, like me, and wanted a sweet badly."

"Then take the cakes and enjoy them as your reward." He couldn't seem to stop himself from reaching out to stroke a partial length of her braid. Once again the image of her honey-colored hair, free and wrapped around him, rose in his mind, and he gently urged her to the far side of the stall, out of the flow of passersby.

Seana hungered to taste the cakes. Only fear of what he would likely demand in payment stopped her from eating them. With the stall behind her, and his broad-shouldered body in front of her, she dismissed the notion of running. His soft voice urging her to enjoy

the sweet tempted her into doing just that. Breaking off a small bit of the cake, she blew on it to cool the sweet.

*Some lord's bastard get.* Micheil silently repeated Jamie's words as he watched every dainty movement she made.

At the first taste of the cake, Seana was assaulted by memories. The last time she had eaten ginger cakes was in Wick, on her ninth birth day. Her mother had despaired of all she had eaten. And with that memory came the sound of her mother's laughter, her sweet voice, and her lovely scent as she had held her daughter close. Seana closed her eyes, fighting to bury the memory.

Micheil was not a patient man, but he stood quietly and watched her savor the first taste of cake as if he had never seen anyone enjoy a sweet before this. Her cheeks were faintly touched with color, glowing with the freshness of youth. The saucy tip of her nose had him longing to run his finger down its length, and the longing was not born of desire. He gazed at the shape of her mouth, caught by his own fanciful thoughts, then lowered his eyes to the curve of her bare throat, where the pulse was barely visible.

When she opened her eyes, he was unable to look away from them. They were gray, misty with a promise he was sure she was unaware of and fringed with thick lashes. They held him as if she, too, were caught by a sense of enchantment. With a rough shake of his head, he looked away to break her hold, gazing at her hands as she continued to break off pieces of cake and eat them. And when she was done, her sigh of blissful

contentment pierced him with the need to hear it
again—from lips sated with his kisses.

"Will you thank me for your treat? And I'll have
your name, too."

"You have my thanks for your kindness. I've already told you I have no coin to repay you." Seana
could not bring herself to look at him. He stood close
enough that the heat of his body seemed to touch hers,
but the nagging warning that was without solid basis
haunted her. She longed to escape him.

"Give me your name, so I can call you something
besides lass!"

It was an order, given in a voice that expected obedience. That he was handsome, Seana did not deny.
Nor did she deny that he was bold. Her innocence was
no match for him. Now she had to leave him, and
quickly. Once more she tried to search the constantly
moving crowd, desperate to find a familiar face.

Micheil's patience snapped. The desire to have her
to himself brought his hands up to her shoulders,
drawing her close. He ignored her startled cry, and
used the smile that had brought more than one lass to
her ruin. Only the deep, piercing knowledge that he
held true innocence curbed his irritation. She had the
softness of a woman, and a sweet scent that increased
his heartbeat as his body responded with intense
longing.

"Your name?" he coaxed, bending his head to rub
his chin against her hair.

For a moment, Seana thought of telling him who
she was. She would take no pride in invoking the name
of Black Micheil Gunn, or in claiming him as her be-

trothed, though it would serve to free her. But it had been kind of him to pay for the ruined cakes, and for her treat. Even as she wavered, she peeked at the firm set of his lips, framed by a thick, dark growth of unshaven hair, and found that once again a warning flared for her to keep silent. Seana heeded it.

With a small half turn, Micheil blocked her view and urged her farther back, toward the end of the stall. When she started to protest, he silenced her. "I'm not done with you. Until then, you'll stay."

The fair was held on the abbey's land, but Seana still had no idea of who he was. His leather jerkin, and breeks of dark green, along with his finely woven linen shirt, made her think he stood high in his clan. She could feel the fullness of his leather pouch against her arm, but he wore no identifying clan badge. His dirk handle was carved, but she could not manage enough space between them to see what sign, if any, was there.

"Do not be stubborn, lass. Give me your name," he coaxed again, pulling her closer.

"You ask for what I cannot give." Her mouth felt parched as she caught his lips forming a knowing smile. For a moment she was trapped, thinking she had longed to see it again. The sounds and smells receded, and Seana grew dizzy with the strength of the yearning that tore through her. She knew he was waiting for her to say something more, but words fled. His muscled body gave off the scents of horses and leather, at once familiar and strange. Liam's scent—but it had been years since her brother had held her close.

His shoulders were broad, and she had the strange sensation that she could set her burdens to rest upon them. Seana's hand rose of its own volition to touch his chest. Beneath her palm, she felt the thudding beat of his heart, and the heat of him. She yanked her hand back as if burned.

"Have you so many men offering for you that you pick and choose? I said I would not bargain your price. Name it. I'll be more than generous with you, lass. There's a look about you that sets my loins to aching." And Micheil could no more resist nudging his hips against her belly to let her feel the proof of his desire than he could have stopped himself breathing at this moment.

"Cease! I've known no man."

"Are the men blind hereabout?" Micheil's grin was a wicked slash, even as he wondered why he accepted her word. She'd bewitched him. It had to be. He'd never allowed himself to be duped before. "Come, lass, tell the truth. No beauty like you could remain unpicked this long. You'd take me for a fool to say as much, and I've no liking to have sport made of me."

"I'm not lying. I've had no company of men. None. I'm not allowed— 'Tis no lie," she finished lamely.

Micheil studied her eyes—they were wide now—and saw for himself the truth that rang in her voice. His body tightened. "Then 'tis a prize indeed that I've found for myself," he whispered. The thought of claiming her and keeping her for his brought a wilder heat to his blood.

"Your look frightens me." Seana shivered in reaction to the sudden darkening of his blue eyes. A frag-

ment of her memory begged her to seek deeper for the sense of danger that rose within her.

"Fear is not what I'm wanting you to feel," he said in a rough voice, ignoring everything around them to lower his head.

Seana reared back, but there was no escape from his lips covering her own. She trembled in shock, and kept her eyes open at the warmth of his mouth pressing upon hers. She saw the thickness of his dark lashes, but his eyes were closed as he held her fast to his hard body. His hands slid down to rub her hips, and Seana bit down hard on his lower lip, shoving at him to free herself.

Micheil lifted his head, but did not let her go. His narrowed gaze dared her to move while he licked his lips.

"You've no right to take such liberties with me. You should not have kissed me. Set me free," Seana begged, struggling against his strength. "You're a stranger, a fine wealthy one by the looks of you, but a stranger just the same. I'm for keeping it so. Release me. I've likely been missed, and will be— Just let me go!"

Micheil had rarely been denied what he wanted. He wanted her, and had no intention of letting her go. He had felt the brief softening of her mouth beneath his before she bit him. If it was true, and she was an untried lass, the reaction was to be expected.

He caught her around the waist, and his other hand closed over his leather pouch. He thought the inducement of gold coin would set her at ease. A warning flashed in her eyes, darkening the gray, and even as the

need rose unbearably to possess her, Micheil thought her look that of a haughty lady. His earlier anger with Fiona, and his bewitchment with this lass, had surely clouded his mind. She was not a fine lady, even if he would rather coax and woo than force any woman.

And he wanted to fully taste the rosy tint of her lips. She had surely captivated him, for never had desire flowed so strong or so hot in his blood.

"Where will you be missed from? Surely you can tell me that?"

"'Tis of no matter."

He caught hold of her chin, lifting her face to his. "I know you will not believe this, lass, but I cannot let you go."

Her gaze fell from the powerful pull of his eyes to his lips, and Seana had to force herself to look away. Why wasn't she screaming? Surely someone would come to help her. But it was the warning of the fear that had slowly receded that kept her from it.

"Please, I cannot tell you more. I'm—I'm promised to someone," she murmured softly.

"Who? Some fat old merchant that'll work you till you're old and ugly and fill your belly with a bairn each year?"

Shocked by his frank talk, Seana knew a deeper pain from the words he spoke. A bairn each year? Not likely. Dhu Micheil Gunn would not let her live that long. But something held her silent, something aside from his being a stranger who should not know such things.

Micheil suddenly wanted her smile as much as he wanted her body. He wanted her willing. Softly, then,

coaxing in a voice like honey, he said, "Lass, I'm not a man to be taken lightly. I've a mind to have you for myself. None will dare touch you then. None but me," he added, seeing the fright that skimmed her lovely features.

"Take me? You cannot! Never think so," she warned him. But temptation, like the need to taste the warmth of his lips, beckoned unbearably. She could beg his protection.

But it would mean his death if he helped her escape, and she could not have that on her conscience, not when so many others had already died. There was his payment, too, that Seana had to consider. For all that she had goaded Fiona's anger last eve with her words about warming Micheil's bed, she knew little more than the words she had spoken.

There was no choice. Seana swirled, ready to run, but Micheil tightened his hold around her waist, drawing her with him around the back of the stall, where none could see them.

"I cannot let you go. Accept that. You've bewitched me, lass. Are you some faerie's get?"

"You're a stubborn man. Take yourself off." But his question made Seana frown. Long ago someone had remarked that she was faerie get...but when? "You make fine sport of me to ask."

His charming smile almost eased her fear. He'd made no move to kiss her again, his touch, while firm, was not hurtful, and Seana found herself wanting that smile for herself.

"I make no jest at your expense. Surely you've been told how lovely you are by others?"

"I have not! You do not believe me, by the look of you, but I swear, 'tis true."

"Have you no clan?"

"None that matters. Are you here with yours?"

"Aye." But that was all he said. Desire unsatisfied, Micheil found that he was developing an intense curiosity about her. Her continued evasions warred with the little truth she told him.

"You will give me your name."

"If you knew whose protection I could claim, you'd not want to know."

Spirit, as well as beauty. Micheil hemmed her in with his big body. "If not your name, then I'll take a kiss in its stead."

He gave her no time to choose, taking her mouth with his, knowing he was fast becoming besotted with her, and bewildered by it.

His hair gleamed ebony in the sunlight, and then his lips touched hers. His taking was not forceful, but warm and sweet, like a caressing breeze that teased her with the desire to know his taste. He was a stranger, this man with his body pressed from her chest to her thighs, but this might well be the only kiss she would ever have. The gentle touch of his fingers shaping her cheek and sliding down to hold her chin eased her fear. Surely there would be no harm in such a sweetly stolen kiss.

He pulled her tight to his hard-muscled body, his hands caressing the length of her slender back with the practiced ease of a man who gave as much pleasure as he took. She was tense, a soft cry escaping her, and he took that for his own.

"'Tis foolish to fight me, lass. Open your mouth for me. There's a wild honey taste to you that I'm longing to savor."

"'Tis not right."

But Micheil knew she trembled in reaction to the heat that rose between them. It was there in her eyes, and the faint blush of her cheeks. The rapid rise and fall of her breasts, the breath she couldn't quite seem to catch, each reflected the same violent and unpretended desire that seethed through him.

"Give me your mouth, lass." His voice was rough with passion. Deeper. Softer. "Once, just once."

The touch of his hand curving over her bare neck was frightening. Seana trembled, her eyes dilating wildly as she met his powerful gaze.

And Micheil felt a hunger so violent he could barely control himself from taking what he wanted.

"Your skin's heated, lass. Like a fever's taken you."

"Aye," she whispered, unable to lie.

"One kiss," he breathed over her mouth, and felt shaken by the shy flowering of her lips meeting his. There was no doubt left about her claim of innocence and his muscles clenched with fierce reaction.

A surging pleasure swept Seana's body. It frightened her, and enticed her to have more. She struggled suddenly, feeling herself drawn into a trap from which she could never escape. And his kiss was no longer coaxing, sweet or gentle. His mouth fed deeply upon hers with a hunger she did not understand. Nor did she know how to ease it.

Suddenly Micheil broke the kiss, lifting his mouth from hers. His eyes were a piercing blue filled with desire as he gazed down at her face.

Seana managed to raise one shaken hand to her lips. "I've never dreamed a man's kiss had the power to make me forget myself." Her body felt empty and aching at once, and her eyes reflected her bewilderment at the sensations that swamped her.

Her words were not coated with sly bargaining. Her candor added to his excitement as a spiking surge of lust ripped through him, gut-deep and burning, her innocence an enticement that he bring her pleasure. His breathing was hard and fast. His hands slid down her back and once more gripped her slender hips. He wanted to draw her nearer, needed to, but a last bit of sanity warned him where he was.

"There's more a man's kiss can give you. More I want to give you. But you've pleased me with the knowing I've given you the first one." His gaze narrowed and targeted the soft red shade of her lips. "You've naught to fear from me. You know I'm already claiming you as mine."

Seana covered his mouth with the tips of her fingers. "You're daft. Say no more." Her heartbeat increased with her panic. She could not draw a free breath without the scent of him filling her. She felt his mouth part, and pressed harder to stop him from saying anything more, only to feel the nip of his teeth on the heel of her hand.

Pleasure shafted deep inside her, and she snatched her hand away. But he claimed her lips, taking both her cry and her breath for his own. He pulled her

close, his palms sliding down to cup her bottom, dragging her into his rigid length. And he fed on her mouth, slowly rotating his head to deepen the kiss.

"Mine," he whispered against her mouth, sweeping her up in his arms, his bold, long-legged stride taking them away from the noise and confusion of the fair.

Ripped from the dreamy pleasure of a few stolen kisses, Seana shook with a fright she had known few times in the past. The farther he walked, the less chance she would have to get away.

"I swear you've naught to fear from me, lass. I cannot let you go. My blood's so hot for you now, I swear I'll be burned till I have you."

"Cease, I pray you." His husky voice, filled with desire, did not inflame her.

"'Tis natural enough to be afraid the first time, but I'll swear, too, that I'll be gentle with you." The promise was wildly given, born of a need so desperate Micheil had never known its like. He ached with that desperation to bury his heated flesh inside her.

Trapped, Seana had no choice. "He'll kill you if you dare take me."

"Kill me? What tale will you spin now? Who would you have me fear?" The strength of her small hands gripping his shirt made him stop and looked down at her. "Give me his name."

Seana met the glitter of his eyes and swallowed. No choice, she reminded herself. "'Tis the betrothed of the laird of the Gunn clan that you think to make free with."

"Sweet Jesu!" The shock, even as his mind denied it, made Micheil set her down before him.

"I swear it true. I've been kept here at the abbey for ten years on his word."

The bitterness of her voice penetrated his shocked state, but Micheil, always quick to order his emotions, could not subdue his desire for her so easily. The vague memory of a child, and another of a rainy night when he'd been forced to track his runaway quarry, had no connection with the full-breasted beauty who stood before him. Her guarded look as she watched him like an animal scenting the hunter had him shaking his head in denial.

It couldn't be! Suddenly her image blurred and his sister Bridget's face appeared. He could not forget his sworn vow of vengeance against the MacKays. Most certainly not the one of family honor he had made to his dying father, the one against Seana herself.

Pain and fury melded in his eyes. But she did not know who he was.

"I'm not blaming you for being afraid of him. He's a savage, they say. I've heard but few of the stories, from travelers to the abbey, and those chilled my blood. 'Tis near five years since I've set eyes upon him, and the night was dark. God willing, it'll be five times five more till I do so again."

Emotions surged inside him. The force of desire and fury rose high, warring with each other. He wanted to throw her hand from his arm, and drag her down beneath him. How dare she look at him with trust and innocence in her eyes?

"Now you know. You understand, do you not? I'm to stay behind the abbey walls, and most likely die there."

"No man who saw you could wish death to one so bonny," he found himself saying, with disbelief. Surely she had bewitched him! He couldn't think!

Her laugh broke like the sweet crystal tumbling of water over rocks. "Bonny? Am I? He would not know what I look like. He has not come to see me. He's of no mind to claim a bride. 'Tis a shroud he'll be offering the likes of me when he's done."

His dazed look brought a rush of compassion to her. She had stopped him, but she was not pleased that she had invoked the hated name of Gunn.

"'Tis a clan feud they began," she offered to explain. "I've never known the full reasons for it, but there's no forgiveness for me."

Micheil could only stare at her, unable to deny her words. He knew he could never forgive her. But he wanted her—that had not ceased—and now, knowing who she was... His large hands raked back his hair, as if to still and order his thoughts. He didn't need to take by force what was his by right. And Bridget had to be avenged. He'd sworn a blood oath, given his word of honor.

"I'll take you back to the abbey, lass. I'll have no harm befall you."

"You cannot," she answered, backing away from his outstretched hand. "I must not be seen with you, or any man."

"'Tis not your choice."

Her shove was unexpected. With a flash of raised skirts, Seana started to flee, only to toss her braids and fling back over her shoulder, "I'll treasure the memory of my first kiss. And be remembering you for it."

Feeling as if he had been physically beaten, Micheil let her go. But when he roused himself, she was long gone. She never heard his promise. "Aye, Seana nic MacKay, you'll be remembering me, all right. I'll be making sure of that before night falls."

## Chapter Five

But Micheil did not rush back to his brothers. He purchased a flask of ale and remained alone with his tumbled thoughts for hours before he sought them out.

They waited with fat purses, and no horses left but their own mounts.

"Micheil!" Davey hailed him. "You missed Fiona in a fine raging mettle when you dinna meet her. She'd still be here demanding to know where you were if Jamie had not decided to tell her you found a lass more to your liking and would not be back at all."

"Did he?"

"Aye, Micheil, I did. 'Tis surprised I am to see you this soon." Whatever more he thought to say to his older brother, Jamie held his tongue. He had witnessed that veiled look in Micheil's eyes too many times. Micheil was barely controlling his black temper.

Davey noticed it, too, but that did not stop him. "Och, Micheil, have you lost the lass? Did she refuse you?"

"Not quite," Micheil answered.

"That cannot be all." Davey glared at his older brother. "Who was she?"

"Aye, Micheil, don't be selfish," Jamie said. "If the lass didn't want you, tell us. I've a mind to go after her myself."

"That you cannot do, Jamie." Micheil touched his horse's powerful neck, his hand gentle as he stroked the gray coat, and so at odds with the fury still churning inside him. He turned to his brothers, his tone harsh. "And Davey should not think of her. She told me she's promised to a fierce, savage highlander."

Both brothers threw back their heads, laughing. Jamie stopped first. "For a moment there, you almost made me believe that would stop you."

"It never has before," Davey added. "You're trying me sorely, brother. You stopped me from having her, and now you tell us we should not go after her."

"Listen to me, both of you. The lass did not blame me for being afraid when she told me his name. I'll admit it shocked me something fierce."

Once again Davey and Jamie roared with laughter. Micheil waited them out.

Davey looked at his adored older brother. "You, afraid? The lass surely wove a spell on you." Gazing at Micheil's eyes, he ventured to ask, "Are you bewitched, man? I've never known you to back off when you're wanting something for your own. And a lass so bonny—"

"Cease!" Micheil ordered. "You'd back off, too, Davey, if you knew who she named. You would," he warned, his voice hard, his features taut, "if you would keep your life."

"Tell us, then," Jamie demanded. "Tell us the name that should make a grown man shake."

"She's mine." Anger and possessiveness rode Micheil's voice. His brother's shared puzzled looks forced him to explain. "The lass I thought to tumble was Seana nic MacKay."

Silence met his announcement. Micheil couldn't blame his brothers for the shocked looks they exchanged. Seana, that sweet, innocent, honey-mouthed witch, would have reveled in the sight of the three of them brought low. But he would not forget she was his clan's enemy. He would never forget it!

"It cannot be," Jamie managed in a dazed voice.

"'Tis true. It was she."

"What will you do, Micheil?" Davey asked.

Micheil looked away. Their bond was strong, and he'd never lied to them. "I have not decided."

"Surely, now that you've seen her, you cannot mean to leave her at the abbey?"

"Why not, Jamie?"

The slow drawl of Micheil's words warned Jamie of his brother's temper. But the remembrance of Seana's lovely face made him speak without thought in challenge to his brother. "'Tis too cruel a vengeance that's planned. I'll not be a part of it."

"Jamie!" Davey grabbed hold of Jamie's arm as Micheil's eyes turned an icy shade of blue.

"You'll have no part in it?" Micheil repeated. "Jamie, keep your mind clear," he warned softly, his hand sliding up to the dirk's handle. He had never used his strength against either of his brothers, but he was willing to do so now. And this sin he laid at Seana's

door, as he did the lust she had aroused and then left prowling his body.

"Who did the lass bewitch, that you'd dare to challenge my word? Are you forgetting that I'm still chief?"

"I'll never forget that." Jamie shrugged off Davey's hand. "But I'd not lie to you. I can't bear the thought of leaving her to rot behind those walls. Think, man. It's not cold stone that should be holding her. 'Tis a man's arms she belongs in.'' Jamie paused, took a deep breath and released it. He knew how far he had gone, but caution suddenly had no place here. "If you don't want her, Micheil, I do."

"You would challenge me?"

Jamie's hand covered his dirk, and he squared off from his brother.

Davey stopped Micheil's forward lunge. He was no match for his brother's strength, and he knew that Micheil allowed him to shove him back.

Micheil, by sheer will, reined in his temper. The emotions that ran through him were a rampant melding of love and hate as he looked at the two brothers who had never before betrayed him. Now he understood how thin the passionate line between love and hate ran. He stood tall, the past generations of proud warriors stamped on his hawklike features. He fought to hide his pain.

"And you, Davey," he forced himself to ask. "Do you feel the same as Jamie?"

"Aye. I will not lie to you. If you have no intent to claim her as a bride, break the vow. There's none left to stop you."

"Break it?"

Davey's eyes darkened to near black. "Break the betrothal. One of us will claim her."

A feral snarl escaped Micheil's lips. "Both my brothers, ready to turn against me over a MacKay! I cannot believe this. She's our clan's enemy." His gaze swept over both their faces, his voice a low growl. "You swore oaths to me, oaths of honor and obedience, when I became chief, did you not?"

"Aye, we did. The clan did," Jamie answered. With a quick shake of his head, he felt himself regain his senses.

Davey nodded quickly, still watching his brothers in the hope they wouldn't fight.

And Micheil, too, seemed to regain control, lifting his hand from his dirk and letting it rest at his side. "I'm glad you're not refuting that, too. Leave this be," he had to warn them again. "'Tis not your brother that's saying this. 'Tis the word of the laird of your clan that orders it."

Neither one answered him. Jamie knew his brother had made men older than themselves, men of their clan, back down with such simmering wrath turned on them when they dared to claim he was too young to be chief.

Micheil stripped his steed's reins from a nearby post. "I will not be questioned about her again. You both ken my meaning?"

"Aye," Davey answered, when he saw that Jamie's mouth had tightened.

The ghost gray stallion stood still beneath Micheil's hand as he bridled and saddled him. Without

another word to his brothers, Micheil mounted and rode off.

"Do you understand his meaning plain, Davey?"

"Aye, Jamie," he answered, feeling an easing of the tension that gripped him. "I do. But I'll be saying this now, I dinna like it a bit."

"Like it or not, Davey, Micheil's right. 'Tis a foolish thing to be setting ourselves against him over a lass. And 'tis a sin, after what happened to Bridget, to take the side of a MacKay, no matter how bonny she is."

"But there was more than her fairness, Jamie. You saw that for yourself?"

"I saw a wench I'd a desire to tumble. Fair, aye, she was that. No denial there. But we can't forget what Bridget suffered at Liam's hands. If you were a wee bit bright, lad, you'd see the truth of it. Micheil claimed his right."

Davey handed the bridles for their horses to Jamie and then took up the saddles. "Micheil's temper is riled nigh on to heaven now."

"True enough. I'd be thinking it best we find him fast, before that black rage of his is loosed on some unsuspecting soul." With a rare insight into his brother Micheil's thoughts, he found himself adding, "Davey, I think Micheil is smitten with the lass, and finding it hard to remember his vow."

Davey lifted his saddle onto his horse. "Do you think he's already tumbled her?"

"Micheil? Don't be daft, lad." Jamie, his own saddle in place, looked over at his brother. "I know Micheil too well. There wasn't time enough for him. Our brother is not a man to hurry his pleasures. I've

never known him to take a quick tumble with a lass when he's been fierce aroused. And Seana did that to him. Nay, he's not like some I could name.''

Davey flushed. He could not help it. Jamie had teased him about it before. And why not, even if it was not his fault? Half the time, Micheil had him leading a raid, or riding out with messages. He took his sport where he could.

Jamie, believing he had succeeded in distracting his brother as he'd meant to, tested him once more. ''If Seana nic MacKay knew who she had met this day, she would not be sleeping well this night.''

Mounting his horse, Davey glanced at him. ''But she did not know. 'Tis only to you I admit that I'll not sleep at all this night, knowing what Micheil plans for her.''

Jamie grabbed hold of Davey's arm and nearly unseated him with the force of his grip. ''I'll add my warning to Micheil's. Don't set yourself against him. She's bonny, 'tis true. There be other lasses as sweet, Davey. Micheil's our chief. Never forget it.''

''I'll remember, just as I remember her. I've naught told this before to any, but I played with her before the wedding. She had spirit, Jamie, and a laugh that made you smile with her. But I will not forget that it was our own clan who named him Dhu Micheil for his savage temper against the MacKays.''

They had ridden but a few minutes, skirting the sprawl of the tents, each keeping watch for some sign of their brother, when Davey mused aloud.

''Do you think it strange that Micheil admitted he had not decided what to do with her?''

Jamie, still trying to reconcile himself to forgetting the young woman who had stirred a powerful lust within him, shook his head.

"Not so strange. And I don't envy our brother his decision at all."

Seana, too, had skirted the edge of the fair at a rapid walk, then had broken into a hard run to reach the safety of the abbey. She was pondering how to slip unnoticed through the gates when she realized the courtyard was filled with carts and horses. Servants and retainers milled about, and she pressed herself flat against the stone wall beside the gate, trying to still her pounding heart.

Someone of importance had arrived to stay at the abbey. Ailis, she knew, would be busy seeing to the guest's quarters. Too busy to notice her. Seana stilled. If ever a time had presented itself for her to make good an escape, she had it before her now.

Gathering her scattered thoughts, Seana knew she was in danger of having a hue and cry raised once it was discovered that she was missing from the fair.

She needed a plan of action. She needed to gather every bit of courage to try. Seana knew it was her encounter with the stranger that had made her spirit chafe against imprisonment and the fate that awaited her.

The more she thought of escape, the more she realized that freedom was something she was willing to risk her life to attain.

Before she could fully formulate any plan, the gates swung open, and two of the younger novices stepped

outside. Seana's barely stifled moan at being caught turned their attention on her.

"Seana, what do you here?" asked the shorter one, her dark eyes filled with concern.

"Are you unwell?" the second asked.

Facing them with panic-stricken eyes, Seana seized upon the excuse they had unwittingly given her for having returned alone.

"Aye. 'Tis the monthly cramps that beset me." She clutched her belly, hating the lie, but determined to carry it through.

"I'll help you back to your—"

"Nay! I'll manage. But, please, the sisters need help with the mule and their purchases. I could not stay a moment more."

"Lilis, you stay. I will inform our reverend mother."

"I can manage to tell her," Seana said quickly. She felt the stone wall behind her, one hand pressed against its rough surface, willing the novices' agreement.

"'Tis a small matter, Seana," sweet-voice Nairna said. "We're sent to fetch Fiona and Janet back from the fair."

Seana breathed a sigh of relief, but as the two walked off, she called out softly, "Why are you sent to fetch them?"

Lilis turned to answer. "Their kinswoman has come."

"Kinswoman?" Seana repeated, a cold knot of tension forming in her belly.

"Aye. 'Tis Ailis's own niece who visits. Bridget, she is called."

Seana paled. Neither Lilis nor Nairna had been here long enough to know what fate awaited her. She heard them urge her to go inside, and thought she nodded as they set off, but for a long moment she could not move. Bridget, here? Why had her brother's wife come, after all these years? Was she sent to fetch her?

Wild thoughts raced through her as she fought the desire to weep. No! Tears would weaken her! Seana struggled to regain control of herself. She stood as still as the stone that supported her. The years of futile pain encompassed her as the violent feelings of terror slowly ebbed.

An icy determination took hold of her. Once before she had attempted escape and been brought back. This time she intended to succeed.

A calmness filled her, and once again she heard the voices of those still milling about the courtyard. Rubbing damp palms over her skirt, Seana reached down to grab some earth and streak it over her face and neck. She was no better dressed than a scullery maid, and that was the role she intended to play.

Last time, she had run blindly, without thought of food or a weapon to protect herself. This time she would steal what she needed and be gone before she was missed.

With her head down, and her shoulders hunched, Seana slipped through the abbey gate.

Keeping to the arched stoneways, Seana blessed the afternoon shadows cast by the stone pillars that hid her flight to her small cell.

The bare-walled room, with its narrow bed, small table and single stool, offered little comfort. But then,

she had not been sent here for comfort. Closing the door behind her, Seana gave one last wistful thought to the man who had offered to claim her.

If she had known that Bridget had come to the abbey, there would have been no hesitation in her accepting his offer. It did not really matter whether or not Bridget had come to fetch her. Sooner or later Micheil would remember her.

She shook with a renewed chill at the thought of being at his mercy.

Mercy? Nay! 'Twas not mercy the Gunn chief would be having for her at all.

Unbidden into her thoughts came the sight of the bold stranger. Slowly raising her fingertips to her mouth, she felt again the warmth of his lips pressed against her own. The fluttering feeling in her stomach replaced the knot of cold. Seana closed her eyes, willing the image of his face to come to mind, knowing she wasted precious time, but knowing, too, that she had to be sure of what she did.

Perhaps it was yet the fear that held her, but all she could recall was the near-black of his hair, and the flash of white teeth that made his grin somehow wicked.

And the nagging sense that she had longed for his smile.

Shaking off such useless thoughts, Seana gathered her few possessions. A warm cloak, stout leather boots, a clean shift, her comb, and the tinderbox. She held the rough wool blanket for long moments, and knew she could not take it. With hurried moves, she shaped her night shift, her second gown and the rolled

straw-filled mattress into a vague figure and covered it with the blanket. If any thought to look in on her, they would believe her asleep.

The kitchen was her next goal, but Seana knew she would have to remain hidden until nightfall before she dared attempt entry. Food and a knife were all that she would take. But where to hide until then?

The answer was so simple that Seana nearly dropped her bundle. Ailis's room! The abbess would toil to see to her guests and would not return there until long after all were abed.

Once again, Seana used care to reach her goal. The abbess's room was slightly larger than the rooms assigned to her nuns. The bed was longer, to accommodate her tall frame, its coverings reflecting the wealth she had brought as a dower to the abbey. The blankets stored in the large chest were of the softest and finest woven wool, and Seana had little hesitation in stealing one. But as she reached for one placed near the bottom of the chest, her hand closed over the gem-encrusted handle of a dirk.

Slowly, she withdrew it, and in the waning light of the afternoon thought of its value and her need of a weapon. She rested the blade across her palm, thinking of her need to go home.

Craigell! Her mind turned away from the memories, not allowing them to rise. She would take the dirk as payment for her lost freedom.

Using the blanket as a cushion, Seana seated herself in the far corner, behind the door, and rested her head against the wall. Liam could not refuse to protect her once she reached the safety of Craigell's walls.

If all was in ruins, as she had been led to believe, perhaps the gems embedded in the dirk's handle would
help restore all the Gunns had stolen and destroyed.
She could forgive Liam for not coming to rescue her
from the abbey. It lay too deep within the Gunns'
holdings. But a cold smile creased her lips at the
thought of Bridget, or the Black Micheil himself,
coming to fetch his bride and finding her flown from
her prison.

That would be sweet revenge. She could have made
good an escape with the stranger earlier, and been long
gone. But she knew the price he would have taken
from her. It was too late to think of seeking him out
and asking for his protection even to leave the abbey's lands. And, she had to remind herself, he had
been afraid once she told him who she was.

Even the mighty Sinclairs, with their ancient
stronghold of Girnigoe Castle, feuded with care
against the Gunns, as did the Sutherlands with their
shifting alliances. And she would have to cross both
their lands to reach home. The enormity of the task
before her struck terror in her heart and mind, but
Seana kept it at bay. To stay would mean her death.
Far better that she attempted escape, for if she succeeded, a freedom long denied her awaited.

She could ask no one for help. But a nagging voice
persisted in questioning—what price would she pay for
her freedom?

"Anything," she whispered. "I'll give anything to
go home."

Ailis's room lay at the far end of one wing, so no
noise or footsteps passed the door. The evening shad-

ows slowly darkened the room, and Seana judged the time right for her to leave when the last bells had rung for prayer. Unless any were too ill, everyone in the abbey would be in the chapel.

Sure of this, Seana nearly cried out when a slender form rose from the kitchen floor. Lit only by the dying flames of the fire, Seana was unsure who stood there.

"Have you come for food, Seana?"

"Ellen?"

"Aye. I've been set to scrub the floor. Like you, I could not hold my tongue against Fiona."

Seana placed her bundle down, hoping that the young nun had not seen it. Skirting the large worktable in the center of the room, she made her way to Ellen's side.

"They all remain?" Seana asked.

"Joined by their kinswoman. Fiona stormed back here, furious over some happening at the fair. Truly, it was not my fault that she chose her path to her room just as I tossed the washwater out. She struck me, and my temper got the best of me. I hit her back. 'Tis a pity that Ailis witnessed my blow, and the words that followed. I could not apologize to Fiona, no matter Ailis's order, so I am sentenced to wash the abbey floors for the week."

"Surely you told Ailis she had hit you first?"

"The sudden arrival of her kinswoman distracted our abbess. They were closeted within her study for most of the afternoon. It seems some event of import is about to happen."

Seana, thinking only that it must have to do with her, grew desperate to make good her escape. She had already spied the loaves of bread left from supper, and knew that Ellen spoke the truth. Ailis was indeed distracted, for otherwise the bread would have already been distributed to the poor.

"Are you done here, Ellen?"

"At last. There's cheese beneath the cloth, and no one will notice a missing slice of the smoked ham. I will not tell you were here." Ellen gathered up her rags and the bucket. "Seana, beware of Fiona. She's a selfish woman, and she hates you. Never mistake her for any but your enemy. I'll be glad when she is gone."

"I know her well for what she is. I was wrong to say what I did last eve. Fiona's arrogance makes her a fitting mate for Black Micheil. Far more fitting than I could be."

Seana moved toward the bread, hoping that Ellen would leave. She felt a warning stir deep inside that whispered for her to hurry. She heard the scrape of the bucket that Ellen dragged close to the back door, sighing with relief when the young woman opened the door and tossed the water out.

But Ellen was not done. "Seana, why have you never tried to leave here? I've not asked, but I've wondered why you stayed and awaited—"

"There's none to help me, Ellen. My clan is scattered, those who are not dead. My brother's wealth is gone, so where would I run to?"

"Where indeed? Seana, be careful."

Frozen for a moment, Seana spun around. She knew! Ellen knew what she planned. But Ellen was

already gone. Indecision rose within her. Should she go after her and beg her silence? Was Ellen even now on her way to alert Ailis?

No. Ellen would not betray her. Two years before, newly widowed and suffering from the loss of her child, Ellen had been in sore need of comfort and a friend. Their bond had formed instantly and quickly. She had waited out Ellen's desperate request to be allowed to take the veil rather than be used for barter in another marriage, lending her shoulder for tears, her prayers, and her support. Ellen would not give her away.

Seana took a clean linen cloth and placed two loaves of bread, a large wedge of cheese and half the smoked ham within before she tied it tight.

Accustomed to the dim light now, she spied the jugs of wine no one had put away. The nuns were indeed distracted, to be so careless. Heavy though it was, one jug was added to her bundle.

A last look as she stepped to the doorway told Seana her way was clear to the small back gate set in the abbey wall. The key hung on a hook next to the gate, and she had no fear of its lock squeaking to give her away, for, like all else within Ailis's care, it was kept well oiled.

The night was chill, and she drew her cloak around her, pulling up its hood. Tossing the key through the gate, she closed it behind her.

Home. She was going home.

It mattered not that she would not go riding out in glory, but rather driven to keep to the shadows in fear.

## Chapter Six

"Gone! You've let her escape your care again? This is the way you repay my protection, aunt? This is the loyalty you give to your clan?"

Summoned from her morning prayers, Ailis faced her nephew. "My first loyalty is to God, and those He entrusted to my care, Micheil. I have done the bidding of your father, and kept Seana here all these years. I have watched over her, and kept her safe. But none could understand the pain that maid has been made to bear."

Black Micheil, indeed! Ailis could well understand how her handsome nephew was called such. He was in a fine, towering black rage now, pacing her office like a great caged cat. As with his father before him, Ailis stilled her temper and let his storming fury play itself out, praying for cooler winds to blow once his wrath was spent.

A soft knock interrupted her musing, and Ailis bade entry. One of the novices came in, bearing the tray she had ordered on her way from chapel. Ailis ignored Micheil's scowl as she lifted a linen cloth from still-steaming meat pastries and poured wine into goblets

of beaten gold that had been part of her dower. She regained her seat once the novice had left them, folding her hands on the surface of her table. She dared not show one sign of her own fear for Seana. It was not difficult to surmise why the maid had chosen to run.

"Micheil, have some wine and calm yourself," Ailis began. "Why did you not send word that you were coming? Why send Bridget here? And Fiona?"

"I had no intent of coming here," he answered crossly. He did help himself to the wine, ignoring both the meat pie and the steaming bowls of hot broth. "No matter what my sister told you, I did not send her here. As for Fiona, she's her own woman, free to do as she pleases."

"She came to be with you."

"Accuse me naught, aunt. I was furious with her sudden appearance. Invite her? Nay."

"And Bridget? She has not come to see me in all these years, Micheil. What reason had she—"

"Ask me not to fathom her mind. I cannot do it." He glanced at her composed features, knowledge dawning. "You think I'd send her in my place? Never! And do not try to distract me. You are certain you've questioned them all? None saw Seana? None know when she left?"

"You heard for yourself what each had to say. You know what she took with her. Little food, and poor clothing. Not even a kitchen knife to protect herself."

Micheil set the goblet down, ignoring the wine that splashed on his hand and the table. "She," he thundered, "was not to be allowed any freedom! Did you

not understand that? I believed I made it clear enough when I was forced to track her down—"

"If you had warned me then that you were coming to take her to see her mother's grave Seana would not have run away."

"'Tis of no matter now!"

Ailis had blood that could run as hot as her nephew's when she was riled. That point was fast approaching. That he would dare forget to whom he spoke! Glaring at him, she forced herself to speak calmly.

"I have kept her safe all this time. Much as I regret doing so. Seana is a sweet-tempered lass, and of a gentle nature. She had to be frightened to run again. And you," she said, her voice driven by anger, "like a warrior beast, would terrify such an innocent maid if she saw you now."

"Terrify her? 'Tis not what I had in mind, aunt. But I've wasted enough time." He turned abruptly, and the blade of his sword caught the rising sunlight.

"Micheil," she pleaded, rising from her chair and coming to his side. "Find her, but I pray you, be tender with her."

"Tender? You ask that of me? Davey saw Sinclairs at the fair late last eve. Do you ken what it will mean if they find her first?"

"But the truce, Micheil, you wrote and—"

"The truce lasted as long as it took the ink to dry, and then they were raiding our crofts again. They'll take her to the Keiths and use her against me."

"By the saints, nephew, let them have her, then. You need not—" His stern, forbidding gaze made

Ailis pause, but she rallied again. "'Tis a shameful request my brother made of you. She is a mere lass, and you'd loose your man's wrath on her."

"You plead dearly for one whose blood destroyed your niece."

"Liam should pay, and he alone."

"But he has, aunt." With an icy demeanor, he stepped away from her. "You know of the raids these years past. He's afraid to ride forth without armed men beside him."

"Aye. I've heard it all, Micheil. And I hear, too, that Bridget rages for yet more vengeance. It is the poor crofters that have suffered the worst of this feud."

"'Tis not enough! I swore my oath to my father in blood. I'll not recant that oath, for all your begging."

"You'll not kill her?"

"No, 'tis not with violence that I want to touch her at all."

"For your soul's sake, I hope you keep to that." Having won this small concession from him, Ailis added, "Go then, with my blessing, and find her. The Keiths ride bold on our borders again, and I do fear for Seana."

"I will find her. Never doubt it," he tersely agreed, stalking with catlike grace to the door, but once more she stopped him.

"Bring her back to me. And think long on letting her take the veil, as I requested. Micheil, she is a maid. Do not forget that."

Insolently he stared at her. Ailis stepped back and hurriedly crossed herself. It was as if the very devil

stood there smiling so wickedly at her. But the smile, cold as it was, could not touch the ice blue of his eyes. Alarm shot through her.

"Do you dare to doubt my word that she is innocent?"

Briefly Micheil closed his eyes and remembered the feel of Seana pressed against him as he'd tasted the sweet honey of her giving mouth. Softly, then, he said, "I'd not question your word. But I doubt the lass herself."

"What say you? You do not know Seana!"

For an instant, his eyes and his smile warmed. "But I do. I was with the maid at the fair yesterday, and she—"

"You dishonored her!"

"'Twas no more than a few kisses I stole from her . . . then."

It was the promise in that last word that made Ailis rush to his side.

"Then? What mean you?"

"I've a mind to be stealing more than a few kisses from Seana when I find her."

Knowing too well the heat of the blood that ran through his veins, Ailis in truth spoke as his aunt, and not the abbess of Deer Abbey. "Then may the devil take you, Micheil, for I cannot countenance what you plan!"

"'Tis not the devil that will be taking me, but Seana nic MacKay herself." His eyes glittered with heat, just like his voice.

He had no sooner quit his aunt's office when he came upon the heavily veiled and cloaked figure of his sister and her serving woman.

"Micheil, I am near ready, and will ride with you," Bridget said.

Anger still simmered within him. "I know not the purpose of your sudden visit here, but make your way home as you came. I've quarry to track on my own."

He moved to brush past her, but Bridget stepped in his path. "I have requested to see her. I told them to bring your bride to Aunt—"

"You're too late, sister. Seana is gone." He started around her, then suddenly grabbed hold of her arm to turn her to face him. "Did Fiona put you up to this?"

"Nay! I came on my own. But if she's gone, you've got to find her, Micheil. You cannot let her escape. You promised me. You promised Da. You must not forget!"

Micheil hated the fear in her voice, and love softened his hold until he drew her against him. "Fear not, Bridget mine, I'll not let her free."

"You swore—"

"Aye," he said, releasing her. "I swore."

Long after he had gone, Bridget stood where he had left her, unaware of the young novice Ellen, watching her and praying that Seana had made good her escape.

Micheil met with his brothers and told them the little he knew. He agreed with them that Seana would not return to the fair. She would attempt to go home. It was a far piece  and held too many hiding places. It

was Micheil's decision not to send for men to help them search.

"The less attention we call to her having gone missing, the less chance a Keith will stumble on the need to find her. If we split up and sweep the land, one of us will find her first. She cannot get far walking."

Once he left his brothers, Micheil spent most of the day riding in a slow arc over the broad, rolling straths that spread from the abbey northward. She had not been this way in nearly ten years, he thought, for he dismissed her first attempt to flee. How much would she remember of the direction she had been taken from? He truly did not know.

Would she head toward the coast? She might know the Gunns rode bold on their own lands. To the south, the Fraser and Grant clans ruled, and would offer her no help. She had to cross open land to reach Craigell, in the far north. Lands held by the Sutherland clan. Instinct guided Micheil then, for he chose to ride east, his eyes ever watchful for a sign of her passing.

Wisps of smoke borne on the soft spring breeze from the scattered crofters' cottages made him swing away from their direction. Seana would seek no shelter among them. This he knew without question. They were Gunn tenants all.

The hours stretched, and still he found no sign of her. As darkness blanketed the land, Micheil knew he had to stop. To continue meant to chance missing a clue to where she was.

He found shelter at the edge of a forest, and with Breac—named for his brindled color—standing

watch, Micheil wrapped his plaid around him and sought his rest.

Sleep eluded him. He could not stop worrying about Seana, out there alone, prey to whoever and whatever might find her first. "Damn fool woman!" he muttered, seeking to turn his weary body and find comfort on the hard ground. "She had not the sense to even take a weapon."

With his head pillowed upon his fine leather saddle, Micheil stared up at the new spring leaves that barely formed a bower above him. The sky was clear, the stars were few from where he viewed them, and the night held a chill.

"Where are ye, lass?" he whispered, the sound of his soft voice bringing an answering snort from Breac. "Rest easy, beastie. We'll find her come morning. But I swear she'll pay for this, too."

But morning's light found Micheil ranging farther afield, without a sign of the path Seana had taken. With every passing hour of the rising sun, his anger grew. Hunger drove him to dismount when he found a small valley, and he crouched near the bank of a slow-moving stream. The water was cold from its mountain home, and once his thirst was satisfied he splashed water on his face. Hard bread and cheese assuaged his hunger while Breac nibbled the sweet young grass. The air was still, and the drone of bees beckoned him to seek the sleep he had forgone the night before.

Micheil was not sure at first what alerted him. A glance at his gray horse showed his head high, ears

perked forward alertly. "Aye, you sense it, too," he murmured, rising with one hand on his sword.

The cry of a curlew was suddenly cut off. Micheil swung himself onto Breac's broad back, heeding the caution that warned him to proceed carefully. He rode out from the mouth of the valley, seeking a sign of the source of his unease.

A hue and cry like that of a hunt made Breac rear. Micheil easily held his seat as the great horse pivoted on his rear hooves. Facing a narrow strip of wooded land, Micheil heard the shouts and thrashing of a chase.

"Easy, lad," he murmured soothingly to his horse. "We've gentler game to run aground this day."

But a deep feeling akin to dread pierced him moments before a broken cry spurred him into action. He set his heels to Breac's sides. It was not an animal's wail of distress he had heard, but that of a woman.

Not knowing what he faced, Micheil gritted his teeth as he drew forth his sword. He was alone, and he forbade himself to use his clan's war cry until he took the measure of what lay before him.

Breac's mighty hooves tore into the turf with a sound like approaching thunder as Micheil gave him his head. He could see them now, three men, running their fleeing quarry to ground between the slender trunks of the trees. A flash of long, fair hair revealed the position of the woman they pursued. Thinking the odds fair enough, Micheil went after them.

"Sweet Jesu!" Seana cried. A darting look revealed that the thundering sound was not the blessed hope of rain to aid her escape, but a rider joining her

pursuers. She was doomed. Veering away from the clear land at the edge of the wood, she relied on instinct that warned it would mean instant capture.

She ran blindly through the stand of young trees. Her heart pounded. She could not draw enough air into her lungs. Walking for most of the night had exhausted her. She had sought rest just as the sky lightened, only to come upon the three men. She had barely avoided them.

With one hand, she clasped her side, as if to contain the painful stitch that pierced her. Stumbling over exposed roots, she held her balance, knowing a fall would bring the men on her like a ravening pack of wild dogs.

Her single plait had come undone. Her hair streamed out behind her as she darted and twisted, making turns and struggling to fight a sense of hopelessness. No matter where she gazed, there was no avenue of escape, nowhere to hide.

She lost track of how long she had been running from them. Her strength was failing. Seana demanded speed from legs shaking with fear. She knew what her fate would be if they caught her.

Seeing that the rider kept pace just beyond the wood, she doubled back into the forest. Low-lying limbs appeared, like treacherous claws about to grab hold of her. She could almost feel the hot, panting breaths of her pursuers as they drew closer.

"No!" she shouted, more to give herself courage than to dissuade them. She had to duck low beneath a thick limb to avoid hitting it. Her hair caught in the tiny branches, and Seana had to twist her body to free

it. A spinning turn nearly brought her to her knees. She jumped between two close-growing trees, only to scream with pain. Fumbling with one hand for purchase to remain standing, Seana saw the jagged rock that had sliced her foot.

She turned like an animal at bay. And, in truth, feeling like one.

Her running was over, her bid for escape gone.

She pressed back against the slender tree trunk and drew the small jeweled dagger from the crude belt she had made. With a trembling hand, she held it out before her. Sweat stung her eyes. It trickled and pooled down her neck into the gaping rent in her gown.

Braced for an attack, Seana shoved her tangled hair aside. She needed strength, wits and clear vision to fight them off. Of the three, she could give herself only the latter, for she had neither the strength nor the wits to use the dagger. Her life was at stake, yet violence was an abomination to her.

A gurgling cry was suddenly cut off. But Seana refused to be distracted. All she saw was two of the men nearing her from opposite sides. The taller, of immense girth, had thick arms, furred with dark, coarse hair where the torn sleeves of his shirt ended. His leering face captured her gaze for a few moments before she quickly sought the other.

Shorter, he appeared a disjointed accounting of bones. His face was shallow, his nose crooked, and spittle formed at the corners of his mouth. Seana's stomach heaved at the low, growling sound coming from his throat. He posed more danger than the other one.

She did not question where the knowledge came from, but had to accept it. Perhaps the Lord had heard her plea for help.

Shivers chilled her flesh. It did not occur to her to ask them for mercy. Seana knew they would have none for her. The stench of their unwashed bodies, their ragged clothing and their lack of clan badges warned her these were no crofters intent on sport, but likely outlawed men, cast out from their clan for some heinous crime.

Men like these would have no honor to govern them.

"Nab," the heavy one cautioned with a motion of his hand, "take care not to harm her. We'll not be paid—"

"Aye, man, you've the right of it there. It's worth your life to touch her."

Seana's gasp was lost in a rumbling growl from the short man. She stared up at the powerful mounted figure, the one she had thought to be among those chasing her. A shaft of sunlight fell through the young leaves and cast his face in shadow. Her gaze dropped to the sword he held in one hand. Its blade edge was dark with blood. A long dagger, unlike the small blade she held, brought the first hope that she would not be at anyone's mercy.

"Away from her," Micheil ordered, nudging Breac forward with a press of his knees. He had his first look at the maid they had been chasing. A possessive rage seethed through him when he recognized Seana.

But Micheil knew the danger of losing his temper. With the two men separating him from Seana, he

dared not put her in more danger by any reckless action.

"There's enough of her to go 'round."

Micheil's gaze slid from the near-skeletal form that had spoken to the other. He did not trust himself to look again at Seana.

"I'm not of a mind to share, lads," he answered. "Step away from her, or your lives are forfeit."

"Nab, 'tis you and me, lad. 'Twas Parlan's cry we heard."

With no more warning than that, the two lunged. Seana quickly looked away from the horseman, the hand holding her dagger following her half turn toward the heavyset man.

She had to fight the searing memory of another time when she had fought for her life. The day of the attack that had taken her from her parents.

But it was the short man, the one called Nab, who swung his fist against her outstretched arm. The bone-jarring blow sent a cry to her lips, but she gritted her teeth, refusing to show even that small weakness. Nab held her wrist in a vise hold, tearing at her fingers to take her dagger.

Seana found herself sinking into a sea of pain as she was yanked away from the support of the tree and her weight came down on her injured foot. She clawed at Nab's hand, finding reserves of strength coming to her aid.

A vicious kick to her knee sent Seana sprawling to the ground. She lost her breath, feeling his sudden weight on top of her. Her ears ran with his continual low, growling sounds, and his stench was overpower-

ing. His fingers crawled into her hair, twisting against her scalp until tears filled her eyes.

Desperate to get him off her, Seana released the dagger, cringing at the keening moan rising in the wood. Nab was using her hair to pull her to her feet. Without thought, Seana grabbed handfuls of the rotted mold on the forest floor. She needed to scream against the agony of her body being dragged to stand.

She heard an enraged bellow, and, not knowing from whence it came, depended on herself and flung the contents of her hands up at Nab.

It took her a long moment to realize she was free. A moment when all she heard was a choked-off growl, and harsh breathing. She lay where she had fallen, terror and exhaustion staking equal claims to a body drained of strength. Only her mind begged her to reach for the dagger, warning she needed to protect herself.

At the touch of hands attempting to turn her over, Seana struck out with one hand, trying to crawl free.

"Easy, lass, I mean you no harm." Micheil gently eased her onto her back, fury rising all over again at the sight of her gray eyes dark with terror. He smoothed back the tangle of her hair, his breathing yet unsteady, for his man had not been easily killed.

He saw her fingers stretch to reach her fallen dagger, and quickly understood her need to hold it. "Here," he said, reaching for it and placing it within her palm. "But you'll not have need of it against me."

Seana clenched her fingers around the rough-cut gemmed handle. His calm voice, filled with assured promise, was reflected in his eyes. Seana closed hers

for a moment, wanting to believe him. His strong arm held her against the warmth of his body, and she heard the thudding of his heartbeat against her ear. Lifting weary eyelids, she saw that his dark hair was damp with sweat and battle had set a light flush across his cheekbones. But it was the slow curve of his lips as he patiently waited out her study that brought the knowledge of who had helped to rescue her.

"You... from the fair..." was all she could manage. Harsh, chilling shivers racked her and she could not control them.

"And you fought bravely for a lass against such odds. I'll be lifting you up, lass. No need to fear. But it's best we're away from here quickly, and that cut on your foot wants tending."

Micheil scooped her up into his arms and rose. Breac snorted, and he stilled. Very slowly, Micheil began to turn, for he felt a warning prickle creep up his spine, as if someone hidden watched them yet. He had killed the three men. They were all he had spied in pursuit of her. Then, as suddenly as the feeling had come upon him, it was gone.

"There's someone," Seana murmured, attempting to struggle.

"Nay. Nothing more is here," he answered curtly.

Micheil looked down on her face. Shadows marred her fair skin, as did small cuts and bruises. He held the chilled body of his enemy in his arms. She had not the strength left to battle a mouse. Yet the glittering spark of spirit that returned to her steady gaze sent heat flooding his body, and chased thoughts of revenge from his mind. She was his, no matter that she re-

mained unaware of it as yet, and all he could think about was her protection and care.

There was no fighting the need. It coursed as strongly as his hot blood did through his body. Not for the first time, he wondered if she had indeed bewitched him, as he set her gently up on Breac's back. Crooning softly to the horse to keep him still despite the unfamiliar scent and weight on his back, Micheil glanced around once more.

He should have kept one alive. There was more here than his eyes told him. Now, with battle lust calming, he recalled the cut-off words about not harming Seana or they would not be paid.

"They'll hang you if you're caught," Seana murmured.

Micheil broke off his heavy thoughts and swung up behind her. "But there's none to catch me, lass." He gathered the reins with one hand, sliding the other around her waist.

Still clutching the dagger, Seana forced herself to accept his hold. Her other hand lay limp on her lap, a throbbing pain coming from her swelling wrist. She tried not to think about her foot, or the aches that made her want to moan aloud as the horse moved out from the wood at a walk.

It seemed to her obscene that the sun yet shone, for the death they left behind had filled her with black thoughts.

Micheil swung Breac away from the wood, thinking to return to the small valley where he had rested.

"Wait, please. My bundle," Seana whispered, trying to rouse herself.

"Easy, lass. Tell me where you left it."

"At the start of the wood. A small cairn of rocks was where I thought to rest."

Without a word, Micheil headed back. Against his will, he was forced to admire the strength of the woman he held, for she kept herself from leaning against him. The sun glinted off the blade and the jeweled handle of the dirk she still held. He knew Seana had proven herself more resourceful than any had credited her. Here he thought she had no weapon. She had the heart of a fierce wildcat, and was as savage as the wolves that roamed the highlands. The challenge of his desire to keep her spirit warred against his sworn blood oath to his father.

Micheil cast both aside for the moment. Seana's soft cry focused his gaze on her scattered belongings. A jug lay smashed, the cloth beneath it soaked red.

Seana cried out in dismay. Micheil stopped her attempt to leap down.

"Stay. It appears there is naught to save." Holding Breac's reins, Micheil made his way to the pile of rocks. He lifted torn bits of cloth with the point of his sword. Once again he had a chill prickling up his spine, but Breac had lowered his head to nibble a few turfs of grass, and a quick scan of the woods in front of him revealed no sign of anything amiss.

This was wanton destruction. Food was mashed into the earth, fumes of wine rose from every bit of ripped cloth, and even her comb had been broken into pieces. Her shoes were ruined beyond salvage by gashes sliced in the leather.

Someone had set those men on Seana. But who?

## Chapter Seven

Micheil raised his head and stared at Seana. The thought of Fiona and his sister, Bridget, at the abbey came to mind. Could they have set those men on Seana's trail? But why?

He sheathed his sword, knowing he would not find the answer he needed here. Without a word, he settled himself up behind Seana, and took hold of Breac's reins.

"There is more than those men trying to catch you for a bit of sport, lass." The words had come unbid, but he felt her shudder as the import of what he said penetrated her numbed state. He hoped for her trust, not understanding why he wanted it. Like the need to protect her, this, too, simply was there.

With fear sliding into the very marrow of her bones, Seana lowered her head. "I cannot ask you to risk your life."

"Do you ask me to leave you?"

"Aye. 'Tis for the best." She spoke the truth, for she knew now what lengths Black Micheil Gunn would go to to have her at his mercy.

"I cannot do that."

Surrounded by the warmth of his hard body, Seana
felt the fear holding her in its grip increase. Dare she
trust him? He would surely have more questions if she
stayed with him. But what real choice was there for her
now?

"Then take me from this place," she told him.

Micheil urged Breac away from the wood and back
toward the small valley where he had rested. He knew
that to continue questioning her while she was drained
of resistance was the best course for him to follow.
Glancing down at her bent head, he warned himself
not to be deceived by her fragile appearance.

"Did ye lie to me when you claimed to be the Gunn
chieftain's promised bride?"

Seana curled the fingers of one hand around her
injured wrist and shook her head. "'Twas no lie."

"You've run from him?"

Seana longed to crawl away and lick her wounds,
not fight the battle his questions posed. How could she
begin to explain her plight? How could she involve a
stranger and risk his life? *But he does not know that
his life could be forfeit. You owe it to him to tell him.*

"I do not know how you found me," she began,
wincing with every jar of the trotting horse. "Nor why
you chose to help me. I give thanks for your—"

"Be glad I did. Thank me by telling me what you
are called. Then I'd be having the answers I asked
for." The more Micheil reined in his temper, the farther he slipped back into the thick brogue of his
childhood.

"Seana nic— Just Seana," she answered after a
moment's hesitation. She looked at the large, well-

formed hands before her, seeing their strength. Yet, unbid, came the gentle feel of them touching her face.

To distract him, she asked, "Do you believe me?"

"I'll not deny that someone's after ye. But look at yourself, Seana. A bride for the Gunn chief? You'd ask much of a man to believe that." The telltale shiver he felt from her slender body brought a grim satisfaction that was gone in the next instant. She still did not know who he was.

"You've not asked my name."

Seana raised her head and saw where he was heading. She was too weary to care what might wait for her there. The sheltering valley they entered offered her respite. Later she would slip away.

"'Tis a wild tale I've asked you to believe, but true. And if you're set on giving me your name, do so."

It irked him that she cared not a wit. Temptation loomed in a mighty force to tell her exactly who he was. That would rouse her quick enough.

Micheil bent his head to whisper in the dainty curve of her ear. "Jamie. Ye can call me that for now."

He pulled back sharply. The name was a common one among the highlanders, that was true, but that did not explain why he had used his brother's name. Admitting to himself that the reasons were twisted tight in a web he had no intent of attempting to sort out now, Micheil let the lie be. His desire for Seana was unabated. If anything, it had grown stronger. Perhaps the blame for the lie rested with the heat of his blood.

She did not acknowledge his name, or the safe place he found for them, in the next hours. She tended to her

foot, only allowing him to use a piece cut from his shirt to bind the injury. Soaking her wrist in the icy waters had helped the swelling.

Her silence bothered him. Even when he managed to snare a plump hare for their supper, she ate only because he forced her to.

With the long shadows of night cast into the valley, Micheil doused the small fire he had made for cooking. Although he caught a wistful look on Seana's face, she offered no protest, and yet he found himself explaining why.

"Even a sheltered fire this small would be a beacon, if there are others lurking about. You can share my plaid with me, since you have none of your own."

The night's deepening chill had nothing to do with the shudder that ran over Seana. "Why are you doing this? You risk your life to help me."

She could not look at him, but she sensed his immediate attention as he mulled over her words. When the silence and the tension became too much to bear, she raised her head and stared at him.

"Why?" she asked again.

"I told you. You bewitched me from the moment I saw you." Micheil rose and shook out the plaid. "Come, it's time to sleep, if we're to be away before first light. I'll admit I will not rest easy until we're away from here."

Seana eyed the soft wool he held, and thought again of the kisses they had shared. Far off in the darkness, a vixen and her cubs screamed. What choice had she but to do as he asked? Weakened from her wound and her flight, how could she hope to escape him tonight?

Patient, simply because he knew she had no other choice, Micheil waited for her to come to him. He placed the blanket on the ground, helping her to lie upon it, then wrapped it around her. With his back to her, he settled himself close until he heard her breathing grow even. Then he turned and drew her into his arms, trusting Breac to warn him of any approaching danger.

With a soft murmur, Seana nestled her head against the warmth that pillowed her. Micheil entwined his fingers in her hair, the measure one of possessiveness, security and need. Resigned to subdue the desire flaring in his loins, he closed his eyes to sleep.

Sliding with the silent menace of a wolf creeping up on a newborn spring lamb, the nightmare came without warning to Seana.

She fought to escape. Her hands clawed at something that held her, trapping her. She could not draw breath, for the weight seemed to crush her chest, and she cried out in a keening moan.

There were faces. Shouts and screams. One stood out from all the others, a woman's, her expression terrified, her scream a wail of despair. Arms reached out to Seana, arms she wanted to reach, for these arms would snatch her back from whatever held her.

Panting now, she heard her own cries echoing in her ears. Her hands clenched around something hard and warm. The face was fading. All the faces were gone. She was alone and frightened. No one heard her cries.

She tossed her head, tears slipping from beneath her closed lids. Hope was gone. She would never be free.

Seana calmed beneath the soft, husky murmurs whispered in her ear. The warmth surrounding her chased the chill from her body, and the scents of horse and leather, of wine and man, comforted her, allowing her to rest more easily now that the nightmare had passed.

She stirred with a sigh as Micheil sipped the salt of her tears from her cheeks before tucking her head in the curve of his shoulder. Only Micheil found that sleep again eluded him. He retained the haunting echo of Seana's voice crying out for her mother. Guilt assaulted him. He had not been with the raiding party that had taken her from her parents that long-ago day. And here, with none to witness his weakness to his clan's enemy, he held her safe through the night.

Deep in the shadowed recess of the arched stone protecting the postern gate of the abbey, a heavily cloaked figure was alerted by a poor intimation of the call of a curlew. As the wiry, short figure crept closer, a smile of anticipation was hidden by the thick folds of the hood.

"Be ye there?" Borve called out, peering hard with his failing eyesight for a sign that someone awaited his message. He had been promised five silver pennies, and had walked all night to earn it. The Lady Ailis fed him well, but he earned his own coin for drink by making himself agreeable to the abbey's wealthy guests. The gentle clink of coins came in answer, and eagerly Borve stepped closer.

"I'll have me coin," he insisted, holding out his palm.

"'Tis done?"

Borve cocked his ear, but the voice was so muffled by cloth he could not tell if it was a man or woman who asked. He was not about to risk losing his coins by telling the truth. Nor would he lie, lest he was held accountable.

"Aye, they found her."

One by one the silver pennies dropped into his outstretched hand. Before he could doff his cap in thanks, the gate opened and the figure was gone.

With a shrug, he set off, clutching his reward, just as the last faint starshine was stolen by the coming day.

Micheil shared the last of his hard bread and cheese with Seana to break their fast. He had not thought it would take more than a day to find her, and he cursed himself soundly for having no other foodstuff with him. He had washed and dressed the wound to her foot himself, thankful that there was no odor of rotting flesh, and that the swelling had come down.

He could not shake from his mind the moment when Seana had awoken, her gray eyes soft with sleep, but darkening the moment they focused on his face. His steady regard had made her turn away. Micheil wondered if Seana had expected to find him gone.

To give her privacy, he drew Breac away from the low-growing bushes to saddle him, knowing that she could not walk far on her injured foot. It amused him that she made a show of settling the small jeweled dagger in her ragged cloth belt, as if that were all the protection she would need from him. But it annoyed him that she retained a thoughtful look as he lifted her

up onto Breac's back. She trembled slightly beneath his hands, and his gaze fell to her mouth as he remembered the sweetness of the kisses he had stolen.

"'Tis a good omen to begin the day with a kiss, lass."

"Prayer will serve as a better one."

Instinct told him he could coax a kiss from her, but when he met her gaze, he found her eyes filled with secrets that he wanted to discover. He gathered the reins and was ready to mount when Seana stopped him.

"Wait. Before I'll ride with you, I beg you to listen. I cannot live with another innocent death on my soul." She spoke softly, but with the force of her need to make him understand the danger. "You will be accused of taking me from my prison at the abbey, and have the clan Gunn after you."

"I'm afraid of no man, least of all Dhu Micheil." He vaulted smoothly onto Breac, filled with tension as his body surrounded her smaller one. "And he'll have to catch me first."

Fear formed her answer. "Then pray he never does."

Unwilling to hear more, Micheil gathered the reins. "When we're away from here, I'll listen to the whole of your tale."

"And you'll be telling me the truth of what you do, who you are?" Seana was filled with strange sensations as she tried not to press against him. She squirmed, and then leaned forward.

"Cease your wiggling! You'll upset the beastie."

Seana tilted her head and looked up at his scowling face. "We cannot ride this way—"

"'Tis the only way." Micheil gritted his teeth. "If I can manage, you'll make do, as well."

Seana flushed and stared straight ahead as he urged the horse toward the mouth of the valley. She wondered which beastie it was that her moving about upset, for his body was as rigid as the wooden kneeling benches in the chapel. At first, when he kept Breac to a walk, it was easy to hold her body away from his, but once clear, he set a hard pace, and to keep her seat she had to fit her body to the curve of his.

Micheil rode hard, with the hope that the wind would cool the fire in his blood. He kept well away from the villages clustered near the coast, seeking less-used tracks. These were Buchan lands they rode through, and while he had naught to fear from being discovered, he wanted no one to give him away to Seana.

The sun rose, and its unfurled warmth filled the air with the fragrant scent of wild thyme. He resisted his desire to brush his lips against Seana's hair, as she dozed against him, only to rouse and once more attempt to maintain a small distance between their bodies. Each time she did so, she looked up at him, and Micheil found himself hard put to look straight above her head.

Seana kept asking herself how she could place her trust in him. She did not know the lands they rode through, as every minute of hard riding took her farther away from the abbey. Her gaze strayed to his hands, firm and strong on the reins. Small scars were

visible, but offered her no clue as to who he was. She thought of the way he had touched her at the fair, and the pleasure of his kisses. He would demand a high price for helping her. There was no doubt in her mind about that. She dreaded the moment she would be forced to make a decision, for she truly did not know what she would do.

Her stomach growled, and she pressed one hand against it to still the sounds. Moments later, when it was repeated and Micheil's rumbled in unison, Seana laughed.

"We are a poor pair of travelers to set off without food."

"Fear not, lass, I'm resourceful, if naught else. I'd be a poor sort not to provide an ease to your hunger."

"Brave words," Seana began, tilting her head to one side to look up at him. Her smile faded, as did his. The desire in his eyes bespoke another hunger of the flesh. Her breath was shallow now. Warmth unfurled inside her as her gaze settled on his mouth, so close to her own. She could not look away. Seana wanted him to close the small distance between them. She wanted him to kiss her again. The thought shocked her. She sensed a hidden power to this man who held her life within his hands, and with the thought came a warning of the danger he represented.

Micheil lowered his head, drawn by the longing reflected in her eyes, a longing he was sure she was unaware of. He had tasted the innocence of her kiss. Hunger rose in him to teach her a man's passion.

Breac tossed his head with a snort, and Micheil drew back. A thin silver ribbon of water sparkled in the sunlight, and it was toward this that he headed now.

"We'll have water, to start," he said. He thought of Pluscarden Abbey, across the river Spey, and the welcome he would find there. But he could not risk taking Seana with him. Leaving her alone to wait was even more of a risk, for he did not trust her.

Seana's cry of delight momentarily ended his problem.

"There's newly ripened cranberries by the burn!"

"A feast for sure, lass."

She ignored his sour note, leaning forward as Breac picked his way over the rocky ground. Her foot throbbed, and she could barely wait to bathe it in the cool water.

The moment he stopped, Seana wiggled down, wincing as she put weight on her injured foot. Limping toward the small stream, she plucked a few of the ripe berries and munched upon them. Once she was seated, she turned back to find that he was standing watching her.

"The berries are tart, but you can pretend they are sweetened with honey. I have done so many a time at the abbey."

"Was the food such poor fare that you needed to?" Micheil asked, joining her on the bank.

"The table in my father's hall was a rich feast at every meal. There were none to compare to the table my mother set." Her eyes clouded over at the memory of her brother's wedding feast, but as quickly as it came, she dismissed the memory.

Micheil moved to hold her long hair back as she bent over to drink the water she had scooped up in her hands. His thumb rested on her bare nape, and he felt the slight tremor his touch caused. Her skin had the color and softness of the delicate inner petals of sweet eglantine. He could not resist the urge to brush a kiss across her bare skin. Leaning back, Micheil held her startled gaze for a moment before he smiled with satisfaction.

"My thirst, lass, needed as much quenching as yours."

The husky timbre of his voice sent a flood of strange sensations curling through Seana's body. She could not answer him. She licked her lips to catch a stray drop of water, unsettled to find that he watched so closely. Thinking only to distract him, she dipped her cupped hands into the water again, holding them up for him to drink.

Micheil tightened his hold on her hair. He was afraid she would bolt and run. He knew she felt the flaring desire between them. It was there in her eyes, but tainted with fear. He lowered his head to sip from her hands, seeing how rapid her breathing was becoming. This, too, added to his satisfaction.

Her hands had not the smooth perfection of a lady's, but he wanted them on his skin. He had tasted wine from lips eager for his kisses, but the cool, sweet water, offered with such seductive innocence, was a far headier brew. He licked the stray drops of water from her palm, and felt the violent trembling this caused her.

Pressing a kiss to her palm's center, he whispered, "My thanks, Seana, for offering so sweet a vessel."

She placed her hand against his broad chest, feeling the thudding beat of his heart, the warmth of his body. "Cease, I pray you. I know not what it is you do to me."

"Then, Seana, I shall endeavor to tutor you." His gaze dropped to the reddened shape of her lips, and Micheil knew a hunger so fierce that his muscles tightened in reaction. He wanted to take her mouth with his, to taste again the unawakened passion of her kiss, and teach her to answer a man's need. His need, and his alone. The rapid rise and fall of her breasts beneath her coarse gown drew both his gaze and his hand. He had to fight against the desire to bring her beneath him and have her yield to him.

"Seana—"

"Nay," she pleaded. The emotions seething within her were too strong, too frightening, and she scrambled away from him.

"Do you want me to kiss you, Seana?" he asked, very softly, his gaze relentless as it targeted hers.

"I want no man. If this is the price you demand to help me return home, be plain and speak it. But I tell you now, I will not pay it."

Micheil let her go. Regret laced his voice. "I'll not demand your body as a price to help you. Stay and bathe your foot." He rose to his full height and looked down at her. "I will gather enough berries to assuage your hunger."

"And your own," she reminded him.

Micheil threw back his head and laughed. "Ah, lass, you've the makings of a temptress. Ripe the berries may be, but they're not the sweet fruit to ease a man's hunger."

Seana believed him. She kept his warning in mind as they rode off and the afternoon wore on. There was no choice but to leave him while he slept this night. Her fingertips touched the handle of her small dagger, the movement assuring her. Seana had little to call her own. Once she was home, she knew, her brother would seek to marry her off to add another clan's strength to aid his fight against the Gunns.

Her virtue was all she had to bring to her marriage. It was not for the likes of the man who called himself Jamie, no matter the quickening beat of her heart at his ever-present nearness.

She was thankful that he had avoided riding close to any of the small crofts they passed. Dusk was closing in, and hunger once more making itself felt.

"Will you be thinking to stop soon?" she asked.

"Aye. Once I've found a low spot to cross the river Spey. The spring rains have swollen the river and I'll not risk being swept downstream."

The river Spey, Seana repeated to herself. Then the abbey at Pluscarden was not far. Now she had a sense of where they were. She would have to round the Moray Firth before she could strike out toward the north and home. Filled with longing to see the places she had roamed as a child, Seana fought to keep memories at bay. She was being lulled by the horse's even gait as he was held to a steady pace in the fading light.

Micheil had not missed her quickened interest when he told her where they were. His prize had thoughts of escape, of that he had no doubts.

But Seana nic MacKay belonged to him. And what Micheil claimed, he held.

# Chapter Eight

The wind rose, and with it came a damp mist off the sea. Micheil veered away from a small cluster of trees that would have served as shelter and rode for the open moor.

Seana fought off sleep. She felt her body ease against him and jerked herself forward. She despaired of his ever stopping. The mist kept her vision limited to the land immediately around them, and without landmarks, she had no way of knowing how far inland he was riding. She was hungry and cold, and her eyes refused to stay open.

"Rest yourself, Seana," Micheil leaned close to whisper. "You're safe with me."

With turbulent feelings still stirring inside her, Seana could have argued that, but she let it be.

It was with shock that minutes later she felt herself lowered to the ground.

"Wait here for me. I'll bring back food."

"Wait?" Seana repeated. She shook her head, uncertain she understood him. "There's naught here."

"Aye. That's the point of it, Seana. There's nowhere to run."

"I'll not wait!" she cried out as he rode away. For a few minutes she heard the thundering vibrations of Breac's powerful hooves striking the earth, and then there was silence.

How had he known what she planned? The fading light and creeping mist sent shivers up and down her spine. She could not see more than a few feet in front of her. No matter what the man believed, she would take advantage of this chance to escape him.

Gathering her courage, Seana turned and started back the way she thought they had ridden. Her steps were slow and cautious, walking barefoot on the rocky ground allowing for nothing else. The chill, damp wind had her shaking within minutes, but even that would not deter her.

No longer was her only reason fear that the Gunns would take her back and cost this man his life. She was afraid of her own unruly reaction to him. She could not deny that there was something strange about this Jamie. If she could even believe it was his name. The doubt came from his boldness in riding where he would, without thought.

Clouds scudded across the feeble rising moon, obscuring what little light she had to guide her. The scent of the sea grew stronger, as did the wind, and Seana forced away tales, oft told, of nights such as this when the witches and ghosts rode the moors.

She tried to think of childhood memories, of places where she had played, of those she longed to see again. The thought that she had been foolish to leave the only safety she knew to strike out on her own rose and stayed within her mind.

From far off came a wild howling, and the marrow of her bones chilled with thoughts of mountain cats, wolves and other beasties that roamed the night. Fanciful tales to frighten a bairn, she knew, but being alone in the mist-shrouded night allowed her to recall them.

But you are free, she reminded herself. Touching the dagger at her waist brought a little comfort. Hunger and thirst made themselves known as she forced herself to keep walking.

Her throat was parched. Her stomach rumbled. Now she knew herself for a fool. She kept thinking of Jamie's promise to bring back food. Even the tart cranberries would be a feast now.

Seana stopped and listened. No sound of rushing water. Nothing but the wind could be heard. She looked back and saw nothing behind her. The mist had covered the land, just as the darkness did. Rubbing her arms against the cold, she forced herself to go on.

At first she thought it was a trick of the wind that sounded like her name. She was faint with exhaustion, and denied it. But moments later she heard it again and knew that Jamie called to her.

She was torn about answering him. She understood the danger she faced alone, but he presented an unknown danger that she did not seem to have a defense against. Once more, she stopped to listen, but his voice sounded no closer.

The scent of wild marjoram brought a slight quickening to her steps. The herb grew close to water. Or was it the wild thyme that did? Confused, Seana

sniffed the air and listened, hoping to hear rushing water to guide her.

A low, vicious growl sent the hairs on her neck up on end. It was close. Much too close for her to run. Her breath caught somewhere inside her. She was too afraid to release it, lest the beast hear her.

*Jamie! Jamie, come find me, quickly!* She repeated the silent cry over and over, not daring to move, for she could not tell from where the growling came.

Drawing her dagger, Seana tried to brace herself against an attack. The growling filled her ears until it was all she could hear.

There was a foul smell of wet, matted fur. Seana bit her lip until she tasted blood. She locked the fingers of her injured wrist around the one that held the dagger to lessen her shaking grip.

Death was near, and she too frightened even to pray.

"Move back slowly, Seana. I'm behind you."

"J-Jamie?"

"Aye. Do as I say. The beast is ready to spring for your throat, lass. Move."

It was the calm in his voice that freed Seana from the fear that held her still. This was not the time to question how he had found her, but only to do as he had ordered.

"I cannot see it," she whispered, taking a step back. She almost cried out to feel his hand on her arm, jerking her behind him. Pain lanced her leg. She stumbled to one knee, barely making out the bulk of Jamie's body. It was all she had time to see, for the beast lunged at him.

Like her brother when he hunted wild boar, Jamie was down on one knee, his sword braced, its tip piercing the wolf's chest. Seana closed her eyes, clasping her hands to her ears to shut out the sounds of death.

Micheil had to plunge his dagger into the wolf's throat before he was able to throw off the body and free his sword. He whistled for Breac, knowing that Seana could not run, and knowing, too, that a pack waited, so he could not carry her.

Seana screamed, feeling an animal's warm breath on her skin.

Micheil wasted no time soothing her. He lifted her up and tossed her on Breac's back, vaulting into the saddle behind her. He dared not give free rein to his anger over the way she had put them at risk, and forced him now to give Breac his head to outrun the wolves howling close to them.

Moments were all they had to make good an escape while the others sniffed at the dead one.

But Micheil had bred his horse from a mare taken from the Moors in the Holy Land. Breac's speed and stamina were legendary, and Micheil demanded them now.

He knew the danger he placed both the horse and themselves in with this headlong flight. At any second, Breac could stumble and break a leg. Fury rose and nearly escaped him that Seana had caused this. The little compassion he had felt when he found her gone disappeared with the growing heat of his anger.

A heat that had not abated when they were safely away and he drew Breac down to a walk.

Seana could feel rage coming from him. "You've a right to be furious with me," she offered, trying to make her voice steady. She waited, and when there was no response forthcoming, she tried again. "'Tis sorry I am—"

"If you value your pretty neck, silence would be most blessed."

Seana could not heed his warning. "Being a man, you did not understand why I had to leave you."

"Being a man? What does my being male have to do with the dim-witted attempt to run?"

"I'm afraid of you," she blurted out.

"And you've good reason," he bent close to whisper to her. "After your fool's escape that nearly got you killed and risks my horse even now, you'll be needing faerie magic to protect you."

He was still shaken at how close he had come to losing her. It was high time she knew who she dealt with.

"Jamie..." she said, very softly, placing her hand over his. "Truly, I am sorry. I cannot tell you all my fears. Believe they are real to me. I did not want to risk your life, or that of your horse. I did not want to lose my own. I seek only to return to my home, free of the accursed Gunns."

"Do you know this Micheil so well that you hate—"

"It does not matter if I know him. I know what he's done. For me, it is enough. My fate at his hands will be my death. Can you understand that?" Seana looked up at him, but his features were hidden in darkness. "Where do we go now?"

"Off the moor" was all he would answer.

"Thank you for saving my life. 'Tis most grateful I am. I wish I had more than thanks to give you."

"For now, your silence would be one payment."

Rebuffed, Seana complied with his wishes. But lurking in the back of her mind was what other payment he would ask of her.

For all Seana knew, he might have been riding in circles. She could no longer smell the sea, and the scent of wild herbs was stronger. Pitifully small clues to where he was taking her. She was not as chilled now, surrounded by the warmth of his body, yet questions nagged at her until she forced herself to speak.

"Did you find food?"

"I did, but it will be cold by the time we eat. I found news, too. You've been discovered missing, and word has been sent out to watch for you."

It was no more than she had expected to hear, yet knowing pierced her with despair. How would she ever reach home?

"The Gunn chief must value you highly, Seana, for he's put a golden price on your head."

"Are you tempted to claim it?" she asked him, unable to hide the bitterness she felt.

He was silent so long, Seana wondered if he had not heard her. Either that, or he was considering it. Her teeth began to chatter from the cold and the shock of knowing her freedom could end at any moment.

"Answer me," she demanded. "'Tis a torment not to know if you'll claim the price he set."

"I've not made up my mind." Micheil rode into a clearing where one wall of a crofter's cottage still

stood. He was still pondering who had set a price on Seana's head. It was not something that his brothers would likely take upon themselves. His aunt would not dare—but Bridget, discovering Seana gone, might have done it.

He dismounted and lifted Seana down, then handed her a sack. "'Tis a cold feast, but a welcome one. The old hag had little enough, but she lightened my purse for the meal. I have a skin of wine, too."

Micheil tied Breac to a low-hanging tree limb, and gathered kindling for a fire. Seana remained standing, clutching the small sack to her chest. He stripped the bark from dried twigs, striking flint against steel until a spark caught. Blowing gently, he fed his small fire, satisfied when it blazed.

"Come and sit, Seana."

The flames cast shadows on his rugged features as he spread his plaid close to the wall. Perhaps for now her fate remained tied to this man, but Seana could not shake off a sense of foreboding. Once more she was struck by the ease of his explanation of having acquired food and news.

Hunger drove her to join him.

She accepted the wineskin, but did not drink deeply, even to quench her thirst. The lady Ailis had allowed no wine at her table but for her guests. Seana remembered how too much could alter behavior. She needed sharp wits to discover the truth behind his tale.

From the sack he pulled out a loaf of bread, freshly baked, by the feel of it. Seana took the piece he tore off and bit into it greedily.

"Wait, there's more," he cautioned, handing over the still-warm breast of a grouse, while taking the leg and thigh for himself. "I've cheese, too," he said, dipping into the sack once again.

"A wealthy old hag, from the appearance of this meal."

"A healer of sorts who claims she receives payments of food from the villagers she treats."

Seana caught the false note, but said nothing more. She ate and shared the wineskin with him, careful to take tiny sips.

Micheil had no reluctance to partake heartily of the wine. He caught her wary looks, and knew she did not believe him. He could not tell her he had purchased food from the abbey, where he had left word for his brothers. Just as earlier he could not tell Seana who he was once she had voluntarily touched him. His ambiguous feelings about Seana perplexed him. Why should it matter if she came to him willingly? She was his by right. Yet, glancing at her to see such a pensive expression on her lovely face, Micheil kept his silence. Studying her, he recalled that day at the fair, and Seana telling him that she did not know the full tale of what had caused the blood feud between their families. Had she lied to him?

Micheil set another handful of broken branches on the fire. He resettled himself with his back against the wall and his long legs stretched out before him. He said naught about Seana's move to keep a small distance between them and yet remain seated on his blanket.

"You've wanted to tell me the whole of your tale, and now the time is here."

"Why?" she asked. "You've stopped me each time."

"I'm not ready for sleep, and if you've no wish to talk, Seana, I shall find another way to amuse us both to pass the time."

The explicit promise in his voice was echoed by the flames reflected in his eyes. Seana looked away. "What is it you wish to know?"

"A wise choice, but not the most pleasurable one," he remarked, tilting the wineskin for another drink. He did not bother to offer it to her. "Tell me how you come to be hunted by the Gunns."

"Bridget nic Gunn married my brother Liam. None wanted the wedding, but there was no denying these two. To ensure the peace, I was betrothed to the oldest son, Micheil. But Bridget demanded too much of my brother's attention, and they fought a great deal."

Picking at the folds in the blanket, Seana stared at the fire, trying to recall the exact events of that long-ago night that had changed her life.

"Are you thinking of twisting the tale before you tell me more?"

"I'm trying to remember. Bairns are not told—"

"But have a way of finding out everything that goes on," Micheil interrupted to say.

"A little, that much is true. Bridget was moody, ofttimes taking long walks alone, but returning the happier for them. Liam was away from Tongue, where our keep stood, meeting with the lord of the North Isle

about our trading. It was Bridget's serving woman who told my mother that Bridget was with child.''

"*With child?*" Micheil could barely speak, so great was his rage at her lie. There had been no child. That was the reason Bridget had been beaten. An inner voice cautioned him to wait and hear Seana out. He drank deeply of the wine to rid himself of the bitter taste in his mouth.

''You appeared surprised that she would be with child,'' Seana said, glancing at him with a puzzled expression. "'Tis a common enough happening after marriage.''

Micheil lowered the skin. ''Are you designing to tell me what passes between a man and a woman?''

There was challenge in his gaze, and more in his tone. Seana shook her head. ''I told you I had kissed no man. I know little of the marriage bed.''

''Finish your tale,'' Micheil ordered, somewhat mollified by her answer.

''When my mother asked Bridget if it was true, she denied it. The next day, she was discovered missing. My family searched for her, afraid that she had been hurt on her walk, but none could find her. Liam returned that evening, furious when he was told what passed. He ordered more men out to look for her, but time and again they returned to the keep claiming none had seen her.''

Seana lowered her head and rubbed the bridge of her nose as a throbbing began. This was so painful to recall, and harder to tell a stranger, for she knew so little of what had happened.

"That's your tale? Surely there's more. How came you to be at the abbey for so long?"

"The Gunns," Seana answered, very softly, "declared a blood feud. That is when we learned that Bridget had returned to them. I was taken a few weeks later from my mother's arms and sent to the abbey."

Micheil would have had to be carved from stone not to be moved by the despair in her voice. He beat back the rush of compassion for Seana that rose, thinking again of the night his sister had returned to their home.

Seana had drawn away from him, closer to the fire, huddled with her arms wrapped around her raised knees. He knew he should let it be, for it was dangerous to probe for more from her. Emotions seething so close to the surface could give him away.

Yet the need to know had him moving up behind her, and he cupped her chin to raise her face. "There's more you're not telling me."

She lifted eyes filled with the sheen of tears to him. Her inhaled breath took in the male scent of him. He sat with his back to the fire, his left hip pressed against her right one, so close that his features were hazy from the tears she fought to hold back.

"Aye. There's more. But I'm of no mind to tell you. 'Tis painful for me to talk of being denied a prayer over my mother's bier, or the deaths that I learned of as the years passed. I've been told nothing of my brother's fate but that he lives."

"Seana—"

"You'll hear it all. The nights I cried myself to sleep, alone and afraid of what would happen. The worst to

bear was being denied my freedom. I'm not daft or dim-witted, I'm desperate to go home where I belong. Where I'll be safe from him."

Micheil's fingers slid beneath her hair to draw her closer. "Seana," he breathed over her lips, "were it in my power to give you what you ask, I—"

"Make no promise."

"As you wish, lass. But let me take the loneliness from you. Let me . . . Ah, Seana, words won't do."

She kissed him, for to deny herself would be to deny the comfort she yearned for. He gathered her closer, lifting and turning her so that she lay across his lap, his lips offering as gentle a wooing as any maid ever had.

His arms were strong around her. His hand, stroking the back of her bare neck, spread a warming glow inside her. The repeated gentle brush of his lips, coaxing her into another kiss, then another, was as heady as the little wine she had had.

She was shaken by the tender feelings he aroused in her. The light score of his teeth across her bottom lip brought a soft moan from her. But Seana could not turn away. She had been alone for so long, and telling him of her past had left her defenseless against his beguiling kisses.

His brogue was thick as his husky, passion-laden voice whispered his desire that she yield to him. Seana cradled his beard-rough cheek, blindly seeking his lips. She knew this was wrong, but the desire he had aroused in her from the first sent need flooding through her.

"Jamie. Jamie, please . . ."

"Aye, lass, aye. I'll please you and myself." He had to silence her cry, for he wanted his own name sighing from her lips. With rough passion, he took her mouth, his tongue delving to find the sweet honey taste of her that he craved.

Seana grabbed hold of his shirt. His every touch was like the sear of fire over her skin. She cried out to feel the heated firmness of his lips slide down her bare throat. Trembling, fevered, she was unable to find the strength to push him away. Tantalizing kisses were strung like a necklace around her throat. She curved her body to the taut fit of his as his tongue teased the pulse there until she felt the heating of her blood.

It was dizzying, frightening, and she was drowning beneath a wealth of sensations she could not have named. No one had told her that desire could raise such fierce need that she would not care if he knew it. He caught her arms and raised them up around his neck. Seana felt his palms slide down her side, pressing her against his broad chest. He traced the curve of her waist, the flare of her hip, only to return to enfold her breast. She froze.

"Ease your mind, Seana. I'll not hurt you," he whispered into her mouth.

"But it does hurt," she answered, hiding her flaming cheeks against his chest. "I cannot do this. If any should find out—"

"Lass, where's your reason? There's none here to see us. I'm on fire for you. I've wanted you from the moment I saw you."

"'Tis lust you feel. I cannot give myself to any man without marriage." Seana struggled to get free of his arms, but he held her tight.

"But you're mine."

Slowly she lifted her head and looked at him. The fire burnished his ruggedly handsome features. Within his eyes was another fire, one of passion that burned hot.

"You're willing to marry me?"

"Och, lass, that's a fool question to be asking a man when his blood runs hot and his loins ache with need." Micheil sought to kiss her lips, but she turned away, and his kiss landed on her head. "Seana, listen. Was I too rough? You cannot lie and say my kisses did not excite you."

"I'll not lie," she whispered, too aware of his fiercely aroused flesh pressed against her hip.

"Then, saints to heaven, woman, what's all this bletherin'?"

"Like all Scots, you've a fierce temper." Seana's shove caught him by surprise, and she found herself free. Scooting backward, thankful that the desire within her was cooling, Seana raised her hand in a pleading gesture. "By the scowl you wear, you prove my point. But your temper is naught to compare to the Gunn chief's. Think, Jamie. Think of what he'd be doing to you, and to me, if he found us out."

*"What he'd do?"* Micheil repeated, realizing what a tangle he had made for himself. How the devil could he punish himself for claiming his own betrothed? The lie had gone far enough.

He rose to stand above her, and Seana lost her breath. Here was the warrior, fierce in his glory. His muscled legs were spread, his hands rested on narrow hips, and his features bore the stamp of an arrogant lord. She had no idea of what he intended, but she scampered back until she was against the wall.

"Do you know who I am, Seana?"

# Chapter Nine

"Aye. You're Jamie. The man who twice now saved my life. A man who, were I free, I would think to give my heart to."

Micheil stared at her. With those simple words she had diffused his anger. The flames turned her tangled hair to a rich molten gold. He saw not the coarse gown, but the pride in her bearing. Steady and direct, her eyes rose to meet his. Truth shone there, as it had in her voice. Her lips, pouty and reddened from his kisses, drew his gaze for a moment before he turned his back on her.

*Tell her! She is your enemy!*

She will cringe and scream and try to escape again. If he held his silence, she would willingly stay with him. They were still days from home, and he'd be a fool to risk finding a dagger in his ribs one night. Glancing back at Seana, to see that she had not moved and still watched him, Micheil raked back his hair, once more staring out at the night. Her nearness disturbed him, for passionate need still ran hot within him. It was a fool's thought that rose and stayed. He was jealous of her caring for Jamie, when she would

plunge a dagger through Micheil's heart. At an extreme, he amended, for he had seen her face when she viewed those dead men.

Seana had no liking for violence. And he lived by it.

"Stay close to the fire," he ordered.

"Where are you going?" she called to his retreating back. The darkness swallowed him up in seconds. What had she said?

Seana repeated her own words, then squeezed her eyes shut when she realized her folly. How could she have told him that he would have her heart if she was free? The man was not looking to claim her love, only her body. A lesson learned, and one she would not forget.

She grew drowsy watching the flames, and settled herself on the plaid with her back against the wall, leaving room for him when he returned.

That he would come back, she had no doubt. Not that she placed so high a value on herself. He had left Breac, and Jamie would not leave his horse. It was her last thought before sleep claimed her.

From the shadows beyond the dying fire, Micheil watched and waited until he was sure that sleep had laid full claim to Seana. It was only then that he sought his own rest at her side.

The abbey was silent as the hours crept toward dawn. The Lady Ailis rose from her prayer bench with a weary sigh. She let her hand fall from the heavy gold cross she wore, for once finding no comfort in its weight.

She was deeply disturbed by the news of three bodies being discovered, but more frightening was the rage exhibited by her niece and Fiona. The wickedness they had planned had been foiled by Seana's escape.

The hope that had flared upon Bridget's arrival that she had finally taken up Ailis's offer to spend her days here in the peace of the abbey, had quickly died. Time and again, she had sent messages begging her niece to come to her, to forget the hate that ate at her soul. But Bridget, obsessed with revenge, would hear naught of it.

For the first time, Ailis wondered if her prayers had any meaning. She could not deter Micheil from fulfilling his blood oath to his father, an oath that never should have been asked of him.

How could her prayers be answered? she asked herself. They were scattered like the leaves blown free from the trees.

She prayed daily for Micheil to cease his violent warring against the MacKays. If his mother had lived, she might have tempered the molding of her son. But she was dead these seven years past and with her had gone any chance for peace.

Her fierce warrior nephew needed a wife, love and bairns to fill his life. Micheil had always been the builder, not the destroyer. But he would do as he was bid, spurred by his love for his father and clan. And Bridget. Ailis could not forget how all three brothers loved their once-bonny sister. None would know true joy while Bridget demanded more and more vengeance be visited upon the MacKays. It was the Lord's work that there were any left alive.

Bridget's viciousness—spurred on by Fiona, Ailis realized for the first time—left no hope that Bridget would ever have peace for her spirit.

Ailis feared that her niece was near-mad. She had shunned the world and its evils, but there was no escape, not even within the abbey walls.

And Seana, she thought, how fared that sweet, innocent maid? Ailis offered prayers for her, too, that Seana had made good her escape. Quandary faced her wherever she turned. If those prayers were answered, Ailis knew, they would bring more bloodshed to her clan. Once Liam had his sister safe, he would no longer be fearful of striking back at the Gunns.

And Micheil would not let Seana go until he had claimed her.

Once more Ailis returned to her prayer bench, feeling an ache within her. She folded her hands together, and bowed her head.

"Truly, my Lord, you have set those I love most upon dangerous paths. I pray only that you guide each of them to choose that which brings joy to the heart. I know not where you intend it all to end. I pray you give strength to Seana, of them all, she is the one most in need of your protection."

Seana woke to a tumble of emotions, held still by the strange dreams she had had. But the more she struggled to recall them, the more they faded from her mind. In those few moments, as sweet birds' trills filled the air, she thought of last night.

It was her last glimpse of Jamie that first came to mind. Jamie standing tall, reminding her of her own

warnings that he was dangerous. *Do you know who I am?* she repeated silently. He had never told her. She had never asked. The way she had answered as she had unsettled her now. Why had she told him she could love him if she was free?

It was the unnatural circumstances that bound them. He certainly had not welcomed her declaration. If anything, his reaction had been a rejection. Seana, coming fully awake, vowed not to repeat her mistake. She would say nothing more to him.

Finding herself curled against his back, reveling in the warmth of his body, was a strange feeling for her. She kept her eyes closed, listening to his even breathing, taking a great deal of comfort in his strength.

Thoughts plagued her. She had given herself into his keeping with absolute faith that he would keep her safe. But who *was* Jamie? Surely he knew of the feud between her clan and the Gunns. Yet, as Seana remembered telling him what she knew of it, she realized he had not said much. The only time he had revealed disbelief was when she mentioned that Bridget had been with child. He'd found that strange, for some reason.

The hard back pressing against her chest grew taut, and his breathing quickened. Seana withdrew from his warmth, knowing that he was awake.

She felt him turn around, and pretended sleep. His musky scent filled her with each inhaled breath. She was attuned to his slightest movement, and sensed he was looming over her. To feel the gentle touch of his hand brushing her hair from her face nearly made her

give up the pretense of sleep. She did not move. She did not dare.

"Are you awake, Seana?" Micheil asked in a soft, caressing whisper.

Her small intake of breath and fluttering eyelids were his answer. He had not meant to touch her this morn, had decided that he had no choice but to remember who she was and the place she held in his life. His enemy's sister deserved no more gentle treatment from him.

Yet the thought of marring such loveliness appalled him, even with the harsh, silent reminder that Bridget had once been bonny, too. He had never been ruled by his passions. The very fact that he had to exert effort to subdue his feelings for Seana angered him.

Seana could not stand the waiting any longer. She opened her eyes and found herself staring up into his. They were a chilling, darkened blue, like ice-encrusted mountain peaks in the dead of winter. What thoughts made his gaze so cold? The slight flaring of his nostrils drew her look, and she took it as a subtle reminder that her scent was ripe. Silently she told herself that his was not the heated muskiness that had aroused her last eve. His mouth thinned, the upper lip curling into a sneer.

"Somehow I have managed to offend you while I slept," she said softly, carefully trying to edge her body away from his. Micheil's arm snaked out and caught her around her waist. Seana did not bother to protest, for she felt the wall at her side.

*Take her and be done with this madness!* Micheil heard the demand in mind and body. He leaned closer,

hovering above her, the very fine trembling in her body acting as a caress to his.

"Jamie," she whispered, "tell me what I've done to make you look at me so?" Seana was afraid to touch him, but the fear his strange look brought outweighed it. She lifted her hands to his shoulders to hold him off. "There's hate in your eyes as you look at me. Why?"

Holding her fearful, wary gaze, Micheil shook his head. He could not tell her. The words were locked within his throat. He wanted passion to light her eyes again, wanted to know that she would come willingly to him. Before he could stop himself, he lowered his mouth to taste her lips.

"'Tis not hate I'm feeling, Seana. Not hate at all."

Wanting it to be true, for her body was already responding to the light press of his, Seana made no move to push him away. The gentle touches flooded her with the desire he so easily called forth.

"The joining of a man and woman can bring much pleasure, Seana." His tongue teased the curve of her lower lip. "Let me show you. Let me give you pleasure, and take my own."

The husky, beguiling tone of his voice brought the slight parting of her mouth. His tongue grazed the inner surface before he kissed the corners of her lips.

"Jamie...why?"

His hand cupped her cheek as his lips continued their gentle tastings of her eagerly given mouth. "Be soft for me, Seana. And softer still." He plied her with kisses, his hand sliding down to her neck, his thumb working behind her ear in light, small circles. Her

breathing quickened as his kisses became more insistent, the heat of his body seeping well within her. She could feel the swell of her lips meeting his, the fullness of her breasts, aching with hardened nipples.

His teeth tenderly held her bottom lip captive, drawing it within the warmth of his mouth, where his tongue bathed its velvet inner surface. Seana could feel the kiss curling through her body, and her hand rose to cradle his bearded cheek. She could not deny the pleasure he gave her, could not deny the shaking that had taken control of her, nor the ache that made her arch her body upward to be closer yet to his.

The rent in her coarsely woven gown allowed Micheil easy access to the lush fullness of the breasts swelling for his touch. Her fingers slid beneath his hair, as if to hold his mouth to hers, but he trailed his lips down her bared throat to seek the sweetly heated flesh he desired to taste.

"'Tis madness you bring with your kisses," she murmured, unable to find the will to push him away.

"Aye, 'tis a fine madness, Seana," he agreed, then added, "one I'm wanting more of."

Adrift in a wash of fierce sensations too many to separate and name, Seana heard a soft moan from her own lips as his strong, scarred warrior's hand held her breast. She shifted restlessly beneath him—seeking what, she knew not. The only certainty lay with him, that he could ease the fire within her as surely as he caused it.

His mouth closed over the peak of her breast and suckled. Like wine spilling into a goblet, heat spilled into her. Her breath caught in her throat, her will to

resist burned away by the flames that burned in her loins. His tongue rolled in honeyed circles around her nipple, and the cool morning air quivered over her skin.

"Jamie? Jamie, think what you do!" she cried out. "'Tis more than my body you claim! You'll steal my heart, and not be wanting it."

She clutched his head, desperate to save herself, but knowing full well that if he refused to stop, she would allow him to claim her.

Micheil lifted his head. Seana's hands slid down, and came to rest across her breasts. In a voice thick with passion, he asked, "Do you deny I bring you more pleasure than you've known?"

"Nay. I cannot say that lie." She gazed at his taut features, sadness dulling the glow in her eyes. "It would shame me to give myself to you...."

"Shame?" he repeated in an incensed whisper.

Seana turned her head away. "I cannot go home with a belly swollen with your child. Can you be promising me it would not happen?"

"A fine innocent lass you claim to be, and talk of—"

She looked up at him, instinctively knowing that anger was the only defense she had. "Aye! I'm innocent! I've told you before, I'm not dim-witted. Many ladies came to the abbey, some to hide the shame of birthing the child of another man." She pushed at his shoulders, but he was as hard to move as solid rock.

"Do I dare return home and have no virtue left, I'd be useless to my brother. My hope for freedom from the Gunn is to wed with another clan." Tears spilled

from her eyes as she tried to make him understand. "I cannot let him destroy me and my brother. I cannot," she repeated, biting her lip and squeezing her eyes closed.

"And if I claim you mine, Seana, what then?"

"Would you give my brother aid? Can you?"

Moments before he rolled to his side and away from her, Seana felt him withdraw. She ached from the need he had stirred, but willed herself to be strong and fight it. From the first, he had claimed that she had bewitched him, but now she knew it held true for her, as well.

"Jamie, will you forgive me?"

"There's naught to forgive. I told you, I will not take an unwilling woman."

As she glanced at the rigid set of his broad shoulders, the keen loss of his warmth hit her. Then he took her by total surprise.

"So it is to bring aid to your brother that you hold to your virgin state. Here I was thinking it was fear of what the Gunn chief would do to you."

"In part that is true." Despair laced her voice. "I will not risk your life if he finds us together and me no longer chaste. It is beyond my ken why the man wants to hurt me. The man does not know me, yet will not release me from a betrothal our fathers made in good faith. It makes no sense to me, and I've pondered it long. Both fathers are dead, and the Gunn chief has cowed my brother, else I would be free. He's stripped my clan of their wealth with repeated raids.

"Why would a man need more? Has not enough been paid?" Seana turned and braced herself on one

elbow, her touch tentative on his shoulder. "Can you be telling me why he's not satisfied? How can any man put such a high price on his sister's abandoning her marriage? She refused to return to my brother. He did not refuse to have her again."

Will you answer her? Micheil asked himself, feeling his skin burn where her hand rested. Will you tell her that you swore a blood oath—not once, but twice—to your father? Was it for her shame that you did not take her? Or does the desire you have for her cloud your thinking and make you forget who you are?

"Jamie, please." Seana inched closer to him, her hand sliding down his tautly muscled back while she laid her cheek against his shoulder. "You're a man. Can you not tell me what makes the Gunn chief do as he does?"

As his silence continued, Seana felt a fear creeping inside her. A fear so strong that she had to give it voice.

"Can it be that you're knowing him? Is that why you will not answer me?"

Micheil twisted around and held fast to her wrist. "Aye, I know him. Know him as well as any man can claim to know another."

"Sweet Jesu!" She tumbled back as she brought up her free hand to claw at his grip. "Let me go! 'Tis all a lie! Are you sent by the savage devil to do what he—"

"I'm sent by no man," he stated, glaring down into her stricken face. "Cease your struggling, or you'll hurt yourself."

"Tell me the truth," she demanded. Fear unlike any other she had ever known seemed to constrict her chest. Bile rose, and she had to swallow it. "You've betrayed me. Lulling me with your lies, when you planned to deliver me to a black savage who rapes and kills at will till they curse his name throughout the land."

"He's not a murderer. He's only killed his enemies in fair fights, Seana. And he's not raped."

She searched his features, and found them tainted with anger. His eyes were the same chilling blue she had first awakened to see.

"Set me free! If you know so much about him, you're kin to him. Will you still claim to desire me and give me over to a man that wants my death?"

"I cannot do that."

"So I escaped one prison to find myself held in another." Bitterness marked her every word, and her blood cooled until she felt the chill settle into the marrow of her bones. "I beg you, Jamie. Free me."

Micheil released her and rolled away, coming up in a controlled rush to stand towering over her. "We've much ground to cover this day."

Seana felt as if the frost of a winter's morning had sealed itself inside her. There was no compassion, no pity, and certainly no blaze of passion, in his eyes. She rose slowly on shaking legs, knowing she had made a mistake in showing any fear to him. But it was beyond her to hide it now.

"How long do I have before you deliver me to him?"

"I've never said that I'd deliver you to him, Seana."

He strode off toward the wood, and she hurried around the broken wall for a few moments of privacy. Hope flared, a hope she did not dare encourage. Did Jamie claim the Gunn as his clan? What did she have to offer him to see her safely away? Lost in thought, Seana did not hear him return.

"Hiding will not serve you, Seana."

She could see Breac, already saddled, at the edge of the wall. Walking out into the open, she saw that he had already folded his plaid and tied it to the saddle. Seana made no move toward him.

"I'm waiting, and you know I'm not a patient man."

Seana raised her chin and stared at him. "I pray the devil takes your soul for your treachery."

If Micheil's gaze was chilling, his smile was more so. "That cannot be, Seana. The devil already owns my soul. Now come."

She glanced from his outstretched hand to his anger-laden features. The last was an order, brooking no refusal, yet she dared to stand where she was. Her heart pounded furiously against her ribs. The limits of her endurance had been pushed too far.

"I think not." She made a grab for the dagger at her waist. Her hand came away empty. With a sweeping gaze, she searched the ground near where they had lain. She raised her head and glared at him. "My weapon—"

"Abides safe with me. Since it was stolen, it's now taken again," he answered. From his leather purse he removed the jeweled dagger. "Sharp enough to slice a

man's throat." He ran his finger along the flattened blade, careful to keep from touching the edges.

"'Tis a pity I've not thought to slit yours. You've given me reason enough."

"My keeping this will ensure it does not happen. Now, come to me, Seana. The day grows light."

The sun was not yet warm, and the chill earth sent its cold up into the soles of her bare feet. She glanced down at them, panic and despair taking hold. What choice did she have? If she tried to run, he would catch her far too easily. They were riding steadily northward, that much she knew, and biding her time would serve to bring her closer to home.

Micheil stepped forward.

"I'll come," she said. For a moment more, her gaze locked with his passionless blue eyes. Her eyes were filled with defiance, but she gave no outward signs of it as she went to him and allowed him to lift her up on Breac's back. The horse turned his head, his warm breath feathering over her bare leg.

"Mark her scent well, my fine steed. We would not wish to lose her now." Micheil vaulted into the saddle behind her, saying nothing when she pressed forward to avoid touching him.

"Hold tight, Seana," he whispered in her ear, pressing a kiss to the lobe. "I'll not have you fall and injure—"

"I will not fall," she snapped, her seat rigid. "But I will escape you."

Micheil slid one arm around her waist, pulling her tight to him. *Never,* he vowed. *I will never let you go.*

# Chapter Ten

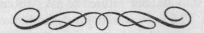

Seana fought to ignore the press of his body and held tight to the high pommel as he set a hard pace through the morning. When hunger gnawed, she thought of betrayal, and beat it back. Nothing would make her ask him to stop.

Moor and forest, burn and cairn, passed by in a blur. She saw with longing the tops of thatched roofs that indicated cottages, but he never stopped. Finally she closed her eyes.

She knew when they crossed a burn, because Breac's mighty hooves kicked up sparkling drops of cool water. Time had no meaning, and she refused to allow any thoughts to surface. She prayed for freedom, and naught else.

It was late afternoon before Micheil stopped to rest. He shared the last of the bread and cheese with her, and only thirst drove Seana to accept a bit of the wine left in the skin.

She said nothing when he finished it and left the skin behind. The carelessness served to remind her that he had a full purse, and stood high in his clan. But was he a Gunn?

The hours stretched with a bone-wearying passage. She saw that he deliberately kept away from the well-traveled roads. Far off in the distance she would catch a glimpse of a cart and know they neared a large village. Only then would Seana turn to look up at him, but the implacable set of his features made hope that he would stop die. She refused to ask, would not beg him again. The Lord would not desert her. A chance would come. She lived for it.

The sun was beginning its descent when Micheil finally broke their strained silence.

"Rest with ease against me, Seana, or you'll jar loose your bones with your stubbornness."

"I'd soon seek comfort with a viper." But the long hours had robbed her voice of heat.

"We'll soon be at the ferry to cross Loch Ness. I'd have your word you'll stir no trouble."

"There's a price on my head, so you say. I've no wish to be placed within that black savage's hands any sooner."

"Your word, Seana."

"Would you trust it?" she asked, curious that he would insist on having it.

"Strangely enough, I would."

She fought against being pleased. "I'll give you my word, Jamie, that I'll cause no trouble."

Micheil drew rein within the hour, bringing forth the blanket to wrap it around Seana. "The less of you seen, the safer we'll be," he gruffly explained.

She could find no trace of caring in his eyes, for the light was fading fast, but she welcomed the warmth of the soft wool surrounding her.

As they approached the ferry landing, a grizzled old man stepped from his small cottage. "You're too late to cross," he called out as they neared.

Micheil dismounted and slid the reins over Breac's massive head to lead the horse. He walked closer, deliberately jingling the coins in his purse.

Seana eyed the rough logged raft, with its single pole railing that bobbed gently against the bank as the currents of the loch flowed by. Her stomach heaved at the thought of crossing the wide expanse of water on so small a raft.

"He'll take us across," Micheil announced, coming to her side to lift her down. "I've told him you're ill."

"Aye, I may well be before this is done."

He threw back his head and laughed. "Are you afraid of water, Seana?"

"Living in the abbey all these years, I would not know."

She was put out with him for laughing at her, and he felt the need to explain. "I was not laughing at your fear. Only your tone. You sounded like a penitent...."

"Aye, that's how I feel. Paying for sins I've not committed."

Micheil's smile disappeared, and he turned to lead the horse forward, ushering her before him. Once he had Breac securely tied, he came to stand behind Seana, wrapping his arms around her, despite the stiffening of her body.

"Close your eyes and I'll hold you. 'Twill be done in minutes, and you safe on earth again."

Thinking of him only as her enemy made doing what he wanted difficult. But Seana would only be spiting herself to deny that having his strength to lean on would help her overcome her fear.

Once she had loved the water, loved swimming in the Kyle of Tongue, where her family's keep stood. But that had been so long ago that, given the chance, she did not know if she could still do it. The loch before her stretched into a shimmering blue that darkened at the far shore. Seana closed her eyes and once more turned to prayer to help her pass the time.

"There's plague near," the ferryman remarked as he plied his long pole to steer them across.

Feeling the man's speculative gaze boring into his back, Micheil strove to keep temper from his voice. "My wife carries no plague." His hand stifled Seana's low cry. "She but longs for her mother's comfort that the illness our first bairn brings will soon pass."

Seana bit the palm of his hand with her need to scream. If he had taken a knife and thrust it into her, he could not have found a more painful way to hurt her. Only the shifting of his body closer to her, so that she felt him molded from shoulder to knee, warned her to cease biting him. But even as she released his flesh from the hold of her teeth, he did not take his hand away.

To the watching man, Micheil knew he appeared to whisper comfort to his wife. But his words were harsh. "I'll remove my hand, but if you utter one sound, I'll have your tongue in payment. If he does not believe me, he'll raise an alarm that you carry the plague. Need I say more?"

He held her so tightly that Seana could barely move her head. She knew they would be run to ground and stoned if any thought they carried the plague. Her release had her sucking in great breaths of the tangy air.

Micheil, to allay any lingering fear, left her for the moment and went to the ferryman's side. "I'd be daft to keep her if she carried the Black Death on her, man. All cats are the same gray in the dark."

"And screech as sweetly," the man agreed.

The raft bumped against the bank, and Micheil hurried to free Breac. He held Seana with one hand and led the horse off the raft.

"Come, love," he said, lifting Seana up. "Our journey's near ended."

"Wean her from her mother's side, man. You'll be the more happier for it."

Micheil acknowledged the advice with a backward look, letting Breac pick his way up the rocky path.

Seana clutched her stomach, feeling a roiling of sickness that she could not contain. Pain lanced through her as she remembered that she would never have her mother's comfort again. She knew the reason for Jamie's cruelty—the man's parting advice told them he had believed Jamie's tale—but the remarks sat ill with her. And what reason could he have for calling her his love?

Gagging, she doubled over.

Micheil drew rein, wasting no time dismounting, but setting Seana down. He was beside her in seconds, holding back the blanket and her tangled hair while she retched.

When the heaving stopped and she trembled with exhaustion, he found a clear space for her to sit. Running back to the bank, he tore off a strip from his shirt and soaked it in the lake. Just as he was about to set off, Micheil caught the scent of wild thyme and found a sprig for her.

Seana remained seated where he had left her. She allowed him to wash her face, and at his order chewed a bit of the wild herb. Its pungent taste rid her mouth of the bile that coated her tongue.

"Can you ride on?" he asked, thankful that the moon had risen full and bright.

She had no choice but to accept his hand as she stood up, but when he made to turn away from her, Seana placed her hand on his arm to stop him.

"You're a compassionate man. I thank you for—"

"I'm not a beast, Seana. No matter what happens, I want you to remember that."

She nodded, thinking the intensity of his voice strange. Once mounted again, she turned to ask, "Have we far to ride?"

"I would see us both rest within a safe shelter this night, and have food to eat."

"Then I take it we have far to go."

"Sleep, Seana. I'll wake you when we arrive."

It was easy enough to do. His chin rested atop her head, his one arm strong and firm around her waist to keep her in place, and next to her ear beat the steady rhythm of his heart.

Micheil headed for the well-worn paths and tracks that would lead him north. Now that Seana was asleep, he veered nearer the coast, unmindful of any

who would see him. The salty tang of sea air kept him awake as he held Breac to a steady pace and rode through the night.

Several times Seana awakened, and he soothed her sleepy query with promises that they soon would be stopping. But Micheil swept through lands held by the Munross clan and circled keeps claimed by the Urquharts. He pushed on, driven to be within the boundaries of those loyal to his clan.

It was near dawn when Breac, more alert than his master, shied in warning of danger ahead. Rousing himself, Micheil saw only the clear track, forested on either side. Silence met his moment of listening, but he trusted Breac's senses.

"Seana. Seana, wake. We've trouble ahead."

Micheil drew Breac to a walk. He needed both hands free, if he had to fight. Still holding Seana around her waist, he wrapped the reins over her hands. His horse needed no guiding hand to see them clear.

"Sit up, Seana. I need my sword arm clear."

She had barely roused herself to cling to the pommel when a ragged band of men rushed them from the woods. Micheil set his heels to Breac's sides, swinging his sword from left to right to keep the outlaws at bay. He kicked out and felt his foot land solidly against one chest. With the flat of his sword he killed another who tried to snatch Seana from the saddle.

Seana twisted around and grabbed the dirk from his belt. Her sleeve ripped at the shoulder as fingers clawed her skin. Blindly she slashed out with the blade and heard a cry. She could see more shadowed figures coming from the wood. Shivering with fright, closing

her ears to the grunts and curses around her, she leaned forward on the horse's neck to recover the trailing rein. One foul-smelling outlaw held the leather fast.

Breac swung his head, and his teeth snapped before the stallion shrilled a challenge. Micheil was fighting with two men. Seana tugged on the leather. Uncertain what to do, she sliced through the taut rein to free Breac.

The horse started to rear, his hooves slashing out, his head swinging to and fro at any who dared to approach. With a shrill whistle from Micheil, the stallion bolted. Seana grabbed hold of the stallion's mane to keep from being thrown.

Micheil made no effort to slow the animal. The back of his hand stung where it had been sliced. As he clenched his powerful leg muscles to keep his seat, he felt the warm trickling of blood. The throbbing in his thigh located the gash for him. But he dared not stop now, though every jolt of the galloping pace released a fresh spurt of blood.

"Seana," he called, cursing his weak voice. "There's a bend in the track. Take Breac across the field and even with the narrow wood."

She barely heard him above the hard-pounding hooves, and wondered if he was daft. How was she to control his beastie, without the use of both reins? She couldn't see him clearly when she glanced behind her, but she felt him sway in the saddle. Certain he had been mortally wounded, she crooned to the horse, using her hold on his mane to draw his head up.

At first she did not think the beastie would obey her, but as minutes passed and the road curved, Breac's pace began to slow.

"Now, Seana, turn him," Micheil ordered.

Seana braced her bare feet against Micheil's legs and stretched out to reach for the headstall. "Easy, Breac, easy now," she repeated, over and over, as the horse's full-blown stride began to lessen.

The field had been freshly plowed, so the weight of the horse and his riders made his hooves sink deep into the earth until he walked.

The sky lightened, and Micheil saw the cut rein dangling uselessly from Breac's halter. His own wound was forgotten when Seana sat up and revealed the deep scratches down her arm.

"I should've killed all the bastards."

"You took lives back there, let that be enough."

"Would you have me hand you over, and Breac, as well? Not to mention my life as forfeit, too?"

"I meant—"

"You meant!" Micheil cut in, disgust evident in his voice. "You're squeamish, like most women."

Seana did not answer him. She looked down to see the blood on her hand and realized she had lost his dirk. The blood was not her own. Shivers of revulsion coursed through her. Jamie was right. She was a woman, and violence was not her way. But she had used his dirk on someone—she remembered the cry. Yet she said nothing to defend herself.

The wood was in sight. "Follow that wood, is that your order?" she asked.

"Aye. There's a burn on the other side."

Breac was at a slow walk, and Micheil slid from the saddle. His leg nearly gave way beneath his weight, and he gritted his teeth, not to cry out. Limping forward, he took hold of the halter and led his horse.

Seana stared straight ahead, refusing to look at him at all. The first rays of the sun rose and glinted off the reddened blade of his sword. Despite her empty stomach, she tasted bile.

The moment she saw the water, Seana scrambled down and ran for the bank. She drank greedily from her cupped hands, then splashed water over her face and throat. She leaned forward to dip her arm in the cool water, bathing the scratches.

Kneeling there, she sat back on her heels. For a moment, she stared at her wavering reflection. Her hair was a mass of thick tangles, and she thought she resembled a wood hag. With a quick shake of her head, she dismissed the vain thought of her appearance and realized that Jamie had not come forward.

She turned her head and saw that he sat beneath a high-grown bush. Farther down, Breac quenched his own thirst.

"Are you not thirsty?" she asked, wondering at his stillness. His eyes were closed, and there was a pale sheen of sweat upon his brow.

"Jamie?"

All Seana noticed was the movement of the hand that lifted to reveal his wound.

"Sweet heaven! Why did you not say—?" Seana stopped herself from saying more. She tore at her ripped sleeve, pulling free the tighter one that be-

longed to her kirtle. She soaked both cloths and brought them to him.

The gash on his thigh was not deep, but, remembering the foul scents of the men who attacked them, she knew the blade that had cut him could not have been clean. She struggled to tear the cloth of his breeks away, and gratefully accepted her small dagger from him.

"I seemed to have lost my dirk when we were attacked."

"A man like you is sure to replace it easily." She did not look at him, but carefully cut the cloth free of his leg.

"A man like me is like any other. My father gifted me with that knife, and I treasured it dear. A man's weapons, like his horse, and his woman, are not easily replaced."

"That's not what you told the ferryman." She was up and away before he said more, once again rinsing the cloths and bringing them back, dripping, to him.

"It's not deep, but an infusion of herbs would ensure its healing. I've naught to use." She folded the sleeve of her kirtle into a pad and, once more setting to with the blade, made strips of the other sleeve to tie it in place.

Settling back on her heels, she looked at him. "Your wound needs washing with heated water."

"Spoken like a true lady of the keep."

"I was instructed in all the ways a lady should care for those who served her husband before I was taken from my mother." Seana glanced at the sword lying by his side, then away.

"Are you hungry, lass?" he asked, watching her intently.

"Weary, 'tis what I am of the game you play with me."

"As am I, but I asked about food."

"Aye, I'm hungry. Little good it does," she added, with a quick look around. "Not one cranberry, ripe or green."

"Then I'd best be off to find something to sweeten your temper. I'll not have it said that you suffered under my protection."

"You're truly daft. Where could you be going, with your leg wounded and not a crofter's cottage in sight?"

"Trust me, Seana. I'll be leaving you here to wait for me while I fetch us something to eat." He caught hold of her hand and lifted it to his lips. "I dare not take you with me and chance having you stolen away. But you will wait here for me."

Seana slid her fingers from his hold and looked down at the dagger lying on the sparse grass. Before she could move to take it, Micheil's hand closed over it.

"Will you wait?"

"Perhaps."

"That's not the answer I want," he softly warned, cupping her chin to force her to look at him. "I will not leave until you promise. Your word as a MacKay is good for that much."

"Aye." She almost spat the word. "It's good." His barbs sunk deep. If the Lord allowed, she would have her revenge upon him.

Micheil let her go and, using his sword, struggled to stand. The cool water and tight padding had stopped the bleeding, and he found that he could put weight on the leg if he used care. A whistle brought Breac trotting to his side.

Micheil handed her his sword. "Hold it for a moment. I know where you'd like to slide the blade, Seana, but you have not the stomach for it."

"Nay. I've not been bred to the violence you enjoy." She saw the difficulty he had to mount, the whitened line of his mouth, the beading of sweat on his brow, but held silent. Nothing she could say would deter him. She had learned little about this man, but of this she was certain.

He leaned forward and caught up the cut rein, tying it with the longer one to make a loop. "Seana, let me warn you, should you think to run off. We're on lands belonging to the Gunn clan."

"*His* clan?"

"Aye." Micheil almost allowed himself regret that he had to mention it. Her face paled to the shade of her torn kirtle, and her eyes widened with fear. He could have hated himself, if he had allowed soft emotion to cloud his mind. She looked up with those gray eyes, pleading for a denial. Her mouth opened and closed without another sound.

"Stop this. I never meant to frighten you so." The words were out before he could stop them. Micheil wondered if he meant them. Her mettle had been tested from the moment he found her. He hated seeing her spirit flee at the mere mention of himself. And he damned whatever devil urged him to reassure her.

"You'll be safe enough here."

"H-how c-can—" Seana swallowed. Her tongue seemed to swell with the terror that held her in its grip. He was so calm, and she grew alarmed at his steady gaze. "How can you be sure? If we are this close— Holy Mother protect me!"

"Cease! None will ride this way. I'll make sure of it."

If he thought to soothe her, he was sadly mistaken. She backed away from him, rubbing her arms before she wrapped them around her waist.

She appeared a wanton, with that wild tangle of hair spread over her shoulders. The deep rents in her coarse gown and kirtle exposed the bare swell of her breasts, and her eyes, meeting his, burned with a hate as strong as passion.

He felt the rush of his blood heating to meet the sudden, violent swelling of his loins. He had desired her, and now he wanted to fling her back upon the ground and satisfy the fire she brought so unwittingly to flame.

"Claim your Judas gold from that savage, Jamie. But I'll curse you until he buries me for your betrayal."

"Seana—"

She turned her back and walked to the bank where she sat.

"I'm not claiming any gold for you."

"Then I thank the Lord for showing me mercy."

"'Tis me and me alone that you'll be thanking. I told you, I claim you mine. None shall take you from me."

Seana bowed her head, fighting not to let the tears that burned her eyes free. There was such conviction in his voice, and she repeated his words to herself, finally forced to turn.

"Who are you, Jamie?"

But he was gone.

## Chapter Eleven

Seana refused to give in to the need to cry. She swallowed the terrified sobs that rose, wiped her eyes, and belittled herself for the mewling whimpers of fear that escaped her lips.

She would not panic. She dismissed the thought of running. If it was true that she rested on Gunn lands, she could be caught and lose a better chance at freedom. As long as she remained free of Halberry's walls, she must hold to thoughts of freedom.

Jamie had to be kin to them. Yet there was no doubt creeping into her mind that he had lied when he claimed he would take no gold for her. She had to get the truth from him.

Rather than allow fear to plague her, she would use this time to bathe her foot and see again to the painful scratches on her arm.

When Micheil finally returned, darkness cloaked the land. He found Seana sound asleep, huddled in a tight ball, and he gently woke her.

Seana was torn from fiendish dreams, and came awake spitting and snarling.

"Easy, lass. Be at ease." The sudden command was not enough to stop her struggles. He caught her up against him, locking her flailing hands within one of his, and felt her shake with terror.

"Seana, cease, I say. You're like a frightened wild thing caught in a hunter's snare. I'll not be hurting you."

Still haunted by the hellish images that had plagued her exhausted sleep, Seana quieted when he pressed a kiss to her temple. She needed no light to see the heat in his eyes. She could feel it. Just as the warmth of his body surrounding her seeped inside to chase the chill that had held her these long hours past.

Her breath caught in her throat, and tension held sway over her body. Moments lengthened and fled, and still he made no move to do more than hold her, his crooning voice meant to calm.

"I'm going to lift you now. I've found us a deserted crofter's cottage to shelter us this night."

"You were gone overlong, and I thought you had abandoned me."

"You need have no fear on that score. I keep telling you, I'll not let you go."

It was useless in her weakened state to try to fight off the last vestiges of sleep. She curled against him, for the moment forgetting all her warnings about him, thankful that she was not alone in the dark of the night. Even after he set her up on his horse and mounted behind her, he held her close.

There was a clean scent to him, along with the tantalizing fragrance of sandalwood. Seana burrowed her face into his neck, comforted. Briefly his lips touched

hers. His murmur was too soft for her to hear. The only clear thought that Seana had ·vas that on some deep, instinctive level she trusted him.

Not until she surveyed the inside of the cottage did she come fully awake. Following him inside, to the heat of a well-burning fire, she realized how chilled her body was as she stood close to its heated glow. She heard him move around outside, then return. The setting of the bar across the door forced her to turn around.

"A feast awaits us," he offered with a courtly bow.

Seana glanced at the array of foods spread on the small wooden table. Her hollow stomach rumbled as she inhaled the aroma of warm mutton pie. But Jamie drew her gaze. He had bathed. His face was scraped clean of the dark beard. A linen shirt the color of fresh cream draped his body, and his breeks, dark as cinnamon sticks, flowed along the muscled length of his legs. She could barely make out a padding where his wound was.

Seana sat on the crudely made stool nearest her. A generous slice of the mutton pie was gone. Beside the pie lay a plate of thinly sliced smoked fish. Bread with a thick, richly golden crust stood waiting to be cut. Sweet creamed butter rested in a small crock. Her gaze rested on each dish in turn—the hard cheeses, the small new apples, the flask of wine, the steepled array of ginger cakes.

She raised her head, her gaze clashing with his waiting one. "H-how—" She had to swallow to moisten her suddenly dry mouth. "Tell me true. Are you a conjurer, or in league with the devil himself?"

Micheil laughed, his head thrown back, his hands coming to rest on his hips. "I claim I'm a man, and no more. Do you not believe your own eyes? The enticing scents of the food before you? Has your hunger been banished so quickly?"

"But how?" she asked again, indicating with a wave of her hand the table before her. "Are you a cook, then? Is that the place you hold with the Gunns?"

The smile in his eyes died. "I'm no cook. Must you have answers now?"

She lowered her head. She had insulted him. As she rubbed her temples with shaking fingers, Seana knew she had to let her queries wait. When she looked up, her gaze fastened on his hand, and the dirk held tight in his grasp. It took her minutes to raise her eyes and look at his face.

"I see you have managed to recover your weapon."

Micheil did not know what to make of her carefully neutral voice. For once, her eyes did not reflect any emotion.

"What I value, I hold."

"Spoken like a true highlander. Will you slice the pie? I vow, I am weak with hunger."

He served her, piling her plate high with food, then took the small bench and sat opposite her. Once he had filled his beaker with wine, he offered to do the same for her. Her nod of acceptance was coolly regal. Micheil began to suspect he had made a serious error in leaving her alone for so long.

He watched her pick at the food. For all her talk of hunger, she ate little. "Is the food not to your liking?"

"It's too much, after the fasting I've had. I do not wish to stress you by being sick again."

"So polite, Seana? It is not a manner that pleases me."

She eyed the hand wrapped around his beaker and took note of the salve spread over his cut. He had taken time to bathe, to clothe himself and have his wounds tended. Now he spoke to her of pleasing him, with all the arrogance of a laird.

*Who was he?* She deliberately lowered her lashes, afraid he would read the fear she felt in her eyes. He moved to take one of the small new apples, and Seana eyed it with distaste. His teeth were strong and even as he bit into the fruit's flesh, and she smiled as he quickly spat it out.

"They're bitter yet, Jamie," she informed him. "Since you'd be knowing so much, you should have been aware of that, too."

"I do now." It sat ill with him that she had to struggle to hide her smile. His gaze locked with hers.

"You did not like the taste of it?"

"Nay, Seana. It's only sweet things my lips would like to taste."

She moistened suddenly dry lips and saw the way he stared at her mouth. A flush began inside her that had nothing to do with the heat filling the small cottage. She sent a searching glance over the table and lit upon the ginger cakes. Reaching out, she lifted one and set it on his plate.

"Here, have this, Jamie. If they're made right, the cake should satisfy your craving for a sweet."

Looking down in mock dismay at the small cake, he then flashed her a wicked grin. "'Tis a tiny bit of sugar you'd think to offer a braw man like myself."

"Take it. 'Tis the only sweet I'll offer the likes of you," she returned in a cross voice.

"You wound me, lass, sorely wound me." His heavy lids lowered, his eyes narrowing, yet his voice, when he spoke again, was soft and oddly warning. "It remains to be seen, Seana, what you'd be offering the likes of me."

Lifting her beaker, she sipped the wine, finding its taste rich and smooth. The same could be said of Jamie. For the first time in days, Seana was thinking clearly. Perhaps it was having enough food to eat and feeling safe within the snug cottage. She thought hard about the man's manner and dress, like those men of the border who traded freely with the lords of England.

Feeling his watchful gaze upon her, Seana ate one cake, then gazed around the cottage. It took but moments to realize that he had lied to her. The cottage was deserted, but the tenants had left but a short time ago. No corner that her gaze rested upon showed any sign of neglect.

The bed, likely mounded dried heather and bracken, was covered with rich, thick furs. A rolled sheepskin served as a pillow. Crocks stood on the wall, and two finely woven baskets hung above them. Disregarding his continued staring at her, Seana twisted around on the stool. The wood box was filled with fresh-cut kindling, and logs were stacked neatly beside it. The hearthstones were swept clean of soot and ash. No

man's harsh hand had tended this cottage, but a woman's loving one, and most recently, too.

Seana turned around and found that he still watched her, with an intensity that darkened his eyes, as if he were waiting. But for what? The silence spread between them, unnerving her, but he sipped his wine, giving her the strange feeling that he was content.

When she could not stand it any longer, Seana tossed back her hair and folded her hands before her on the table.

"You have made yourself, and me with you, at home here. Tell me how you dare, if we are so close to the Gunn's keep, and you deny that you're kin?"

"Leave the matter be, Seana." Annoyance sharpened his voice. "I told you, you have naught to fear from them. Not while you're with me. Believe and trust me on this."

"Trust you? You ask much of me. But, once more, I have little choice. Yet you did not answer me. Are we close to their stronghold?"

"None will dare to bother us here."

She nodded, her worse fears confirmed. He had to be of their clan. He could not state that fact, otherwise. And she would be wise to say naught of it now.

"'Tis late, Seana," he remarked, setting aside his beaker.

"Aye, so I ken."

"A long day," he said, rising and adding, "I did not get much rest."

"You cannot blame that on me. 'Tis your own fault. I slept well enough."

Her smile, that tiny secretive smile, was an irritating sight. He glanced at the small bed, then back to her face. Her eyes held a strange glitter, gone the moment she saw him looking at her.

"Am I to wager that you're thinking to share that with me?"

"'Tis an appealing thought."

"Well, you cannot! There's no wind chilling either of us tonight. I've no need of your blanket. I've no need of you." Seana rose and began to clear the table.

Micheil's hand snaked out and caught her wrist. "You may not have a need, Seana... but I do."

"This was your end all the time." Her voice accused him, her eyes glared hate. "You'll ruin me for some foul purpose of your own."

His fingers tightened their grip for a second more, but then Micheil let her go. "There's naught foul about a man wanting a woman. Or her feeling the same desire."

Seana made a dash for the door, clumsily trying to raise the large wooden bar. Her frantic struggles lent her no strength to lift it. She cast a panicked look over her shoulder at him, and found a smile of amusement lighting his face, before he rose and stood behind her.

"'Tis not heavy. You can lift it, Seana. But you might try untying the leather thong that binds it closed below."

The fact that he mocked her, and made no attempt to stop her, sent a flood of fury through Seana. She refused to look at him, and concentrated on freeing the tightly laced knots. Beneath her breath she swore

an oath that he had tied them too tight. The stubborn leather refused to yield.

"Are they proving stubborn to your attempt, Seana? Aye, I can see for myself, they're as stubborn as you are to me."

"Why is a woman called stubborn to cling to her honor? I seek to remove myself from Satan's own temptation."

"Women know naught of honor," he whispered against her flaming cheek. "And it wounds me, Seana, that you see me as Satan. I'm not a devil." When she refused to turn, and kept trying to untie the leather, he commanded her to cease.

"'Tis a foolish errand you set yourself, for I will not let you go. I'm a man, Seana, one of flesh and blood, whose body sings hot for you."

Seana quieted and stilled. Passion had thickened his voice to the beguiling tone that warned her she would not escape him easily. With his hands stroking her arms and then coming to rest on her shoulders, she knew she would need her wits about her. The callused warmth of his palm against her bare flesh sent a piercing arrow of desire quivering through her.

Her protest died unspoken at his dark whisper in her ear as he pulled her back against his chest. His wine-warmed breath fanned her cheek as he slowly drew her hair back. Like a hot brand taken from a fire, his lips scorched the exposed skin of her neck when she tilted her head to the side, away from him.

Seana trembled then, every second he held her bringing her senses alive and attuned only to him. Every moment was an agony of waiting as his lips

parted and she felt the first rough, heated caress of his tongue begin its descent down the length of her neck.

Micheil slid his hands within the rent neckline of her gown and pushed the cloth down her arms. He murmured to still her whispered refusal. He traced the flare of her hips and narrow waist. He counted the rapid beat of her heart, for its measure kept cadence with his.

"You cannot deny the passion in you, Seana. It's for me you rise hungry as any trout to the bait. It's the same for me, lass. Fire, Seana. A fire so hot, it'll melt the strongest of swords."

"Jamie? Jamie, 'tis not fair what you do—"

"As you to me? Nay, 'tis not fair at all." The sound of her quickened breathing filled his ears. Or was it his own?

His fingers splayed wide over the flattened plane of her belly, and the sound of her breath catching before she released it brought his lips to the shell of her ear. He traced the rim with the tip of his tongue and felt the ensuing shivers like a caress over his own aroused skin.

Holding her to him, pressing her against his own violently aroused flesh, his palm kneaded the tension from her while he gently cupped her breast with his other hand.

"Jamie?"

"Tell me. Tell me what will please you most."

"You must—" Seana lost the thought. His hands caressed her body until her legs felt boneless. She was fevered. Naught else could account for the dizzying swirl that had her shaking her head to and fro. She

ached. To stop him, her hand covered his on her breast.

"Ah, Seana, tell me what it is you want. Shall I make my touch softer still, or does your pleasure demand a harder caress?"

"Aye...nay... I know not. I ache, Jamie. I—"

"I want you till I burn with need." His thumb rubbed the hardened peak of her breast, his tongue replaying the same circling movements as both his hands. Gently then, he suckled the soft flesh of her lobe.

Seana drew her other hand up—to stop him or to aid him, she did not know—but he held the full weight of her breasts within his palms. The sensations sent flame flickering its heat along her skin, and her bare toes curled as her legs grew weaker. She feared if he made one move to release her now, she would surely fall.

Never had any man touched her. She knew it was wrong. She allowed him liberties with her body that belonged to none but a husband. But Jamie knew that. He had to, for he laughed softly when she moaned and fought to lean even closer to him.

"Yield to me, Seana," he softly coaxed, scattering kisses at the sensitive joining of her neck and shoulder. He lightly nipped her, sensing that she was held in passion's thrall and would not feel a lighter touch. "Aye, yield to me. I've not met a wench that fired my blood so."

His hands slid slowly down over her rib cage, spanning her slender waist as he rocked her against his body, then rising again to enfold the swelling fullness

of her breasts. Her lips parted on his name, ending with a moaning sigh.

"I said I'd be the first to have you, Seana. Do not be denying me now. You cannot tell me," he huskily demanded, "that you'd be wanting me to stop." He nipped her lobe, whispering dark murmurs and his breath into the small pink shell until he felt her shivering delight.

"You're ripe for a man, Seana. Will you deny yourself the pleasure I'll teach you?"

Denying herself was impossible. She had not the will. Denying him—where would she draw the strength to do so? Hunger to know what he promised simmered dangerously within her. Her head arched back to rest on his broad shoulder. Her whole body was weak and trembling against him.

He raised his hand to her chin, his thumb pressed against the corner of her mouth as he lowered his for an achingly sweet kiss. The pressure of his thumb opened her mouth for him. The moment she gave in to his silent demand, Micheil thrust his tongue inside, deeply, completely. Seana tried to pull away. He refused to let her move. His mouth promised, his tongue softly probed and teased as he slanted his lips, first one way, then another, to drink in her whimper of protest.

No longer gentle, his mouth was hot and hungry, and his tongue claimed hers in a wild tasting that forced her to learn the taste of him, as well. His kiss inflamed her. Both his hands captured her hips, turning and molding her to the fit of his.

The rich, smooth taste of the wine they had shared had the added enticement of being heated. Seana felt the wildness take hold as her tongue dueled with his. She tried to struggle when he pinned her against the door, but he locked her thighs between his spread legs, entwining his fingers with hers and slowly raising her hands above her head.

There was no part of her body that did not know the hard press of his. His tongue drove in and out of her mouth, matching the driving rhythm of his hips, until her body strained toward his.

"Yield, Seana, say you're mine."

"Will you leave me naught of myself?"

"Naught," he whispered in a near-growl. "I would have all from you, and call it mine. If I am bewitched, then you shall be. *Will you yield to me?*"

Seana looked up and stared into the glittering blue of his eyes and knew she was lost. "How can I deny you, with your lips on mine? I yield all to you, Ja—"

He cut off the name she would have whispered with a kiss that burned him to his soul, and scooped her up in his arms to carry her to the bed.

Her coarse gown tore beneath his hands, as did the thin cloth of her kirtle. Micheil stripped off his shirt and kicked free of his soft leather boots. His eyes never left Seana, bathed in the fire's glow, the wild tangle of her honey-gold hair spread over the rich, silky furs. Her lithe body was a feast for his gaze, passion-flushed, with a fine sheen of desire's mist that matched his own heated skin.

His ragged breathing slowed as he tried to regain a measure of control, but she held up welcoming arms,

and his breeks tore beneath his need to sheathe himself within her.

He came to her whispering dark, seductive promises that made her quiver with need. Soft as velvet, his voice stroked, as surely as his hands as he blanketed her body with his. She gasped to feel the heat of him, and somewhere in the deep recess of her mind she was pleased to hear the low, groaning sound he made before he captured her mouth with his.

It was a kiss that demanded complete surrender. And Micheil knew he had bent her will to his when she arched up against him. He left her lips to seek sweet flesh to suckle, closing his lips around one taut peak as he lay at her side. His hand stroked the trembling length of her, wanting to set more of her passionate nature free to overcome her timidity. The feel of her hands, fingers digging deep into his shoulders, brought a grunt of satisfaction from him.

He feathered the golden nest that hid the sweet, hot treasure he longed to claim as his. Every touch coaxed her thighs to part, and he felt their restless stirrings, clenching his jaw with the demand for patience he made on himself. He rolled his tongue in honeyed circles around her distended nipples, praising her as her back lifted in offering to him.

She was as wild, and as wanton, as he had thought her to be, a woman to match his strong passions. The seductive, supple movement of her body drove him to near-madness.

Nothing was enough. Yet Seana thought it all too much. She was awash in heat, fire consumed her. She knew nothing but his searing mouth and the caress of

his hands until she believed her body was no longer hers. Her fingers furrowed into the thickness of his hair, dragging his mouth up to hers with a demand that shocked her, but brought a groan from him.

She searched his mouth with her tongue, and felt the drag of his hair-rough chest against the sensitive peaks of her breasts. It was not enough to ease the ache inside her. The heel of his hand shaped her, drawing a long moan that was caught up in his praise of her. She squeezed her thighs tight at the invasion of his touch, and tore her mouth free.

"'Tis pleasure I would have you feel, Seana. Pleasure that I'll give you, and myself, as well. Yield once again to me, love." He would not be deterred. She sank her teeth into his shoulder as he stroked the tender folds. She was sleek and hot, and so damp he nearly lost control.

Her body betrayed her. Seana fought to keep her treacherous thighs from parting. She heard his voice, but not his words, for he made ashes of her resistance with his slow, gliding penetration.

"Och, lass, you're tense and tight. Let me ease my way." She shivered and twisted beneath him, inflaming him with every restless move that brushed her body against his aching flesh. A shudder rippled through her, and he deepened his touch until she cried out.

"Jamie!"

"Hold me. Just hold me."

She clutched his shoulders, her hands sliding down the straining muscles of his arms as he parted her thighs with his knees.

"They say the pain is great!" she cried out.

Micheil knew there was naught he could say to ease her fear. He stroked her as he made a place for himself between her quivering thighs. She whimpered low in her throat, burying her face against his chest as he lowered his body to hers. The muscles in her body tensed and he knew he should take more time, but his blood threatened to scald him with its heat and demanded that he make her his.

Seana felt the tremors that rode her body and held him close, feeling the taut pull of his muscles that echoed the tension in hers. He shuddered and let the full weight of his body cover her.

She felt the first burning stretch as he entered her. Her body coiled like a whip as his legs spread her thighs wide. There was no warning. His mouth captured hers, just as the powerful surge of him drove into her.

He drank her cry, and stilled for a moment to allow her time to adjust to his invasion. His possession was near complete. "Sweet Jesu, Seana, do not move. You're so tight."

The yearning and the promise of pleasure were gone. The tearing burst of pain had swept it away. Silent tears slid down her cheeks from beneath her closed eyes.

"'Tis done," she whispered.

"Nay, sweeting. 'Tis not yet begun."

He kissed the tears from her cheek and dipped to taste lips swollen with passion. "I'm sorry I hurt you, but only this once, Seana."

He claimed her mouth, delving deep to capture the sweet taste of her, holding himself deep within her

until he felt the first tiny tremors begin. Slowly, then, he began to move, giving her time now, waiting for the wild passion to come alive once more.

She raised her hips to ease his way.

He wanted to be gentle now, as he had not been before.

Hunger drove Seana to hear again the low groan from his lips. She held his head and brought his mouth to hers, not knowing the right or wrong of what she did, only acting on instinct that came from within. She held him close, feeling beneath her stroking palms the damp sheen that covered his body. The quickening rush of his breath was all she longed to hear. Woman to man. Two halves of a whole. A mating born in fire that would surely consume them. The disjointed thoughts ran through her mind as he brought her to a splendor that made her cry out.

Micheil knew she was innocent. Never had he felt such overwhelming passion. She would not know what a blessing had been bestowed on them, that her fulfillment came in a rush even as his release did.

She was everything he could want in a woman.

And she was his instrument of revenge.

In a final act of rage against what his oath had set him to do, he spilled his seed deep within her.

## Chapter Twelve

In the minutes when the storm yet held sway over her, Seana held to the fragments that slowly seeped into her awareness. The heated scent of sandalwood. The silky feel of his hair, crushed against her neck. The ragged sounds of their melded breathing. Tremors still shook her. The warmth and weight of his finely hewn body, covering her, offered a haven of strength and safety.

She stroked the taut, damp skin of his back, feeling the small, rigid scars that marked him as a warrior. As she felt branded his, so she wished to mark him hers. And with that thought came the understanding of the enormity of what she had done.

Her eyes closed as if to shut out thought, but with every moment that passed that became impossible. She had yielded all to him....

The feel of her hand, suddenly tense, fingers digging deep into his skin, made Micheil rouse himself. Had he ever felt this completeness before? This sense of utter peace? He knew he had not, but these were not things he could speak of to a woman. Most especially not to this woman.

"Seana?" he murmured, shifting his weight, feeling her inner tightening as she sought to hold him within her yet. "I fear I'll crush you."

Her answer was to hold him closer, afraid that his move would allow him to see the tears in her eyes. "Abide within me a moment more." Even she heard the shaken forerunner of a sob that rose from her throat. A sob she quickly swallowed as she turned her head away from his.

With tenderness that was as strange to him as the fierce protective urge he had felt toward her from the first, Micheil drew her hand to his lips, turning it so that he could press a kiss to the center of her palm. Without withdrawing from her, he raised himself up on one elbow, and sought the pulse in the hollow of her throat with his lips.

"I treasure thy giving, Seana. Never was a handsel so sweetly offered."

*A first gift.* He named her yielding to him a gift. But when she turned to speak, his lips sealed hers with a kiss of such infinite seductive wooing, her thoughts scattered like wheat before the wind.

For Seana, passion did not shimmer awake slowly, it rose like an engulfing wave to sweep over her. She could feel the hardened press of his flesh in the center of her being. His whispered dark murmurs of yet more pleasure to be shared clouded her mind. And the cherishing he offered with every kiss stole into her heart.

Along with the desire he invoked came her need not to think of the damning result of her yielding to him. Eagerly she banished the twinges and aches of her first

joining and welcomed his deepening thrusts. Welcomed the fire and, with it, the fierce hunger to be one with him.

Micheil could no more have resisted her siren call than he could have ceased his breathing. He knew the strength of her passion easily equaled his, and he reveled in finding so perfect a mate. He knew, too, that the hunger raised and fed this night would never be fully sated.

As he once again defied his oath and poured his seed into her, there came the stunning realization that she was not alone in yielding all.

In the act of withholding naught, of surrendering all, Seana demanded its like measure from him. And Micheil, with a prayer that she remained unaware, heeded her silent demand. For good or for ill, she had branded his soul hers.

The kiss that sealed her cry of joy was harsh, as if the overwhelming need to punish her for making him vulnerable could no longer be contained.

"Ah, love," he whispered, caught up in passion, "'tis a fitting mate for Black Micheil you'll be."

Had he pierced her with his sword, the thrust would have been more merciful by far. The shock of his meaning, his poisoned words, held her still. As she repeated them to herself, repeated them and grasped the treachery behind them, great, icy shudders racked her body. She could not bear to look at him. The need to be away from him rose with a threatening tide as fury overcame all else.

She lashed out, her fingers curled like claws, wanting him gone, and wanting, too, to shred his flesh as surely as he had flayed hers.

Micheil rolled onto his side. Aware of what he had said, he did nothing to stop her fists beating him.

Seana's fury was soon spent. Pain encompassed her, robbing her of that solace. She scrambled to her knees, drawing up a fur to shield her nakedness. She was unable to draw in a full breath, so tightly constricted was her chest. Whipping her head from side to side, setting the wild tumble of her honey-gold hair to flying about her face and shoulders, was the only denial she made.

Not a sound came from him. Not one move did he make to stop her.

A green piece of wood fell into the glowing coals of the fire, its sap popping loud enough to startle her. Raising a hand that seemed leaden and devoid of strength, Seana pushed aside the tangle of her hair and opened eyes that were as darkly gray as a storm-tossed sea.

She saw before her, not the grace and lithe body of the lover who had demanded her surrender, but the taut, powerful body of a hunter who had snared his prey.

His gaze held hers with eyes that were narrow and cool in their silent appraisal. Only his hands, clenched at his sides, gave evidence of the rage she knew had to be simmering inside him. His very stillness alarmed her. He just lay there, watching her. And waiting.

Her teeth scored her lower lip—it was swollen from his drugging kisses—and she tasted the lingering af-

termath of the wine they had shared, and with it the passion. She could not stand the strain of holding his gaze. But, as much as she desired to look away from him, she could not.

She had felt the scars on his back, and picked out the small ones that hid beneath the dark whorls of hair matting his chest. *Warrior.* How had she dared to let herself ever forget? Like polished bronze, his body had been cast by a master's hand. The burnished shadows cast by the fire's glow enticed her gaze lower.

Seana tried to summon shame for her bold appraisal. Tried, and failed. Her study went beyond virginal curiosity. She, who had never viewed an unclothed male, was desperate to find a reason why she desired him.

His scars did not repulse her. They were a warrior's badges. She sought fault in his narrow-flanked hips, in the muscled length of his legs, even the greater size of his foot. She saw that his wound bled through the new linen. But it was not a fault. She forced herself to tear the last veil of innocence from her eyes, and brought them to bear on his rampant sex. Black, curling hair nestled it between his firm horseman's thighs. A weapon to tear her asunder. The proof of her virgin state lay in a dark stain, a match for the blood he had spilled this day. Deep within herself, Seana felt an involuntary tightening of sore muscles.

"Seana—"

"Do not speak," she commanded in a hoarse whisper. "I cannot stand the lying poison of your voice." She closed her eyes, fighting the emptiness that spread inside her.

Micheil had borne her silent scrutiny, his teeth gritted in frustrated fury. Did she dare to believe he could be dismissed so easily? She *had* cast a spell of witchery upon him, that he forgot all in his need to spill his seed in her womb. He saw the stains on her torn kirtle where their blood mingled. She huddled, shamed, eyes shut tight against the sight of him, but he saw again the sultry passion that had shimmered within them. Peeking through the tangled length of her hair was the silky cream of her shoulder, a darkened mark of his passion branding the flesh. He saw how tightly her fingers held the fur as a shield before her, and felt them clawing his back, making her demands known. And her mouth... How eagerly those sweet lips had flowered open beneath his. A blaze stirred in his loins, and Micheil, hearing how his voice was now poison to her, rose from the bed.

At his move, Seana opened her eyes, quickly turning away from the sight of the marks she had made on his back. But her gaze beheld her torn kirtle, and the red stain. She would not cry. Her virtue was lost, and none at fault but herself.

She heard him tilt the flask to a beaker, and her own parched throat tightened with need of moisture. She would not ask him for wine or water. She would never ask him for anything. Clutching the fur with one hand, she reached out to gather her kirtle and gown.

Micheil emptied the beaker of wine and poured another. "If you're in sore need of modesty now, wear my shirt."

"I'd sooner wear a viper's skin."

"Spit and snarl all you wish, Seana, you'll not change what's passed."

Pride came to her aid, and the good Lord knew she had little of it left. "I cannot wish the time back. But I will do penitence and offer prayers that this night will bear no fruit."

"You'd think yourself cursed if my seed took in your womb?"

If her senses had been less alert to him, Seana would have missed the rage that underlay each word, though his voice was soft, almost too soft.

Before she could answer, Micheil spoke. "Do not vex yourself about it, Seana, I'll be adding my prayers to yours."

Easily said, but even the wine would not take the bile from his mouth, for he had risked his honor.

She clearly saw she had provoked him. His mouth thinned, and, as this morning, his eyes turned the chilling blue of the deepest part of a loch.

Her mocking laughter was unexpected. Seana made no effort to stop it, not even when tears ran down her cheeks. "Kin or not, the Gunn chief will have your head for this night's work, and my life, as well."

"What makes you sure he'll kill you? Were you told this by someone who claimed to know?"

"You're a fool," she said, wiping the wetness from her cheeks. "Why else lock me away for all these years in a place to keep me chaste? Mayhap he practices the ancient religion, and has need of a virgin sacrifice. There's reason for him to kill you. You've stolen my worth."

With razor sharpness, Micheil returned her knife thrust. "And mayhap he'll reward me for a saddle-broke mare."

*Do not let him see the pain!* Seana held the fur so tight that she tore hairs free. In a dull voice, for she had used all her remaining courage and strength, she answered him.

"The truth comes at last. You intend to bring me to him." Much as she hated it, her sigh was both weary and an admission of defeat. "You played a fine game of cat and mouse with me."

"Games are for bairns, and you're no longer an age to claim that safety."

"I claim naught now. You have taken my honor."

"And I told you," he stated, his voice rising, "a woman knows nothing of honor. 'Tis a man's word. His oath. His vow to keep."

"Will you leave me?"

"Why?"

She flinched at the harshness of his tone. "I want to wash."

"Ask me."

She looked at him, looked and hated. "Never."

Unconcerned with his naked state, Micheil went to the fire. He hunkered down, and fed it with logs until he had a blaze going again. The flames were no less hot than the hate in her eyes. Honor? She dared to talk to him of honor? Damn her black heart! She was a MacKay! They knew naught of honor!

He had only to envision Bridget's face and know the truth of that. But the flames brought no image of his sister. He saw within them only the honey-gold length

of Seana's hair, framing her face. He closed his eyes, but her image would not leave him. Seana tossing her head back...defying him...refusing him... Seana yielding, so sweetly, with untaught passion. Why? Why now? He had told her they were on Gunn lands. He had used that as a threat against her. Why had she come to him now?

For a long moment, Micheil fought against the answer that whispered through his mind. He had no choice but to hear it. She had surrendered to him in the hope of using him against the Gunn chief. Naught else made sense. Like a harlot, she sought to use her body to bargain with him for her freedom.

He rose to his full, towering height and stared at her. She had not moved from her huddled position. Little did she know she had failed. If anything had been accomplished this night, it was only that Seana had bound herself to him more tightly than if he had wed her.

"You have decided then what you'll gain," she said.

"I've always known. You, for the start, Seana MacKay."

She was drawn to look at him. She was held speechless by the naked flame of desire in his eyes.

"I've never denied wanting you. Believe me or not, 'tis true. You'll still be innocent of how a man thinks, I ken that, but I want you for my own. Willingly you came to me once. I'll wait for you to come again. But, Seana," he added, "I'm not a patient man."

"I know that well." But she had been thinking as he spoke, and she nearly cursed herself for a fool for not having seen the answer all this time. Jamie had his own

debt to pay to Black Micheil. And he had used her to do it. Somehow he had learned of her presence at the abbey. Naught else made sense. Who knew what devilry he planned with her? Perhaps her life would be forfeit. He could cheat the Gunn chief of his revenge.

Her gaze swept the cottage, seeking a weapon.

Seeing only the fear that had returned to her eyes, Micheil forced himself to speak with calm. "I said I will not force you. Seek your rest. I'll not bother you again."

Warily she watched him make a bed by the fire, tossing down sheepskins he took from a small wooden chest. She closed her eyes when he reached for his breeks and boots.

"Wear the shirt till I replace your gown."

She made no move to touch it. Minutes passed, each one dragging. The even sound of his breathing seemed to fill the small, confining space. She sat and watched him. Cold drove her to slip the ruined garments on, and, using her teeth, she tore the remaining kirtle sleeve free to use for a crude belt. The flames drew her gaze, but his shadowed body, lying before the fire, disturbed her too much for her to look at them for long.

Then the sweet, clean scent of heather drew her head down, and before she knew, she had fallen asleep.

Seana often dreamed. Some of her dreams were horrors that made her wake bathed in a cold sweat. Others left behind fragments that often made no sense. But none had been like this . . .

She was alone on a moor, and within the mist behind her, the cold gray stones of a mighty fortress
stood. She had never seen its like. Wet, chilled, and
breathless from running, she held to the thought that
she must flee. She was weak, her last reserves of
strength were needed to keep her burden safe. The
cloth held something precious, and she moaned with
the need to see it.

Behind her came the thundering of hooves. She
knew who was chasing her long before she could
clearly see his face. She tossed and turned to deny it.
But it was Jamie. Jamie, who had never before looked
at her with such black, killing rage filling his eyes. Nor
had his lips ever been so grim, so determined a slash
of anger.

His hands were clenched on the reins of a huge steed
as he drew to a halt beside her. She struggled to hear
his words. There was naught but the movement of his
lips. A terrible feeling of unbearable pain filled her as
he went on and on.

She was begging him. Down on her knees, implor-
ing him to relent. But for what? All she could see was
his bare head, black hair slick with mist, tilting back
with the force of his devilish laughter.

She jumped and awakened with her hand clamped
over her mouth to stifle a scream. Cold sweat bathed
her. Almost afraid to look, she slowly turned her head
to see that in the dim glow from the dying embers,
Jamie was still sleeping soundly on his side.

Without a wasted motion, she eased from the bed
and found his dirk, still lying beside the bread. Holding it securely in her hand, Seana reached the door.

Casting looks over her shoulder to see that he slept on, she began to saw at the leather binding. Minutes later, drenched in sweat, she released a small sigh of relief as they came free.

She tucked the dirk into her cloth belt, needing both hands to lift the bar. She froze when it slipped slightly and one corner hit the floor. Surely the sound was not as loud as she thought. She shot frantic glances at Jamie as she eased it down onto the floor and rested its end against the wall.

Still as a fawn hiding from the hunter, Seana saw that he stirred. She shook with a chill of fear. He was turning, restless, and she held her breath, lest that sound give her away.

He finally settled, but still she waited, for now he lay facing the door. *Have mercy, Lord, and do not let him open his eyes!* Her breath escaped her in tiny pants, and she had to force muscles taut with tension to move.

Easing open the door just enough to slip through, Seana took her first breath of freedom. The cool highland air, filled with the scents of pine and wild herbs, was as heady a draft as any wine.

Truly, the Lord smiled upon her, for the moon was fat and full, brightening her path. She went quickly to the small shelter against the back wall, struck by the strangeness of it. Most crofters would bring their animals inside for their added warmth.

She did not dare whisper to Breac as she slowly made her approach. Holding out her hand before her, praying that she would have both her scent and that of

Jamie—much as it galled her that she carried it—
Seana murmured the beastie's name.

The horse lifted his head, ears perked forward,
alert. Seana stepped closer still. He arched his neck,
his warm breath fanning over her outstretched palm.
With a snort, he pawed the earth. She touched his
velvet nose. Breac reared back, as did Seana—right
into Micheil's waiting arms.

# Chapter Thirteen

He snatched the dirk from her belt before she thought to grab hold of it. "Would you become a thief now, Seana?" he asked, with a softness that belied the heat of his anger. "I'd not expected you to run."

Incensed that he had caught her, Seana twisted around within his loose hold and slapped him. "You're a bastard, Jamie!" she spat.

He caught hold of her hair, forcing her head back, and held her upper arm with the other hand until he felt skin and muscle give way to bone.

Despite the stinging of her palm from the force of her slap, Seana raised her hand to him again.

"Dare it, Seana," he said, his words grating from between clenched teeth. "Just dare to raise your hand to me again."

"None but a coward would raise his hand to a woman."

"Aye, and who would know that better than a MacKay?" he leaned close to whisper. Micheil closed his eyes briefly against the blinding rage that swept over him.

"You lie, Jamie!"

His grip on her arm tightened until she cried out, and even then he only eased his hold, but did not release her.

"I lie? The whole of the north Highlands knows your own brother treated Bridget nic Gunn so gently that none but her family have seen her face."

His voice and his words were whiplashes. "Nay. 'Tis not true. Liam would never raise his hand to her. He loved her! You lie!"

Micheil released her hair, only to grab hold of her other arm and haul her up against him. "The truth, by all I hold dear!" He shook her to make her cease her screaming denial.

Her stomach roiled with sickness. It could not be true. Liam had loved his wife. She had left him. She had denied their marriage and refused to return. She'd listen to no more poison from Jamie's lips.

"And you're no better than that skulking coward you call brother. I know why you yielded to me, Seana. You'd play the harlot for any man who'd take you home."

"A harlot?" she repeated in a stunned voice. "Aye. But first I had to find a fool of a man to teach me." His biting grip on her arms made her cry out again. The moonlight cast shadows, and enough light for her to see the scowling fury that stamped his features. Seana grew quiet as terror took hold.

Her heart pounded until she thought it would burst. She could not even close her eyes against him. Not a sign did she see of his intent. He shoved her roughly from him. She stumbled, but managed to keep her balance, and stood there, rubbing her arms.

His move to the dirk brought a catch at her chest and a gasp. Sweet heaven! Did he intend to kill her? But he bent swiftly to tuck it in his boot.

"Go inside, Seana."

She refused to feel compassion at his weary tone. Just as she refused to obey him.

"Stubborn to the end. This is not Breac, but his near-twin, Ciotach. Neither of the braw beasties would let you ride them. You're blessed with the faeries' own magic that he did not kill you. I've traded dear to have them trained to kill my enemies. Now, come inside, where it's warm." He stroked the horse's outstretched neck, then looked at her. "You've not the sense of a wee one, for you're shaking with cold."

His rage she could deal with, but this seeming calm confused her. All the time she had tried to be so quiet, he'd been awake and aware. Unable to bear him touching her again, Seana led the way back inside.

She poured a beaker of wine, sipping it before she went to the fire. Her hands were shaking, and she believed she would never be warm again.

"If you'd but asked, I would have poured wine for you," Micheil said, coming up behind her. He reached out to touch her hair, but snatched his hand back when he saw what he was doing. Offering more comfort to an enemy? How far would she unwittingly have him betray his clan?

He tossed kindling on the coals, then set the small cut logs on top. When he was satisfied they would soon blaze, he rose to stand beside her.

"Why did you run, Seana?"

Even if she had wanted to answer him—which she did not—there would have been no way to tell him of her terror-filled dream. She could not give him more weapons to use against her. It was enough that she had desired him, that she would never forget the feelings he invoked by his very nearness. If she knew where on Gunn lands this cottage lay... but she did not.

Bitterly she reminded herself that ten years locked in the abbey, shut away from all she knew, left her with little memory of land markings to aid her in her quest to reach home.

"I asked for an answer. Now I'm demanding one."

"I'm not a thing you own."

She finished her wine, coughing at the last, and set the beaker down on the hearth stone. Her gaze locked on the visible handle of the dirk.

"'Tis the one you lost when the outlaws attacked."

"I told you I treasured it. What I cl—what I think of as mine, I fight to hold." Micheil waited, hoping she would not notice his slip. He almost stated the words emblazoned within his hall.

She looked up at him. "You went back there to claim it."

Since it was not a question, he felt no obligation to answer her.

As he walked away, Seana cried out, "I had to run. I need to be away from you."

"Much as I hoped your feelings would lie in another direction, I will not hold this against you. I warned you, and you chose not to believe me. I cannot have you wandering about these lands. You'd be found by a man loyal to the Gunns.

"Seana?"

She turned and found herself hauled to her feet. He locked both her wrists with one hand, the other reaching above her to pull several leather strips from a peg. The wine had dulled her senses. He had her wrists wrapped and tied while she looked on in disbelief.

"Will you hobble me, too?"

"Such a tart tongue. Aye, it's my intent." Lifting her, Micheil brought her the short distance to the bed and laid her prone. Two leathers dangled from his hand. "If you dare to kick me, I'll—"

"Would it serve to free me, I'd unman you if I could."

"If I did not know I gave you pleasure, Seana, I'd take that as an insult." He bent to her ankle, making a noose that was not overly tight, but one that could not slip easily off. When he lifted her other foot, he frowned at the healing gash.

Seana watched him walk to the chest and take from it a packet of linen. He glanced around, as if searching for something. Then, with a shrug, he lifted the flask from the table.

"Your foot needs bathing before I use this salve, but you'll forgive me for not walking to the burn. It'll sting."

With no more warning, he poured a bit of the wine over the cut in her foot. He held her ankle firm against her instinctive tug away. Micheil saw her toes curl and knew it hurt, so he made short work of spreading the salve before he noosed her ankle and tied the leathers together.

"I'll find you shoes, too." He yanked two furs from beneath her and used them to cover her. Drawing one up to her chin, he grazed her breasts with the backs of his hands. He met her resentful look with wry amusement. The bindings would not be overly tight unless she struggled. He knew she was at a loss for words, else he would be having his ears blistered.

"Your own wound wants tending."

"Concern for your enemy, Seana?" She had surely said it to annoy him and prove him wrong.

"I'd not have you die from so paltry a wound. Not when I want it to be by my hand."

"Such a fierce little warrior maid. I'd lose sleep—"

"Maid no more," she snapped.

"Aye. Sleep well, little cat." He leaned over, wishing her eyes widened with something other than fear. "'Tis a true sign of enchantment that I wish you sleep at all. This is yet another night that you've stolen mine from me."

Her lips set in mutinous silence. She refused to look, but heard him settle himself before the fire once more. All too soon his even breathing made a lie of his accusation that she robbed him of sleep.

But he was the thief of hers.

Him and her fear of returning again to the terror-filled images of her running, only to be caught like a *tod.* She was no fox, even if they were claimed to be wily creatures. She'd be free, or die trying.

If she had never run from the abbey, and the only safety she had known, she would not have found herself trussed like meat for the spit. The soothing salve on her foot made her turn her head to look at him.

Never had she heard the lies whispered about her brother. And they *were* lies. No matter the strong conviction of Jamie's voice. He did not know Liam. Her brother was a man of strong will and passion, but he would never strike a woman. What lies had Bridget told her clan?

Round and round the questions circled in her mind. She turned to prayer, her only comfort. Begging for help to escape, she added pleas for mercy, that she not bear a child. Why had she yielded to him?

She fled to the safety of sleep not to learn the answer.

Streaks of sunlight, warm and butter yellow, filtered through the narrow slits of the cottage wall. Seana yawned and stretched, her eyes gritty and burning as the shaft of sunlight drew her gaze. The sun—more fool she! The lands of the Gunns lay to the northwest, and home lay to the east.

Coming fully awake, she understood she was no longer bound. A sweeping look showed that Jamie was gone. Seana needed no urging to run for the door. He'd been so sure of her that he'd left it unbarred.

But when she lifted the wooden latch, the door would not budge. Barred from without! He had locked her in to await his return.

If he returned....

Panic took hold.

What if he had gone to bargain with the Gunn chief?

Or to fetch him here?

She gouged the wood, uncaring of the painful splinters that pierced her skin. Freedom and safety lay on the other side of the door. She had to get out!

Within the ancient stone walls of Halberry, Micheil sat at the high table in the great hall. He could smell the spice of the sea above the sweetness of thyme and roses scattered in the rushes. He closed his eyes, listening again to the echoes of his childhood where the sea lapped at the rocks below the promontory where Halberry stood. The cold salt tang came with the late-morning sunlight through the slits high in the wall.

He drank deeply of his ale and set the gem-studded goblet down, annoyed that Peigi insisted on using his father's cup to serve him.

As if his thought had conjured her, Peigi, short and round as a keg of ale, bustled her way before him. Meeting her sharp, raisin-dark eyes, Micheil knew he would be berated for not doing justice to the meal she had set before him.

His gaze followed hers on its progress from dish to dish. Salted, smoked and baked salmon, broth, stewed beef, and mutton pie. Hard cheeses and bannocks, along with brose—a personal dislike of Micheil's, for he'd yet to have the oatmeal porridge served without lumps—all remained untouched.

"Were the bannocks burned?" Peigi asked, fingering the thick, flat cakes made from coarsely ground barley.

"Not so I could tell."

"You did not eat your brose, lad. 'Tis no true Scots blood within ye."

Micheil eyed her askance. Her age gave her privilege, for Peigi had ordered the kitchens and castle from the time of his mother's death. But even she stepped over the bounds when she berated him as if he were yet a wee bairn still in swaddling.

"Ye're troubled over the lass."

"Have you done as I ordered?" Micheil asked her, knowing she had true sight. His voice was soft, for he knew the old woman meant well, but his churning thoughts were not to be shared.

"Aye." She sighed, and glanced around the hall. "I've set young Moibeal to clean the tower room. Will ye fetch her home this day?"

"Seana MacKay will not call Halberry home," he reminded her.

Peigi poured him more ale. "I'd not be expecting to have a *reiteach* for her."

"Keep it to mind, Peigi. She had her betrothal party the cursed night Bridget wed her foul brother. There'll be no *failte* here for her."

"Would the laying of a fire in her room be too much welcome for her?"

"You sore test my patience. Have you no chore to tend but to plague me?"

Rattling the keys to his storerooms, which hung from the belt that Bridget refused to wear, Peigi nodded and took herself from the hall.

His thoughts turned to Seana as he had left her sleeping. She'd be long awake. Her discovery that she was locked in the cottage would likely have her attempting to tear down the walls. If he left now and rode hard, he could be back with her this night.

Bridget had yet to return from the abbey. But her progress would be slower. From what Peigi had told him, she had taken it upon herself to fetch Seana from the abbey. He had been in such a hurry that day, when he saw his sister, that the fury of Seana's escape held sway and he never thought to question her why she had come. He liked it not that Bridget felt the need to usurp his place and begin the revenge he was sworn to do.

He lifted his gaze and found himself staring at the curved stone lintel above the massive oak doors to the hall. There, carved in the stones, was his family's motto: I claim I hold.

The touch of a cold, wet nose broke his reverie, and he looked into the shaggy face of an enormous hound. "Ah, Jennet, where's your mate and your master?" It was Davey's whimsy that named his hound after a small horse, but then, she was of a size for a child to ride. He gazed at her soulful brown eyes while he obliged her nudge and scratched her behind her ears.

"Well, big beastie, where in tarnation be your mate? Not far from you, I wager."

A loud bark announced Cudgel, so named for his reiving any stick he found. The hound loped into the hall, and behind him came Davey and Jamie.

"Have you come to stay, brother?" Davey yelled, hurrying to the high table. "We've news. Old Lachlann found two sheep gone this morn. Jamie and me rode out, and I'd swear the tracks we followed led toward MacKay's holdings."

"Has he any left?" Micheil asked, feeding bits of the stewed beef to both dogs.

"Peigi won't be pleased to see you feed them with her finely cooked dishes."

Micheil merely glanced at Jamie and continued to feed the dogs.

"Have you come with the lass, Micheil?"

"Nay. I left her locked in Iain's cottage. Davey, set her from your thoughts and tell me about the stolen sheep."

Davey took a long quaff of Micheil's ale and helped himself to a bannock. Jamie sat on the edge of the table and filled a plain silver beaker with mulled wine.

"I'm waiting," Micheil reminded his brother.

"There's not much to tell. Lachlann found his sheep gone, sent word, and Jamie and me left Crisdean, Gabhan and Marcus to find them."

"Do you think the MacKay knows about his sister?"

"I could not care less, Jamie." Micheil felt Cudgel nudge him for more food, but the beef was gone. "You've had enough. Go beg from your master." He rose from his place, his gaze resting on the massive, double-edged claymores and single-edged broadswords mounted on the side wall. Many of the hilts were inscribed with ancient runes and gems large as quail eggs, but his own personal favorite was a plain iron hilt and single-edged blade forged from one length. They were the weapons passed down from Olav the Black, the Norwegian King of Man and Isles, taken as his plunder.

Davey's hand on his arm roused him. "Micheil, will you listen without anger to what I say?"

"'Tis such a grave matter that you need ask?"

"Aye, Micheil. The first is Niall. He's been seen with a Keith. They're growing bold again."

"When are they not?" Jamie interrupted.

"Aye." Micheil agreed, "When indeed?"

"We've never told you this, but the night Bridget wed, George Keith and Niall were deep in talk. I liked it not then. Niall's purse is ever empty and you need beware."

Micheil placed his hand on Davey's shoulder. "'Tis a true brother you are. Set Lucas to watch him. He's got no liking for Niall."

"And with good reason. Niall took his leman." Jamie met Davey's gaze and nodded.

Impatient now to be gone, Micheil saw the looks they exchanged. "Tell me."

But it was Jamie who answered. "Davey's been having the dreams again."

"Lovers in fire?" Micheil would not hurt his younger brothers by dismissing Davey's dreams. Some had come true. Peigi defended Davey, claiming he had the sight. He waited until Davey raised his head and met his steady gaze.

"More. There's a storm, and she's running—"

"Who?"

"Seana, Micheil. The lass is well? She appears weak, and cannot run. She carries some bundle clutched to her chest, but I did not see what she holds. There's thundering and great slashes of lightning, but the sound that comes is the pounding of hooves."

Micheil felt a chill walk up his spine. He recalled Seana thrashing about, the cries that had come from

her and awakened him before she tried to flee last night. And when he asked why, he'd known she was unaware of the terror that briefly darkened her eyes. Did she dream as Davey did?

His aunt would have known, and she had said naught of it to him. But then, his meeting with her had not allowed her to tell him anything about Seana. If it was true, it was no wonder he thought himself bewitched.

"Micheil?"

"I need to get back to her, Davey."

"Does she know yet who you are?" Jamie asked, walking alongside Micheil.

"Not yet. But she will."

Davey joined his brothers. "It's not like you to play a cat-and-mouse game with her."

"Are you talking to her when the dreams come upon you, brother? I swear she accused me of the same only last eve."

The dogs went flying past, Jennet in the lead, with a mouthful of smoked salmon, Cudgel hot on her tail as they bounded out the doors.

"Dinna be yelling about her thievery, Micheil," Davey said defensively. "She's swelling with a new litter."

"Mayhap Bridget would like—"

"Bridget cannot abide them. She's been obsessed with having the MacKay lass here. That's why she braved going to the abbey. She claimed you were dragging the time out, Micheil. She intended to bring your betrothed home."

"Our sister forgets that she does not rule here. And Seana is my enemy, Davey, naught more. Take lesson from Bridget, and never forget it."

Micheil took hold of Ciotach's reins as the stable lad led the horse forth to the foot of the steps. He looked out over the courtyard, seeing that all was in order. Smoke rose from the bakehouse, the blacksmith's forge rang with his blows, and a cart rumbled on the cobbles, drawing away from the stable where his prize horses were kept. He saw Peigi, with Moibeal following, head for the storehouse.

Ciotach tugged at the leathers Micheil held, and he mounted. The horse was as eager as he to ride free.

"Do you bring her back this eve?" Jamie called out.

"Aye. It's long past the time she knew who I am."

Jamie saw the pained expression on Davey's face and quickly took his brother into the hall.

"Did you hear him, Jamie? Hear how he named her enemy? Micheil is still reminding himself of that." Davey grabbed his brother's arm. "Micheil's made her his leman."

"God's bones, Davey! Never say you saw them become lovers, too?"

Davey let his hand fall to his side and turned away. He could not answer Jamie. He would not tell Jamie or any other of the terrible battle Micheil waged to remember that Seana was his, but only for revenge.

He had seen a pair of lovers in flames. Now he knew that the flames of passion had burned. He need only await the flames of fury to sear all before them to ash.

Then it would be over.

Davey never felt Jamie catch him before he fell.

"What have you seen, brother mine? What awaits us all?"

## Chapter Fourteen

Seana heard the coming of a lone horseman. She had made good use of the hours she had been alone. A thorough search had yielded needle and thread, so her kirtle and gown were roughly mended. The leather thongs that had been used to bind her served to hold the tangled length of her hair. When her senseless attempt to tear apart the door was finished, she had used the salve to ease her bruised hands, and had discovered a cloak at the bottom of the chest.

The foods left from their meal had been redistributed, and she glanced at them, sure the hidden cheese and smoked fish would not be missed. All was as ready as she could make it.

With an outward show of calm, she folded her hands on her lap, and sat on the stool to wait. Instinct told her that Jamie had at last returned to her.

Behind her a merry fire blazed, but Seana stared at the door and heard the sounds of her prison being opened.

Micheil eased the door open slowly, uncertain of his reception. Seana had a fine temper when aroused. Leaving her alone and locked in might earn him a hail

of missiles flung at his head. She sat meekly behind the table, the signs of tears clearly visible, and he had to stifle the rush of compassion he felt, knowing he had frightened her. There was no longer any choice but to take her to Halberry and make good his oath. That he constantly needed to reaffirm this sat ill on his mind. After all, she was a hated MacKay...was she not?

"There's many a highland man who'd be wishing to find so meek a goodwife awaiting his return," he said by way of greeting as he entered the cottage.

"I'm not your wife, Jamie."

"The hours alone have not sweetened your tongue."

"The stench of the food spoiling has not sweetened the air in here, either."

"In that, I agree," he returned, his nostrils flaring as he neared the table. "We'll not be staying, Seana. I've come to fetch you."

Her fingers tightened their hold around each other. His mocking smile and jaunty step showed him pleased with himself. Once more he was richly dressed in fine linen, his black hair gleaming where the last rays of the sunlight were caught and held within its length. There was a strong, arrogant air about him as he hooked his thumbs in the belted leather girdling his hips. The dirk rested within, but he wore no sword. He truly thought himself in command of her and all else he surveyed, if he felt he could go forth without a weapon.

"Did you not hear me, Seana? I've come to fetch you to your proper place."

For a moment, hope flared that he meant to take her home. But as she raised her gaze to the hard cast of his

features and looked at his eyes, Seana knew that was not his intent. So be it.

"Despite what you believe, *Jamie*—" and she deliberately placed a most heavy emphasis on the use of his name "—being alone did not addle my hearing." Her gaze dropped to the open laces of his shirt, which revealed his throat and offered a peek at the black whorls of hair on his chest. Seana gave herself a mental shake. This was not the time to be thinking of how the whiteness of his linen made his skin alike to the tawny coat of a lion, or his eyes brighten to the blue of a loch on a calm day.

He leaned closer, and she inhaled the scent of sandalwood. It offended her, for it served as a reminder of her own ripe scent. He was groomed like a peacock for show, and she a beggar maid for his bidding.

"Seana, what is it? You're deep in thought. It's not like you to ignore—"

"You do not know me, Jamie. Do not be making that claim."

"You were crying."

"Need you sound accusing? Aye, I shed tears. 'Tis not every night I go from maid to...h-harlot." She hated that he knew the name troubled her, but he said naught, and even looked away for a moment.

Seana looked away, too. Toward the bed. She fought the images that came to mind. She did not want to remember how she welcomed him, yielding all and begging for release.

"Seana?" Micheil saw for himself that her thoughts had taken her where his had gone. He had seen hope

flare and die, and now, for a heartbeat, there was longing in her eyes, too quickly veiled.

"If you believe I will meekly follow like a sheep led to the slaughter wherever you intend to take me, disabuse yourself of such a daft notion. I will not go."

There was regret underlying her words, regret that this man, who had aroused her and shown her an all-consuming passion that stole into her heart, was truly her betrayer. His betrayal set her on a path from which she could not turn. That she would live the rest of her days with the dark chasm of desire he branded upon her soul was her burden to bear. She knew she must never reveal it to him.

"'Tis not a choice I'm giving you." Micheil sat on the edge of the table, his hand on the carved handle of his dirk. "Do not make me hurt you."

She glared up at him. She longed to slap his face. "Will it matter? What more can you do to mark me soiled in the eyes of my clan? I yielded—ah, you did not think I'd admit that, but it's true—and in yielding left Dhu Micheil without a weapon against me. What can you do that will not be done by him?" Her laugh was false and mocking. "Proceed, Jamie. If you take my life, I'll not be cursing you. I'll bless you with my dying breath for saving me from the Gunn's revenge!"

"A most serious mistake on my part to have left you alone." Micheil felt as if a lifetime passed in those minutes when he looked upon her. Rage slid into his blood even as his loins stirred. Her carefully mended kirtle and gown could not hide the slender curves within. They were his, burned in memory of the

sweetly heated passion he had taken and been given in turn. Her ripe breasts rose and fell rapidly—with anger or desire, he did not know—but her hands were clenched tight, and a quiver rippled over them.

He wanted her. Even as her last words sounded again in his mind, he wanted her. And she would suffer death, gladly, rather than be claimed by him.

Micheil slipped from his seat at the table, turned his back on her and walked to the open doorway. He stared out at the land he loved, heaths rich with purple and gold, the thick, greened woods, the crags and valleys, the mist-laden moors, all as wild and raw as his feelings.

His soul cried out for peace. He wanted to visit his lands without arms, without men riding at his back. He longed to lift one crofter's child in his arms, and see no fear in that child's eyes. He yearned to be free of the wailing of widows, free of the burning of crops and the hunger. He hated the death toll that had mounted over the years as he kept the blood oath he had sworn. The blood oath Bridget never allowed him to forget.

The abrupt sound of the stool scraping against the earthen floor told him she had risen. He felt the glaring hate from her eyes stabbing into his back.

"Jamie, I ask you one last time. Will you let me go? I'm not a thing to be used by a man, like a beast from the field." She looked to see his large hand clench on the wooden doorframe. Seana found the courage to continue only because he did not turn around. She had to try, before he forced her into what she was ill-suited to do.

"I do not ken if you be doing this to me to help or hinder that black savage. I do not care now." She could not help the desperation in her voice—it was all that filled her.

"Kill me or free me!"

*I cannot kill you!* But the words went no farther than his mind. "Freeing you will not save you, Seana. You know what your clan will do to you."

"Only if they know I've lain with you."

"I am asked to keep silent, then? Of course, why else would you say such? But what if there's to be a bairn?"

Too desperate and distracted to hear the wistful note in his voice, Seana cried out. "I will not let there be!"

Micheil cringed. He knew the ways of potions and herbs that ofttimes would kill a woman as soon as rid her of an unwanted child. He often wondered if Fiona had used them, for not once in the years they had lain together had she come to him claiming to carry his seed. True, he had been careful to hold himself away from her at the last moment of release, but many a man had been snared, just the same.

So deep in his thought, he turned and found her behind him. Her eyes should have warned him—narrowed and glittering, like those of a golden feline ready to strike prey—but she lifted her face toward him, and all he could see was the mouth that had known no kiss but his own. He reached for her, despite the warnings his mind cried out, for the tide of savage need rushed through him.

"Seana, I claimed you, lass. I cannot let you go."

"'Tis sorry, so sorry, I am to hear that." She rose on tiptoe to press her lips to his. The moment he closed his eyes, seeking to deepen the kiss, she raised the log she had hidden behind her back and smashed it against the side of his head.

Seana caught him as he fell, dropping to her knees to cushion his body. "I did not want this," she whispered as she carefully lowered his head to the earthen floor. "You brought me low, with no way out but to meet violence with violence."

Her hand shook as she sought his heartbeat, for her intent had never been to kill him. Finding the faint beat brought her quickly to her feet. She skirted his body and peered outside, making sure that he had come alone. When her fear receded, she stepped outside, slowly making her way around the cottage, sending her searching gaze over the land to make sure no one waited to trap her again.

The Lord had answered her prayers, and Seana set to work quickly to ensure her successful escape. From his belt she took his dirk and, remembering his warnings about his horse, stood well to the side while she cut free the leather that held him.

Dashing back inside, she removed the bundle she had hidden in the chest—the cloak wrapped around the food—and this she set outside. Now for his body. She had to drag him out of the cottage. A thought easier come than the deed accomplished. She stood panting from her exertions when she had him clear of the cottage.

Seana hardened her resolve as she went back inside. She tried not to think of the woman whose lov-

ing hands had tended this home. She thought of her own clan, of the crofts that had been burned, and with them all possessions. She tore the dry heather and bracken free from the bed and laid a trail to the fire. She placed the stool directly on top, added all the kindling and wood from the box, then snatched up the log she had hit him with. Rolling out the glowing embers, she saw to the start of the flames. Smoke rose and filled the air.

She walked out without a backward glance. Lifting up her bundle, Seana gazed down at Jamie's face. "I'll not be forgetting you."

She had only his word that they were on Gunn lands. Fire should draw the clan to stop its spreading. If the Lord would show her mercy, she would make good this escape.

Jamie restlessly drummed his fingers against the high table. The torches flared at his order long after they had supped. Davey lingered by his side in the hall as they awaited Micheil's return. Jamie's gaze fell on Niall. His arrival had been unexpected, no excuse offered. Hard upon his heels, Fiona came, with Bridget. He liked not her presence, nor her flirtatious manner with Niall. Och! Would Micheil never come and send them all fleeing!

"Jamie!" Davey whispered, his head thrown back as he stared blindly upward. "It happens now."

"What—" Jamie's question remained unasked. The door burst open.

"They've signaled Iain's croft's in flames!"

"Kill the MacKay and be done with it," Niall declared, rising even as Jamie did.

"The MacKays haven't ten horse left to mount men. They'd not dare to come this far on our lands." Jamie eyed Niall's dress sword. "Micheil's there, and if you think to ride with us, *cousin,* fetch a sword that'll cleave a man's body, not that toy a lady fancies."

Niall colored with unspoken rage. He nodded and hurried from the hall. *Someday that pink-cheeked bastard will beg for his life!*

"Davey! Davey, lad, can you ride with us?"

Jamie hauled his brother to his feet and pressed a goblet of wine against his lips. He ignored the nearness of Fiona, with her cloying scent of gillyflowers and musk.

"Why was Micheil at Iain's? You said he was to fetch that MacKay bitch here."

Jamie tightened his lips and saw that Davey had finished the wine. "Can you ride?"

"Aye. I must come."

Fiona dug her fingers into Jamie's arm. "Answer me, or I'll tell Micheil you insult me."

"Tell him. Now, stand aside, or I'll order you taken from Halberry, Fiona."

Meeting the fierce, dark-eyed gazes of both brothers, Fiona lowered her head. She twisted her fingers within the finely wrought links of the necklace Micheil had given her.

"Forgive me, Jamie. I feared for him, and did not think before I voiced my concern."

Casting her a mocking look as he rounded the table with Davey at his side, Jamie could not resist a part-

ing remark. "I'll be sure to tell Micheil. Pray we find our brother unhurt, or blood will run."

Outside, men filled the courtyard. The shrill neighing and restless stamping of the horses blended with shouted orders. The flaring torches revealed Niall mounted on one of their prize grays.

Crisdean came forth. "I had to give him a fresh horse. His poor beaten beastie was done for."

"'Tis our misfortune he rides with us at all. Help my brother to mount, and stay close by him." Jamie sought his own black, Killen, and once mounted announced, "Any man found not of our clan is to be slain!"

"Bring the dogs," Davey ordered.

"Why, mon?" Crisdean asked, stilling the restless prance of his steed. "We've no need of dogs to track reivers, no matter whose badge they wear."

"'Tis not reivers, but a lass, we'll hunt this night."

Seana kept the setting position of the sun behind her as she set off for home. Every step on the spongy earth, bursting with new shoots, filled her heart with a joy she had not known for too long. The wind drifted by, carrying with it the smell of the burning croft, but not once did she turn around.

In her mind's eye she held the image of the heathered moors of Cape Wrath. She could see the heather blooming purple under the deep blue sky where the hawks reigned supreme and floated with wings outstretched until prey sent them hurtling toward earth. It was a harsh place, the stones of their keep appearing to rise from the pitiless cliff that fell straight to the

sea. Had the battering white-tipped waves eroded the
stones as the Gunns had eroded all the MacKays'
pride?

She prayed not. And allowed no more thoughts but
those of her survival to occupy her.

Her soles had toughened somewhat, and a raider's
moon allowed her to put a good distance between
herself and the burning cottage. But it was time to find
a safe place to rest for a few hours.

Nearly an hour later, she found a shelter in an out-
crop of rocks. The hard cheese she ate sparingly.
Wrapped in her stolen cloak, she grabbed handfuls of
bracken to pile around her. Safe within her nest, she
fell into a deep slumber. Exhaustion left no room for
dreams this night.

Davey saw the danger first, as the party rode toward the cottage. He had to call off the dogs when
they attempted to go near Micheil's prone body. There
was naught to save of the cottage. A glance showed
that Micheil had tried to go inside. But had been
forced to draw back. Ciotach screamed and reared.
The stallion's hooves lashed out, his eyes rolling
wildly, his hide rippling with tremors of fear as the hiss
and crackle of the flames blazed high and he stood his
ground to protect his master.

"Jamie, come talk to him," Davey ordered.
"Micheil's hurt."

It was Jamie, whose voice most resembled Micheil's easy croon, who slid from his horse and cau-

tiously approached the pawing steed. Ciotach arched his neck and snapped viciously at Jamie.

"Easy. Come, my fine braw laddie. Come away from the fire," he crooned. Jamie held out his hand, walking very slowly around the horse so that Ciotach was forced to turn away from the fire.

Jamie could not spare a glance at his brother Micheil, but he heard his groan. And then, in a soft voice: "Davey, try to pull him back from the fire." He continued coaxing the animal, who snorted and pawed the earth, quivers still visible across his gray hide, as the men used their swords and plaids to beat down the fire. By the time Jamie had caught hold of the reins and led the horse away to one of the men, Micheil was sitting up.

"Dinna try to move, brother," Davey cautioned, his dark eyes filled with concern. "You've a nasty gash swelling like a hen's egg on the side of your head."

"Aye, I feel the devil's own pounding," Micheil groaned. "Seana?" he asked, closing his eyes against the smoldering ruin of the cottage.

"Och, Micheil, there was no chance of saving her. The blaze engulfed the cottage by the time we arrived. Here, have yourself a drink of—"

Micheil shoved his hand away. "I've no need to be cosseted, Davey."

"Have the drink anyway. Something needs to sweeten your tongue and your temper."

"I'm not hurt badly. 'Twas the smoke that laid me low. I cannot believe she did this." Micheil felt for his dirk, and found it gone. A shout near the blackened ruin made Micheil tense.

"There's no sign the lass burned within!" Crisdean yelled, waving his sword high.

"She's run, then?"

Micheil eyed Davey, holding his aching head. He coughed and accepted the flask that Davey held out to him. The fiery liquid burned down his throat. He winced as he ignored his brother's offer to help and, swaying slightly, stood to survey the blackened ruin, where small fires yet flared.

"'Tis the grace of God that you came when you did, Davey."

"You dinna arrive as promised. The watch called the fire, and we rode—"

"You saw no sign of Seana?" Micheil sipped again, and felt the warmth in his belly. Rubbing his head, he admitted softly, "More fool I, to think she would come meekly."

"Would you have, Micheil?"

"Nay. But I'd not be leaving an enemy to burn alive in fire."

"When we came you were lying toward the cottage, not away from it. 'Twould appear—"

"I roused and thought her within." Micheil touched his aching head and felt the blood on his hand. "You set a high price on yourself, Seana."

Davey saw the way his brother's eyes narrowed, and a shiver walked up his spine. "Micheil, come home and have your head tended. She'll not get far this night." Davey hesitated, then leaned close, so that none but Micheil would hear him. "Take this as an omen to let her go, Micheil. Naught good can come from having her."

"Do not dare ask me to have pity on that MacKay spawn. 'Tis more than the injury done, more than stealing my dirk, 'tis my pride she dares, brother."

"Nay, 'tis the hunger she stirs." Davey closed his eyes against the darkness, but it waited within his mind. "None need know that the lass bested you. Let her go. No matter she dinna know who you are. She did not try to kill you, Micheil."

"She's not got the stomach for shedding blood."

"She shed yours," Davey reminded him, looking again at the dark savageness of his brother's face.

"As I did hers. 'Tis my shame that she bested me, and I'll have my payment in full for this night, and for Bridget." Micheil looked at Davey and lifted the flask for another drink. "I'll not sleep till she's found."

"And I'll be riding with you, Micheil," Jamie said as he joined them. "She left you for dead, I vow. She can't get far on foot. Set the dogs on her, Davey."

Men's voices chorused behind them. "Aye, set the dogs on her!"

"She thought herself imprisoned in the abbey. She'll have a true taste of prison when I find her." Micheil tossed the flask back to Davey, and with Jamie's help mounted Ciotach.

"Have a care, Davey," Micheil warned. "None of her sorcery can make you forget she's a MacKay. Never." The last was soft, but held a note of danger that boded ill for the MacKay woman.

"I'm not forgetting. I only warn you in turn, Micheil, that she's set you on a reckless path." Davey left him to call the dogs to him.

Micheil eyed his brother's retreating back before turning to Jamie. "I'll not deny she sets fire to my blood. But she pays for the sins of the past as I swore."

Quietly listening and waiting far back of the mounted men, Niall smiled. *As will you, Micheil. As will you.*

The keening of the wind awakened Seana. Her body ached, yet she heard the warning whispering through her mind. *Flee! Hurry!* She shook her head, and the minutes passed, spinning out time as slowly as the feeding of thread through the distaff. The warnings only intensified.

From the far distance, she heard the baying of hounds.

"Sweet Lord, they've set the dogs on me!" She needed no more urging to rise and run, leaving behind her small nest and her food.

The rest had served her well, and her blood pumped with alarm. The thought of being caught and dragged before the Gunn chief hardened her to the pain of the fresh cuts and bruises on her feet. She could not allow her freedom to be stolen from her now.

She ran like a wild thing, until she could no longer hear the dogs, until pain lanced her side and she stood panting, with her head hanging down, against a stunted tree. Drawing and releasing great lungfuls of air, Seana knew she was hopelessly lost. She was beaten beyond thinking, as well. There was a scent of rain in the clouds that scudded across the moon.

Not that, she pleaded, casting her gaze heaven-ward. Her stomach rumbled, reminding her that she had run off without her food store.

"Curse you to Satan and the fires of hell, whoever you are, Jamie!" but she could not summon the strength even to raise her fist to the sky. She sagged against the rough bark of the tree, forcing herself to calm.

She needed to gather her strength and go on. There was no other choice. She could not face that betrayer yet again. Not after what she had done to him. Shame rose, that she had given herself to him. Covering her mouth with shaking hands to keep herself from screaming with rage, she forced the sight of him that rose too fast back into the deep, hidden reaches of her mind.

Rage served where fear could not. She rose and started walking. She would not be caught again! She would die first!

Sometime later, she stumbled into a burn. The shock of water, chilling her to the bone, roused her. She satisfied her thirst, trembling with cold as the day broke on a gray, misting rain.

Seana dragged her sodden cloak around her and once again started off. She would not be beaten.

'Twas smoke she smelled, long before the crofter's hut came in sight. She implored all the saints in heaven to let her find safety and warmth within. If not, she prayed, grant that I've found a far outlying farm of the Gunns'. One where they will not be aware of the hunt for me.

She cautioned herself to proceed slowly before she revealed herself. She eyed the thatched roof, and its welcome smoke, but saw no one stir.

Knowing she could go no farther without warmth, food and rest, Seana ignored the niggling warning that surfaced as she stared at the small grove of trees at the hut's side. As if she had willed the decision to be taken from her, a wizened old man came from the trees, his thatch of white hair a target for her gaze. His shirt and breeks were ragged. Before she could stop herself, Seana limped forward.

"Have you naught to spare for a weary traveler?" she called out.

With a hand shading his squinting eyes, the man stared at the wraithlike creature coming through the mist toward him.

Half fainting, Seana held out a pleading hand. "Quick now, tell me whose lands these be?"

"'Tis me own earth." Pity stirred for the lass. She was in a sorry state. But his eyes had witnessed as much and more, these long years past. "Come by the fire and warm yerself," he offered.

"God's mercy, I have need for you to send for aid," she whispered, sinking to her knees.

"Here, now, lass," he said, coming forward to help her stand and get in out of the wet. "Ye're done for, by the look of ye."

Blessing him for his kindness, Seana leaned heavily on him as he led her inside. She huddled close to the fire, lacking the strength to do more than plead with him.

"Can you send to the MacKay to come?"

"Och, lass, he'll not be one to give ye protection, if that be what yer seeking. He gives little enough to his crofters."

The refusal made her close her eyes. She needed to bribe him, and had naught. Sliding her hands inside the wet cloak, Seana touched Jamie's stolen dirk. A finely wrought weapon should bring her what she needed.

"Liam will come, I tell you. Tell him that Seana comes home. Aye, say that to him, old man. Tell the MacKay his sister is here."

The sheepskin he had been about to cover her shoulders with fell unheeded to the floor. He crossed himself and stared at her.

Seana turned and opened her eyes at his silence. She almost gave in to the wild laughter rising inside her. He was peering at her as if she were a ghost. Crossing himself again and again, muttering under his breath. So he thought her dead? Likely many thought it so. But not yet, she reminded herself, feeling warmth creep back into weary limbs. Her freedom depended upon her convincing him, and quickly, to get her aid from her brother.

"I'm not a ghostly being. I've been kept prisoner at Deer Abbey all this time. Please, give me a name to call you. I would thank you, and remember you for all my days in my prayers."

"Angus I'm called." Her hunted appearance, and the haunting fear in her gaze, made pity rise again, but he had to ask, "Are they after ye then?"

"Aye. Not long behind me. I will not go back. Is there no one you can send to the MacKay?" She glanced down at her feet. "I'll not be able to walk another step." When she still did not hear the words she longed for—that he would go—Seana withdrew the dirk. "It's yours to keep," she said, pushing it into his hands.

Her avid gaze watched him turn the inscribed dirk over and over, studying it, hefting its balance. She knew it was a weapon to covet. "Take it as a token, and in payment for the aid you'd give me."

He looked up at her. His dark eyes gleamed. "Aye, lass, I will have it. Me daughter's lad tends the sheep, but I'll fetch him. His legs are strong." And he remembered well the reason why. "Rest ye an' abide here. Yer safe."

"Safe?" Seana closed her eyes and repeated the word to herself. She heard him leave, and vowed that safe she would remain. Weary, she let her sodden cloak fall from her shoulders and dragged the sheepskin closer so that she could lie down.

With no idea how much time had passed, she roused herself from her exhaustion when she heard the sounds of horses. Her heart beat with joy. A glad cry rose to her lips, and she rushed to fling open the hut's door.

A mighty force was bearing down on the hut. "Liam!" she called out. "I'm home, brother. I'm ho—"

"God's blood, Micheil! The lad was right. 'Tis the MacKay woman that's fallen, ripe as fruit, into your hands."

From the center of the group of horsemen, Micheil rode forth until he could see the terror dilating Seana's eyes.

"I claim, I hold," he stated, releasing the devil's own laughter.

"Whoreson! Coward!" Seana screamed, her soul denying what her mind told her was true.

"I've killed men for saying as much, but my revenge on you will be sweeter by far, till you wish for death. Naught else will free you."

## Chapter Fifteen

The men's laughter shamed her, and with it went her heart's denial that she had given herself to her enemy. Jamie was indeed the Gunn chief. Over and over she heard them claim it as they all dismounted. None made a move toward her. Seana grabbed hold of the doorframe to keep from fainting. She'd not show them weakness. But even as her gaze skimmed the crowd and lit upon one fair of face who stood at Micheil's side and commanded the dogs to silence their yapping, she knew she was doomed.

Ripe fruit? Nay, she had fallen into a nest of vipers. She found the old man and hate ran deep for his betrayal.

As if she had willed it, Angus came forward and drew forth the dirk, and with it, another. "Look ye! Look upon the murdering blade that pierced my lass's heart. I'd not give aid to MacKay were it a wee one," he spat, vemon alight in his eyes. "Ye know that blade, dinna ye?"

Seana recoiled as he held it up, so close to her face that her eyes would have to cross to keep the blade in sight. *In his lass's breast,* he claimed. Just as he had

claimed to hold the land as his. A terror so chilling that she could not speak or move gripped her. She knew the dirk. It was her brother Liam's own.

"Beaten about the face she was," Angus growled, shaking the dirk back and forth. "Killed her, he did, after he had his way with her. And she, poor lassie, not yet seen her fifteenth summer. 'Tis your fate, as well, the Dhu has promised. Your kind—"

"Enough!" Micheil's command rang out. The devil's wrath burned in his eyes as he beheld Seana. "Angus, you served us well this day. Davey will see to your reward."

Madness lit Angus's eyes. He lifted Micheil's dirk to his lips and kissed the blade. "Show me this drenched with her blood, and that's reward enough," he said handing over the dirk to Micheil.

"Aye," Seana whispered softly, "have done, and kill me now." But even to her own ears the words rang false. She did not want to die. As long as she kept herself alive, she could have hope of escaping him.

"You know the penalty for thievery, Seana."

She looked down at his hands, the hands that had taught passion to her body, and clenched her own at her sides.

"'Tis my right to demand you pay for stealing—"

"Then take it!" she whispered furiously. "Take what little you've left me."

"Micheil," Jamie came forward to warn him, "you've granted these lands to Angus, but they lie too close to the MacKays' for us to linger. Should word reach them that she's alive and—"

"Wise counsel, brother." Micheil snagged Seana's wrist in an iron grip, pulling her along behind him.

Seana shivered at what she read in his eyes. He hated her, hated her and yet still wanted her. She knew that look of his too well. She was powerless to stop him, and yet so close to reaching home.

Crisdean held Ciotach's reins while Micheil tossed her over the saddle. He surveyed his clansman with a cold eye as he bound her wrists together and left her hanging facedown. Micheil moved around to bind her ankles. Crisdean glanced at Jamie, who stood beside him. "I like not the taking of her. If it were any other, Jamie, I'd join in celebrating her capture and rape her along with the rest. But she's bewitched Micheil. I've not seen such a look in his eyes for another."

"He'll not betray his oath, Crisdean. Micheil won't let her live, should she bring him to that."

Micheil settled his plaid over Seana. He grabbed hold of her hair and raised her head. "Do not think it a kind gesture that I cover you. I'll not have you dead before I lock the gates of Halberry behind you. And you'll find little comfort there."

Seana wished she could summon the moisture to spit at him. He let her head down and vaulted on Ciotach.

"I'm for home, lads. Who rides with me?"

There were wild yells, and beneath them Crisdean leaned toward Davey and whispered, "I like it not. It's a devil's witch he brings among us. You *know*, Davey. He could have been done with it all right here, and taken her to the very walls of MacKay's keep. That sniveling cur of a brother couldn't rouse himself from

his drunken state to come after us. There's no enough
horses to mount ten men among the MacKays."

"Micheil orders us to ride, clansman," Davey replied, his heart heavy. He knew the sorrow that would
come. He knew Micheil had his mate, no matter how
his brother denied it.

Within the ladies' solar of Halberry Castle, Bridget
paced like an angry tigress, waiting for news that
Seana had been caught. Her dark veil was turned
back, for she waited alone, having sent Fiona and her
serving woman away. Wine and sugared nutmeg cakes
remained untouched as her agitation increased.

"Soon, let it be soon that they come," she whispered, touching the scars that ruined her face. She
stared out through the wide slit in the wall, but darkness lay over the land. Below, she could see the flare
of torches. Many awaited Micheil's return. Many
would demand a piece of the MacKay woman's flesh.

A soft knock made Bridget quickly lower her veil.
"Come," she called, clasping her hands in a death grip
and hoping it was the news she longed to hear.

"Mistress, your cousin Niall begs to see ye. He said
to tell you 'tis verra important news he brings."

"Niall? What could he— Tell him I cannot see
anyone now, Moibeal." But as the buxom maid turned
to go, Bridget changed her mind. "Bring him here to
me."

When Moibeal had been ordered from the room,
leaving the two alone, she sought out Peigi. "He's up
to no good. The laird will not be liking him whispering with that one."

"Hush! She's our laird's sister, mad or no, and don't ye forget it." But Peigi marked this meeting even as she sent Moibeal off and made her way to the door of the solar.

"'Tis not true!" Bridget shouted. "You're lying for some purpose of your own, Niall. Micheil would not be caring for that spawn of the devil. She's an enemy. He'll have the revenge he promised my Da and me. He'll have it, I tell you!"

Peigi took herself in a hurry back to her kitchens, cursing Niall for the vile cur he was. The only good news he had brought was that the laird was unhurt, though the cottage was in ruin. Peigi set her lips. The laird should know what Niall had told Bridget. But Micheil would not hear a word against his sister. Davey was then the one to tell, for he could tread with Micheil where others could not. With a rough shake of her head, she set herself to getting food ready for the men's return.

Seana no longer felt the pins and needles in her limbs. Blood roared in her ears, and she kept her eyes closed as the ground rushed by. If the Gunn thought she would beg to sit, he was mistaken. She would bite her tongue before she begged a crust of bread from him. A groan rose as her stomach rumbled, and she cursed him for keeping her dangling like a sack of grain across his horse. She could feel his hand at rest on the small of her back—no lover's caress, but a firm hold to make sure she could not wiggle free. As if she

would see herself crushed beneath the beastie's hooves!

*Death before dishonor.* The thought came, but Seana had to reject it. She turned her thoughts inward, for she truly could not face the knowledge that Jamie was her feared enemy.

Between the pounding of the hooves and the rush of blood to her head, Seana stopped fighting the blackened void that beckoned. She welcomed the dark that sent her spiraling down until there was nothingness.

Micheil felt the tension slip from her body, but he dared not move her, for it would be taken as a sign of weakness.

Mere minutes later, Davey came abreast of him, riding alongside for a pace before he spoke.

"Your legs must be numb, carrying her weight over them, brother. Give her over to me." When Micheil did not even cast a look his way, Davey tried again. "She'll make poor, pitiful sport if she cannot even stand."

"I'll drag her, then."

"Och, Micheil, 'tis not like you to cheat them all of seeing her cower in fear of you and let her lay the cause on limbs robbed of feeling."

Micheil slowed and gave into Davey's urgings, making the transfer quickly. He said naught to his brother when Davey wrapped his plaid around the both of them, or when he held her upright in his arms. The sight of her limp body was too much, and he spurred his horse to the front of the men.

It was the familiar scent of the sea that roused Seana. She saw the flaring torches on the ramparts,

reflecting the massive stone of Halberry. *I will die here.* Hearing Jamie—no, he was not Jamie, he had never been Jamie, she forcefully reminded herself—call out to have the gates opened for them, Seana stifled a sob.

She tasted the sea spray and the salt of her tears, fighting to control herself before any saw this weakness. *Do not show your fear. They'll tear you apart like a pack of wolves.*

But she knew her own warning came too late, for the man who held her felt the trembling of her body.

Before Micheil took her from Davey, he slashed open the tie on her ankles. The torchlight burnished all with both golden light and shadow as the sea breeze sent the flames wavering in the courtyard. Seana stared at him, aching from the inner pain of his betrayal. When he reached for her, all she had left was her scorn.

"Are you satisfied now, savage highlander? You caught me, but only with the aid of beasts like yourself. How will your mighty Gunn pride stand hearing the tale of the chase? Will that mocking laughter of yours ring clear over the moor when the jesting begins in whispers?" Husky, and filled with hate, her voice rose as she leaned down. "How will you defend the truth, savage? That you needed the aid of hounds and near fifty men to bring the MacKay lass to bay?"

Micheil lifted eyes filled with a feral gleam to meet her gaze. "Will you still dare mock me now?"

"Aye. 'Tis all you've left me."

"And will you be alive to hear any tell of this day, Seana?" He could see the new fear his question raised,

but he thought of the fire, of her leaving him to burn, and he hardened his resolve. Her face blanched, her eyes widened, and yet she still defied him.

"I would die, and gladly. I would be a whore to the whole Highlands, rather than be raped by the likes of you."

"Lass, lass," Davey moaned in her ear, "'tis a reckless taunt. Take it back."

But Micheil laughed, and as his mocking laughter washed over her, Seana wrapped her pride around her and refused to take back the words.

"Did you mean those words, Seana? Will you make your own damning end?" Micheil forced himself to ask.

"Aye. I meant them," she spat.

"So be it. I'll not rape you," he stated in a near-growl. "But I'll not be offering you my protection. Halberry's walls will contain you, and you'll be free to seek your way, with none to blame for how it ends."

"Micheil! She dinna understand." Davey held her shaking body close, his voice low.

"Then tell her, Davey. Tell her what the fate is of a woman captured from an enemy clan."

Seana felt as if her soul were shredded by his threat. She wanted to shut out Davey's voice telling her she would be used by one and all, with none to stop them.

"Would you have me beg you for mercy, Black Micheil Gunn?"

How he hated the sound of his name on her lips, filled with that defiant scorn. He hated it so, he snarled in reply, "Aye, beg me, Seana. Beg for mercy, for a crust of bread, for your very life."

He grabbed her away from Davey and set her before him, one of his hands gripping her hair, the other forcing her head high.

"Who among you," he shouted over the milling horses as the men stood listening beside them, "has no need for a taste of revenge against a MacKay?" A damning silence came in reply. With a piercing gaze, Micheil sought out those of his clansmen who had suffered the greatest losses. He began naming them, and the wives, daughters, sons and parents dead these years past. He named a killing, the burning of a farm, the loss of livestock. All the while he totaled the grievances against her clan, Seana trembled in his hold, but her proud, defiant gaze touched each man in turn.

Jamie moved among the men, silent as a shadow, and saw that Davey did the same. To each man he whispered a warning, and when he saw that his cousin Niall stepped out from the hall's doors, he hurried to him.

"Don't utter a sound, Niall, when Micheil asks," Jamie ordered. "Once his fury cools, he'll kill any man that dared to touch her."

"If you're believing that, Jamie, then it's you who plays the fool. She tried to kill him. Micheil will not forgive her."

As Seana waited in dread for the last, she looked to the walls of the fortress, and knew this was the place of her dreams. These were the walls she had run from, from where she had escaped. And with the remembrance came the intense pain of seeing again that Micheil followed her, his words still shrouded in si-

lence, but hurting her nonetheless as she clutched her bundle and ran.

Micheil paused and drew his dirk. Still holding tight to her tangled hair, he slit the leather binding her wrists without once looking at her.

"Here's the MacKay woman. When you've had your fill of her, I will take her back to her clan, shamed as Bridget was shamed, broken as my sister was broken, so that no man would have her. Since I am her betrothed, and blessedly not of her clan, I still claim the right of her punishment. Here's your prize, then, if any want it."

He released her and stepped back. Seana did not know where she found the strength to stand there, the waiting and the silence an agony to bear, feeling herself stripped by the men's gazes.

From the steps leading to the hall came a woman's scream. "Is there not one man among you to avenge me?" Bridget, her veils fluttering, rushed from the steps, and before any could guess her intent, she shoved Seana to the cobblestones. "I'll claim her. I'll have my own revenge!"

She raised her hand to strike Seana, but Micheil caught her wrists. "Bridget, lass, 'tis not for you to soil your hands with the likes of her. Jamie! Take her inside!"

But it was Niall who came forth, Niall whose arms Bridget welcomed as she once more faced her brother.

"If none will use her, then I remind you of your sworn oath given to Da and to me, Micheil. 'Tis for you to do what must be done to her. I'll have no peace

till you do." She did not wait for him to answer, but clung to Niall as he took her back to the hall.

Seana summoned her last reserve of strength to force herself to stand. One by one, she watched men turn away to lead their horses to the stables, until she stood alone with the three brothers.

"Micheil?" Jamie said.

"Take her from my sight," Micheil ordered, turning away from her.

"Come," Davey said, taking hold of her arm.

Seana shrugged off his hand. She would walk by herself to whatever waited for her. Hate, she had learned, was almost as powerful a force as passion. And she hated Micheil, hated him as she thought of his lies, the false promise of his kiss... *Cease whipping yourself. It will defeat you where he cannot.*

Her bravery fled when she entered the warmth of the great hall and saw the high table set with food. She could do naught about the rumbling of her stomach, and she knew both brothers heard.

But the thought of having to beg for sustenance brought bile to coat her mouth.

"Peigi," Jamie called out, keeping Seana at his side with his hand at the small of her back as he led her toward the table. "Seana MacKay, our prisoner," he said to the woman as she came forth. "Micheil asked to have the tower room ready for her."

"Aye. 'Tis ready." Peigi saw the bedraggled state of the young woman between the brothers. The lass was near done in, she thought, for she could not hold her head up now.

"I'll have Moibeal light the way."

"Peigi," Davey said, "have food brought to her. I would have her away from here."

The woman cast one look at Micheil's black, scowling face, where he stood near the hearth, talking with Crisdean and the just now returned Gabhan. The latter had rode after reivers riding the north lands, and looked none too happy about his report to Micheil. She nodded and motioned for Moibeal to get the torch.

It was Davey who helped her up the winding stair. Seana knew she should thank him, but the words could not come past the lump of fear in her throat. The room was as bare as her small cell in the abbey. But a fire blazed warmth, and Moibeal open the shutters to a view of the sea.

"I'll be serving yer needs," the young girl said as she set the torch in its holder near the door and lit two candles on the table. "Will ye be wantin' water—?"

"Of course she does, Moibeal," Davey answered. Impatient, he sent her from the room. Seana had moved to stare out at the sea.

"I'll have her bring you clothing once you've washed and eaten."

"I want naught from you, or any Gunn."

"'Tis a bairn's stubborn talk I'm hearing now, when I thought you a woman to be admired for her spirit, if not her good sense."

She rounded on him. He was Micheil's brother in his features, yet his dark brown eyes were kindly, and the firelight gilded his brown hair with red glints. But Seana knew there was little help to be had from him. She saw it there in his eyes that he would not inter-

fere, would offer no hope to escape. They were all bound by the ancient laws that governed the blood feud, even as those very laws remained unwritten. The fire beckoned her to its heat, and she stood with her hands outstretched, seeing the marks of her captivity.

"There is little sense in any of this. I am made to pay for sins I've not committed," Seana said, then sighed. "I would throw myself into the sea, had I the courage."

"Life is infinitely more precious. But I warn you not to taunt Micheil as you did this night. He's bound by oaths of honor a woman little understands. If you claw him with your reckless tongue, lass, he'll be forced to retaliate, lest he be thought too weak to lead the clan. Think upon that this night."

Davey heard Moibeal and opened the door to her. "Where is the food and water?"

"She's not to have any till she begs." His dark eyes flashed, and Moibeal hurried to add, "Your brother says it. I dare not disobey."

Davey glanced over his shoulder to where Seana stood. He saw the slow straightening of her weary body, the tight set of her lips, the impotent rage in her gray eyes. Compassion moved him. It was naught else, he told himself.

"She's begged food and hot water, as well as clean clothes, from me, Moibeal. Tell that to my brother, should he ask."

The moment the door closed, Seana lashed out. "Do not think I'll thank you. I will not beg."

"I dinna think Micheil will care when he comes to you."

"Comes to me?" she repeated.

"'Tis the way, lass. He'll have to come to you to-night. You did not listen when I explained?"

"He'll—" She could not say it, could not bear to have him watch her give way to the terror that shook her. There would be no sweetly heated kisses, no touches to set her on fire. If Black Micheil came to her tonight, he would rape her.

Davey thought to say more, but if he did he would betray his brother. And it would not matter what he said, the die had been cast. He left her then, but did not return to the hall. He sought out his sister to discover where Fiona had gone, little knowing that Fiona waited in an alcove off the stair, until the way to the tower room was clear.

The door opened again, but Seana did not turn from where she stood by the window. And when she heard Fiona's voice, she was glad that her back was turned toward her.

"So, for all your running, you were brought to ground, Seana. He plans to rape you. You should have stayed safe at the abbey. In time, Micheil would have forgotten you."

"If you have come to taunt me, Fiona, spare yourself. I know well the fate that awaits me. You've reminded me of it twice now."

*Where was the fear that should have Seana trembling?* Fiona eyed her bedraggled state. An unholy suspicion formed.

"You were alone with Micheil for all this time? Mayhap he has no need to force you? Is that the reason you dared to play the—"

"I play at naught, Fiona. As for the other, are you asking or telling me? It matters not. You'll have no answer from me." For all her brave words, Seana trembled inwardly at the thought that Micheil had sent Fiona here to torment her. *I'll not be offering you my protection. You'll be free to seek your way, with none to blame for how it ends.* Micheil's words came to taunt her.

"Much as I have hated you from the moment the auld laird betrothed Micheil to you, I would not see any woman left without a choice. I have brought a gift to you, Seana."

Metal clattered on the bare stone floor. This time Seana, with reluctance, turned around. Her gaze fell on a *sgian-dubh.* The boot knife's hilt gleamed where the firelight caught it. Her fingers curled at her sides with the need to grab hold of the weapon. But Seana made no move toward it.

She glanced at Fiona, leaning against the door, her gown a rich blue cendal that shimmered with her every breath. Gold threads embroidered the neckline, sleeves and hem of the gown, a finely wrought chain graced her neck, and a golden girdle circled her hips. She remembered how Fiona had flirted with Micheil the night of their betrothal, and remembered the sense of danger she had felt. She could not trust this woman. Seeing for herself the avid feral gleam within Fiona's eyes as she touched her netted flaming-red hair, Seana gazed toward the fire. *Keep silent,* she warned herself, *and let her goad you. She will reveal more.*

"'Tis not the choice you were hoping for, is it, Seana? A clansman took pity on you and begged me

risk much to bring it to you. There's yet time for you to cheat Micheil, and keep the stain of your blood from his hands.''

''Why, Fiona? Why do you dare his wrath to aid me? Am I not your enemy, too?''

''I'm not denying that. But I love Micheil. I've loved him all these years, as he has loved me. His da made him swear a blood oath the night Bridget was returned, beaten near to death and scarred for life. Then again, when the auld laird lay dying, he forced Micheil to oath again. As his lover, it's to me that Micheil shows his gentle side. I know how his sister goads him when he would seek some end to this feud.''

Fiona's eyes glittered, for she had seen her claim of being Micheil's lover, find its mark. Seana had no skill in hiding her thoughts. A smile creased her lips.

''Take the—''

''You are wrong to believe that Liam would have beaten her. He loved her beyond reason. If Bridget claimed such happened, she lied, Fiona.''

''The deed is done, these long years past. None care to know more. Take the *sgian-dubh,* Seana. Its blade is finely honed. Spare yourself what comes. If you die by your own hand, not to face dishonor, there is yet a chance to end it all. For, despite Micheil's oath to return you shamed and broken, there's many here who want you dead.''

Seana did not watch her leave, but the moment the door closed she snatched up the weapon and hid it beneath the pillow. For now, it was a safe place.

When Moibeal and another young girl came to bathe her and wash her hair, Seana mulled over all that

Fiona had said. She sat on the stool before the fire, unable to eat more than bread dipped in ale as Moibeal combed the tangles from her hair.

To be cosseted and clean, dressed in a sheer shift and a soft wool robe the shade of new heather, both finely made and richly embroidered, aided Seana in letting her mind rest. She had not worn such rich cloth since she was taken from home. The pleasure of not having to haul and heat her own water, as she had done at the abbey, helped the tension ease from her sore body.

She thought of what was promised, and as the candles melted slowly and she was left alone to wait for Micheil, Seana gazed at where the *sgian-dubh* rested. Fiona had been wrong. There was another way for her to find freedom, and it would not be by the sin of her own death.

She needed but the strength and the courage to do it.

Violence bred violence. Bloodshed bred bloodshed. There was no more hiding behind innocence. And if her heart murmured of love, her mind replayed Micheil's laughter, and the cruelty of words.

Choices? Were there truly any left to her?

# Chapter Sixteen

When Micheil could no longer ignore the demands of his clansmen that the deed be done, he climbed the tower steps, bitterness filling his heart, vengeance sharpening his mind. He saw that the bar had been left lowered, and wondered if she even waited within for him. The door opened to reveal the candles gutted and the fire mere glowing embers outlining Seana, seated on the stool before the hearth.

"So you waited for me?" he said, prowling into the room, his voice soft. "I'd thought you would take refuge in sleep, Seana."

"And have you think I waited in that bed for you? I'll not make this deed easy—"

"You'll have no say in how it's done."

"I know," she returned, in a whisper so soft, Micheil had to step close to hear her. The faint scent of sweet heather rose from her hair and her skin. Micheil had steeled himself for this, steeled himself to fight the remembrance of her passionate giving. There would be no yielding to him. He ached to stroke the honey-gold hair that rippled down her back and

touched the floor. He ached for much, and knew he would find none of it within this room with her.

"I thought you had more courage and fire than to meekly await me. You make poor sport for a man, Seana."

"Poor sport? It is the only way to cheat you. And do not be so free in calling yourself a man. You're a savage."

"That's my lass. Reckless, and a fool. I'd not expected to be entertained," he said, reaching out to stroke her hair.

With a graceful twist of her body, Seana ducked and jumped from the stool to evade his touch. She found that she could not sit meekly still. She backed away until the wall behind stopped her.

"What pleasure can you have to take me?" Seana looked at him, but her gaze went no higher than the undone laces of his shirt at his neck.

"Once I could have answered you there is none. But that was before you left me for dead to burn in the fire."

"Left you to burn? Nay, 'tis not true. I dragged you out. I did not want your blood—"

"Like the witch I named you, you'd still whisper lies?"

She looked up then, and found his features as hard as the stone her fingers clawed behind her. "'Tis no lie I speak. I cut your horse loose and dragged you from the cottage." She had naught left to fight him with, and defeat filled her voice. "I am at your mercy, and you have none for me. Do what you will. It matters not."

Micheil hesitated. There was truth in her eyes. Seana did not lie well. He recalled Davey telling him that he had been facing the fire. And he recalled his own answer to his brother. He had tried to find Seana within. If he had had the strength to crawl out... Micheil looked at her bent head, saw the fine trembling she could not hide, and knew she spoke the truth. She had no stomach to spill blood. She had not known who he was, only that she did not trust him, due to his own carelessness. She would not have left Jamie to burn.

He came to stand before her. It mattered not, just as she had claimed. There were too many who waited in the hall below to hear their enemy's screams fill the night. He dared not show her mercy.

But as he moved to cup her chin and raise her head, she twisted away again.

"Do not touch me!"

"Not so meek and resigned to your fate, I vow. Mayhap you need taming, witch, but first you'll learn obedience. I've no intent to chase you round and round, Seana. Come here to me."

She darted for the door. Only his warning stopped her.

"The stair is well guarded. Would you have my men drag you back to me?"

Goaded, she turned like a wild thing held at bay. All her carefully made plans flew from her mind. She could not let him touch her. She knew her body would betray her. And hate rose at the knowledge that he could so easily control her passion.

"I'll not add more to my shame in having yielded to you."

"There was no shame in the honest giving we shared, lass."

"Do not give me your sweet-talking tongue! I'll not have you!"

"'Tis not your choice."

She watched him come to her, rooted to where she stood. *I cannot beg him. I will not,* she vowed, unprepared for the striking movement that snagged her wrist and pulled her to him.

"I will not have you!" she screamed, struggling against him. With both hands shackled by one of his, Seana tried to kick him.

Lithe and graceful as any dancer, he avoided her weak blows, impeded as she was by the shift and robe. Over and over she repeated her cry that she would not have him, until, spent and panting, she quivered against him.

Her head lifted and her gaze sought his. "I know well that you will not have me." If she had not looked away, she would have seen the understanding for her plight within his eyes.

He grabbed hold of her robe, and she came to life once more, snarling and clawing for his face. Shoving him, Seana heard the ripping of cloth, but all she cared about was reaching the bed and the weapon she had hidden there.

Micheil tossed the robe to the floor, stripping off his shirt and breeks while she rounded the bed. Seana felt as if his glaring gaze goaded her to redouble her feeble effort to fight him off. A cold, gnawing fear snaked through her, and she closed her eyes against the sight of his body.

He approached the bed, and Seana blindly reached beneath the pillow for the blade, all her plans forgotten. She could not let him have her. She felt the dip of the bed as his weight came down, and she pulled forth the blade, opening her eyes and raising the weapon high.

Her arm trembled. She beheld fury in his eyes as his lips drew back in a snarl, and a strange, masculine beauty in the body that had taught hers desire.

"Use it, Seana. I will still claim you mine as my lifeblood flows."

Her gaze darted to the weapon she held, and Micheil caught hold of her shift, tearing it as he yanked her down on the bed. One hand locked over hers, which still grasped the blade, the other tangled tight within her hair to hold her head still as he lowered his body to hers. She cried out at the force of his hold, but a surge of blinding rage burst inside him, and he took her mouth with his. Uncaring of her whimpers, he roughly held her hair, forcing her head back, bruising the mouth he had tutored in the ways of desire. With his greater strength, he forced open her fingers, one by one, until he threw the blade across the room and held her wrist in a bruising hold as he lifted his head and stared down at her.

He wanted to punish her for stirring his passion when he sought to keep this a cold act dictated by necessity. But with each surging thrust she made to struggle against him, a fever spread to sheathe himself within her and loose the black lust that had risen.

All for naught! Seana silently cried, twisting her head from side to side. Her frail strength was no

match for him. She knew he waited for her to wear herself down, knew it and yet could not stop. Her gaze caught the newly opened wound on the side of his head, and she cringed, trying to bury herself against the drops of blood that fell to her cheek. A haze enveloped her, and she screamed.

With choking terror, she felt his hardened knee part her thighs.

"I curse you to hell!"

"Aye, I'll meet you there," he returned in a weary voice. His gaze locked with hers. *Pray God she cannot see how this sickens me.*

"Do not do this to me!"

Her eyes glittered with the threat of tears, and he felt her quiver beneath him like an animal about to be slain. He had wanted to shame her. He needed to have his revenge upon her. Suddenly he understood what it was she ran from, what she truly feared. It was not a brutal taking. There, within her wide dark gray eyes, he saw the same fear of betrayal he fought against.

"Mine," he whispered, lowering his head to capture her mouth once more, delving deep with his tongue to claim again the sweetness he alone had tasted from her. He sought what she fought to withhold, coaxing and tormenting her with the kisses that would make her yield. Over and over, he drank her cries, until his lungs begged him to draw breath, until he wrung a moan from her and felt her lips, heated now and trembling beneath his.

He rose above her, his fingers entwined with hers to hold her hands on either side of her head.

Ashamed of the desire that threatened her will, Seana shuddered. "Have done," she pleaded. What more could she say to goad him? She had to keep her hate alive. And his... Sweet heaven! She had to fan his rage again. "Surely 'tis not an act you cannot perform, savage? There must have been wails aplenty after you raped and pillaged the MacKay lands. Can it be you've no taste for any but virgin flesh. Have done, you cowardly—"

"I'll have you turn traitor on yourself, Seana. And when I'm done, I'll have all from you."

She closed her eyes against the blaze in his. "Spend your rotten lust quickly."

"Nay. 'Tis not the way to have my revenge on you."

She felt the silky glide of his hair rubbing against the skin of her throat as she arched her head away from him. His lips trailed heated kisses down the taut cord, finding the madly beating pulse in the hollow of her throat. Her hips rose in a feeble attempt to push him off that only served to spread her thighs wider for him. Her helpless struggles galled her. She shuddered at the way his teeth lightly nipped the delicate curve of her collarbone, flushing her with heat. She tried to bite back her gasp as his tongue flicked her nipples. Slow, aching need began to build inside her, and there was no escape from the hard, masculine length of him pressed against her.

All for naught, she repeated to herself, knowing this would be no cruel, savage assault. His mouth suckled her, and she could not summon the will to strain against him.

"Jamie! Jamie, do not—"

"Not Jamie, Seana. *Micheil!* And you'll purr my name with longing afore the night is gone."

She bit her lip, afraid to let a sound escape, afraid it would be no curse that passed her lips, but a moan for the pleasure his mouth imparted to the aching fullness of her breasts. And when her heart beat at a faster pace and she shuddered weakly, Micheil teasingly licked her ribs, moving down to her belly.

Seana only realized he had freed her hands when she found herself stifling a cry by biting her knuckle. She made a grab for his hair, attempting to stop the kisses he placed along the flesh of her thighs. There was no warning of his intent, and she cried out, feeling the soft roughness of his tongue slip into her. Not even her hand could hide her cry. She hated the sound of it, hated the tremors of pleasure that made desire flame against her will.

He brought her to the edge, the very edge that threatened to snap his own leashed control. He knew he had aroused her to the same fever pitch of need that clawed inside him. Once more he loomed over her.

"Look at me, Seana. Say my name, and know who you yield to, or I will leave you."

She knew he would do it. Just as she had known she would lose this battle from the first moment he touched her. But a last remnant of pride rescued her.

"Could you slake the desire for me on another? You made me turn traitor to myself. Let that satisfy your need for revenge."

It was not enough, but he sheathed himself inside her, feeling as accursed as she, for it was only the lust he had aroused within her that made him welcome.

As he surged powerfully into her, time and again, he knew how tightly passion ensnared her, for only that driving force could have made her claw his back as she cried out.

But Micheil at last had a final revenge on her. With every tremored release he brought her to, he fought the near-maddening enticement of her tight, gloving contractions that begged him to spill his seed.

Never again would he give her that pleasure.

And in those last seconds, Seana turned to look up at him, knowing as he withdrew from her there would not be the full measure of the pleasure they had known.

He left her the moment he could, and Seana winced as she heard the bar drop into place, locking her in. The sobs came then, great racking ones that left her drained. She did not know how she found the strength to rise and find her torn robe. With its warmth around her, she made herself feed kindling to the fire. Dragging the furs from the bed, she made a place for herself on the hearth. Just before she lay down, Seana saw the gleam of the blade in the corner.

She slept then, clutching the hilt as the tears dried on her cheeks.


Micheil woke to pounding rain, its beat a mate for his aching head, the sullen weather a match for his mood. He knuckled bloodshot eyes, tasting the foul coating in his mouth that came from drinking too much wine after he left Seana.

The pounding intensified, and Micheil squeezed his eyes closed, drawing the pillow over his head to shut

out the noise. It was then he realized someone banged on his door.

Spilling curses and oaths, he yelled a command to enter, and heard the frantic return of Peigi's voice telling him he had barred the door from within.

Peigi spared his rumpled state a glance before she launched into her reason for waking him. "'Tis Bridget, gone to the tower room, with Crisdean sent to hold her off. She's carryin' on somethin' fierce about seeing the MacKay lass. An' from the look of ye—"

Micheil rushed past her, taking the stone steps two at a time in his bare feet. He took in at a glance Crisdean's effort to stand his ground, and ward off his sister's attacks, both verbal and physical.

"Bridget! Och, lass, do not vex yourself. Come away afore you do yourself harm. That scurvy baggage within is not worth—"

Bridget rounded on her brother. "Prove you fulfilled your sworn oath to me! Let me see her! You've locked her in and set someone to guard her like she was precious to you, Micheil!"

He drew her into his arms, stroking her shoulders and whispering reassurances. Over her head he eyed Crisdean. His reddened cheek showed where Bridget had slapped him, but the man merely shook his head.

"Come away, lass. Come tell me what brought this about. How could you be thinking I'd value an enemy so?" He led her away and down to her solar, calming her until Peigi came with Moibeal and Cuíni, Bridget's serving woman.

"Stay with her till I've rid myself of the stench that fills my nose."

But Peigi followed him down to his room. "I'm not a bairn that needs help, woman," he snarled at her.

"Surly, are ye? I only come to ask if I should fetch the lass food. Crisdean served you well. He would not let me in."

"Let her work for what she'll eat. I'll not have any say I've cosseted an enemy beneath my roof."

"You'll break her, then?"

"Leave be, Peigi. Leave be."

"I'll be needin' clothes for her."

"Do you mean to drive me mad with this concern? Dress her in sackcloth and ashes, for all I care."

"Aye, my lord. As ye wish."

Peigi did not bother him further about Seana. But she made certain that the MacKay woman was kept far from him. She set her to work in the wash shed, for it was one place no man ventured. It was done not out of kindness for Seana, but to ease the burden her presence caused Micheil.

Seana surmised as much, once she was dressed in the coarse woolen gown and fed the remains of the morning meal after the spit lad had eaten in the kitchen. The brose had been thinned with water, and she could barely force herself to eat it. Only the thought that starving punished no one but herself made her swallow the cold mess. If Peigi knew that she had strapped the *sgian-dubh* to her thigh with a torn length from her shift, she gave no sign. But Seana followed her out to the wash shed, feeling safer knowing she could protect herself.

The serving women greeted Peigi's announcement that she was to work with them with silence. One spat at her feet, another made the sign of the cross and muttered curses under her breath, the rest ignored her as she set about scrubbing linens.

It was late when Moibeal, accompanied by one of the men who had been in the hall last night, came to fetch her.

"Peigi says to go with Gabhan Roy."

Seana eyed the thick stock of red hair that had added *Roy* to his name, and met eyes cold as the steel against her thigh. He was not as tall as Micheil, but heavier-muscled. And his sword, hanging from his right side, marked him a deadly foe.

"Where does he take me?"

Flanked on either side, Seana repeated her question. Grim silence came in answer. Under the cover of darkness, as they walked toward the hall and her tower prison, she felt for the hilt and eased her fear.

She heard the laughter, music and shouting from the hall the moment they entered the kitchens. The aromas made her lick her lips, and she glanced with longing at the platter of coffined lamprey made the way she loved it, with fine milled bread and a wine-and-ginger syrup. But she knew better than to look too long.

"Move on," Moibeal said.

Seana knew she would have to pass through the hall to gain the tower stair. Fiona would be there, and Bridget, who had once called her bonny. She rubbed her damp palms against the coarse wool of her cloth-

ing and kept her eyes downcast as she followed Moibeal. Behind her came the dour-faced Gabhan.

She was spared being seen, for they walked single
file behind the great tapestry that hung from the rafters behind the high table. Seana wished she could
close out the sound of Micheil's voice coaxing Fiona
to sing for them.

Moibeal lifted a torch at the end, and Seana hurried to catch up. She was filled with relief when they
barred the door behind her and she was alone.

A cup of broth, two bannocks and ale waited for her
on the table. Seana fell to her meal hungrily, for she
had worked hard. Once done, she saw that the soiled
robe and shift were gone. Tonight there was no
steaming bath, no water at all. She saw at a glance
there was a smaller fire burning, and no kindling to
keep it high all night. It was no more than she had expected, but tired as she was, a restlessness made her
pace the confines.

She opened the shutter, and her sleeve caught on a
ragged splinter, pulling loose a few threads. Picking
them free, Seana untied her knife and worked loose
more threads from the hem of her gown. Seated by the
fire, she began to weave the threads together to make
a tie for her hair, plucking more free as she needed
them. The faint sounds drifting up the stair were a
world away from her, and she welcomed the solitude.

The women had been set to watch her, she knew, for
each time she attempted to step closer to the door to
survey the lay of buildings and land, she had been
motioned back to work. It had been difficult to see

anything in the dark on her return. Of Micheil she refused to think about at all.

As the firelight grew dim, she saw the long passing of the time and rubbed her eyes to finish the last bit. Not knowing what morning would bring, she finger-combed her hair, wincing each time she pulled free a tangled knot, then making one single plait, she wove the center of her tie into the end of the braid, securing it tight. She removed her gown and closed the shutter before once again taking the furs from the bed and making her place by the hearth.

"Please, Lord," she prayed, "do not let him come to me."

In the hall below, Micheil turned from his sister and echoed Seana's prayer that he would not give in to the need to go to her. He smiled and drank yet another toast, for they celebrated another successful raid against the MacKay and Keith holdings this night.

His hardened stare caught Peigi's eye as she bustled forth and placed a mound of sugary nutmeg cakes in front of him. He would not forget her curt reply when he had asked in passing how Seana fared. *"She earned her supper."* And not another word would pass her lips.

"Will ye no have one?" she asked him now. "I made them special for ye. To sweeten your black temper."

"'Tis too late for that, auld woman," he answered, and drained his cup. "One day you'll goad me too far, and I'll show you the side of my temper." He set his cup down and saw that Peigi motioned to have it refilled. "What mischief is brewing?"

"Leave her be, Micheil love," Fiona whispered at his side. She lifted the cup to her lips, holding his gaze with her own. "I'll share this and more with you."

He eyed the spill of her milk white breasts over the low neckline of her gown. Fiona was lusty enough to cure him of any lingering desire for the MacKay woman. And once he would have hardened at the thought of bedding her. Once. But there was Seana standing between them now. Micheil discounted all the other women who had taken his fancy over the years. Fiona had learned to be undemanding, or she would be welcome no more within his hall.

Her hand glided along his thigh, her eyes filled with promise, but Micheil found himself lifting her hand above the table and filled it with a cake.

"Gordie," he called to his harper, "come play for us."

"I would play, too, Micheil," Fiona murmured, licking the sugar from her lips.

He saw that his cousin Niall watched Fiona, much like a cat that coveted a caged bird. He leaned close to her ear. "Take pity on poor cousin Niall. He hungers for a taste of you." When she would have tried to turn, he held her arm to the table. "Gently, now. I'm not the fool you take me for. You bed him often, Fiona."

"If you cared for me, you would never suggest—"

He cupped her cheek and made her face him. "I do care, in my own way. But it's never been love I've felt for you. You knew from the first the way it was between us. Go to him. He'll welcome your attentions as I cannot."

"It's her that takes you from me!"

"Lower your voice. You're daft, and I'll hear no more."

*Och, you will hear more, but not from me, Micheil,* she vowed.

In her solar, Bridget listened to the sweet song from Gordie as he played. She stood close to the window, ignoring Cuíni, who sat and mended by the fire. Did Liam know that his sister lived, and that Micheil held her? It was a question she had repeatedly asked herself all day. Peigi refused to tell her where the woman had been sent, only that Micheil's harsh orders were being carried out. She had to be content with that. But it was not enough.

She reached beneath her veil and touched her scars. Once she had told Seana that she would be as bonny as she herself if she lived to her young promise. Seeing how lovely Seana was only stirred the hate within her. She wanted Liam to wail and moan, needed to hear him cry out as her da and brothers had when they saw her face.

Micheil, she feared, played some deep game with her. Who knew better than she how little time it took to break a woman's will? She shuddered as the events of the past came rising from memory.

"Come away from the window," Cuíni called. "I'll build the fire higher, for I can see how chilled you are."

"Aye, do that," Bridget answered. "And close the shutter. There's evil air about this night."

When Cuíni returned to her stool and picked up her needle, Bridget thought how long and well the girl had served her.

"Your ma's skilled with herbs. I need ask her to give me a potion to help me sleep."

Lifting her sweetly rounded face to look at her mistress, Cuíni smiled. "I'll see to it first thing."

"Aye. And Cuíni, tell your ma to make it very strong." Bridget leaned her head back against the high wood carving and watched the flames. She could play her own deep game. No one was going to rob her of her revenge.

# Chapter Seventeen

It was the next night when Seana was roused from a sound sleep to hear a thud outside her door. She snatched up the blade, forcing herself to stand and back away from the door. The latch was wiggled, and she held her breath. But the moments passed, and no one entered. Yet a feeling of deep unease remained, no matter how she tried to dismiss it, for she was certain that someone other than the man who guarded her door was out there.

When she grew weary, she crept back to her place, and just as she laid her head down, the soft, taunting laughter of a woman reached her.

"Who goes there?" she called out.

Silence.

She shivered, despite the warmth of the night. Not a sound did her guard make, and not a moment's more rest did Seana have.

She told no one what had occurred, for who would believe her? And even if she was believed, who would care that she was frightened?

It should have made her fear ease to know that Micheil rode out the next morning. She judged it was

to hunt, for he and his brothers wore the thick leather gauntlets that protected their hands from the claws of the falcons that rode proudly on their wrists. She knew little about the hunting birds, for her father had never kept them, deeming the expense too large to keep mews, a master falconer to train the birds, and a well-stocked henhouse to feed them. But she had seen a little more of Halberry, and she knew Micheil's wealth was greater than Liam's. Would that his sister had been prevented from having her brother to wed by reason of his clan being the poorer.

A foolish, wasted thought. She tossed out the washwater and went to the steaming kettle where Peigi waited.

Noting the dark circles beneath Seana's eyes, Peigi knew she had not slept well. The cause was not to be laid at Micheil's door, for she had kept his cup full until Davey helped him to his bed. She could feel no compassion for the MacKay woman, having lost both sons to her clan. Yet Moibeal said the lass had cried out when she opened her door this morn. In her place, Peigi thought, she would not be sleeping well, either.

"I'm to keep ye with me in the kitchens, the laird says."

Seana lowered her head to hide her excitement. There was talk to be heard there, talk that could lead to her escape. She merely shrugged her shoulders, and followed Peigi's waddling figure.

Her labors were no more than those she had oft-times done at the abbey. True, the enticing smells kept her stomach rumbling, but she kept her gaze away from the foods that Peigi oversaw the making of to

serve when the hunting party returned. She ate by herself, after the other servants had their fill, and once more set to work kneading bread.

Seana did not know what made her realize that someone stared at her. She looked up and found the man leaning in the hall's entrance, the same man who had led Bridget away the night she was captured. He was slender-boned and richly dressed, his features even within a frame of dark brown hair.

She tried to name him, and could not. His penetrating gaze made her uncomfortable, and she kept her eyes on the dough, which was near ready for baking.

"Peigi," Niall said, coming into the kitchen. "Bridget requests your presence."

Seeing that Cuíni came in behind him, Peigi gave no thought to leaving Seana alone. Mumbling beneath her breath, she took herself off.

Seana noticed the darkening bruise on Cuíni's cheek and, thinking her in the same position as she, wiped her hands and asked what she needed.

"The sugar cakes," the girl answered, shooting a look over her shoulder at Niall.

Seana caught his nod, but, not understanding the reason for it, dismissed him. That he had come deeper into the kitchen, so that she could see the gleam of his crested ring, disturbed her.

"Peigi set them high on that shelf there. The ones covered over with the linen." When Cuíni claimed she would not be able to reach them, Seana pulled over a stool and climbed up. She was very careful handing down the silver plate to Cuíni. And as she stepped down, she felt the bit of sugar coating her finger.

Seana, with the curse of her sweet tooth, licked it clean.

The blow sent her reeling to the floor, as did Niall's shout of "Thief." She glanced from one to the other, too bewildered to understand what she had done. That Cuíni fled with the cakes and left her alone with Niall made Seana's throat and mouth parch with fear.

She reached up and felt a sticky wetness on her cheek. Her fingers came away with streaks of blood.

"'Tis a taste of what Bridget had done to her. And there's none here who'll rise to your defense."

Cold and calculating, his gaze stripped her where she lay. He caught hold of her long plait and used it like a rope to pull her toward him.

"There's damn little of you to go round for all who seek to avenge themselves against you. But mark my words, MacKay woman, I'll have—"

"Here now, what's she done?" Peigi bustled forth and eyed Niall's hand until he dropped Seana's hair. "Cuíni said the girl stole a cake."

"Aye, 'tis true enough. The moment she saw your back, she ran for the cakes that Cuíni was sent to fetch. She would not listen to our warnings. I tried to stop her, but she stumbled from the stool and fell upon my ring. Didn't you?" he added, glaring down at Seana.

None would believe the word of a MacKay. Seana hung her head.

"Answer me!"

"Och, Niall, get ye gone from my kitchens. 'Tis for the laird to decide her punishment." Shooing him out,

she turned to Seana. "I'll have to tell him when he comes."

Swallowing and trying not to feel the sting of her cheek, Seana nodded. "Aye, I ken the way of it."

Peigi did not trust Niall, but Cuíni would not lie to her. She had raised the girl herself, and taught her to be a maid to Bridget after she had come home to stay. Micheil would not like this.

"Go bathe your face and finish the bread."

Micheil waited until everyone had bedded down. He had borne with the demands that he drag the thief forth and set her sentence tonight. He cooled the heated blood with a promise that on the morrow her sentence would serve the same sport as the hunt had today. But he knew the whispers that ran through the hall, from the lowest table to his own.

Fiona's feral gaze, Niall's secretive one, Jamie's, offering little comfort, and Davey, the only one who dared to meet his anger. He had marked them well.

He stood in the center of his room, glancing up, honor and his position as leader demanding that he carry out the same sentence he would give to any thief he caught.

That Peigi had not been there to witness Seana's stealing bothered him. Cuíni he had to dismiss, but Niall... Ah, his cousin Niall, as Davey and Jamie had warned, bore careful watching.

Not so easy to dismiss was Peigi's swearing that she had twice more asked Seana if what Niall said was true. And twice she had neither denied nor admitted it.

He thought of how she had craved the sweet ginger cakes at the fair, eating them greedily and paying with a kiss. Had Niall demanded that and more from her? But how could he, or any, know of her craving? They had not been at the fair.

He walked slowly to the door of his room, knowing he had waited long enough. So deep was he in thought that Micheil never saw the shadowed figure that hid within the alcove. He passed as close as a hand away, and never knew he was being watched.

He roused the snoring guard with a kick to his ribs. "Is this how you stand watch, man?" Micheil waved off the mumbled excuses, never seeing the beaker near the man's foot. He unbarred the door himself and opened it.

Warned of his coming, Seana sat clutching a fur to hide her nakedness. Peigi had given her a basin to wash with, and she had rinsed out her shift when she was done.

Micheil faced eyes that were near-black in a face leached of color. The rippling waves of her hair shielded her, but the side turned toward the faint embers of the fire revealed the pale gleam of her bare shoulder.

"Does your lust need slaking, savage? Is that why you come like a reiver in the night?"

"Curb your tongue." Micheil closed the door and leaned against it. He had not come with the thought of bedding her, but the desire rose, strong and hot, to take her.

"'Tis the only weapon I have left . . . lest you cut it out. Am I to be allowed no peace?"

"You've been accused of stealing from my larder, Seana. A punishment befitting the crime is demanded by all."

"Sweet Jesu! Then you've come to torment me!"

"Nay. 'Tis not my intent. I want the truth of what happened from you."

She needed no light to see him as he stood, proud and tall, his arrogance of carriage evident even in his voice. Lord and master here. She glanced away from him to the coals that glowed like evil red eyes amid the ashes. There was temptation to tell him the truth, but if he did not believe her and Niall found out, he would do worse to her the next time. There had been a cold, malicious glaze to Niall's eyes that warned her to silence.

Even if he did believe her, she knew the thirst to see her beaten down and broken by one and all. He would have no choice. But her silence would protect her. Mayhap...

"Seana? Remember, I'm not a patient man."

"There is naught to tell you. Do what you must— what you will. I've told you, it matters not."

"Stubborn wench! Will you lay bare your hand for my sword? I would give you this chance to tell me."

She turned to him then, some note in his voice catching her attention. She was weary from all she had endured, and confused, as well. He claimed hate, yet desired her. He came to her now as if he could stop what he had set into play. Was this all new torment to break her? What madness had made her believe she could ever trust him?

"Your silence damns you," he warned, in a voice as dark as the despair that filled him.

A strange sense of loss filled her. "The paths we each walk were chosen long ago. You cannot believe a woman has any honor to uphold, but that's not true. I am a MacKay. I'll never have any say that I begged or pleaded for mercy from a Gunn."

"You found it easy enough when you thought me Jamie."

"Aye, I did. But he was a lie, and all that came with him was a falsehood that shattered any innocence I had left. You used me in the foulest way a man uses a woman. There is naught more to say."

"If I'd raped you, you would have cause to claim as much." His reply was heavily tinged with sarcasm. "We both know that to be the biggest lie of all." He watched her keenly, seeing her head bend as if the weight were too much to bear.

"Is there no other," she whispered, digging her fingers into the fur, "that would serve as sport for you? Must you rob me of sleep, as well as peace?"

"As you steal from me?" Micheil crossed to her swiftly, hauling her up by her slender shoulders. She threw her head back, and he felt the silken fall of her hair across his hands send the blood pounding through his body.

"Seana, I—" He saw it then, the darkening bruise and cut across her cheek. She cried out as his fingers tightened till flesh met bone. "Who dared to mark you?"

"Why do you care? 'Tis a mark for all to see, unlike the ones you branded on me!" Reckless now,

fighting against the fury she felt coursing through him—for it awakened her own, and she knew that would not serve her well, she cried, "'Tis the same end you seek. For all that you claim not to be a patient man, you've dragged out my fate. Have done with it."

"Are you begging me?" He roughly shook her, incensed by her refusal to tell him.

"Never. I cannot do it."

"When I find out who it was, I will kill the whoreson for touching you."

Soft, menacing, and filled with promise, his voice spiked her with new fear. "No more blood. No more deaths."

"Then you beg for his life, this coward who struck you?"

She sagged in his arms, the fight leaching from her. "I will never beg you for aught."

Micheil stared at her upturned face, saw the hair, a golden cloud, framing the eyes that pleaded as her lips would not. His loins blazed with a desire so intense, he caught his breath. He wanted her, wanted that savage beauty as he had first known her, all soft, welcoming heat, sinking its claws deep inside him, taking away the despair of walking a path others had set for him.

He caught her hair and forced her neck to bare to his lips, and there marked her his with teeth and tongue until a soft whimper of need filled his ears.

*You hate him!* a voice screamed in Seana's mind as his lips sealed hers with a kiss that stole, as well as gave. Beneath the fierce roughness that fired her own smoldering passion to life, there was an ardent tenderness that held her more securely than the stones of

his keep. Though honor's pride demanded that she name him enemy, she had taken him into her heart and her body with the first stirrings of love. And there was a need in him, as desperate as her own, to find some haven away from what had to be.

Micheil sensed she stood on the brink of yielding all to him, and kept silent. He coaxed and wooed her surrender, knowing nothing would be changed. Her need was his. As he bore her down to the furs and tore free the lacings of his breeks, he knew that the power of what lay between them would have him yield all as well.

When she cried out in the stillness of the night, there were few who heard. Those who did turned and grunted with satisfaction that revenge was being well served. Only one knew it was a cry not of pain, but of passion's fulfillment, that spilled from the MacKay woman's lips, and that beneath nails impotent with fury flesh tore.

Morning brought Seana a respite. Micheil had ridden out with a troop of his men. None would say why. Moibeal had sickened with cramps, and Peigi had Seana take her place serving in the hall. It was a grave error on Peigi's part, for none would be served from her hand. There was cruelty in every jest, and Peigi was forced to remove her.

Seana fetched water from the well, and there met with bairns spitting hate with words while they pelted her with stones. Not one voice was raised in her defense. She was afraid to be out of Peigi's sight—not that the woman ordered any to cease, but her mere

presence brought a lessening of the tormenting—and she felt terror each time she saw Niall watching her.

When night came and Peigi took the torch to lead her up to her room, Seana broke her silence.

"Is there nowhere else I could bed for the night?"

"There's none that would have ye," came Peigi's sharp reply. "Up with ye now. Me weary bones fair cry for rest."

Dread marked every stair for Seana. She could not explain the fear that had grown and doubled throughout the day. When Peigi stood waiting with the torch held high to light Seana's way into the room, she knew she had to try one more time.

"Let me bar the door from within, Peigi. I cannot sleep, knowing any can come inside."

"That's not what the laird ordered. I'll be sending Marcus to stand watch tonight. He'll not let any pass." Peigi handed the torch to Seana. "Light yer fire, and I'll bar the door meself."

Protesting would gain her nothing. Seana heard the bar fall into place and stood listening at the door until she heard the heavy footsteps that told her the guard was there.

She spied the pitcher and beaker on the table, and found it filled with wine. Seana glanced at the door, then shook her head. Even if she asked the guard, Peigi would not come. The auld woman had likely sent this up earlier, out of pity for her haunted look. And Seana drank the wine greedily, wanting the oblivion that sleep would bring.

She had barely made it to the bed, sick and dizzy, before she thought herself running through a black

tunnel, running from the taunting laughter that pursued her.

"*Would you have her?*"

"*I want only you.*"

"*And you shall have me when you slay her. But not as yet. I need more.*"

Voices swirled within Seana's mind, the laughter faint now, the darkness everlasting, as she fought her way free.

With a scream, she jerked awake. The stone walls echoed the sound. And no one came.

Seana staggered from the bed to the window, struggling to open the shutter, dragging in gulping breaths of the salt air. She clung to the stone sill, cold sweat drenching her body. And there she remained until the mist over the sea lifted and she heard the cries of the sea gulls as they dived for their morning meal.

Shivering from both the terror that lingered and the chill of the air, Seana turned around. The pitcher and beaker were gone!

Had she dreamed it all? Mercy, Lord! she prayed. Let this not be a madness of my mind. Raising up her arms to implore and pray, she saw the livid marks on her skin as the loose sleeves fell back.

No dream, then! But who? Fiona and Bridget both had reason to hate her. And Niall... But the guard... And within her mind she heard again the taunting laughter.

And Seana found herself wishing for her enemy's return. Better to face the devil she knew, night after night, than to fear the sleep she craved.

Peigi's pinched mouth was the only sign that she noticed Seana's listlessness as she tended the chores as she was bid. That the lass did not eat one morsel or drink any but the water she herself had drawn from the well raised Peigi's anger.

"Do not think any here would use a coward's poison, no matter how they wish *ye* dead."

"I sickened this morn," Seana answered, seizing the reason Moibeal was once more absent. "Mayhap 'tis akin to what ails Moibeal."

With a shrewd eye, Peigi looked her over. "Ye'd best pray not. Moibeal's quickening with a bairn."

Seana felt the blood drain from her, then return with a dizzying rush. She swayed where she stood.

"If ye only laid with Micheil—"

"Aye! No other has touched me." *Would you have her? I want only you.* The voices that had haunted her last night came back to her with a vengeance. Dearest Lord! Sickness roiled, and Peigi made no move to stop Seana from finding a corner to retch in. She could not be swelling with his child! It was the wine, that was all, she swore to herself once the heaving had ceased. Peigi was wrong. And Seana clung to that.

It was late afternoon when Seana learned from Davey where Micheil had gone. Peigi had gone to the buttery and left Seana alone in the kitchens. Davey, annoyed that Peigi had not answered his call for ale, came seeking her, as well as to see how Seana fared.

The innocent loveliness that had first attracted him was gone. And yet the features his eyes beheld were honed to a haunting beauty. Gowned like the meanest thrall, she still carried a prideful air as she turned and

faced him. Davey's eyes narrowed to see the barely closing cut on her cheek, and the dark shadows that filled her eyes.

"You've naught to fear from me," he said, making no move toward her, afraid she would bolt and run.

Seana studied him, remembering his gentle touch and the kindness in his brown eyes the night she had been brought here. He repeated again that she had nothing to fear from him, and this time she answered him.

"You're his brother. Do you not despise me for the sins of my clan?"

"I know well who you are, and again tell you there is naught to fear from me. I'm not Micheil. The burden falls to him, or to Jamie. I pray their health remains strong and no enemy's sword finds it mark on them."

He helped himself to a beaker of ale from the barrel on the back wall. He noted how warily she watched him. The moment he crossed the room, she had put distance between them. This was no longer the defiant lass who had stood and faced mounted men, taunting Micheil that he needed dogs and a troop to bring her to bay. He had had no more dreams of her. But he knew she had been tormented. None but a fool would deny it, seeing the results before him.

"Would that I could grant what you desire most."

"Only death or your sainted brother can give me that."

Davey eyed the fowls she rubbed with wild thyme and lard before she spitted them for roasting. He cut

himself a wedge of cheese, and once more found her watching him.

"Why do none call it stealing when you take food as you please, and I'm to lose my hand— I prattle and forget myself."

"Are you hungry, lass?" He caught the hesitation before she lowered her lashes and shook her head. Davey sliced off another wedge of cheese and tossed it to her. "I've no liking to eat alone."

Like the animal she felt reduced to, she ate the cheese too fast, casting a look from his face to the door. Davey started talking to her, once more being free with the cheese, telling her that Micheil rode the highland tracts of the Gleann na Guineach, in the parish of Kildonan, where the Sutherlands' border lay.

"My brother would treat with one and all to buy peace for our clan, but there are many against him."

"He's a warrior, and knows no other way but shedding the blood of guilty and innocent alike."

"'Tis not true, Seana. You need understand that Micheil wanted no feud. He wished to challenge your brother, but my da, as laird and father, made Micheil swear a blood oath of how he wanted the revenge taken. It's not easy for a lass to ken the ways of a man's honor."

"He says that often."

"Micheil talks to you of honor?"

"Only to tell me that as a woman I cannot have any." Seana shrugged, and wondered what kept Peigi so long. If Davey had not come, she would be here alone, like the last time Niall had found her. Against her will, Seana found comfort in Davey's soft, lyrical

voice, telling stories of the brothers' boyhoods. She came to understand that Micheil had always walked a path alone, apart at times from his brothers and his father. All that had ended when he was chosen by the clan as laird after his father's death. Unlike a man's wealth, which was passed to his heir, the clan chose the one who would be their leader and the one who would hold the coveted position of *tanist*.

As Davey continued, Seana created a younger Micheil in her mind, one who loved his horses and his lands. His undemanding presence made her venture to ask a few questions that had plagued her. Questions whose very words were hard to force past her lips, for the intimate nature of them.

"Davey, I have known no man but your brother, and much as it pains me to ask, what would be the fate of any bairn I had?"

"Are you carrying his child?"

Seana set aside the pot she was scrubbing and turned to him. She kept her gaze on her hands. "'Tis too soon to know."

"If he wished to claim the child, naught would stop him." Rather than pleasing her, his words brought distress. "I cannot say for sure what my brother would do. I do not believe he would allow a bairn of his blood to be named bastard."

"And the mother?" she asked, clenching her hands in the folds of her gown.

"He claimed you still his betrothed, the night he brought you here. If Micheil loved you, he'd marry you."

"Your brother knows naught of love. For to have love, one must trust. Only a daft woman would believe a man like him knows how."

"But he's a braw, bonny man, Seana. There's many who would claim his heart. Micheil's—" He stopped himself from telling her what he knew.

Her laugh rang out. "What lass wants to lay her love, trust and honor before a man who would lay waste to them, Davey?"

He tilted his head to one side, a wide smile making his face boyish in appearance. "I've not heard you laugh since that day at the fair. I vow, Micheil would enjoy—"

Seana interrupted him. "It matters not. I have work to do." She caught the shadow of someone standing outside, listening to them. But, though she watched, no one entered.

Seeing her deep in thought, Davey took his leave. "If you have need of me, send word with Peigi. I would trust her with my life."

She nodded, but grew pensive as she thought of the one burning question she had not asked him. What would happen if his brother refused to claim her child?

Seana had three days of peace, and owed it to Davey's company, for he sought her out, no matter what chores Peigi set her to do. There were no more dreams filled with the laughter that taunted her for her plight, and if many still spat or turned their skirts as she came near, Seana bore it in silence.

When Seana came at his call and found him in the far corner with two young clansmen, she fetched the ale they wanted, and lingered to watch their play.

Seeing her interest, Davey motioned the others away and taught her to dice.

"But you wager on each throw," Seana protested. "I've naught to wager."

"I'll settle for a smile. Learn the throws, then we'll see if you bring me luck."

"I'd learn the throws in a trice if I had something to win."

"What would you have, Seana?"

"A walk on the moor," she answered without hesitation. "To wager for coin would not serve me. I've been locked within these walls, and hunger to breathe air filled with the scents of new summer."

"You ask that I go against Micheil's order. I cannot do—"

"A walk, Davey. A few minutes of freedom is all that I ask."

Peigi stood at the hall's entrance and saw Seana in profile, her smile and shared laughter with Davey bringing a worried frown to her brow. The lad played with fire, she told herself. It boded ill that he was so taken with her.

And from the shadow of the stairwell, Niall, too, watched and listened. He did not frown with worry, but smiled coldly to see Seana flirt with Micheil's brother.

## Chapter Eighteen

Niall came forward to join them, ignoring Davey's scowl. "Teaching her to wager on the roll of the dice? Micheil will not be pleased. He might wonder, as others do, what the MacKay woman wagers in return."

"Take your foul thoughts and like mouth away, Niall."

Seana backed away, twisting to avoid Davey's move to keep her beside him. She held the unholy light in Niall's eyes for a moment, before she turned and fled the hall.

"If I hear whispers, Niall, I'll know who caused them."

"Davey, think what you do. Your sister is beside herself that her own blood refuses to honor the oath sworn to bring her peace. You coddle an enemy, Davey. I'm not alone seeing it. Micheil—"

"Can go to the devil!"

Niall's gaze was thoughtful as he pulled up a stool and joined his cousin.

Seana glanced back once to see the earnest expression on Niall's face as he sat, deep in conversation with Davey. She longed to scream that Davey should

beware of all he said, but just then Peigi summoned her. And, for all his kindness, she should not forget that Davey was a Gunn.

Jamie returned with the wounded that night, and Seana's offer to help tend them was shunned by all. She did not know by whose order she was sent to her room long before the meal was served, but she welcomed the respite.

From her window, she watched the calm sea, and as the sky darkened the starshine's reflected glow. Sea gulls wheeled in flight, and she envied their freedom. Thanks to Davey's generous sharing, she was no longer hungry.

When a new serving girl came with a tray, Seana eyed the rich portion of sliced beef it held, its juices drenching the manchet of bread beneath it. There was a ripe apple, too, and a cup was filled with barley-bree. She poured the cup down the stone wall, and tossed bits of the bread and meat to the gulls. For a little while she forgot where she was, and how she came there. When the last crumbs of soaked bread were gone, Seana left the shutter open, the gulls' cries filling the empty silence of her room.

It was to silence that she awakened. Seana had taken to sleeping with the shutter open these warmer early-summer nights, and most mornings the gulls' cries woke her long before someone came to fetch her.

She lay on her bed of furs, trying to sort out the strange feeling, akin to dread, that chilled the very marrow of her bones.

Slowly she turned and looked toward the opening. What did she dread to find? The not knowing drove

her to stand and walk to the opening. Below, through the mist, she could make out the whitecaps topping the waves and the darker shadows that rode between the swells. She recoiled from what her eyes saw there, and retreated back into the room.

Later she heard the whispers of the evil omen brought by the strange deaths of the gulls found in the sea. Seana redoubled her efforts to get Davey to give her freedom beyond the walls. She was desperate to escape and was not careful.

"Since you're so fond of wagering, let the dice decide," she told Davey. "One throw to determine the answer."

He refused, but a few hours later a message came that the Sinclair wished to meet with Micheil. In his absence, Davey made preparations to go in his brother's place.

Seeing her last hope and refuge prepare to leave, Seana no longer had a choice. She sought him out in his Spartan room, and told him all that had happened.

"If you leave me here, you sign my death warrant, and mayhap that of your brother's child." She did not yet know if it was true that she carried Micheil's child, but she would use any weapon she could in her bid to escape.

"Dinna vex yourself, lass. I will set those I trust about you."

"Davey, I'll not touch a morsel of food or drink. Your brother will not be thanking you when he returns to find me dead."

Davey could not deny the ring of conviction in her voice, nor the frantic, haunting look of her eyes. If she told him the truth, he could not leave her here. Cursed sight! Why did it not come to him now, when he had need of it?

"You'll go to your brother, Seana? He'll not have protection to offer you. Many a time there's been talk of battering down what's left of the keep."

Seana went to her knees. "I swore I would never beg. I break my word and do so now to you. I beg my life. If your brother still wants me, he'll come, and none will stop him. But give me the chance to live. Give the bairn I may carry a chance, as well."

It was a devil's choice for Davey. But if she died . . . He turned and rummaged in his chest. "Here," he said, "put these on. You'll pass as a lad. You'll wait by the stair till I summon Peigi to me in the hall, then make your way to the stable. And, Seana," he added, his voice grave, "if you're caught, there's naught I can do to save you."

Davey took his leave of Bridget and, with her, Fiona. When asked where Seana was, he replied, "I've ordered her kept in her tower room. 'Tis time I remembered who she is. Peigi will tend her." And he saw, with sickening dread, the slow, satisfied smile Fiona shared with his sister, and the way that Bridget's hand reached out for the other woman's and held tight. Knowing that Seana had been right to think they wished her dead did not ease his mind as he made his way to the stable. He still betrayed his brother.

He chose two men who had little reason to suspect what he was about. Mounting Seana, it dawned on

him that he never asked if she could ride. It was too late now, for only with hard riding he would be at the Sinclairs' by nightfall.

Seana bore easily with the men-at-arms' jests about her clumsy seat. But they thought naught amiss, for the very danger of what she did lent her the strength to manage the horse. The most frightening time came as they approached the first guardhouse, before the drawbridge. She was sure they would be challenged, and she hunched low, making sure her cowl covered a good part of her face. With every strike of hoof against wood plank, she expected an alarm, and it took her minutes to realize they rode free of Halberry.

Davey set a hard pace, riding for almost two hours before he slowed and drew rein to motion Seana to his side.

"You'll ride north, lad, and bring my brother this message."

She watched him ride off, unable to give him a word of thanks, and broke the seal. He had drawn a crude map for her to follow.

Home! At long last, she rode for home!

They brought a wounded Micheil across the drawbridge at Halberry that very night. His fever raged, and there was concern for naught but saving his life. He had taken a sword thrust in the side, and it was Fiona's steady hand that picked the wound clean of the broken bits of mail embedded there, and Bridget's and Peigi's skill with herbal infusions that nursed his fever.

Three days passed before any gave thought to the tower room, and the woman locked within.

It was Niall who sounded the alarm, then came forth to tell Micheil of his brother Davey's betrayal.

Jamie was sent forth to bring his younger brother home, caught square in the middle of what would come.


Seana's homecoming was far less than she had dreamed. Liam, her adored brother, appeared a broken man. He could not rouse himself from his drunken stupor to greet her, in fact did not know who she was for almost two days. She came home to charred, empty lands and a hall of filth and cobwebs. But Seana's trials had sharply honed a core of strength within her, a drive for survival.

She found an ally in Leites, a woman who had come here when her mother was a bride, and a foe in Maille, who named herself Liam's leman.

Holding Maille at knifepoint, Seana searched for the coin that kept her brother supplied with sour ale. It was Leites who showed her where Liam kept it hid, and Leites who brought her down into the storerooms where Seana discovered the small jewel chest that Leites had hidden upon her mother's death.

"Ye'll need coin to fight the Gunn, lass," the old woman told her. "Take this to the Keiths. They're very greedy, and will help ye for a price."

"Are there no clansmen left, Leites? Have they all run off?"

"The years we thought ye dead, lass, have been hard ones. Dughall, Calum, Sim and Angus remain loyal to

yer brother. The others made their way to the Keiths, for they could offer protection when Liam could not."

"I've learned much of the world and its ways. The Keiths will not treat with a woman. You'll have to help me sober my brother. He is going to tell me the truth of what happened with Bridget and bring our clan back together. I swear, Leites," Seana declared, one hand splayed over her mother's jewel chest, "I'll not be taken again, and I'll see every MacKay's death avenged."

Seana found within her a wild courage and daring that lent her strength when she shamed the few clansmen assembled in the hall. She begged their aid, called on their pride, and demanded they fulfill the oaths once sworn within the keep's walls.

With Calum's and Dughall's help, Liam was denied all drink but water, and Maille threatened with banishment when she attempted to sneak him ale. Seana bullied and harried each one by turns, knowing what precious little time she might have before the Gunns descended upon them. She sent Sim with jewels to buy aid from the Keiths, listening to Leites's wise counsel that she be wary in her dealings with them, for there were branches of their clan that had treated with the Gunns over the years.

The days of summer passed, and Liam grew stronger. Seana believed that her prayers were answered, for no Gunns were seen within their borders. As she quickened with Micheil's child, she remained unaware that he lay ravaged by a fever that brought him close to death.

When George Keith arrived, Leites kept silent, lest she burden Seana's fragile health, for the lass drove herself and all around her hard, slowly drawing crofters back to the empty farms. Seana, thankful that her brother was able to meet George with a clear eye and a steady hand, set aside the tormenting dreams of the man who had ravished her body and stolen her heart, and would, she feared, forever possess her soul.

None questioned her right to sit and hear the terms that Liam and George worked out between them to treat with the Gunns. She suspected naught amiss when Liam requested her to leave at the conclusion of their talk to bring refreshments. Seana would not have protested, anyway, for her brother had promised to tell her all that had happened in those last fateful days before Bridget left him.

Seana was reminded again of Leites's warning to be wary of the Keiths as she gathered a repast from their meager stores. It was Maille, sauntering into the kitchen with her malicious smile, who brought news that nearly crushed Seana's hopes for peace.

"The Keith men-at-arms say the Gunn chief lies near death. The clan has gathered to await word. If he dies, they'll ride against you," Maille informed Seana.

Moments later, Seana confronted George and her brother.

"Aye," George answered, "'tis true. Jamie, as *tanist,* will not make a move till he knows if Micheil lives or dies. Liam thought to keep the news from you. But I'll still go forth and meet with Jamie."

Pressed by a need to be alone, Seana sought a corner near the seawall. Rarely did she allow thoughts of

Micheil to surface, but now, hearing that he lay dying, she had to face her own feelings for him.

Her hand cradled the slight swell of her belly. She knew the child she carried formed a bond between them that was stronger than the passion they had shared in creating the child.

She lost herself in memory of the gentleness he had shown, the laughter they had shared, and knew that he was as torn as she. Only Leites knew that she swelled with Micheil's child. But her secret would not remain so for much longer. Seana did not know what her brother would do. He could cast her out, if no other would claim her. To prove himself yet a strong leader, he would be given no choice but to cast her out from the clan and have all turn their backs on her. None would offer her shelter or a crust of bread, once it was known that she carried a child with Gunn blood.

She could not put herself at the mercy of the Gunns, for they would take her child and have her death, with none to protect an innocent bairn.

She had to pray, then, that Micheil lived. Pray that he would find it within himself to sue for peace. Perhaps then there would be a chance for them.

Her mind called her a fool to dare dream, but her heart and body knew there would be no other for her. While she stood there, staring out at the sea, which touched the Kyle of Tongue as it did the far reaches of Halberry, Seana understood that, no matter what happened, she had to protect her child.

A calm unlike any she had ever known filled her. The sea seemed to offer a benediction, for the sea breeze was softly combing back the length of her hair,

and below, the breakers were gentle swells that came to meet the stone cliff, much like a lover come to woo.

Across the rocky ridges and steep, narrow glens, between barren peaks and broad, rolling straths, came the voices of the Gunn clan as word reached them that the fever had broken and Micheil would live.

There had been times, while the fever raged, that Micheil had sane moments and asked for Seana, and, being told that she was gone, lapsed back into the delirium that laid waste to his once powerful body. He did not know that it was then that Davey came to him, having been forbidden his brother's bedside, so great was Micheil's rage to know he had betrayed him, and, once there, whispered to Micheil to fight to live, so that he could reclaim the woman who held his heart.

The fever finally broke, and Peigi nourished his body with rich meat broths and possets. Micheil had time to understand that he would have Seana, no matter the cost. He dreamed of her, felt her soothing hand upon his brow, heard the whisper of her voice calling to him to live. When Peigi told him she believed Seana quickened with his child, none had to coddle him to get him to rest and eat to get well.

"I've word that George Keith wishes to set a meeting with you, Micheil," Jamie informed his brother. They stood on level ground outside Halberry's massive walls, where Jamie had left his brother and Crisdean working with their broadswords. Not an hour had passed, and yet Micheil sweated profusely with his weakness.

Micheil would never admit he welcomed the interruption, for Crisdean had slipped under his guard twice in the short time they practiced. He cursed his body, which healed far too slowly for him, and motioned Crisdean to take the sword that weighted his arm. Slinging an arm around Jamie's shoulder, Micheil walked off to where the shade of trees offered both respite and coolness.

"I should be the one to go and hear what he has to say, Micheil."

"Jamie, I need you here to defend our borders. I cannot send Davey, for I'll not forgive him for his betrayal."

"Och, Micheil, I speak as your brother, and no other, now. You can't blame him. Mayhap Seana bewitched our young brother, as you claimed she did you from the first."

Closing his eyes and resting his head against the rough bark of the trunk, Micheil inhaled the salty sea air and felt the cooling of his body with the steady breeze. Softly, then, he began to speak.

"'Tis more than our three combined ages since the battle of Stirling Bridge, where Wallace led us to defeat the English. Three weeks hence is the date to mark the treaty of Paris, between France and our bonny land. A good omen. What say you, Jamie? Shall I set the date?"

"Nine days shy of All Hallows' Eve?"

"Aye." Micheil opened his eyes and leaned forward, hooking his arms around his upraised knees. "'Tis not an easy admission for me, but I want her back. Not for revenge. I want her truly mine. There is

a peace she brings me such as no other has. I crave it as much as I crave the taste of her sweet lips again."

Jamie laid his hand on his brother's shoulder. "You risk all for her, Micheil?"

"Aye. I risk all for her. Are you with me?"

"Always. But it fair tears me to see you estranged with Davey. He *knows* what comes."

"I'll not have him in my sight. Mayhap, once Seana is returned to me, I can forgive him, but do not ask that of me now."

Sliding his hand away, Jamie, too, sat forward and locked his hands around one knee. "Who will you choose to meet with George?"

"Our cousin Niall."

"He's a viper you nurture—"

"Cease, brother, cease. I ken your feelings toward the man, but I owe him. I cannot forget it was I who forced him to take up the *crois taraidh,* and laid the curse of death upon him."

"Och, Micheil! The man's hail and hearty. Poor swordsman that he is, he could best you now. Trust him not."

"You and Davey both claim he treats well with George. Did you not warn me of such?"

"Aye, but—"

"Then who better to send to George?"

"None," Jamie answered, then heaved a weary sigh. "Do you choose him for the pestering our sister gives you? 'Tis hard to believe how he finds such favor with her."

Micheil rose in a controlled rush to his feet and stood glaring down at his brother. "Have you such a

mean spirit that you'd deny Bridget joy where she finds it? Niall brings her laughter. 'Tis jealous you are, Jamie. I'll hear no more against him. He alone came forth at a risk to himself to tell me what Davey had done. None other can make that claim.''

"Nor will you," Jamie avowed. He rose and left to do his brother's bidding.

Micheil finally had word of the planned meeting, but it was long past the date he had set. Strange storms had swept the Highlands, and it was close to Saint Andrew's Day, at the end of November, when he set out with eleven others to meet with a combined force of like number from the Keiths and MacKays. He had thought the terms odd, couched as Niall related—no more than twelve mounted horses from each side. Armed for battle, he lead his clansmen forth, knowing he left behind a great deal of dissension. There were those in his clan who had called for him to relinquish his place when he told them he intended to sue for peace.

He calmed flaring tempers with the logic that while they had suffered lost lives, the MacKays losses had totaled the larger share. The Gunns' purses had been fattened over these years, as had their bellies, by livestock stolen, while there were few, if any, MacKays who could stand in a strong wind.

His sister's cutting voice, denouncing him within the great hall, had pierced him like a sword thrust, but even her pleas would not stay him from the course he had set.

He would have Seana and the bairn she carried, he would have peace—uneasy alliance though it would be—and he would have both on his terms.

He saw that Crisdean and Gabhan rode with wary eyes on either side of him as they approached the burned-out kirk that was the meeting site. Micheil heard the clink of swords and dirks alike being loosened in the case of ambush.

Micheil had told no one that, even now, Jamie rode with a large force to take George Keith's heir from where he was fostered. Should treachery be the game played this day, the boy's life would be forfeit.

Micheil tried to keep Breac to an even pace, but he was himself anxious to know what message came to him from Seana. Niall had promised him she would send word by George for his ear alone.

He had to crush the yearning that rose to see her, and hold her near. To gaze upon her loveliness, and hear her sweet voice... and see her grow round with his child.

Seana cradled her rounded belly, having watched as her brother rode forth to meet with George. From there they would ride to meet Micheil. She had impressed upon Liam that he must, if they were to survive the coming winter, sue for peace. It was only her slight build and the layers of cloth she wore that prevented him from yet realizing that she was with child. Leites had only whispered this morning that Maille had raised the question to her. If her brother's leman even hinted of it to Liam, Seana feared her fate.

The day had begun clear, but a mist was rolling off the sea, spurred by strong winds. Yet she remained

near the seawall, praying, resentful that this would always be a woman's lot.

She thought of seeing Micheil again, having come to terms with who he was, and able to use his name. She knew the crushing blow she had to deliver when she told him the truth she had learned of his sister's lies. But, living in the same fear as had Bridget, Seana fully understood why the woman had chosen the path that she had. She was not condoning the blood shed and lives lost, it was simply a woman's way to survive the harsh dictates that governed the clans.

A wild hawk rode the wind, and Seana turned to follow the bird's flight inland, wishing she could rise above and witness the first meeting toward peace.

"'Tis not peace but our lives they seek, Micheil!" Gabhan cried out as they entered the broken wall around the kirk. There came twelve horses, as the terms stated, but upon each rode two men, doubling the number who came at them with swords drawn.

Each of the Gunn clansmen was set to fighting a man on foot, as well as one mounted. Micheil caught a glimpse of a man he thought to be Liam MacKay on a hill above the kirk, standing alongside a mounted man. He swore bitterly for the treachery he had walked into like a lamb, even as he fought for his life.

Liam, with a sword point at his back, heard the curses rain down upon him as George Keith's trap was closed. The cutting wind did not chill him, for the malt that George had pressed him to drink in toast after toast to their success warmed his blood, just as George's voice shamed him.

"You're a weakling and a fool, Liam. Not fit to wear a clan badge. 'Tis blessed you are that I have saved you this day."

"Whoreson!" Liam shouted, ducking and spinning to avoid the sword George wielded. "'Tis my sister's death warrant you signed this day!"

There was no real fight between them, Liam having no weapon and the liquor he had consumed aiding the shove from George that sent him sprawling.

Micheil, fighting to keep his seat upon a rearing Breac, lifted his bloodied sword and killed the foe who would have felled Crisdean. Since his friend had been unseated from his own steed, Micheil bent low and offered his left arm to Crisdean so that he could mount behind him.

Breac, prancing in place, his neck outstretched, snapped viciously as an enemy's horse neared. Micheil, caught leaning out as his horse pivoted, felt the searing pain as a dirk pierced the mail at his shoulder. Crisdean found purchase in the closing melee, and swung into place behind him, acting as a shield.

Spurring Breac free, Micheil headed for the hill where he had spotted Liam. But it was George Keith who rushed forth on his steed to meet him.

"Hold your sword!" George yelled halfway down, stopping his advance. "I've a message for you from Seana. Try and take her and you'll be met with steel and blood. She told you once, she'd be a whore to all in the Highlands afore she'd let you lay claim to her. Never forget your lesson this day!"

Micheil swayed in his saddle, whether from shock of wound or shock of words, but he knew not and

cared less. In a blinding fury, he turned Breac back to the few men able to stand and fight.

"Bring me a MacKay!" he shouted. "To me! Dead or breathing, it matters not!"

Seeing that Crisdean's steed lay gutted, Micheil drove Breac toward another riderless horse.

"Grab hold, Crisdean. You'll need a mount for the ride ahead."

"Micheil, let me ride with you. Your wound needs—"

"I'll not ride for home till I have that MacKay woman."

George Keith, thinking they turned tail for home, called his men to him, leaving two wounded MacKay men, Sim and Calum, at the mercy of the Gunns.

Liam was forced to cower as the Keiths thundered past him. Not one looked at him, or offered him a weapon to defend himself. Believing that none of his four clansmen were alive, Liam saw that there were yet six mounted Gunns, milling about the dead. The treachery of the day would be laid upon him. Yet he knew he would not play the fool by calling out and offering himself as a target.

Retreat was the only path open, and one it shamed him to take. He had to get back to Seana and tell her what was done this day.

It was dusk when the overwhelming urge to step outside the keep's walls came upon Seana. She rose from her chair at the hearth, setting aside her sewing, and began rapidly walking toward the doors.

Leites, coming from the kitchen with a cup of hot broth to tempt Seana, cried out in alarm. "They've not returned, lass. What ails ye that ye fair run?"

"I know he's near, Leites. I hear him call me."

"Who, lass? Who calls ye? Is it Liam that comes?" But Leites queried an open door, for Seana was gone from sight.

Not all of the wall had been repaired, and Seana crawled over a low spot, driven by an inner voice that beckoned her forth.

Something was wrong. That was all she knew. Her gaze was searching as she walked out on the cleared land, returning twice to a grouping of stunted trees that led to a narrow glen. Even as Seana headed toward them, she thought she heard a faint voice calling her name. There was no caution within her as her steps quickened, for she knew it was Sim's voice she heard.

She saw Sim clinging to a twisted tree trunk and rushed to his side. His voice was weak, and blood matted his plaid.

"Sim! I'll call for help. Tell me quickly— No, wait to tell me—" Seana felt a darkness close in on her. For Sim was shoved free to sprawl at her feet, and Micheil stepped out, holding his dirk.

# Chapter Nineteen

For one blinding instant, Seana stood frozen. Then her eyes filled with joy as she beheld him. Without saying a word, without giving thought to why he had come, she flung herself against him, her slender arms encircling his shoulders.

There was no mistaking the sticky wetness her fingers touched as anything but blood, or the rigid tension in his tall, powerful body as anything but rejection.

Confused, she stepped away, staring down at the blood covering her hand, before she frantically wiped it against her gown.

"'Twas a meeting of peace," she whispered. *Why do you stand there, as if in judgment of me, Micheil?* She turned away, her thoughts scattering, and felt him close by. Then the prick of his dirk was at her throat.

"Do not cry out, Seana," Micheil warned, in ever so soft a voice. He drew in the scent of her skin, anointed with roses, and a hunger rose within him to know again the sweet oblivion he found in her arms. But she had betrayed him, time and again. He needed to see her face, the face that had haunted his sleep and

his waking moments, needed to hear from her lips the lies that would condemn her.

Micheil withdrew his dirk. "Look at me, Seana. I've waited long for this moment."

A bitter wind wrapped itself around them as she did as he bade, and turned. Her gaze went to his lips, the mouth she had longed to touch with her own, despite every denial she tried to make to herself. The very lips she had wished to hear speak of the desire that bound them beyond all else. But his lips were not the softened ones, sensuous with the promise of a lover. In the haze of the rising moon, she saw his mouth thinned with anger, and she forced herself to meet the wrath that churned within the chilling blue depths of his eyes.

She recoiled from his rage, and from the sudden sense that the stench of blood surrounded her. Bile rose, and only her resolve to never again show him weakness enabled her to swallow.

Sim moaned, and Seana made a move to bend to him. Micheil's hand gripped her arm, hauling her up and away.

"Leave him, Seana. I've come far to find out why you betrayed me yet again."

"He's wounded. Let me—"

"As I am. 'Tis lucky we are, for others lost their lives at this *meeting of peace.*"

The one name she yearned to say—his name—was not the one that passed her lips. "And Liam? What of my brother?"

"A sniveling coward, as ever. He did not soil his blade, but ran when he thought us beaten by the treachery you two planned."

Seana stepped back in alarm. His voice, though yet so soft, held a steel blade of fury directed at her.

Micheil came forward until he had backed her against the gnarled trunks of the stunted trees. He could feel himself weakened from the loss of blood, and not even Crisdean's whispered warning from below, in the narrow glen where the others waited for him, could force him to leave.

Still holding his dirk, he caught her long plait at the back of her neck and forced her head back so that she could not look away from him.

"I made you a promise that what I claim, I hold. From the first you were mine, and still you refuse to believe me. The passion in you is the mate of mine, Seana. I'll have it, though it destroys me. I wish the hate that runs so hot you cry out to spill my blood was a love as fierce."

"You dare speak of love and betrayal in the same breath? Aye, I had a hand in forcing my brother to sue for peace. I loathe the violence by which you live. And if any have betrayed you, Micheil, look to your own house. Look to your sister, who began this with her lies." The clouds were scudding quickly over the moon, shadowing them both, hiding his eyes from her. But the trembling of her body betrayed itself in her voice.

His grip tightened, and he bent close. "'Tis you who lie. You'd protect that whoreson coward of your brother, and deny me! I should have slain him."

"And me, Micheil? Would you slay me, as well?" *I carry your child,* she longed to scream. *Against all reason, I have loved you. Micheil! Och, Micheil, you cannot have peace so long as you deny the lies Bridget spoke.*

"I cannot kill you," he whispered against her lips. "I would sooner take a knife to my own flesh. For we are bound together, Seana, though I be cursed into hell for still wanting you."

"You'll destroy us both with your blindness. I would give you a passion more grand than you dare to dream of, but you cannot have the love you claim to want without trusting me."

"Then I'll settle for what I take from you, till you cease your damn haunting," he lied, wounding her as she did him.

From the glen below came the hissed warnings of his men that riders approached.

Seana refused to struggle, afraid that, with the fury shaking him, he would hurt her and injure her unborn babe. If she dared to speak, dared to tell him of the child, he would take her with him, and cost her two lives. *But did he not see? Didn't he know?*

*Mayhap,* a devil's voice whispered, *he does not care.*

"Micheil," Crisdean called, coming forward. "Take her, or let us leave. You risk too much to linger."

Micheil caught her chin with a biting grip and crushed her tender lips beneath his. He allowed her no breath as he bruised her mouth, driving his tongue inside to pillage her softness. There was a hunger upon him to have her submission, to have her yield all and

be unable to deny him aught. He wanted her snared as helplessly as he felt himself to be by the need he had for her.

He wanted to break her, to have her resist and fight him, but she defeated him with the softening of her mouth. He fought the tenderness that nearly made him ease his brutal kisses, hearing again the whispers of Bridget and Fiona. *She betrayed you. Davey set her free. What had she to give him but herself? She bewitched him. She is your enemy. Always your enemy...*

Crisdean, fearing for their safety, for there were none among them who could stand and fight for long, grabbed hold of Micheil's arm. "Now, mon! We'll all be slain."

From below came yet another warning. "Are ye so sheltered ye cannot feel the snow?"

Micheil tore his mouth from hers. "I should take you. But I'll leave you to wait and wonder when I'll come for you again, Seana. Or your need of me will drive you back to the only man who's your mate. There is no other who will have you." His laugh was cruel and mocking, aimed at her and himself. "You once warned me, wee bairn though you were, that when you had grown to your promise I'd want no other woman. Witch that you are, it's come to pass. And as you lay claim to my heart, so I claim yours. As my body hungers to find the passion and peace you alone give me, so will you hunger. If you deny me again in this life, Seana, I swear by all I hold dear, I will follow you into hell itself."

He released her, and had already turned away when she called out, "Micheil, do not—"

"Do you beg, witch? Will you recant your words that any man but me can have you?"

"I cannot beg you, Micheil," she whispered, as sorrow tore at her. "You cannot trust me. On the day you do, I will give you the love I hold." *As I hold dear your unborn child.*

"What of this one?" Crisdean asked, kicking at the limp body of Sim.

"Slit his throat, or leave him. I care not," Micheil returned, staggering so that he needed Crisdean's shoulder. He turned once more as they descended into the glen, and saw that Seana knelt beside the body of her clansman. The first flurries of snow touched his cheeks, but Micheil did not feel their icy caress upon his flesh. It was no match for the deep cold that spread inside him.

She had cost him his faith in one brother, a broken trust with his sister, and the lives of yet more clansmen. And she dared set terms to him. Trust her, and she would give him her love. *Trust her, and you'll lose your clan, mayhap your life.*

He almost turned back to her, but the sounds of horses and men nearing the keep made him remember that he risked what was left of his peace party. Crisdean and Gabhan closed their horses with his, and Micheil retreated.

For now.

Seana roused herself and pledged to get help. Sim was muttering, but she made her way quickly back to the keep and came upon the horsemen. It was the

ghostly gray of the lead rider's horse that made her stop. These were no Keiths or MacKays, but a small band of Gunns. She was caught out in the open when she heard her name called.

"Davey?"

"Aye! Where's Micheil? I know he rode this way." He dismounted and ran toward her. "Where is he? I *saw* what happened. He's hurt again."

"You were there? You saw who betrayed—"

"Not there, Seana. I've seen much of what was to come, and yet more remains hidden. Tell me quickly, what befell my brother?"

"He's ridden off with your clansmen." She shivered as the wind rose in a howling glee, the light flurries of snow increasing. "I've a wounded clansman there, by the trees," she said, turning to point.

Davey stepped closer and offered her shelter of his plaid. "Micheil believes I betrayed him. He'll not listen to the reasons why I set you free."

"He's cast you from the clan? Oh, Davey, 'tis sorrowing I am to hear this." She touched his cheek and looked to the men who watched at a short distance. "I know not what fate befell my brother. Micheil claimed it was a trap, and that Liam ran, believing them slain. I cannot believe him. Liam swore he wanted peace."

"As did Micheil. He would not listen to Jamie when he told him not to trust Niall. Ever has our cousin dealt on the sly with George Keith. Fiona and Bridget filled him with lies while he lay stricken with fever. I feared for you, as well as my brother. While he will not listen to me, he's not cast me from the clan. Few know

how you escaped. What hold Micheil used to keep Niall, Fiona and my sister silent, I know not."

"Come and warm yourself and the others at the fire. Liam is not there, but I will not have shelter denied to you after you helped me."

Her uneasy glance at the men with him made Davey hurry to reassure her. "They feel as I do, that Niall has ever set himself against Micheil. 'Tis the only reason they ride with me. I would take up your offer, Seana, but I must find my brother."

She sought to hold him, a strange sense of approaching doom coming upon her. "Tell me, Davey. Something more has happened."

"Micheil is not the trusting fool. He sent Jamie to take George's son where he fostered at the tower of Dirlot. The boy was taken easily enough, without a fight, but as they rode for Halberry his horse bolted and the boy was thrown."

"He's dead?"

"Aye. All swear they know not how it could have happened. But his neck was broke, and the Keiths will be rising for Gunn blood."

"Go then, Davey. Find Micheil. He's wounded, and the men with him are weary. Keep him safe," she whispered, hugging him.

Davey mounted, then leaned down from his saddle. "The bairn?"

"All's well," she answered, splaying one hand over the rounded swell of her baby. "The Virgin keep you safe."

Maille turned from the low, broken place in the wall. She knew there were those who thought her mind

dim as any animals'. But she had an animal cunning
that surfaced when her survival mattered. She knew
that what she had overheard and witnessed was secret, and she hugged it to her. She had much to pay
Seana back for. So she would wait and watch. Her
time would come. She giggled, and smothered the
sound with her hands, running lightly over the ground
and back into the keep. She would pay and pay!

Leites eyed Maille as she entered. "Did ye not find
her? I thought I heard horses. Is it Liam that's come?"

"Nay. I saw no one." Keeping her eyes downcast,
Maille made her way to the fire and stood warming her
hands. "The snow comes," she added, seeing that
Leites had donned her cloak and hurried to the doors.
But the old woman was muttering to herself.

Seana pushed open the door and told Leites to fetch
the kitchen lads to help bring Sim within the hall.
Seeing that Maille watched them, she refused to answer Leites's questions.

"Later we will talk."

But the time did not come, for once Sim was tended
and resting by the fire in the hall, Liam arrived home
with Calum and the bodies of Angus and Dughall.

Liam was frozen to the bone, for the storm had
come upon them with a slashing fury, and it was late
when he finally told Seana all that had happened.

Kneeling on the hearthstone, Seana rested her head
against her brother's knee. "George paid dear for the
treachery he practiced this day. His son is dead."

"And will you now claim to have the sight, that you
could know such?"

Seana heard the weary forced amusement in her brother's voice and looked up at him. "Liam, Davey came. He has the sight. He knew the meeting was never for peace, and tried to warn Micheil, but he would not listen. He does not trust Davey. He knows it was Davey who set me free."

Liam shook his head.

Seana covered his hand with her own. "Listen. I would hold no secrets from you." And so she began to make her confession of hate turned to love, of Micheil's torment, and his visit. Of his threats and his promises. She made Liam understand how she had tried to tell him of Bridget's lies, and his refusal to hear one word against his sister.

Liam, who had had the pride stolen from him this day, the pride his sister had fought so hard to give back to him, found he could summon compassion for her. He, too, had loved, with a blinding passion that had brought his clan to ruin. He stroked Seana's hair as she shed the tears she had withheld these many months.

While she took the comfort her brother offered her, Seana knew she should tell him about the child. But one look through tear-filled eyes at the weary lines that ravaged Liam's once-handsome face, and Seana kept silent. Her brother needed no more burdens, and she would force his hand to tell him now about Micheil's child. With the winter coming, she would perish if banned from here.

"Liam, have you never thought to appeal to the king?"

"Robert? A man who sows unrest? Our quarrels are too petty for him. He'd not help the likes of us. We've

no wealth to enrich his coffers. No army to stand for him. We are doomed to be a branch of the MacKays wiped from memory. Och, Seana, I wish I'd never set eyes upon Bridget. I wish I had listened to wiser counsel, and not the passion that set us on this path to ruin."

"Lay the blame where it belongs, Liam." Seana spoke impatiently, for she hated it when her brother took all fault upon himself. "If she had been a true wife to you—"

"And I not constantly gone from her side," Liam cut in. He placed two fingers over his sister's lips. "No more. My head aches, and I'm sorely in need of rest. We sit here and bleat like sheep, sister. Between the Keiths and the Gunns, we shall be crushed, unless the Lord shows mercy. Go find your bed and leave me mourn my loyal friends' deaths. Maille! Maille, come, lass!" he called.

Seana rose awkwardly to her feet and saw the girl come from the shadows. Her gaze was for Liam alone, and Seana left them. It mattered not what the girl overheard. There were none she could tell.

As the cold gray dawn fell upon the land, the rage of the storm continued with unabated fury. Within the keep of George Keith, so, too, did the keening wail of the bagpipes remain steady, playing the pibroch, the song of grief for the young boy lost to the clan.

Night after night, George sat within the chapel, the wavering light of candles throwing shadows on the stone walls and alcoves, where so many dead were laid to rest. He refused to hear the whispers that he had

none to blame but himself. But his mind played with the revenge he would have to see Micheil Gunn mourn the loss of his child. Mourn the loss of what he held dear. He wanted to see that bastard stripped and banished. And there was only one who could help him bring this about, for it would satisfy him, as well.

Death for Micheil, he decided in his arrogance, was a blessing he would withhold. Far better would it be to see him broken.

As the days passed, George, blind with what he alone could see, noticed naught of those who made the sign of the cross against the madness in his eyes, or covered their ears against the mutters passing his lips.

He often stood on the ramparts, fist raised, cursing the snows that fell without cessation.

And the heavens laughed at man's impotence, blanketing the Highlands with blizzards the like of which none in memory could recall.

Within the walls of Halberry, Micheil kept his brooding self away from Bridget's solar, where Gordie often played and sang for her and Fiona. He kept his own counsel as to what the spring would bring to bear. Bridget no longer plagued him with his broken oath to her and their father. Had he been less deep in thought of Seana and his regret that he had not taken her that fateful day when the first snows came, he might have paid attention to his sister's sudden joy.

He saw little of Niall, and less of Davey, for he had yet to forgive his brother. Jamie stood by him, and for that he was most thankful.

Did Seana carry his child? He would spend hours staring out at the storm-tossed sea and repeat the question over and over.

In the evening, he sat at the high table, surrounded by his clan, knowing that some wished him gone, yet were not strong enough to wrest control away from him.

The snows fell, and there was no word from beyond the walls, for travel was nigh impossible. Fights broke out, over real or imagined slights. Poor Peigi was beside herself to vary the meals she prepared.

Micheil watched it all, waiting. Waiting for spring.

An uneasy truce existed between Seana and Maille once Liam had been told of his sister's coming child. They were isolated from any news, and Liam had not the heart to punish his sister. Sim's wounds healed, as did Calum's minor ones, and Liam ofttimes jested that the highlanders healed the quickest. Leites would cackle with glee, telling each one it was the blessed water that fed their crops and animals and brewed their ale that made their blood strong.

Seana would laugh, seated by the fire, her hand always filled with sewing for the babe that kicked so vigorously. Sometimes Liam would prevail upon her to set her woman's work aside and cheer them by playing the *clarsach*. The harp had sat unused since their bard had been killed, and while he should have been replaced, none mentioned that Liam had failed in his duty to do so.

By the light of the fire, Seana would pluck the strings, she and Liam singing together. Then Maille

would want to dance, and Liam would join her. It was a far cry from the *ceilidhs* Seana remembered held within this hall from her childhood. She tried her best these days to keep every thought a pleasant one, for Leites told her tales of women who worried themselves into birthing monsters.

Seana grew clumsy, and the babe seemed to sap every bit of her strength. Leites always gave her the choicest morsels at meals, and while Seana saw that Maille resented it, the girl held her silence.

Calum presented her with a cradle, and Liam soft furs to line it. Seana's eyes filled with tears at their gifts, and her thoughts turned to Micheil. It would be a great and gay company filling Halberry as the Yule season began the celebrations that led to Hogmanay. There would be no worry that stinting was needed to have food enough for the New Year. The daft days, Seana recalled with a smile. And to chase her saddened mood, she demanded that all had to present their bare feet so that they could choose a proper "first-foot" among them. Even the kitchen lads were drawn in, for the person chosen had to be male, and dark-haired. When the lads hung back, saying they had no gift to bring, as was proper, Liam promised he would provide one.

It was most important that the first-foot have a high arch so that water could run beneath his foot, and Calum won the honor. There was much teasing and laughter that night as they recalled years far past, when they were young and the coin purses full.

Seana rested contented that night, a sense of peace and of waiting filled her. All her thoughts turned to

the child. Leites swore she would have a son, for she carried him low, not high and round. Seana suspected Leites slipped out to leave her small offerings beneath the trees. The old woman could trace her family back to those who had practiced the old ways, the ones who had worshiped the sacred oaks and made blood sacrifices.

Wrapped as she was on her bed in furs, Seana wished that the ache in the small of her back that plagued her at every day's end would leave. And she longed to have Micheil know that she cradled and nurtured his child.

The dream came to her that night, the one in which she fled Halberry. She awoke without the fear and cold sweat, for now she knew what it was she held tight to her breast to protect. Seana still did not know what words Micheil spoke to her as he rode after her, but she had dreamed of the face of her son.

And none would be able to deny who had fathered him.

And so she, too, waited for the coming birth.

Maille was sent to collect the branches of juniper that had to be kindled in every room. All doors and windows had to be sealed, so that the smoke from the burning of the juniper would protect all those within from harm in the coming year. Not only were those within the keep treated to this, but the animal pens and stables, as well.

Calum brought spiced ale and, together with Leites, broke the sowens and sprinkled the sweet on the doors and windows. Liam blended an infusion of spirits and sweetened ale, so that they would have their hot drink

on the last night of the old year. Sim brought the fresh hide of a cow they had slain, and he was the one chosen to wear it. Only Liam, Calum and the lads were allowed to belabor Sim as he went three times around the hall, following the direction of the sun, and sang his cry as they struck him with switches.

Strips from the hide were removed without the aid of a knife, and each was handed one strip to burn. Seana watched that none of the strips were extinguished, for it was a bad omen, not only for the one who held it, but for the house, as well.

Seana had to bid them good-night, for she grew tired. To Maille she gave a hug and a kiss, thanking her again for the lovely length of ribbon the girl had given to her. Seana, in turn, had parted with a small silver brooch that she had come across in her mother's chest. It had little value, but she hoped the girl would treasure the spirit she had given with it.

The land lay hushed and waiting as the New Year began. But within many keeps, it was time to hone the blades that would be needed once the snows melted and the moors turned green, for revenge tasted somewhat sweeter when cold and deadly.

# Chapter Twenty

Maille chafed at every chore Leites set her to do. Seana kept to her room these days, and the old crone swore her time was near. Maille yearned to have it be so. Of late, she knew, she was losing favor with Liam, ever since the night of *Calluinn*. So much had happened that New Year night. Just thinking about what she was daring to do, and right beneath Liam's and Seana's noses, brought a cunning smile to her lips.

"Here now, what's got ye wearing that bletherin' look?" Leites asked, coming upon Maille. She squinted, shaking her head, thinking her eyesight was failing, for the girl lost her smile and poked her foot in the rushes. "Done with all I gave ye?"

"Aye. See for yerself." Maille hid her face, her gay mood replaced by a sullen one. "I've needs of my own to tend." She ran for the cloak on the peg near the kitchen door.

"Needs of her own?" Leites muttered, cuffing the lad who turned the spit for good measure. "She'd best tend to the master's needs, or she'll find herself without a bed."

Maille, having snuck back, for she often heard the choicest bits when others thought her gone, stuck out her tongue and cursed the old woman. Careful that none watched her, she went round the stable and squeezed her slender body between the stone wall and the thick wood that formed the stable's back. She did not believe that any remembered the missing stone that she could crawl through. If she had not been set to watch the hens when they lost a few to a fox, she never would have discovered this means of escape.

The hole slanted down, for it was close to the cliff, and she tasted the salt spray. Keeping on her hands and knees, she crawled along until she reached the stunted trees where she had spied on Seana. Now she could stand and run down into the narrow glen.

"I've near froze my arse off waiting for you!"

Caught in a bear hug from behind, Maille giggled and squirmed until she could press her lips against the man who held her.

She welcomed the hard thrust of his tongue as she welcomed his greedy, rough fondling of her breasts. "Enough!" she said, pushing him away. She had learned her lesson well with Liam. Never again would she be generous with all her favors before she had her payment.

"Show me what you've brought for me."

From beneath his plaid, George Keith withdrew a delicately linked silver chain that his wife would never miss. But as Maille made a grab to pluck the chain from him, he shackled her wrist and pulled her hard against him.

"The pretty is yours, soon as you tell me what I came to hear."

Pouting, Maille quickly thought better of lying. This was not Liam. George would hurt her if she made him angry.

"The old woman tells us her time is near."

"You said as much the last time I risked life and limb to come."

"Ye cannot hurry a bairn's coming!" she snapped back.

"You can, but it takes a skilled hand," he muttered to himself, releasing her and letting her pluck the chain free. "How near?"

"A week or less. She's fat as a cow, an' ugly as well." Sliding the chain around her neck, Maille tried to see herself, but the chain was too short, and she knew she dared not wear it.

George caught her chin, and smiled with his lips. "You didn't forget what you're to do the moment the bairn is born?"

"I'll not forget. You can kiss me again," she offered, pressing up against him. "I keep the red wool ye gave me hid well from all eyes."

George pecked her cheek and ignored the flash of anger in her eyes. "Go, lass, before you're discovered. I don't want anything to happen to you. Your reward awaits."

"'Tis grand?"

"Aye. Like none have given you before."

He watched her run back, spat, and wiped his mouth. "Aye, 'tis a grand, grand reward I've planned for you."

* * *

The snows were melting, and any traveler was made welcome, as those within keeps were eager for news. At Halberry, all knew of the estrangement between Davey and Micheil, and none remarked when Davey, learning that the roads were passable, set out. Jamie knew where his brother went, but since no one asked him, he did not say.

The long winter had left him with a bitterness toward both Micheil and Davey, for neither would listen to his oft-given counsel, and both refused to come together and make peace. For Micheil it was enough that he did not banish his younger brother, or let others know what he had done. And Davey, with the same bad-tempered, stubborn streak, refused to go on bended knee to Micheil unless he would hear all that he had to tell him.

What Davey was about to do smacked of madness, yet Jamie had helped him pack provisions for his journey and map the best route to take him safely to the Kyle of Tongue. He wished he could have accompanied his brother, but someone had to stay and guard Micheil's back, for Niall yet remained at Halberry.

Despite the favor Bridget showed to Niall, Jamie trusted him not. And he trusted Fiona's new demure manner even less. They plotted, he would wager his life on that, but even Gabhan, who had taken Cuíni as a leman, offered no hint to the schemes they hatched in Bridget's solar.

Jamie, to turn aside his bleak thoughts and remove himself from the hall, where a tense air of waiting prevailed, went in search of Micheil.

He found his brother walking the seawall, as was his habit of late. Observing him, Jamie thought Micheil was as finely honed as any blade, and if the plotting for the coming attacks by the Keiths had robbed him of youth and sleep, the lines added a new maturity to his face. Jamie was struck by the close resemblance of Micheil to their father. The sea wind combed back the length of his black hair, revealing his profile. As ever, Micheil gazed out on the sea, and Jamie could stand and wonder until long past Candlemas what his brother found there. Unless Micheil wished to open his heart, none would know.

"Has he gone, Jamie?"

"Davey left nearly two hours ago."

Micheil nodded. He longed to share the thoughts that plagued him with Jamie, and even, in a weak moment like this one, with Davey, too. He missed having the friendship of his youngest brother. But to forgive him . . . It was more than Davey helping Seana to escape. It was the whisper that came upon him, catching him unawares, that Davey had taken what he held dear. Did Seana carry *his* child? *Trust me and you shall have my love.*

Abruptly Micheil turned from his contemplation of the gray sea. "He has gone to her."

"Would you have me lie, brother?"

"Nay, Jamie. I hear enough lies, or truth so twisted it would take a better man than I to sort it out."

"Davey said her time is near. Candlemas approaches. A fitting time for a bairn to be born, brother. A true sign to celebrate spring. As for the lies and twisted truth, Micheil, you need look no further

than who speaks them to you. I hold no claim to be wiser than any man, but I can see clear that a lie serves no purpose but to the one who tells it.''

Micheil's gaze, naked and anguished, met Jamie's. ''Then tell me, brother, who is served by the telling that Davey lay with her? Whose bairn does she nurture? Who is served by the telling that my brother betrayed me?''

''Look to your heart for the answers, Micheil.'' Jamie held his gaze steady on his brother's face. He could almost see the torment that Micheil abided with, and wished a word could end it. It saddened him that Micheil turned away in dismissal, but Jamie decided not to leave him.

''I would offer her a devil's choice, Jamie,'' Micheil said softly, almost as if he spoke aloud to himself. ''I would give her a ring for marriage, or a sword to end her damned haunting of me. She dared to set terms to me, Jamie. Dared to tell me to trust her. I have broken my oath to Da and to Bridget, and that witch still sets more terms to me before I can have her.

''Would that I could cast her out from heart and mind. But like the witch I call her, she has burned a brand upon my soul, and chained me to her, though leagues keep us apart.'' Closing his hands over the edge of the stone wall, so that his knuckles whitened, Micheil added, ''I refused again the only gift that Bridget asked for the New Year.''

Micheil hunched his shoulders, his whole body sagging forward to let his arms take his weight. ''Bridget, too, sets a devil's choice for me. I cannot destroy

Seana. I cannot kill her. And, by her terms, I cannot have her.''

Jamie saw the rage and longing that came upon Micheil's dark visage. He stood quietly, letting Micheil find his own pace, and his own way of spilling the torment that plagued his nights.

But Micheil remained silent, and Jamie, afraid to let this chance slip by, forced himself to speak. "If you harbor the belief that Davey betrayed you with Seana, why didn't you slay him? Ban him? Challenge him, Micheil? And why, brother, have you threatened those who first set the whispers to haunting you to keep quiet? You have not once made Niall account for his part in that foul meeting that nearly cost you your life. Why, Micheil? What hold has Niall on you?"

Micheil spun and advanced on Jamie, his hands clenched at his sides, his blue eyes blazing with temper. "Do you think I've not asked myself these questions? Davey's my brother, my blood. I can no more spill it than willingly spill my own. Aye, I threatened him, and Fiona and Bridget, to keep their tongues still. The belief is Davey's own acts and words in defense of her from the moment I set accursed eyes on Seana.

"As for the other, Niall has ever played a deep game with me. 'Tis better, Jamie, to keep the viper in view than to wait for its strike in some hidden place. He goes among the clansmen, pretending sorrow for me, and with a sly tongue goes about asking if it would not be best for the clan to choose another."

"I didn't think you knew." Jamie offered him a crooked smile. "Our *dear* cousin has lofty ambitions." Thoughtful for a few minutes, Jamie crossed

his arm over his chest and with the other cupped his chin. "I ponder this, Micheil. How does Niall twist that near-fatal meet to his own ends? All know he spoke for us. You made much of toasting him that night in the hall, though there were many sickened by it."

Micheil's laughter, low and mocking, was unexpected. He clapped a hand to Jamie's shoulder. "Do you ponder that? Och, he's as wily as the fox, Jamie. With great show, Niall confesses his anguished part in warning me upon his return not to trust the Keiths. And I, great arrogant beastie that I am, paid my wise cousin no heed, thinking myself above the laws that rule men."

Jamie clamped one hand on his sword hilt. "Name the whoresons who believe his lie."

"Rest easy, brother. You know them well, just as you know those who stand loyal by us have come to tell me. Our clan is no different from another. Ever are there factions who will strive to gain control. If a leader worthy of being laird presented himself, I believe I would gladly hand over—"

"Say no more! You can't do it, Micheil! Da would turn, nay, he'd rise and haunt Halberry."

"He comes and sits judgment on me often enough, Jamie. Has not Davey told you how he *sees* Da? 'Tis accursed we are, from the moment Da allowed the marriage. We all sensed it would bring doom. And it's not finished. Till I have Seana mine, it will not be finished."

"And the bairn, Micheil? She could carry your heir. Will you let the child be born a bastard?"

Jamie did not need to have Micheil walk away to be suddenly alone. That quickly his brother withdrew, his face devoid of expression, his eyes shuttered. He would have no more answers this day, and so it was Jamie who left.

Micheil was forced to remember how he had sworn he would never spill his seed within the MacKay woman, never allow the blood of the Gunns to mingle with hers.

An easy oath to give, when all he could remember of Seana was a bairn with the look of faerie's get about her.

Alone and facing the sea, for it somehow brought Seana closer to him, he allowed a smile. Even that long-ago night she had dared to set the terms of his behavior to him. He had threatened her with a taste of the taws, and she had countered that when she was full-grown, and met the promised beauty all could see, she would bring joy to his hall.

With a rough shake of his head, Micheil turned aside from an oft-walked mental path. He looked to the sky and watched the flight of a sea gull who wheeled and dived time and again, but came away with nothing.

Micheil knew he, too, held naught. There was an empty place inside him that defied all reason and cried out to have Seana.

Watching Micheil from the tower room, Bridget cursed her brother. "Come witness Micheil laid so low by that bitch, he moons at the sea, as if she'd come sailing back. Come look, Fiona."

"Do you want all ready for when *she* comes?" Fiona snapped with a sharp bite. "Come help me scrub the soot from the hearth so that she'll have no cause to complain and refuse us."

Bridget, ever mindful of her scars, lowered her veil before turning. "Cuíni should be set to—"

"Cuíni isn't *one of us,* Bridget! Time and again I have told you. You have the blood. Have we not shown the power that can be yours by following the ancient ways?" With a narrowed gaze, and a sly smile, Fiona rose and went to Bridget. "Don't you like having a strong man warming your bed again? With none to know?"

"Hush!" Bridget glanced around the empty room, fear rising so that she gripped Fiona's arm. "You must not ever speak of it."

"But you will never give it up. Help me now, Bridget. I have seen her powers. What she will do to Micheil this night will cost him dear, and give you pleasure. Never again will he hold any dearer than his sister while you live."

Fiona was quick to resume her scrubbing. It would never do to have Bridget suspect how well she was being used.

Seana dreamed. Halberry's hall, ablaze with torches and candles. Micheil at the high table, she standing proud and defiant before him. She could hear jeering voices, but from faceless forms that hovered just out of sight. He rose, coming around to her, drawing her into the circle cleared for dancing.

With a cry, Seana tossed and twisted, trying to block the images that came, faster and faster.

Micheil's eyes, glinting with a wicked challenge, the direction of his gaze forcing her own to follow. She could feel the swirl of confusion as the image of herself looked upon the gleaming blades of two swords that formed the cross for the sword dance.

Micheil, lithe and powerful, coming forth to take his place as the music played. The music swelled, drowning out the voices that cheered him on. But Micheil danced for her. His blue eyes held her own, as surely as he held her heart. Time and again she wanted to see his booted feet moving in the intricate steps as the pipes wailed high. Somehow she knew he never once touched the blades. He danced for her, in lust and in challenge, but not with the love she yearned to see.

And, when done, there was a sudden silence as he lifted one sword, then the other. He came again to stand before her, offering her one sword. And there, gracing the tip of the other, gleamed his heavy gold ring. He laughed, low and mocking, to see the confusion on her face.

Within her bed, Seana felt smothered, and powerless to move. Whatever brought this dream to her, it had to be played out. But fear consumed her.

"In love?" she heard herself ask Micheil's handsome countenance. "Do you offer me a ring of marriage with love in your heart?"

"Love? Marriage?" He mocked her, and invited all to join in his laughter. "'Tis a small banding I offer you, Seana, in place of the thrall's collar you should wear. You vowed you'd whore for the Highlands—"

"Will you never forget?"

"Never! Seana, make your choice. The sword or the ring."

"Death or dishonor!"

"You have no honor. None. Where's my bairn, Seana? What have you done to our child?"

Fighting her way through the smothering darkness, Seana awoke. "What have I done?" she repeated, her hands curved over the tight, swollen mound of her belly. She could still hear Micheil's demand, but laughter, too much laughter, drowned out the sound of his voice.

And within her room, so far from Halberry, there lingered the scents of sandalwood and juniper. "My babe!" She choked the words out, her voice hoarse, as if she had screamed and screamed till her throat was raw. "Micheil? Micheil, what befalls us now?"

But the stones of the Kyle of Tongue had no answer for her.

"Seana? I cannot see you. I hear you call. What ails you, lass?"

Smoke rose from herbs and powders cast on the fire, and Bridget was beckoned closer yet again to see her brother's agony.

"Micheil stumbles, yet naught is there to trip him." Bridget spoke in a hushed whisper, as if the image of her brother that came through the flames could hear her. He cocked his head, as though to listen, and turned toward her. She recoiled. Micheil was blind! Gone were the searing blue eyes that seemed to know her every secret. "What have you done to him?"

"Only what you desire to see."

"You cannot stop it now, Bridget," Fiona leaned near to say. "'Tis all there. Watch and learn the power you have given yourself to. None shall be stronger. And Micheil will pay at last for thinking so little of your honor that he cast aside his oath for her. Lost, Bridget, ever shall they be lost to each other in darkness."

"And the bairn?" Bridget dared to ask, the lure of the flames too much to resist. And she laughed then, laughed till tears ran from her eyes, as she saw the final end.

While Bridget was held enthralled by her visions, Fiona slipped from the tower room and entered Micheil's bedchamber. She stood leaning against the closed door, smiling to hear his hoarse mutterings.

"Cry out for her, Micheil. Cry all you wish. I will bring her to you. Bring you the scent of roses and the sweet spring heather. Birdsong and soft breezes. Make her welcome, Micheil. Show your love what awaits her in your arms."

Fiona carried forth the goblet she held, sipping from it, then kissing Micheil's lips. She passed the liquid to him, time and again, until his will was hers.

When Micheil caught her flaming red hair within his hands and drew her near for his kiss, he held not Fiona's hair, but Seana's honey-blond tresses, to veil their lips.

But he thought to take her sweet mouth with the need and tenderness he held in his heart, and as from afar beheld his savage attack. Her body gleamed with

a pale sheen, supple, and as wanton as the whispers that passed her lips.

He was repelled, and yet drawn to have and master what she promised. Each time he tried to call her name, her lips sealed his and offered him a taste so rich his blood flamed anew. She rode him as he had ridden Breac to break him to the saddle. She beckoned him to do the same.

Naught satisfied her. And the same wild hunger drove him to break her. It was no longer enough to have her yield all. It would never be enough.

He struggled to keep her with him as the dawn light broke the dark line of night. He had not the strength.

Micheil called to her. He called to Seana with an ever-weakening voice, pleading with her to come and stay. He heard an odd echo of mocking laughter.

Davey awoke half in and half out of an ice-encrusted burn. The sun was high, and he last remembered having stopped to break his fast. Half his body was numb, the other so chilled he could barely move his fingers. He tried to call for his horse, thinking to grab the reins and have the beastie pull him clear of the sodden bank.

His head ached as if he had taken a blow, and he squeezed gritty eyes closed, trying to remember what had happened to him. The visions came in a disjointed rush, and he saw himself apart, kneeling by the water, about to scoop up a drink with one hand, when he was felled by the power that swept his mind.

Micheil? Or Seana? He lay square between them. Who did he try to warn?

By the blessed Virgin! What had Bridget set in motion?

And what could he, who had not yet even removed himself from the numbing cold, what could he do?

## Chapter Twenty-One

Micheil had to be roused to awaken. His mouth held a foul taste. His body felt wasted, as if ravaged by long illness. He sent all away, for he could not understand why they stared, then turned from him.

Truly, he thought, if I look a bit like I feel, 'tis no wonder they act so. He struggled to shove off his furs and sit on the edge of his bed. Had he drunk so freely of wine last eve that the very devils pounded in his head?

He had to shield his eyes from the sun's glare, coming through the unshuttered window. He puzzled for a moment that it was open, for while the day marked Candlemas Eve, there was no sweetly heated spring air covering his naked body.

"God's wounds, I ache," he muttered, his blurred eyes staring down at his thighs. He rubbed his eyes and looked again at the bloodied furrows that marked his skin. There were more to be seen on his arms and chest, even on his belly. Micheil smelled the roses—a faint, oh, so faint trace that came from his bed—as he turned and stared where his sword yet rested.

He held out a trembling hand for his weapon, making himself stretch across the bed. And there rose from his furs the scents of mating.

"She was not here! 'Tis madness to think I possessed her!"

He snatched the hilt and came off the bed. His quick, searching gaze showed naught amiss within his room.

"What demon have ye set upon me now, Seana? For surely only a fiend would have me dreaming this."

But his voice was pitched low, for if any should hear him, he would be cast within the dungeon below.

Leites brought Seana the sheaf of oats. "Ye be the mistress here. 'Tis for you to dress the sheaf in yer clothes, with Maille and me to help ye. Best do it now, Seana, for the bairn shall come any day. Ye cannot forget that we need make Briid welcome."

Weary from the torment of the night, Seana made no effort to move from her place by the fire. "You do it, Leites. You and Maille."

"Yer not like yer ma. She could not be kept still." Leites had to lean down very close to see Seana's face. "There's dark circles ringing your eyes, lass. It bodes ill for ye."

"I did not sleep well. You had best get Maille to fetch the basket, and wooden club, as well." Knowing the deep caring Leites had for her, Seana patted the old woman's wrinkled cheek. "I will come help, and be rested to walk with you two. I would have no ill omen come upon us now."

Seana slept then, no dreams troubling her rest, though she longed for their hall to be blessed by a priest this Candlemas Eve.

Liam found his sister in his own chair by the fire late that afternoon. His anger that she carried a bastard was raw upon his features as he called out for Leites and Maille.

Seana stirred at the sound of Liam's voice, and she smiled as he bent to her.

"Where are they? I've come with a fierce hunger, as do Sim and Calum, Seana, yet there is naught ready for us to eat."

"Leites and Maille make ready the basket for Briid."

"And let the fire in the kitchen go dead?"

Seana struggled from the chair. She knew that Liam tried to avoid touching her, now that her time was so close. "I cannot say what has kept them. But I can still feed you." She thought it strange that Leites had left the cheese uncovered, and the fire, as Liam said, was out beneath the kettle of soup. Bending over to grab a handful of kindling, Seana cried out as a knifing pain lanced across her lower back. She held her hands flat against the still-warm stones of the hearth, waiting for it to pass, waiting, too, to regain her breath.

She was not afraid. Leites had schooled her in what was to come. Her room had all she needed in readiness, but she would need Liam's help to get there.

Poor Liam, she thought, his meal would yet have to wait.

But he did not answer her call and Seana was forced to find him. He stood at the far end of the hall, locked

in an embrace with Maille. From the moans of the girl, whose back was toward her, Seana knew Liam was not going to welcome her interruption. She felt the pain gather itself again, and placed the back of her hand against the end of her spine as the pain built and built. She knew she had made some sound, for when she looked up, Liam and Maille stood watching her.

"The bairn..."

"Fetch Leites," Liam ordered his leman, rushing to his sister.

"I have not seen the old woman all day. She sent me to find a proper club for Briid's coming."

Seana clutched her brother's arm. "You have not seen her? But I need Leites. The bairn's coming. She's to help me birth my babe."

Maille came forward. She smiled and touched Seana's long plait. "Don't worry. I'm here."

Seana closed her eyes, hoping her brother would think her chilling shivers came from the beginning of labor. Maille? All she had was Maille?

"Liam, find Leites and bring her to me. I want her with me."

"Aye. Aye, don't vex yourself. Let me carry you up, and I'll find the old woman."

Maille ran back to fetch the large basket she had dropped near the door when Liam greeted her with fierce kisses. Never losing her smile, she ran to *help* Seana.

Seeing his sister's pale face, and hearing her moan as another pain gripped her swollen body, Liam bolted from the room. "Take care of her, Maille."

"Maille will not fail ye." She bore his quick, hard kiss, and entered the room.

From the bed, Seana watched ner enter, seeing the large basket she carried. "What have you there, Maille?"

"What I need for Briid." She saw the pain take Seana again, and stepped closer to the bed. "'Tis the basket for carrying the sheaf of oats dressed like you. And the club. Look at it, Seana. See what a fine one I found."

Against her will, Seana looked down into the basket. There, nestled on a folded length of red cloth, was a club. Its wood was marred with dark stains. And she had to gaze up into Maille's staring eyes.

"'Tis a war club you've found. A club for killing."

"Aye. Don't ye think it fitting?" Her short, stubby fingers caressed the wood before she lifted it out and set it on the floor, just beyond Seana's reach.

"Maille? Maille, go help my brother find Leites. The pain's not bad now. I'll manage alone. Go find Leites!"

"I can't do that. Leites is gone. There's only me to help you birth your bastard bairn, with its accursed blood." She looked again to the club, then at Seana. "We'll need a fire. And a knife. A sharp one."

She crooned her list, but Seana did not hear any more. She stared at the club, and the one stain that seemed darker, almost fresher, than the others. Her scream filled the room.

Liam heard her. He stood outside and listened to the scream that went on and on. Hurrying to the stable, he

found that Sim and Calum were more than eager to ride out with him.

Birthings were best left to women. As they passed through the newly repaired gates, they shared a smile when the screams abruptly stopped, and Liam said, "Seana worries for naught. Maille will see her through this. But I'll have a strip of that old woman's hide when I find her."

Turning from the window, Maille took the length of red cloth from the basket. "He's gone with Sim and Calum. None are left here."

"Maille..." Seana forced herself up from the pillow, her ragged breathing making speaking difficult. "What do you do with the cloth?" She tried not to think of being at the vacant-eyed woman's mercy. The blessed Virgin had seen her safe until now, and she would protect her unborn child. Seana would not believe otherwise.

Rubbing the soft wool against her cheek, Maille ignored Seana until she shouted her question. "Don't vex yourself, Seana. 'Tis naught but a shroud." She pulled the stool close to the hearth and started the fire. And there she sat, holding the cloth, dreaming of all the fine things George Keith would give her as her reward for helping him.

Seana blessed and cursed the pains that came, wave upon wave. Her babe was eager, impatiently so, to be born. The quicker he came, the less of her strength he sapped. And she would need her strength, hers and all that her fervent prayers could garner, to protect her child, and herself, as well.

To distract herself from her great thirst, she thought of the honey ready to be rubbed on the child's palate to clean the inside of the babe's mouth, and with the sweetness of the honey to gift the child with taste. The rose oil that she had hoarded was for bathing the child. She heard again Leites repeating over and over that the male babe needed strong rubbing with the oil, for his limbs had to be made tougher, for hard work. And the cradle that stood ready in the dark corner of her room, where the babe must needs spend the first hours in the same darkness as the womb, to protect his sight and ward off the light that would hurt its eyes.

And the songs. She had to remember the songs to sing. But the words escaped her as the pain left her drenched in sweat.

Feeling Maille's hand on her taut belly, Seana bared her teeth and hissed at her. "Get back, you witch!"

"It won't be long now."

Seana did not need Maille, or any other, to tell her that. Her body felt torn asunder by pain so great she did not think she could bear it.

*A helpless babe. Micheil's child . . .* Aye, she could live. She *would* live.

Och! If only she knew if Liam had planned this.

She had to grab hold of the furs and lift her upper body. The babe was coming! Prayers spilled from her in a senseless jumble. And at the last, when she thought the child would rend her in half, she screamed for Micheil.

Micheil, crossing the courtyard with Gabhan and Iain, suddenly stopped. He felt the hairs on his neck rise, and spun around.

"What ails ye?" Iain asked, seeing the fierce look of Micheil.

"Do you hear the cry?" he asked them, staring up at the almost crystalline perfection of black sky and brilliant stars.

"You're daft man. 'Tis naught but the wind you hear, in the caves below the sea." Gabhan shifted uneasily from one foot to the other, waiting for Micheil to come to his senses and return to the hall with them.

"Aye, daft," Micheil muttered, but he took one last look at the sky. Someone had called him. *Someone, or something.*

It was Jamie, leading a patrol in search of stray Keiths, who discovered Davey stumbling across a field. The snow yet lay upon the ground, but each day saw its melting. Seeing that his younger brother appeared as if outlaws had attacked him, Jamie spoke alone with Davey, away from the other men.

"I know not what befell me, Jamie. How many days have I been gone from here?"

"Three."

Davey wasted no time bemoaning the time gone. He told Jamie all that he had envisioned, and blessed this even-tempered brother, who listened and offered a way out of the corner that Davey believed himself in.

"Micheil's had something happen to him from the night you were gone. Niall has gathered a following who speak out against Micheil that he has not slain Liam MacKay. If he were to think that Liam attacked you, Micheil would ride against him. Micheil need not

know the truth of what you saw, Davey. He'll know well enough once we reach the Kyle of Tongue.

"None will think to stop him, even if the Keiths have begun their raids. But tell me, Davey, what of the bairn? What happened to Micheil's child?"

"I know not. The bairn is born. That is all I saw."

"And Seana?"

"She cries Micheil's name. In curse or in plea, I know not." Taking Jamie's offered hand, Davey leaned on his brother. "You have more faith than I that Micheil yet holds my life worthy of his personal challenge to Liam."

"Trust me, Davey. He'll be ready to run the distance, so great will his desire be to slay his foe."

"You cannot tell him about Bridget. 'Tis not the time."

"As you are guided by me, so shall I be guided by you. Between us, we'll make Micheil a whole man again."

Davey watched from the shadowed alcove as Jamie approached Micheil where he watched a dice game. He saw Micheil in all his tempers, the blending of his powers, his harsh manner, his recklessness. Just like their da. No man would ever control him, and no woman fully tame him. And none would ever lay claim to knowing all that he was.

Jamie, of a height with the black-haired Micheil, was ever loyal and steadfast to their bond as brothers and to the clan. He had the same pride as Micheil, but his nature would have him always seek to see all sides presented before he acted.

Davey left himself out of his thoughts, and knew he dared not let them stray to Bridget. He sensed no evil here, unlike the night he envisioned, but the sight of Fiona sweeping into the hall on Niall's arm made him reach for his dirk, until good sense took hold and stayed his hand.

He had to remember that Micheil was the key. Micheil had to be healed, and then the others would receive their just rewards.

"Davey," Jamie called, "we ride at first light."

"No questions? Micheil believed you?"

"He grabs, as does a drowning man, at any reason to ride on MacKay lands."

Davey glanced to where Micheil stood watching them. "Does he yet believe that Seana betrayed him with me?"

Grabbing hold of his arm, Jamie demanded, "Leave it be. We ride with a small group on the morrow. Come, you need rest and food to be able to ride with us. I've a feeling Micheil will set us a killing pace. And we've more plans to make, brother."

They set out long before the sun had burned the mist off the land, a handpicked group of fifteen men. As Jamie had predicted, Micheil set them a killing pace. The men were fully mailed and armed, ever aware that Keiths would be riding for their blood. Jamie rode at Micheil's side, but neither brother spoke. It had been Jamie's decision to take a small group of men, for he wanted to leave a strong force at Halberry. Without Davey's sight to know what would happen, he would take no chances that their castle

home would be in danger. The larger force also allowed Gabhan, who had been left in charge, to send out fresh relays of patrols day and night.

Davey hung back, thinking again of the plan he and Jamie had, wishing as he had other times, that the sight was a gift he could summon at will. If they failed . . .

He dared not let his thoughts dwell on failure. But the worry was there, and his gaze, like those of the men he rode with, searched for signs of enemies, not the coming of spring upon the land.

Davey looked at Micheil, who had yet to say one word to him. What thoughts spun through his mind as they rode toward the lands that Seana loved?

At that moment, Micheil's thoughts were on his youngest brother. Davey would understand the turmoil within him. Davey, ever the gentle one of the three, would know how the constant strain of guilt stole pieces of a man, and could threaten to snap every thread of every relationship he had.

How could he refuse to ride against Seana's brother? He had wanted to do this from the first. The winter months always took their toll, and the spring set fire to men's blood and aroused their lust. Micheil knew himself to be no more or less than any other man. If he could not cool the lust that stirred his loins with the one denied him, he could cool it with battle.

But the prospect of destroying that which he knew Seana held dear, not only her brother, but her lands, as well, filled him with a loathing he could share with no one.

He could not go to her with her brother's blood on his hands. He could not live with himself, if once more he allowed Liam MacKay to live after touching one of his own. And to set upon Davey as he lay helpless, and leave him without a weapon, a horse, or provisions, was the act of a coward. It mattered not that Liam had not slain or wounded him. He had attacked a Gunn for the last time.

It was the crofters who ran shouting the warning that a troop of men crossed their lands. Liam, returned from yet another unrewarding search, knew that they had come for him. He gazed up at the blackened rafters, and wondered if his sister knew. What would she do if forced to choose?

Seana roused herself when the first shouts sounded, and rushed to stand by her window. Two crofter's lads stood on the stone wall, shouting the childish rhyme she, too, had ofttimes repeated.

"A Gunn, a Gunn. They come, they come. Hide the beasties, but never run!"

The pickings were poor, if they had come to raid. Her mother's jewels had helped to replace some of the lost cattle and sheep, but the spring lambs had yet to be born, and the cattle were thin without the sweet spring grass to graze upon.

She wanted to turn away, but her eyes hungered for a sight of Micheil. She could not make them out, but then the sun's rays fell upon the ghostly gray horse and the gleaming trappings of sword and armament. Seana felt the quickening beat of her heart and her hand rose to cover her aching breast.

*I betrayed all for you, Micheil, and you cared not.*

Slowly she let her gaze rest on his tall figure as he rode closer. Then she closed the shutter and dropped the bar in place, as if she could keep him out. Did he not know he came too late? There was naught left for him to take. Had she the strength, she would take up a sword against him herself, for all that he had stolen from her.

Though she had barred the shutter, she did not move away, and she clearly heard the arrogance in his voice as he issued a challenge to Liam.

Without giving her brother time to answer, she again heard the gut-bitter fury of Micheil's voice demanding Liam meet him.

"Come, you whoreson coward! You've made your war on women and weary men. 'Tis time to see the hour of your death, MacKay. I mean to keep my sworn oath to my father, and have the very stones of your keep litter the moor, and your blood nourish it!"

The need to know what happened had Seana spinning and unbarring the shutter before she could stop herself. Micheil stood alone, his men well back from the clearing before the gates. Seana picked out Jamie, and then Davey, mounted alongside him. The squeak of the wooden gate that Sim opened drew her gaze to her brother.

*Liam, no!*

Her brother went forth dressed in leather jack and shirt, breeks and boots, his sword held in his hand. He faced a man fully armed for combat.

She heard the snarl in Micheil's voice.

"Think you to shame me, MacKay? I'll fight you, dressed or naked as a newly born babe!"

"Ever was your temper one easily fired, Micheil." Liam buried his sword point in the earth, and then stepped back. "You've men aplenty to keep watch while you rid yourself of mail. I'm less the coward that you call me. I'll wait."

Seana clenched her hands helplessly at her sides. How could she bear to watch them? Yet how could she not?

She refused to release the sudden tears that burned her eyes. For Liam she would do this. And if he was slain . . . Nay! She would not think of it.

Two men came forward to help Micheil divest himself of all but his breeks, boots and shirt. He took up his sword with one hand and his dirk in the other.

"To the death, MacKay."

"To the death," Liam echoed, and took his sword from the earth. He thought of Seana, of her loss, but seeing that Micheil had no room for mercy, he refused to ask any for his sister.

They were of a fair physical match, Liam having had his body honed by the lean years, and Micheil ever quick and graceful, with his deadly moves. Seana swallowed her cry as the clash of steel rang out. She leaned forward and saw that Sim and Calum stood armed outside the gate. Two against so many.

She could not watch the quick, slashing swords, the scrape of blade upon blade ringing in her ears as the two men she loved thrust and parried, their booted feet moving with a strange grace, like that of a deadly dance. There was the sheen of sweat upon their faces,

muscles straining in their forearms for the strength that was needed to wield the heavy weapons.

Low voices taunting one or the other into a lunging move had Seana straining to hear. Micheil slashed at Liam, and caught his upper arm. Blood welled up to stain his linen shirt, and she had to press her hands to her mouth not to cry out and distract her brother.

Why did Liam still protect Bridget? Why did he not tell Micheil the truth about his sister? And why had she not rushed down to do it herself?

Seana knew the answers. Micheil would not listen. Micheil would not believe. And so the payment continued for Bridget's lies.

Micheil pressed his attack, driving Liam back to the stone wall. He heaved to with a mighty stroke, and sparks flew from the blade striking against the stone as Liam twisted free. There came a blinding flare as torch after torch was lit by the crofters drawn to watch the combat.

Now it was Micheil's shirt that was ribboned with red, the flaring torches making the blood appear near-black. Liam closed on him, their sword hilts locked together as each tried to force the other to give way. Liam was the one who stumbled, and Micheil broke away. For a moment, Seana thought he would deal her brother the mortal blow, but he stood, chest heaving, as was Liam's, waiting for her brother to resume.

Seana lost all sense of time, closing her eyes, only to have to open them again. How much longer could they stand?

She knew she could wait no longer. The dread came upon her suddenly that Liam would die. She rushed

from her room, ignoring her own pain, fleeing across the rush-strewn floor of the hall and outside.

Sim caught hold of her, but she fought free. Liam fell to one knee, his arm, his sword arm, dangling uselessly. Micheil was raising his broadsword for the killing blow.

"Spare him!" Seana cried, rushing through the open gates to plead for her brother's life. "For eleven years you've wreaked your vengeance upon us. Cease now. Micheil, I beg you."

The words were themselves bitter gall, for she had sworn never to beg him. Calling upon the remnants of her pride, she stood tall until her gaze met his.

The highland warrior's eyes were bleak, targeting her now-slender form.

Liam was forgotten. Micheil swayed where he stood. "The bairn?" he mouthed across the distance that separated him from Seana. His features hardened when she did not answer, but looked stricken that he dared to remember. Before he could move, before he fathomed their thoughts, his two brothers rushed forward on their steeds and caught Seana up between them.

There was the whispering of swords freed as the Gunns held their weapons ready.

Seana's cry was cut off, and her struggles were immediately stilled. Horrified, Micheil saw Jamie press his dirk to her bared throat.

"Nay!" Micheil cried. Without a thought to what he was doing, he dropped his sword, and turned his back on his enemy, Liam. Seana! They meant to kill her! Micheil started to run.

"Hold, brother!" Davey ordered. "We can all see that the bitch has whelped your bairn. Hear me, Micheil? Your bairn, and no other's. Now Jamie and me will have an end to your torment." Davey held tight with one hand to Seana's arm, and controlled his mighty horse with his knees. With his free hand, he gripped a length of her honey-blond hair, forcing her head back until she had to look up at him.

"For your life, and that of your worthless brother, give the bairn that carries my brother's blood over to us."

Seana cast the two men frantic looks. Not Davey! Not the only Gunn to befriend her! She felt the pinprick of the dirk's point at her throat, and lost what little breath she had left. There was no moisture left in her mouth for her to speak. Her eyes drifted closed in defeat and despair. Was this then to be their final revenge? Her life, and that of her brother, in exchange for her child? She could not do it!

She longed to spit out curses against Bridget. For their lying sister, they had raised their clan and destroyed hers. So many lives lost. So much blood shed. And now they dared to demand her child.

"She'll not tell us, Micheil," Jamie declared. "She leaves us no choice." Jamie's smile was terrible to witness, without mercy. "And will you not be thanking me, brother, for ridding you of the witch that haunts you?" His jeer brought no response but a strangled sound from Liam. Micheil stood frozen.

"Och, Davey, 'tis not the fitting end our father decreed, but 'tis well served." Jamie gazed again upon his older brother. "Agreed, Micheil?"

"Are you blind, Jamie? He cannot speak. He cannot move." Davey's laugh was mocking. "He'll thank us once the deed is done. Wait no longer, Jamie. Slit her lying throat. Rid Micheil of the MacKay witch."

# Chapter Twenty-Two

"Stay your hand, Jamie! Stay it!" Micheil shouted. He pulled free his dirk and tossed it aside. "My life for hers!"

"And mine, as well," Liam added, in a battle-weary voice.

Micheil did not look at any but Seana. And at Jamie's dirk at her throat, where the pulse beat with her lifeblood. He stood in hell as the moments spun past and no sound was heard, no move was made. He would murder his brothers for what they dared. But first he had to get them to release Seana. Her eyes, God's wounds, but those dark gray eyes pleaded with him.

"Her life for yours, Micheil?" Jamie taunted him. "Do my ears deceive me? You hate her. You curse the day she set her eyes upon you. She's a MacKay, Micheil! Yet you claim to be willing to give your life for hers. She has betrayed you, man. Have you forgotten that?"

Davey took up the taunting. "She whispers lies about Bridget. Did she not, Liam? Micheil will not

believe any. But you know. And Seana knows, Micheil. I *saw*.''

"As did I, the night I carried her broken and bleeding into our hall. I am the one who heard from Bridget's lips the name of the man who beat her and left her to die. But I'll hear your tale. I'll swear any oath, give you whatever you wish to claim, but free her," Micheil bargained.

"Why?" Davey held his brother's gaze. He almost pitied Micheil, was almost sorry for what he and Jamie did to him. Almost. "Tell us, Micheil. Why do you wish her life? She's naught—"

"She's mine!"

"That cannot be, brother, for we hold her now."

"I claimed her first," he whispered in desperation. What did they want from him? Seana's skin was leached of color. He could see her body sag within their grip.

"She's mine," he repeated. "My betrothed."

"Jamie, what say you to that? Reason enough to let her go?"

"Not for me. You need more reason, Micheil. She's a comely wench, I'll not deny, but the Highlands are filled with others as lovely. And none so recent brought to bed for a birthing."

"She's mine, I tell you, Jamie. My half to make me whole. Kill her and slay me with the same stroke. I love her. You cannot kill her, for I love her!"

Micheil rushed forward just as they let her go, and swept Seana up in his arms. But Seana never heard the last, for she had fainted.

With the help of Sim and Calum, Liam was brought to Micheil's side. "If you love my sister, then find her bairn. She's near mad with grief, and not yet a week from childbed. We've searched our lands, and no sign is found of the bitch that took the babe and left Seana to die."

"What say you?" Jamie demanded, dismounting when he saw that Davey did the same.

Liam told them what he could. "We found Leites's body the next day, down among the rocks by the sea. She was old, and could have fallen, but Maille may have killed her. She was with Seana through the birth. I rode off, and none other was near. When I returned, there was no sign of Maille. She took the babe. Seana knows it was born alive. She remembers its cry, and her own, as it was torn from her."

Seana stirred and moaned. She lifted lids heavy with fatigue and looked up at Micheil. "You would have given your life for me?"

"I've no life without you, Seana."

"I tried to protect our bairn. I fought her, Micheil. I did not want her to take my babe. I did not have the strength to stop her."

"Hush, Seana. We'll find the babe. I swear this to you." He could not stop himself kissing away the tears that slowly fell on her cheeks, bending low so that none could see the wetness of his own. She claimed no strength, yet fought as bravely as any warrior for what she held dear. The guilt was his, that he had not been with her, giving her and his child the protection that was their right.

"Liam?" Seana called.

"They've taken him inside," Jamie answered. "To bind his wounds," he added, seeing her panicked look. "Micheil, your own need to be tended." He made a move to take Seana from his brother, but Micheil's look was so forbidding, he backed off. "After you, Micheil."

"Wait," Seana pleaded. "Micheil, I would have your word that you enter the hall in peace. I love you, and hearing the same words from you, words my heart has yearned for, makes me bold. I will be yours," she whispered, cupping his cheek and holding his gaze with hers. "There is no more precious gift than to be loved."

"'Tis a lifetime of vows and honor you ask me to put aside. I can promise no more than to try. I want to hear what Liam has to say."

"I'll ask no more."

Two of the crofter's wives came forth to help, for Seana was weakened from her ordeal. She saw that they followed her orders to fetch Leites's herbs and cleaned the wounds of both Liam and Micheil. Davey helped hold her hand steady as she stitched Liam's wound closed, then bound it with a poultice.

After they served spiced ale, the women left as quietly as they had come. From his pallet by the fire, Liam saw that they waited for him to speak. He beckoned Seana closer, and she slipped from her chair to kneel beside him. Holding her hand, Liam took both strength and courage from her.

"As I love my sister, I swear on her life that I never raised a hand to Bridget."

"Then if not you, man," Micheil demanded, "who beat her and left her to die."

"Tell him, Liam. 'Tis long past time for the truth." Seana gazed from her brother's sweat-sheened face to Micheil. "My father thought Liam coddled her, and sent him off to trade. Each time, Liam was away longer. Bridget grew restless, and took to riding out alone, despite my father's request that she not."

"You were a child yourself, Seana. You cannot expect me to believe you knew what happened."

"Nay, Micheil, I make no such claim. Leites told me, when Liam would not. She's dead and cannot speak, but as my brother swore on my life, so I swear on his, that this is the truth."

"Seana's right," Liam said, struggling to sit up, for he felt vulnerable, lying before the Gunns. "Bridget warned me when I returned that if I didn't spend more time with her, she'd take a lover. I forbade it, forbade hearing such from my wife, and left her on clan business yet again." Liam looked away from the three brothers and stared at the fire, gripping Seana's hand.

"Bridget was young, and restless. She had a temper, but I was arrogant enough to believe that she would obey. I thought she needed time to settle. If I had told her I was planning to take her with me, if she— Och!"

Seana ached for her brother. His pride had been beaten, just as he had been, and now he was being asked to lay bare his soul. She took up the story.

"Her serving woman told my mother that Bridget might be breeding. Bridget denied it, and refused to cease her rides. None knew where she went, only that

she would be gone most of the day. Leites said they whispered that she had taken a lover, but again, none saw them. When Liam returned and was told, he confronted her. He knew the child could not be his. She—"

"Seana!"

"I cannot stop now, Liam, though I know the pain I cause you. Micheil and his brothers have a right to know. This is a feud based on lies, terrible lies that brought the deaths of our parents, and countless others from both clans. If you will not say the rest, I will."

She looked at no one but her brother, pleading silently with him, trying to make him understand that she knew how this shamed him. When at last he nodded, Seana glanced at Micheil.

"Bridget refused him her bed the last two times he was home. He had not slept with his wife for almost five months. The child could not be a MacKay heir. He fought with her, but never did he strike her. She ran. It was the last any saw of her."

"There was no child." Micheil's deadened voice was a whisper. "She named you, Liam. I held her in my arms, begging to know who had dared to beat her, and she named only you. It was near three days before my father and I stood again by her bed, her face already veiled to hide the scars she lives with. She told us you cast her out because she could not have a child. That you beat her and left her to die."

"I loved her! I loved Bridget enough to defy you all! You were there, Micheil. You knew. You saw it. Never

would Bridget be denied what she wanted. Never,"
Liam ended, in a hoarse broken voice.

Seana comforted him, but a chilling dread once
more came upon her as she repeated Liam's last words
to herself. She caught Micheil's gaze. His eyes were as
tormented as she felt. But it was Davey who gave voice
to what they all were thinking.

"Bridget has longed to see Seana beaten and
shamed. If she cannot have Seana, she could have the
bairn."

"Niall, that cursed whoreson!" Jamie declared,
rising and pacing over the rushes. "Ever has he envied Micheil. And of late he closets himself with
Bridget and Fiona. And there, brother," he said,
coming to stand before Micheil, "is yet another viper
harbored within Halberry's walls."

Micheil rose and Jamie had to step back. "Aye, I've
kept them close. And if it is true that Bridget holds my
child and they helped her, I need seek only one place.
Order the men, Jamie. We ride for Halberry now."

Struggling to rise, Seana was torn. She could not
leave her wounded brother. But this was her child they
sought. "I would ride with you."

"You cannot, Seana." Micheil went to her and held
her close. He smoothed the hair back from her face,
cradling her cheeks and gazing down at her. "There's
a storm gathering within your eyes, but quiet it, love.
We'll need to ride hard and fast. You would slow us,
for I'll not have you lost to me now. 'Tis too much to
ask of me. I've yet to forgive myself that you carried
my child and bore it alone. There is much yet unre-
solved between us—"

"All I want is my babe returned, Micheil. I ache to hold my child. Bridget doesn't want the bairn. She wants me."

If Micheil could have been granted a wish at this moment, it would have been to see that child within Seana's arms, and his own holding them both, close and safe.

"I cannot allow it."

"Davey! Jamie! Make him see. You know I'm right. It is me that Bridget wants to harm. This may be her plan. She must know I would come."

"You'll be safe here," Micheil insisted. "And do not be pleading with my brothers. I've yet to forgive them for what they did to you."

"Stubborn highlander!" Liam exclaimed. "Don't you see it was the only way to force you to speak what was in your heart."

Both Micheil and Seana turned to look down at her brother.

"Aye, well might your eyes share the same disbelief. But ask them. Ask them, Seana."

"Davey?"

"It's true. We lied to him. We told him Liam robbed me. He needed a reason to come to you. I provided it. But he gave us no chance to talk. Jamie knew you could not stay away from the fight. We seized the chance to have an end of it."

Seana laid her head against Micheil's chest, her hand resting beneath her cheek to feel his heartbeat. Softly, then, so that no other could hear, she spoke to him.

"I have grieved for the loss of you, Micheil. I grieve for the loss of my child. Ask me not to wait alone, in fear for both your lives."

Micheil held her tight, pressing her head against him, hearing her plea and yet knowing he should stand firm on this. Once more Liam spoke, drawing their attention.

"What if you are wrong? What if even now an attack is being readied for here? I cannot protect her. Sim and Calum are the only fighting men left to me. You have us all at your mercy, Gunn. Though it galls me to admit it."

"Micheil?"

"Aye, lass. He's right. I cannot leave you here. But we face other danger, Seana. I would have your word that no matter what I order, you will obey me."

"You have my word, Micheil. Till we are all joined and safe, I will obey you."

Within the hour, they were ready to ride. Micheil carried Seana out to where the horses waited. He brought her to Davey—not an easy task for him to do, but one that added a measure of safety for Seana.

"I entrust her to you, Davey. Guard her with your life."

Without further words, the breach was healed between them. Seana longed to touch him one last time, but he had wrapped her in furs, cloak and blankets, insisting that she be kept warm, and cushioned from the hard ride.

Micheil took his place and, with Jamie at his side, rode once more for Halberry. There was no speech, for

voices carried, and each man had come of age raiding these lands.

Twice Micheil led them off onto a wooded track to avoid roving bands. Without light to see by, they could not know if they were friend or foe. Micheil would not risk being engaged in battle. He had yet to come to terms with all he had been told. That Bridget had lied to save herself from being cast out of the clan, without thought to what a blood feud would cost them all, set his stomach to churning.

The hoofbeats seemed to echo the questions he asked himself over and over: Who was her lover? Who had she lied to protect, besides herself? Had he been harbored within Gunn lands all these years? On and on the questions came, as the horses ate up the leagues.

Deep as his thoughts were, it was Micheil who signaled them to halt when he smelled smoke. "Jamie, pick two to ride with us, and leave the others here till we see what we face."

Micheil rode up the rocky slope and saw the dying flames of a crofter's hut. The *tigh dubh*'s thatched roof was gone, and smoke curled from the inside. The bodies of those slain lay scattered like broken dolls. The work of the Keiths, he knew—expected, but still sickening to witness.

"Jamie, leave the men to bury them. We ride on."

Davey kept Seana's head turned away as they rode past. She knew, of course. He felt her tears against his neck.

"Did you know that Micheil dreams of a day when this will be no more?" he asked her, in an effort to turn her thoughts from death.

"He dreams high, Davey."

"But what is a man without his dreams, lass? Are you cold? I feel you shivering."

"I but think of what is to come. He listened to us, but does he believe, Davey? Micheil loves Bridget, as he loves his clan and his honor. I pray only that he finds the strength needed to do what he alone can."

"As I do, Seana. As I do."

Exhausted as the horses were, they sensed the nearness of home and stable, and carried their riders forth toward the high, forbidding walls of Halberry. The rising sun lit one half of the castle with sparkling brilliance, while the other half remained buried in the night's shadows.

Micheil hailed the watchtower, looking back to make sure that Seana was secure with his brother. The moment the drawbridge was down, he spurred his horse across, and rode into the courtyard.

Lads were just leading horses away, and Crisdean hailed them from the steps leading to the hall. "We, too, have just now returned. The Keiths raided. Gabhan is tracking them."

"Any news of a child?" Micheil demanded, dismounting and taking the steps at a run. "Have any come with terms for ransom?"

"I've not been here." Crisdean watched the others dismount. He shook his head as he realized it was Seana that Davey handed down to Jamie. "So you've brought her back!"

"Crisdean, she's the *a ghraidh mo chridhe*. To dishonor her is to dishonor me."

"There are many who will fight you over this, Micheil."

"Aye, I know." But his gaze was for Seana, refusing all aid to come stand at his side.

"Has he news of our child?"

"Your child!"

"Aye, Crisdean, mine. 'Tis a long tale, and one I've no time to tell." Micheil hugged Seana close. "He has no word, love. But do not despair. Are you sure you want to come with me? My sister—"

"Wants to hurt me, Micheil."

He turned to Crisdean. "I want Halberry searched from the towers to the meanest hut."

"I'll call out the guard."

"Nay, my friend. Quietly. I do not know who is foe among us. I would not have the child in more danger. You are certain that none demanded admittance? None came to see my sister?"

"Not while I was here, Micheil."

"Micheil, please, I beg you to seek out Bridget."

"Aye, Seana. Together." He lifted the hood of her cloak so that none seeing her would give any alarm. With Jamie and Davey behind them, he and Crisdean kept Seana's body shielded on either side as they entered the hall.

Men just returned milled about as Peigi ordered food and drink to be set on the long tables. Micheil beckoned her to him, asking her the same questions he had put to Crisdean.

"Bridget has forbidden me her rooms. She and Fiona have closed themselves off, and when I tried to query Cuíni, she would not speak to me. Micheil, ye should know that we found Moibeal, beaten and raped, with a dirk through her heart."

"Like old Angus's daughter," Jamie whispered.

"The one Liam was blamed for?" Seana asked.

"'Twas my brother's dirk the old man claimed had pierced her heart, and I denied it could be Liam. If my brother would use violence on women, would he not have beaten me? Slain me for coming to him with a bastard child in my belly? Do you see now, Micheil, how deeply run the betrayal and lies that kept this blood feud alive?"

"What more would you have from me, Seana? A promise to slay my sister? I love you, lass, but you've had time, and I've less than—"

Jamie shouted and ran when he saw his cousin at the stair. "Niall!"

Micheil shoved past Seana and took off after them. Jamie had Niall flattened against the stone wall, his dirk at his throat.

"Tell us! Does Bridget have Micheil's child?"

"You're too late. She's up on the seawall. None can reason with her."

"I should kill you where you stand, you bastard."

"Leave him, Jamie!" Micheil took the steps with a heart that felt as if it would burst with fear. He heard the others come behind him, and had the presence of mind to stop them at the door leading out to the walk.

Handing over his sword to Jamie, he ordered them to wait. "Bridget must be mad. Let me reason with her."

The moment he stepped out, he saw Fiona. She ran to him, clutching his arms.

"Micheil, thank God you've come back. I cannot talk to her. She's beyond reason. Bridget thinks the child is hers."

"And who gave my child to her?" He pushed her away. "Never believe you will not pay for your part in this, Fiona."

Micheil forced himself to walk around the tower, praying that he would be in time, praying, too, that he would be granted the words needed, for this was not a place where his training as a warrior with weapons would aid him.

Bridget stood at the far corner, her dark cloak billowing out like the wings of a huge bird of prey.

Micheil saw her lift a swaddled bundle high with both hands, and he froze, afraid to breathe, lest she send the babe plunging to its death on the rocks below. He heard the soft shuffling of those yet behind him, and motioned with his hand for them to stay as he started forward.

"Bridget, lass," he crooned, in a voice like the one he used to gently break his horses. "Come away from the edge, lass. 'Tis cold for you."

"I'm hiding, Micheil. They've come for my babe. But I will not give it over to Liam. The man doesna love me. He cannot have the babe."

"Och, lass, I will never give the child over to him. You know I'll protect you with my life, Bridget. Have

I not always been there to shield you? Come nearer me, Bridget. I would look on your babe.''

She turned then, watching his approach with an animal's wariness. "You will not cast me out? You'll let me keep my bastard? Fiona tells me you'll have to kill me, Micheil, for I bring dishonor to our clan. Da will make you do it. I know. 'Tis why I had to— Come no closer!''

"See? I stop here. But you do not need to be afraid with me, lass. 'Tis Micheil, Bridget. Have I not loved you best? You can trust me. I cannot hurt you.''

"But they told me—''

"They lied to you, Bridget. Fiona, Niall, and the other.''

"The other?'' She gazed down at the mewling child. "You cannot know about the other. Hear, Micheil? My babe cries for milk. I have none to give the poor babe.''

Sweet Jesu! Micheil shook his head, feeling the sweat that broke out on his body. *Help me! Lord help me!*

"Bridget, I'll find a wet nurse. But you'll need to come down to your solar. Even now, Jamie is gathering them for you to see. Someone you approve of, lass. So come,'' he coaxed, holding out his hand, seeing that it trembled, but unable to stop it.

"Nay, you cannot, Micheil. Da will kill it. The babe's not Liam's. Da will kill me.''

Seeing her once more gazing at the child, Micheil closed the distance between them—stopping the moment she looked up.

"Fiona told him I was unhappy. He brought me pretty gifts, and told me I should have been his bride. But the babe, och, how he raged about the babe. I had no choice, Micheil."

"I ken, lass. I ken more than you know." Micheil thought he would rather face ten armed men alone than hear these words that sealed his sister's death. Betrayal—he had never known such. His yearning to hold that child, to see what he and Seana had created in a fire of passion, and had near lost by the raising of swords, spurred him to continue.

"Bridget, tell me what you want. I will grant you all I can to see you happy."

"But you know. I wanted Seana beaten and shamed, as I was. You refused me, Micheil. I set the witch on you. I *saw* you with *her*. Will you slay her for me, brother? Will you do it now?"

"Anything!" he cried out, growing desperate when she began to laugh and once more faced the sea. "Seana! Bring her!" he yelled.

Seana needed no more urging to rush forth and fall to her knees, baring her throat for the dirk Micheil held. He gazed down at her, anguish in his eyes as he set the blade to her throat.

"Bridget! Look! Here she is! I'll slit her throat, but come away from the wall. Come bring me the child, and I'll grant your desire."

In agony they waited until Bridget turned once again and beheld her brother and his leman. She set the babe on the stone before her, ignoring its weak cries, and slowly stood tall as she lifted her veil.

Only the knife at her throat kept Seana from crying out as she beheld the twisted scars that disfigured Bridget's once breathtaking beauty.

But Seana's eyes gave her away, for Bridget threw back her head, stripped off her veil and laughing, let it float out for the sea wind to take.

Micheil did not need to see that Seana's lips barely moved. He could hear her plea within his mind, the same plea that beat through him. Save the babe...

The sight held Jamie and Davey, and Fiona was able to slide past them, running for Bridget. "They'll kill you! They only come for the child! You know what must be done. Hurry, Bridget! Hurry, before he comes and finds what you have done."

"*He* comes?"

"Aye, even now. With an army he rides to rescue you. Didn't I promise you that? Didn't I show you? But kill the child! You must kill the child!" Fiona bent and tried to snatch the babe, but Bridget reached out and caught hold of Fiona's hair.

"Swear it! Swear that George comes now. Swear that witch will make me beautiful for the Keith again. Swear it, or it will be you who meets her death."

As Fiona swore, babbling, Micheil motioned to his brothers. Bridget seemed possessed of strength they had never known, for she had Fiona bent back over the wall, the babe forgotten.

Seana rose, and for a moment leaned against Micheil, taking courage from him. Her babe's weak cries tore at her. She knew what they intended to do without listening to the hushed exchange.

"You lied!" Bridget screamed, shoving at Fiona to push her over the edge. She tore at Fiona's hands to free herself, but the other woman held to her. Wild laughter erupted from Bridget.

The moment Jamie and Davey rushed toward their sister, Seana ran with Micheil to snatch up her child. She turned away at the sound of ripping cloth and the brothers' cries, melding with keening wails as the two women plunged to their death on the rocks below.

Seana was torn, her joy at holding her babe for the first time diminished by the grief that left her love stricken.

She saw that Jamie and Davey neared, but at a shout from the door, they all turned.

Crisdean came forth, his eye swollen, his lip bleeding. "I tried to stop him. I know you wanted Niall alive, but he fought free and used my dirk on himself."

"Temper your grief with forgiveness, Micheil," Seana whispered. "'Tis done. There's new life that awaits us, love. Will you come meet our child?"

Micheil turned to face her. "You've a gentle strength that becomes a hard sword for me to fight against, Seana. Aye, I wish naught but to see my— What have you borne me? Son or daughter?"

"I know not, Micheil. The babe was taken as it was born. Will it matter to you?"

"Take her below, Micheil," Jamie said. "We all come to see. 'Tis time for joy within our hall again. The mourning can wait."

# Chapter Twenty-Three

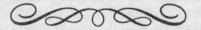

Seana was surprised when Micheil continued down the stairs and into the hall. He led her to his place at the high table.

"I know you would wish this to be a private time for us alone. But this hall reeks of the stench of death and lies. I would share the joy of this child, and the promise it holds with all, Seana."

She looked up at him and thought of the dream in which she had clutched her child and run from him. No more. As he wished to share and proclaim before those gathered close that here was their child, she could not deny him.

Seana laid the babe to rest on her cloak, and with hands that shook she began to unwrap the cloth. She marveled at the tiny features, and the small, perfectly shaped hands. She saw that Micheil was enchanted, too, for he set one finger within the babe's palm and watched those little fingers close tight to hold him. She stroked the downy hair and leaned down to place a kiss, the kiss of welcome she had longed to give her child.

Micheil, ever impatient, stilled his urge to remove the cloth that bound the child's legs. He saw the need that Seana had to touch the babe, shaping the ears, brushing the pale cheek, but his brothers had no such reluctance, and called out for her to hurry and let them know if they had a new lad or lassie among them.

"Och, Micheil," she whispered, "look at how tiny the toes—"

"Toes?" Davey roared.

"Toes!" Jamie echoed. "God's wounds, lass, show us the last. Are we to drink to more bairns or brawn?"

The cry was taken up until the hall filled with it.

Seana unwrapped the last, lifting her child and holding the babe out to Micheil. "Will you accept this babe as yours, *mo ghraigh?*"

Micheil beheld his son, and the woman who called him her love. He held his child, this tiny being he would give his life to protect, and slowly brought the babe to his lips. "A son," he whispered, then lifted him high for all to see. "A son!" he shouted.

Peigi elbowed her way to his side. "Here, give over that lad. Ye two have not the sense God gave the dumbest creatures. Can ye not tell the poor mite needs feeding?" She rounded on Seana. "Have ye got milk for the babe?"

"Peigi!"

"Don't *Peigi* me. Can ye feed the mite? Come along. Leave them to their drinking. I've helped raise this braw lot, an' I'll no be cheated of seeing this one growed."

Micheil gave the child over to her and watched as she kept Seana in tow to take them from the hall. He

drank one toast, then retreated to be with Seana and his child.

Peigi stood guard at his chamber door. "A word with ye. Treat the lass gentle. She's had a hard time, and yer a mon that doesn't know his own strength." With a gnarled hand that had soothed many a tear, she reached up to touch his cheek. "Ye need the love, lad. Open your heart. 'Tis all within for ye."

Micheil beheld Seana, lying upon his bed nursing his son. His gaze held only love as he closed the door behind him and shut out the world. Someday he would tell her of the dreams that had haunted his nights here. But not now. This was a time for them alone, a time of peace.

Seana lifted one hand, and beckoned him to join her.

"Come, love. Help me nurture our child, after his rough beginnings. I know your thoughts are troubled still by all we did not know and may never have the full story about, but I wish only this time for us."

Micheil came to lay beside them, enfolding them both in his arms. "*A ghraidh mo chridhe,* how I have longed to call you the love of my heart. You have given me a son, and I pledge I'll keep him safe for you, love."

Seana's eyes filled with tears. Her world was complete. She felt the babe's mouth grow slack upon her breast, and lifted him away. Micheil caught the tiny pearled drop from his son's lips and brought it to his own.

"Will you marry me, Seana? Will you pledge me your love, and the fire that burns bright within you,

as I pledge you my own and my sword to keep you and our bairns safe?"

"Aye. Aye to all," she whispered, leaning as Micheil did, to form a sheltering arch over their tiny son's body as their lips met freely with love.

\* \* \* \* \*

# COMING NEXT MONTH

**#247 DESIRE MY LOVE—Miranda Jarrett**
In the continuation of the Sparhawk series, Desire Sparhawk enlists
Captain John Herendon to rescue her brother, but finds the captain's
motivation far different from her own.

**#248 VOWS—Margaret Moore**
The seventh book in the Weddings, Inc. promotion, *Vows* is the story
behind the legend of Eternity, Massachusetts, the town where love lasts
forever.

**#249 BETRAYED—Judith McWilliams**
Coerced into spying on her British relatives, American heiress Eleanor
Wallace finds herself in a trap that could cost her the man she loves.

**#250 ROARKE'S FOLLY—Claire Delacroix**
When obligations force a landless knight to become a weaver's
apprentice, he discovers he has an affinity for trade, as well as for the
man's fiery daughter.

## AVAILABLE NOW:

**#243 FIRE AND SWORD**
Theresa Michaels

**#245 ANGEL**
Ruth Langan

**#244 THE TEMPTING OF JULIA**
Maura Seger

**#246 TAPESTRY OF FATE**
Nina Beaumont

**Award-winning author**

# BARBARA BRETTON

**Dares you to take a trip through time this November with**

## Tomorrow & Always

How fast can an eighteenth-century man torn with duty and heartache run? Will he find the freedom and passion he craves in another century? Do the arms of a woman from another time hold the secret to happiness? And can the power of their love defeat the mysterious forces that threaten to tear them apart?

...Stay tuned.

**And you thought loving a man from the twentieth century was tough.**

**Reach for the brightest star in women's fiction with**

MIRA™

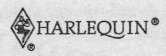

## VOWS
## Margaret Moore

Legend has it that couples who marry in the Eternity chapel are destined for happiness. Yet the couple who started it all almost never made it to the altar!

*It all began in Eternity, Massachusetts, 1855....* Bronwyn Davies started life afresh in America and found refuge with William Powell. But beneath William's respectability was a secret that, once uncovered, could keep Bronwyn bound to him forever.

Don't miss **VOWS,** the exciting prequel to Harlequin's cross-line series, **WEDDINGS, INC.,** available in December from Harlequin Historicals. And look for the next **WEDDINGS, INC.** book, *Bronwyn's Story,* by Marisa Carroll (Harlequin Superromance #635), coming in March 1995.

WED7

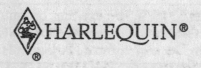

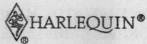

# HARLEQUIN®

Don't miss these Harlequin favorites by some of our most distinguished authors!
And now you can receive a discount by ordering two or more titles!

| | | | |
|---|---|---|---|
| HT#25483 | BABYCAKES by Glenda Sanders | $2.99 | ☐ |
| HT#25559 | JUST ANOTHER PRETTY FACE by Candace Schuler | $2.99 | ☐ |
| | | | |
| HP#11608 | SUMMER STORMS by Emma Goldrick | $2.99 | ☐ |
| HP#11632 | THE SHINING OF LOVE by Emma Darcy | $2.99 | ☐ |
| | | | |
| HR#03265 | HERO ON THE LOOSE by Rebecca Winters | $2.89 | ☐ |
| HR#03268 | THE BAD PENNY by Susan Fox | $2.99 | ☐ |
| | | | |
| HS#70532 | TOUCH THE DAWN by Karen Young | $3.39 | ☐ |
| HS#70576 | ANGELS IN THE LIGHT by Margot Dalton | $3.50 | ☐ |
| | | | |
| HI#22249 | MUSIC OF THE MIST by Laura Pender | $2.99 | ☐ |
| HI#22267 | CUTTING EDGE by Caroline Burnes | $2.99 | ☐ |
| | | | |
| HAR#16489 | DADDY'S LITTLE DIVIDEND by Elda Minger | $3.50 | ☐ |
| HAR#16525 | CINDERMAN by Anne Stuart | $3.50 | ☐ |
| | | | |
| HH#28801 | PROVIDENCE by Miranda Jarrett | $3.99 | ☐ |
| HH#28775 | A WARRIOR'S QUEST by Margaret Moore | $3.99 | ☐ |
| | (limited quantities available on certain titles) | | |

| | |
|---|---|
| **TOTAL AMOUNT** | $ |
| **DEDUCT: 10% DISCOUNT FOR 2+ BOOKS** | $ |
| **POSTAGE & HANDLING** | $ |
| ($1.00 for one book, 50¢ for each additional) | |
| **APPLICABLE TAXES\*** | $_____ |
| **TOTAL PAYABLE** | $_____ |
| (check or money order—please do not send cash) | |

To order, complete this form and send it, along with a check or money order for the total above, payable to Harlequin Books, to: **In the U.S.:** 3010 Walden Avenue, P.O. Box 9047, Buffalo, NY 14269-9047; **In Canada:** P.O. Box 613, Fort Erie, Ontario, L2A 5X3.

Name: _____

Address:_____City: _____

State/Prov.: _____ Zip/Postal Code: _____

\*New York residents remit applicable sales taxes.
Canadian residents remit applicable GST and provincial taxes.

HBACK-OD

# COMING NEXT MONTH

**#1615 TERMS OF SURRENDER—Shirley Rogers**
*Dynasties: The Danforths*
When Victoria Danforth and rebellious David Taylor were forced into close
quarters on the Taylor plantation, former feuds turned into fiery passion.
But unbeknownst to all, Victoria was no farmhand—she was the long-lost
Danforth heiress! Could such a discovery put an end to their plantation
paradise?

**#1616 SINS OF A TANNER—Peggy Moreland**
*The Tanners of Texas*
Melissa Jacobs dreaded asking her ex-lover Whit Taylor for help, but
when the smashingly sexy rancher came to her aid, hours spent at her
home turned into hours of intimacy. Yet Melissa was hiding a *sinful*
secret that could either tear them apart, or bring them together forever.

**#1617 FOR SERVICES RENDERED—Anne Marie Winston**
*Mantalk*
When former U.S. Navy SEAL Sam Deering started his own personal
protection company, the beautiful Delilah Smith was his first hire. Business
relations turned private when Sam offered to change her virgin status.
Could the services he rendered turn into more than just a short-term deal?

**#1618 SHEIKH'S CASTAWAY—Alexandra Sellers**
*Sons of the Desert*
Princess Noor Ashkani called off her wedding with Sheikh
Bari al Khalid when she discovered that his marriage motives did
not include the hot passion she so desired. Then a plane crash landed
them in the center of an island paradise, turning his faux proposal
into unbridled yearning...but would their castaway conditions lead
to everlasting love?

**#1619 BETWEEN STRANGERS—Linda Conrad**
Lance White-Eagle was on his way to propose to another woman when he
came across Marcy Griffin stranded on the side of the road. Circumstances
forced them together during a horrible blizzard, and white-hot attraction
kept their temperatures high. Could what began as an encounter between
strangers turn into something so much more?

**#1620 PRINCIPLES AND PLEASURES—Margaret Allison**
CEO Meredith Cartwright had to keep playboy Josh Adams away from
her soon-to-be-married sister. And what better way to do so than to throw
herself directly into his path...and his bed. But Josh had an agenda of his
own—and a deep desire to teach Meredith a lesson in principles...and
pleasures!

SDCNM1004

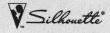
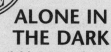

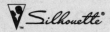

**Silhouette®**

# Desire

is thrilled to bring you

Three brand-new books in
## Alexandra Sellers's
popular miniseries

Powerful sheikhs born
to rule and destined
to find their
princess brides…

**SONS**
OF THE
**DESERT**

Be sure to look for…
## SHEIKH'S CASTAWAY
**#1618 November 2004**

## THE ICE MAIDEN'S SHEIKH
**#1623 December 2004**

## THE FIERCE AND
## TENDER SHEIKH
**#1629 January 2005**

*Available at your favorite retail outlet.*